MONSIGNOR WILLIAM BARRY MEMORIAL LIBRARY
BARRY UNIVERSITY
PS3569.H3862 D3
Shaw, Russell B dn   010101 000
The dark disciple.

0 2210 0049887 5

 Y0-CJG-016

PS   144771
3569
.H3862
D3

Msgr. Wm. Barry Memorial Library
Barry University
Miami, FL 33161

SHAW

DARK DISCIPLE

THE DARK DISCIPLE

THE
DARK DISCIPLE

BY RUSSELL B. SHAW

DOUBLEDAY & COMPANY, INC., GARDEN CITY, NEW YORK   1961

Barry University Library

Miami, FL 33161

All of the characters in this book are fictitious, and any resemblance to actual persons, living or dead, is purely coincidental.

Library of Congress Catalog Card Number 61–8904
Copyright © 1961 by Russell B. Shaw
All Rights Reserved. Printed in the United States of America
First Edition

PS
3569
.H3862
D3

144771

THE DARK DISCIPLE

ROBBIE BOND TURNED THE VOLUME OF MATTHEW ARNOLD over fondly in his hands and tilted his chair back from his desk up against the wall with its peeling green paint. The ancient fan on the floor beside him rattled and wheezed, sending a current of brackish air flowing over his tubby, perspiring body. The bald top of his too-large head shone with sweat. He sucked on his pipe and thumbed happily through the book of poems. Of all the Victorian poets, Arnold was his favorite. He knew well enough that the Victorians were considered passé by many today—but out of stubbornness or sentiment he clung to his enthusiasm, cherishing it even as a symbol of the sensitivity which preoccupied moderns had lost. He paused over "Dover Beach," reading parts of the poem half-aloud to himself:

> And we are here as on a darkling plain
> Swept with confused alarms of struggle and flight,
> Where ignorant armies clash by night.

"A darkling plain," he repeated. How lovely! One could see the mellow sunset falling upon a Hellenic scene of grassy meadow and crumbling columns. He would have to remember to call that particular image to the attention of his elective class in Victorian poetry. The students had so little appreciation of beauty these days. They were fact-crazed, he reflected. If you couldn't measure a thing or touch it or count it, then it was to be dismissed as inconsequential. But there was so much, Dr. Bond thought, gently setting down on the desk the beautiful old-fashioned book in its green and gold binding, that couldn't really be measured.

Dr. Bond untilted his chair and glanced at his watch. Ten-thirty. Time for Christopher Gavin to be here. He looked absently around at the large room occupied by the English faculty of Webster University. A jumble of desks and bookcases, books and papers heaped everywhere in disorderly piles, dirty green walls with stains at the top where the rain had leaked through. The hot September sun beat down on the roof just above and made the room an oven. Perhaps, had he been a dynamic person, Robbie Bond, as chairman of the department, would have wangled more satisfactory quarters for his faculty from the reluctant administration. But he was not, by any stretch of the imagination, a dynamic person. Rather, he preferred peace and quiet, the preservation of the *status quo*—unless, of course, it became absolutely intolerable. And, he told himself, rising to open several more windows in hopes of coaxing a stray breeze into the room, the English department's quarters did not fall into that category. Though some of the older English faculty grumbled now and then, and some of the younger men insisted on displaying their untidy personal habits in public—cigarette butts on the floor, dirty shirts thrust unaccountably into odd corners of the bookshelves—Dr. Bond rose above the inconveniences of the arrangement and, on the whole, rather preferred things as they were. As he annually told his colleagues when they met together for the first time at the start of the school year, it meant a chance for that daily personal contact so essential to the stimulating interchange of ideas. And the interchange of ideas, Robbie knew very well, was the essence—the very *sine qua non*—of a university. Even of such a nondescript university as Webster, a struggling city college, neither the faculty nor student body of which could claim much in the way of distinction.

Robbie Bond seldom alluded to the university's deficiencies, even with himself. It was not, of course, that he was a stupid man.

Rather, he had simply trained himself, defensively, to be unaware of whatever was unpleasant. He had developed an automatic optimism that depended largely upon the habit of thinking clearly about nothing. Coupled with a zeal for paper work, a meticulous enthusiasm for getting things done on time, and a horror of giving offense, this made him an ideal functionary in the administrative set-up of the university. He was a thoroughly satisfactory, if uninspired, head of the English department.

It was in this role as chairman that he was sitting this hot morning, a few days before the start of the fall semester, in the English department office. He was waiting for the newest member of his faculty, a young man named Christopher Gavin, who was due in town that morning. It was one of Robbie's current embarrassments that he had never met Gavin, but had hired him sight-unseen by mail, on the basis of an application received the spring before. Such a procedure, he recognized, was hardly ideal. But circumstances had made it necessary. One of his regulars, a teacher named Barry, had defected abruptly only a month ago, surrendering at length to the blandishments of his father-in-law, who had been urging him for some time to join him in the insurance business. Robbie Bond bore no grudges against Barry—he had two children already, and his wife was pregnant again. Family finances had made the difference, Robbie knew—a problem which hardly bothered him, being as he was, at fifty-three, a confirmed bachelor. But Barry's sudden disappearance from the scene had left him, barely a month before school was to start, quite without anyone to take over the two freshmen and two sophomore English classes which Barry had handled with uninspired competence for three years. A flurry of calls to the various young men who had applied earlier for positions established the fact that most of them had long before located jobs elsewhere. All, in fact, except Christopher Gavin. Their negotiations had been quick and to the point. The young man seemed delighted at being offered the position—so delighted, in fact, that he had not even bothered to ask about salary—and Robbie, for his part, had been delighted to get him.

Delighted at first, that is. Later, after the signed contract had been returned and Gavin had announced his day of arrival, he had begun to have his doubts. If all the other applicants had already been hired, then why had not Gavin? He chided himself for asking the question. But it remained in his mind. He returned to the young man's application. References, excellent. He had taken his master's degree—at a good graduate school—and was well along on his doctoral dissertation. No teaching experience, granted. But that was hardly a handicap these days. Then why——? Dr. Bond had pondered the problem, a little apprehensively. He wished there had been time for an interview, a more careful appraisal on the basis of a face-to-face meeting. But of course, he told himself, there was almost certainly nothing to worry about. Nothing at all. And in this frame of mind he was ready and eager to give the young man the benefit of the doubt. He puffed out a cloud of smoke from his pipe. He was prepared to find in Christopher Gavin a real gem.

The door to the English department swung open and a tallish young man walked in with modest firmness, carrying a shabby suitcase. The door knocked sharply shut behind him.

"Dr. Bond?" he said, looking at Robbie with an expression of solemn but not unappealing curiosity.

Robbie Bond rose from his desk. "Yes, that's right," he said cordially. "I'm Dr. Bond. And I suppose you're Chris Gavin?"

The young man nodded. "I'm very happy to meet you, Doctor," he said with a smile. He extended his hand and Robbie took it automatically, smiling in return.

"Let's sit down," he said, guiding Gavin to his desk by a gentle pressure on his elbow.

Gavin settled himself into the straight chair beside the desk. He put the suitcase down in front of him, and then looked up with the same expression of intent but polite curiosity at Dr. Bond.

"Well now, Chris," Robbie said, resuming his seat, "you must be rather tired. I see—" he nodded at the suitcase, "—you haven't been to your apartment yet."

"No, not yet. I got in about seven—in time for Mass, you know. Then I had a bite to eat, looked around town and before I knew it, it was time to come over here."

The word *Mass* struck Robbie a little jarringly and not altogether pleasantly. He was not accustomed to hearing anyone refer seriously to his religion. Not, of course, that he had any prejudice. Every man had a right to his own beliefs, Dr. Bond was convinced. But it seemed to him to be somehow more decorous if one kept his religious beliefs to himself. However, he was prepared to allow a few slips to one of Christopher Gavin's evident youth and inexperience. And it would, moreover, have been impossible for him to feel any real animosity toward the young man, for Gavin's innocence hung upon him like a chasuble. Christopher had sandy red hair, clipped short. He wore an unfashionable double-breasted blue suit a little too small for him. His appearance appealed to Dr. Bond's protective instinct. His handsome face with its square jaw, regular features and intense blue eyes had not acquired the art of concealment. While speaking with him, it was as if one could see his thoughts and emotions through a clear pane of glass.

"We'll have to get you settled, Chris," Robbie said. "I think you'll be pleased with the apartment I got you. It's an efficiency, but really rather nice. Oh—and do you like Arnold?" he asked, noticing that Christopher had turned the book on the desk toward him to read its title.

"No, I don't," the young man replied absently.

"Why not?" Dr. Bond was always ready for a literary discussion with one of these young people. It kept the mind keen, helped one to avoid dogmatism and stuffiness.

"I don't like people who feel sorry for themselves," Christopher said abruptly. "All the Victorians did, and then they wrote poetry about it. They saw themselves on a cooling world under a dying sun. It's foolish."

His words both unsettled Robbie and slightly irritated him. "But if one has reason to feel sorry for oneself?" he prompted.

"What reason does anyone really have though?" Christopher fixed him with a peculiarly intense stare and smiled. "The problems we have are those we make for ourselves through our ignorance. Once we know the truth, we can solve our problems. And since the truth is only there for the taking—why, we have no right to complain if we fail to take it."

Robbie stirred uneasily. "But who knows what truth is?" he asked. "Not many people would presume to say."

"Yes, that's so, Doctor," Christopher conceded, leaning suddenly closer to him. "Very few people would. But what does that matter? If you are sure, as I am——" He gestured, as if to say that words would only be superfluous. "I wish everyone could know what I know."

Involuntarily Robbie shifted his weight to lean away from Christopher. "Most of us are afraid of self-delusion," he said. "Especially when it comes to these ultimates about which no one can be sure."

Christopher's face darkened into a scowl which seemed not to be directed at Robbie Bond, but through him and beyond him at old enemies. "You can be sure," he said in a low voice. "People only doubt because they want to."

"You can say the same about belief, can't you?" Robbie remarked, his irritation rising to the surface. "People believe because they want to."

Christopher started to speak, then stopped. He looked instead at Robbie in silence. As Robbie returned his gaze, he saw with chilling clarity that in these few moments he had been appraised and rejected—for what, he did not know. Christopher leaned back in his chair and spoke with nonchalance. "I can see we'll never convert each other, Doctor. We share no common ground." He smiled, but it was a smile which failed to hide contempt.

Stung, Robbie looked for a means of retaliation and picked up the book of poems. "To return to the Victorians," he said stiffly, "you must admit at least that what they wrote is beautiful." He opened the book at "Dover Beach," where the pretty green ribbon marker lay.

But unexpectedly Christopher reached over and took the volume out of his hands. He glanced down the page, then began to read, rather loudly, in the tone of a prosecuting attorney producing damaging evidence.

"Listen! you hear the grating roar
Of pebbles which the waves draw back, and fling," and so on. . . .
"The Sea of Faith
Was once, too, at the full, and round earth's shore
Lay like the folds of a bright girdle furl'd.
But now I only hear
Its melancholy, long, withdrawing roar,
Retreating, to the breath
Of the night-wind, down the vast edges drear
And naked shingles of the world.
Ah, love, let us be true
To one another! for the world, which seems
To lie before us like a land of dreams,

*So various, so beautiful, so new,
Hath really neither joy, nor love, nor light
Nor certitude, nor peace, nor help for pain;
And we are here as on a darkling plain
Swept with confused alarms of struggle and flight,
Where ignorant armies clash by night."*

Christopher dropped the book back down on the desk. "It speaks for itself," he said. "How can you take anyone seriously who asks you to feel sorry for him at the same time he's enjoying feeling sorry for himself?"

"We were speaking of beauty." Dr. Bond felt the desperation of a man leaping across a pond on stones which keep slipping out from under his feet. He had not wanted to dislike this young man. In fact, quite the opposite, he had been more than ordinarily predisposed in his favor. But there was something so—so *fanatic* in his callous self-confidence! He seemed not merely to be careless of the amenities, but virtually unaware of their existence. He was capable of affronting without knowing it. Nor was there any indication that he would have been more amiable had he been aware of the impression he made. There was nothing about Christopher Gavin to suggest that he cared in the least what other people thought of him. His inner resources, unspeakable though they might be, were quite obviously boundless. With a sick feeling Robbie realized that the mystery of his unemployment had been solved. "My point was that at least the poem is beautiful."

"Well, what about beauty? Granting it's there—and I'll certainly defer to your judgment in that, Doctor—" Christopher's smile was perhaps meant to be ingratiating, but its patronizing condescension only made the other man bristle, "—still, what good is it? If it covers something ugly or petty, then it's no better than a fresh coat of paint on rotten wood. It's dangerous, because it hides what's underneath. Of course, there's an attraction in it, but one has to be careful. It's the same way with sin. One has to be careful."

Robbie hesitated, and at that moment the door opened again and a large man about thirty walked in. He glanced curiously at them.

"Mark—what a surprise!" Robbie exclaimed, jumping up in evident relief.

The man by the door looked quizzically at Dr. Bond out of amused, heavy-lidded eyes. "Well, it's not as if I'd just gotten back from the moon, Robbie," he said. "We were only down at the shore for a couple of weeks." He had a round face, tending to fat now from too little exercise and too much self-indulgence. His sandy hair was beginning to thin out at the temples and in back. A faint and slightly mocking smile flickered around the corners of his rather thick lips. Robbie took him cordially by the arm and led him over to where Christopher Gavin sat, watching the two of them with composure.

"Mark, I'd like you to meet the newest member of the English faculty—Chris Gavin," Robbie said. "Chris, this is Mark Brodie."

Brodie extended a fleshy freckled hand. Christopher rose and met it with his own pale bony one.

"You picked a damned hot day to arrive, Chris," Brodie said. He pulled a handkerchief out of his pants pocket and dabbed with it at his forehead and around the open collar of his sport shirt.

Christopher smiled. "The heat doesn't bother me," he said.

"Good for you." Brodie slouched into the chair Robbie had dragged up for him. He took a cigarette from a pack in his shirt pocket and lit it. His fingers were deeply stained with nicotine. "Oh, excuse my manners," he said, extending the pack to Gavin. "Care for one?"

"I don't smoke, Mark. Thank you anyway."

Brodie nodded in approval, a little too vigorously. "Good again," he said. "You don't smoke and you don't get hot. I'm afraid I have both vices." He turned to Dr. Bond, who had sat down once more behind the desk. "I suppose you've been filling Chris in on dear old Webster?" he said.

"Well——" Robbie began.

"Actually," Christopher interrupted, "we were talking about Matthew Arnold."

"Arnold?" Brodie said, picking a shred of tobacco off his lower lip. "Can't stand him. The man's a prig."

"Well, you two have something in common," Robbie remarked in a slightly offended tone. "Neither of you likes poor Matthew Arnold."

"Triply good." Mark bowed his head ceremoniously at Christopher.

"Mark teaches freshmen and sophomores too," Robbie explained to Chris.

"I'll have to get some pointers from him," Gavin said.

"Speak softly and carry a big stick," Brodie remarked, blowing out a cloud of smoke which hung for a moment in the tepid air, till a breeze from the fan caught it and sent it scattering in all directions.

"Yes, you two ought really to have a great deal to say to each other," Robbie enthused. "It's something I'd forgotten—but of course you're both Catholics."

Brodie looked up, almost angrily. "Really, Robbie—I'm afraid you have me confused with two other people."

"Well, I know, Mark—you aren't what they call a 'practicing Catholic'—that is the expression, isn't it? But I thought——" Robbie glanced a little nervously at the two of them. "Well, after all, don't they say 'once a Catholic, always a Catholic'?"

Mark Brodie tapped cigarette ashes onto the floor. "Hardly," he said. "Don't try to be a theologian, Robbie. I'm sure Chris can tell you that's a lot of crap."

Gavin smiled, sitting straight as a ramrod. "Dr. Bond may not be a theologian, Mark—and of course I'm not either—but I'm quite sure that he's right."

Brodie shrugged. "Have it your own way. I've got a maiden aunt who thinks the same thing." He heaved himself up abruptly and crushed out his cigarette in Robbie's ash tray. "Well, I just came up here to get a few books out of my desk, so if you'll excuse me——" He crossed to a battered desk in the middle of the room and began rummaging through its drawers.

"Mark——" Robbie said.

"Yes?"

An idea had occurred to Dr. Bond, a way of escaping from this young man. It would not do, of course, to omit taking him on a tour of the campus, but he had had enough of Chris Gavin for one day. The young man would, he had already realized, take some getting used to, and he had no desire to hurry the process in his own case. "Are you in a rush, Mark?" he asked.

Brodie straightened up. "No," he said. "Why?"

"I was just thinking— I have a few things to take care of. An appointment with the dean a little later, you see. So I wondered—

if it's not imposing too much—could you possibly show Chris around the place?"

Mark shoved one of the drawers of his desk shut with a bang. "Delighted," he said.

Robbie was deliberately oblivious. "Fine," he said. "Chris, you'll learn a lot from Mark." He rose and smiled at Gavin.

"I'm sure I will," Christopher said.

Mark sauntered back across the room to them. "We'll learn a lot from each other," he amended.

"And that—" Brodie said, pointing up the flight of steps to the large pseudo-Grecian building outside which they stood, "—is the library."

"Very impressive," Gavin said.

"Uhh," Brodie grunted without enthusiasm. He flipped his cigarette butt away and it rolled over the edge of the curb under the wheels of a parked automobile. "At least they managed to get it air-conditioned—God knows how. It's the only inhabitable building on the campus during the summer. Come on, let's go in." The two men walked together up the broad steps.

"You weren't joking about not feeling the heat, were you?" Brodie said, nodding at the shabby suitcase which Gavin still carried. "You've been toting that thing all over the place and you're still cool as a cucumber."

"Temperatures don't usually bother me much one way or the other," Christopher said. "Anyway," he added with a little laugh, "I suppose you'd say I travel light."

"Commendable." Brodie pushed through the revolving glass doors with Christopher behind him. Inside he stopped and, as he had done repeatedly, pulled out his handkerchief to wipe his forehead. "Damn this weather. Let's sit down."

They crossed the foyer to a cluster of clumsy-looking overstuffed chairs covered in red plastic, chipped and torn in places. Brodie settled into one of the chairs with a groan. Christopher sat down next to him. A few students strolled into or out of the building, while a janitor in what looked like Army fatigues swept the floor.

Mark pulled out his habitual cigarette and lit it. "So that's about it," he said abruptly, blowing out the match. "Webster University. There're a couple of places I haven't shown you, but hell, you'll see them for yourself sooner than you'll like. Well, how does it strike you?"

"Pretty much as I'd expected," Christopher said.

Brodie grinned. "What a beautifully noncommittal statement. Tell me then, what had you expected?"

"What I found." Christopher grinned back. "Seriously though, I think anyone can see the place isn't exactly top-flight. I mean, several of the buildings looked pretty rundown to me. Still, I suppose any school could use more money."

Brodie leaned back and crossed his legs. "That isn't all dear old Webster needs," he said.

"No?"

"'Not exactly top-flight.' That's good. Myself, I'd say the place was decidedly second-rate."

"In what way?"

"Faculty, administration, students—you name it."

"Perhaps you're hard to please, Mark."

"I don't think so. I just see things the way they are. And as for Webster—it's just a struggling little city college trying to make a go of it. The only reason the students are here is to get their degrees, then get out and make some money. And most of the faculty are just time-servers, or people like me."

"What do you mean—people like you?"

Mark shrugged. "Men who thought it would be a first step—and then decided after they'd been here a while that it would be too much trouble to take the second step."

"That doesn't seem like a very good reason for staying."

"It serves. And there are compensations. After all, a comfortable little rut like this doesn't come along every day. Opportunity only knocks once, you know."

"I'm afraid I wouldn't regard that as opportunity," Christopher said.

"Really—why?"

"I like to be doing things."

"I don't," Mark stated flatly. "I suppose you'd call that reprehensible. Still, I like to think I'm preserving some sort of balance in nature. You do things—I watch. It works out very nicely."

"That is reprehensible," Christopher said. "A man ought to use his talents."

"I have a talent for watching." He flicked his ashes onto the floor. The janitor shot a dirty look his way, and Mark grinned blithely back.

"I appreciate having your appraisal, Mark. Still, I'm not sure I should take it without a grain of salt."

"Oh, you haven't heard anything yet," Brodie said. "I haven't even touched on personalities."

Christopher smiled. "I don't believe you'd be unbiased."

"On such a topic—who is?"

"Perhaps I'd do better to get my own impressions firsthand. I'd rather start with the assumption that everyone is well-intentioned."

"Oho, my boy!" Mark chortled. "You haven't been around school faculties very long, I can see that. There's no place in the world that beats a school for sheer petty cruelty. It's the same anywhere."

"I hope not. At least, I'd like to think *I'll* be given the benefit of the doubt to begin with."

"Oh, they'll be all right at first. But that's only because you've just enlisted—and they don't know on whose side yet. But once you commit yourself, you'll have to start warding off knives in the dark like the rest of us."

"Are there factions in the faculty?"

Mark enjoyed gossiping. He puffed his cigarette contentedly. "Well, you mustn't make the mistake of thinking the school is split down the middle between the Guelphs and the Ghibellines. Our alliances are a good deal more fluid than that. As a matter of fact, except for a relative handful of sworn enemies, it's possible for anyone to join up with anyone else. For a while. It all depends on the issue. By the way—who knows?—perhaps you'll have the honor of being the first issue of the new year."

"I?"

"Well, after all, the issue we like best is a personality—pure and simple. Though I suppose the bone of contention will be just how pure and simple you are."

"I suppose—if you're right and I do become an issue—I suppose it will be because I'm a Catholic."

Mark straightened from his slouching position, suddenly serious. "No it won't," he said. "The fact that you're a Catholic won't affect things. Webster isn't that way, at least, thank the good Lord! So don't start feeling persecuted. You won't have any trouble about your religion unless you try to press the point."

It was Christopher's turn now to sit back and cross his legs. "I suppose that's your secret, Mark—you didn't press the point."

Mark crushed out his cigarette in annoyance with the toe of his shoe. "Damn Robbie and his big mouth," he said. "Look, Chris, for the sake of cordial relations, just forget that stuff he was telling you about me."

"You mean you're not a Catholic?"

"Of course not. Oh, I was brought up in the Church, all right. But that was all over years ago."

Christopher looked closely at him. "You know better than that, Mark. Being a Catholic is something you can't ever give up."

"Don't be naïve, Chris. I'm not going to argue with you about it— but just remember that you're looking at the matter from your side of the fence, and I'm looking from mine. And what each of us sees from his point of view is not at all the same as what the other sees. Anyway—" Mark lapsed once more into the role of advice-giver, "—remember what I told you. You'll get along a lot better here if you don't try to make an issue of your religion. After all, you don't want to scare us all into thinking you're out to convert us."

Christopher smiled a noncommittal little smile. He leaned forward slightly and said in a low voice, "Do you want to know a secret, Mark? That's exactly what I do want."

Brodie stared at him in surprise. For a moment he was not sure whether the young man was in earnest, or merely having a joke. But the expression of fanatic certainty in Gavin's eyes dispelled the notion that he was anything less than deadly serious. "Very laudable," Mark drawled. "But I'm afraid you've lit upon some awfully barren ground."

"Why do you joke about everything, Mark?"

"Why not? I've never found anything that absolutely required me to be serious."

"But if you did, what would you do? Do you think you'd know what to do?"

Mark shifted in his chair. "It's a pointless question. I never will."

"Perhaps you already have."

"Look, Chris, let's stay off my religion."

"Certainly—if you're so sensitive about it."

Brodie snorted impatiently. "For God's sake, don't be so damn smug," he exclaimed. "You want to know what I believe?—all right, I'll tell you. Once and for all. Then maybe you'll drop the subject as a waste of time."

"Maybe," Christopher said.

"Well then, in a word, I just don't care especially about religion, one way or the other. If some people like it—well, fine, let them have it. If others don't, that's all right by me too. And you know why I don't care? Because I just don't think God—if he exists—cares either. After all, assuming there is a god—what possible difference could it make to him whether I believe in him or not? It's like saying *I* care whether an ant under my feet believes in me. If you think so highly of your god, then at least do him the courtesy of realizing that he must have more important things on his mind than who fornicated with whom last, who blasphemed a week ago Tuesday and how often, who did this and who did that. After all, if we don't care about God, why the hell should he care about us?"

Christopher frowned. "That's disgusting," he said.

"I didn't say it for the sake of pleasing you," Brodie replied frostily.

"You people——" Christopher seemed almost to choke on his words, but then got control of himself. "You talk and talk and that's all you want—talk. Just playing word games—'believe,' 'disbelieve,' 'God.' I don't think you're capable of enough sincerity to believe in anything you say."

"You asked me and I told you. If you don't like what you heard, don't blame me."

Gavin considered for a moment. When he spoke it was without the contempt—hatred, almost—that he had shown before. "The thing I don't understand," he said, "is how it happened to you—*you*, a Catholic."

"Oh, come now, Chris. Even you must have had your doubts sometime."

"Never."

Brodie raised his eyebrows skeptically. "Now you're going to make me think you're not very bright," he said. "Really, in all these years——?"

"It hasn't been so long," Christopher cut him off. "I'm a convert. I've only been in the Church five years."

"Ohhh," Brodie nodded as if it were clear to him now. "I see. The good old convert zeal. That explains a lot."

Christopher glanced coolly at him. "I'm glad you think you understand me. I wish I could say the same about you."

"I'm not such a puzzle. If you'd just take my words at face value——"

"You're married?"

Mark hesitated a moment. "Yes."

"Tell me, is your wife a Catholic?"

The query annoyed Mark. But they had gone so far already that he felt it would be a sign of weakness for him to refuse to answer now. "Not that I see any relevance to the question—but no, she isn't."

"Does she practice any religion?"

"Julie? No, she doesn't. Fortunately for her, she had parents who were a good deal more enlightened than mine. They didn't fill her full of all that nonsense."

Christopher nodded thoughtfully. "I see."

Mark glanced ironically at him. "Do you? That's nice."

Abruptly the young man got up. "Well, it's been an interesting talk, Mark," he said. "We'll have to do it again some time."

Brodie did not rise. "Sure."

"And I appreciate everything you've told me. About the school and—the other things." He stooped and picked up his suitcase. "Very enlightening."

"Glad to hear it."

"So, I'll be seeing you around," Christopher said. He turned and walked away.

Mark watched him go, straight and stiff. One could almost see the aura of alien impenetrability about his spare ramrod figure in its shiny blue suit. Mark shook his head a little and lit another cigarette.

MARK BENT OVER FROM BEHIND AND KISSED HIS WIFE LIGHTLY ON the neck as she stood at the sink dropping ice cubes into two glasses.

"Give Robbie a stiff one," he said. "He's got the wind up."

"That's not hard for Robbie. It doesn't take much to wound his sensibilities." She looked up at him with a smile. Julie was a pretty girl with thick black hair, a fair complexion, thin but attractive features and lively gray eyes. She was quite small, hardly coming up to Mark's chin, and looked fragile. In her pert apron over a white blouse and blue skirt she reminded one of a little girl playing house.

"Don't be hard on him," Mark said. "He's a good fellow—even if he did pull a dirty trick on me today."

"Oh? What trick?"

Mark frowned slightly. "Leaving me to show the new English teacher around school."

Julie poured bourbon generously over the ice. "That doesn't sound so bad."

Mark rolled his eyes. "You don't know the half of it," he groaned. "You'd better make that two stiff ones."

"Don't worry. I know how to handle you and Robbie." She handed him the drinks with a playful gesture, stepping away and holding them out at arm's length.

"You know how to handle everybody," Mark grinned. "That's what worries me."

He took the drinks and walked through the narrow hall with its dirty yellow wallpaper into the low-ceilinged living room of their small apartment. Robbie Bond sat on the couch, his legs crossed. One moccasin-clad foot jiggled up and down rapidly.

Mark put the drinks down on the glass-topped coffee table that wobbled because of a short leg, then lowered his big body into a frayed overstuffed chair. He was at home, comfortable, contented—except that the disturbing memory of his talk with Gavin would not leave his mind. He rubbed the yellow down on his growing bald spot, lit a cigarette, picked up his drink. "I didn't appreciate that trick you played on me," he remarked.

"Trick?" Robbie repeated, focusing his attention with an effort. "Dropping Gavin in my lap."

"Oh, that." Dr. Bond blushed. "I'm sorry, Mark, but—well, I'd had him to myself for quite a while before you came in." He sipped his drink.

"And you'd had enough for one day?"

"Yes." He seemed about to go on, but hesitated.

"What happened?"

Robbie avoided his eyes. "That would be hard to explain," he brought out at last. "It wasn't so much anything he said—though heaven knows that was bad enough, what with his harping on religion and truth and what have you—but his whole attitude. The terrible thing is, Mark—" Robbie looked unhappily over the rim of the glass. "—I seem to have hired a fanatic. That awful superior self-assurance of his, as if he had the key to all truth and simply felt contempt for everyone else—the symptoms are unmistakable, I think." He shuddered slightly.

"But what exactly did he say?" Despite himself, Mark could not help feeling an uneasy curiosity about Chris Gavin.

"We were discussing Matthew Arnold." Again Robbie hesitated, and a look of reminiscent horror came into his eyes.

"And?"

"And before I knew what was happening he started talking about truth and belief and—and I don't know what other nonsense. What he said just didn't seem to mean anything."

Mark looked skeptically at him. "You seem pretty upset about it then."

Robbie ignored the remark. "I asked him if he didn't see any beauty in Arnold's poetry. Oh, I know, you won't yourself admit 'beautiful' as a critical term, but that's just a question of semantics as far as I'm concerned. Only Gavin's objections weren't along those lines at all. Apparently it's his idea that beauty in a work of art is irrelevant, and the real test is whether the work adheres to some theological party line or other."

"Excuse me for interrupting." Mark and Robbie looked up at Julie, who stood in the doorway holding a drink. She smiled brightly at them. "Excuse me for interrupting you," she repeated. "The dinner can look after itself from here on, so I thought I'd join you."

"By all means, my dear," Robbie said, rising and offering her a place on the couch. She sat down beside him, looking thoughtful, and then said:

"I do think it's interesting—that point of view you were talking about, Robbie. It sounds so very certain."

"Exactly," said Mark. "It's certain. But that's about all it has to recommend it."

"Oh, it's interesting, my dear," Robbie conceded. "There's a fascination to it, in fact. But fanaticism is always such a gross oversimplification."

"But suppose the fanatic were right, Robbie?" she asked.

"How is one to decide? We have only his word for it. The fanatic is always sure that for the first time in history truth has stood still—for him, and for him alone. And for that reason he has the right to set out to convert the rest of us. But truth obviously doesn't stand still."

"Of course," said Mark. "Whatever truth is, it's something living—an organism. It's not a diamond to be quarried out once and then distributed to the end of time in little slivers of infallibility."

"Very good," Robbie agreed. "You put it very well, Mark."

"I suppose you're right," Julie said. She frowned slightly.

Mark laughed. "You see how much weight my opinions carry here, Robbie."

Julie seemed hardly to have heard him. She was still thinking.

Like many young women she seldom concerned herself with abstract thought, but when she did her mind stuck to a problem with a bur-like tenacity. Mark and Robbie exchanged a look of embarrassment, as between serious men whose discussion is being delayed by a woman.

"Well, Julie?" Mark said at last in a slightly ironic tone.

She looked up in surprise. "Were you waiting for me?"

"Weren't you going to say something?"

"No—at least—well, I was thinking."

"Might I inquire what?" Robbie asked with coquettish gallantry.

"I think sometimes that you're afraid to be certain of anything," she said simply.

Mark laughed in genuine amusement. Robbie smiled—not quite pleased—and asked: "Why should we be afraid to be certain, my dear? I admit it makes an agreeable paradox—rather feminine, if you'll pardon me—but after all one must be logical. I believe one would be more likely to be afraid of being uncertain."

"Perhaps." The slight frown still creased her forehead as she concentrated intently. "But I really think it would depend on which you were to begin with."

"I'm not sure that I follow," Robbie said.

"What she means—" Mark's eyes still twinkled with fun, "—is that a person can become as dogmatic about uncertainty and indecision as about the Trinity or the Virgin Birth. If your whole life is devoted to an unquestioning belief in uncertainty—to unfailing assent to the proposition that some questions simply don't have answers—why, then I imagine it would be a pretty shattering experience to find out that the answers did exist."

"On the contrary," Robbie said with some heat, "the essence of your position and mine—incidentally, I prefer to call it open-mindedness—is willingness to recognize truth whenever and wherever one finds it. In that way life is a constant series of discoveries. New truths cancel out the old ones or coalesce with them to form new patterns. I can assure you I don't feel 'shattered' to discover a new truth where formerly I had felt only uncertainty."

"Of course you don't," Mark said. "But that's because you're very careful about the truths you discover. Literature, history, economics—they're safe enough fields and I dare say you've become convinced of a few things there in your time. But after all, Robbie, when have you ever tried to discover a truth in religion? Do you even admit that there are 'truths' there? I suggest," Mark concluded with a hint of mimicry that escaped Robbie, "that perhaps it's just there that your open-mindedness shuts up tight."

"Really, Mark, sometimes you betray your early training!" Robbie Bond was hurt. He had the look of a dog who has received a rap on the nose and a sharp word.

Mark noticed this and reminded himself that the joke had gone far enough. "I can't help it, Robbie," he said. "Jesuit education is an indelible thing. It's like the mark of Cain." He paused, then went on, unable to resist pulling the other man's leg. "But it does permit me new heights of open-mindedness. I can be devil's advocate in the cause of agnosticism. But you, Robbie—never."

Julie made a nervous, vexed movement. Mark looked at her, still grinning. "Sometimes I wish——" she said. "I wish——"

"What do you wish?"

"I don't know. That you could be more serious, I think." She glanced toward the kitchen. "Things must be about ready," she said, rising. "Why don't you go into the dining room?"

Julie went to the kitchen. Mark and Robbie looked after her in surprise for a moment before finishing their drinks.

FATHER JEREMIAH KIRSCH SAT AT HIS DESK IN HIS TINY OFFICE IN the administration building, looking out the window at some students playing on the tennis courts outside. He had enjoyed tennis himself years ago and he took a vicarious pleasure now from watching the young men. He had, of course, he reminded himself, set aside this time—the early afternoon, when neither students nor anyone else was very likely to come in—to read his breviary, but he much preferred to watch the tennis game. He could read it tonight—no services, no meetings, it was a free evening. He recognized with wry amusement one of his habitual weaknesses cropping up again—the fatal reluctance to cram activity into every waking minute that kept Jeremiah Kirsch—"a very bright fellow," his teachers and fellow seminarians had all said—from being anything more than an assistant in a number of pleasant dull parishes, and now Newman Club chaplain at Webster University. It was really too late to begin to change now, he told himself. He had always done everything that was asked of him and done it with good will. If someone wanted to see him tonight—well, he'd spend as long as was necessary and then stay up till midnight with the breviary. Perhaps the Lord would forgive him for not being a go-getter. Besides, he had always thought himself that the only thing that could spur him on to greater activity was ambition, and, recognizing its seeds in his own spirit as a young man, he had long ago decided that it might be a smaller sin to be easygoing than to be self-seeking. "And may the Lord have mercy on my soul if I'm rationalizing," he murmured. "Good shot!" he said as one of the players, having run his opponent ragged with drives to all corners of the court, now sliced the ball just beyond the straining racket.

The suppression of ambition was of course not the only key to Father Kirsch's failure to live up to expectations, although it was the readiest solution and was therefore the one most often put forward both by himself and by his acquaintances. Beyond any mere self-centered diffidence, however, he was possessed by an idealistic fastidiousness, an insistence on purity of motive so rigorous as to make action all but impossible for him. Friends told him his attitude was foolish and self-defeating. The pure of heart, they insisted, were under obligation to contend with the less pure and the impure. Noble ideals were all very well, they said, but when carried to the point of altogether precluding action they ceased to be a virtue and became an affectation instead. The priest was ready enough to agree in theory and sometimes had even rebuked himself for his failing. But when it was a question of hard, concrete fact, a demand that he take positive and unpleasant action, Father Kirsch inevitably found himself vacillating. Counsels of perfection, urgings to turn the other cheek, crowded upon him. And he hearkened to them and did as they commanded. He had turned the other cheek so often that it was for him a reflex gesture. But still, he told himself, it was what Christ Himself had commanded. Love, after all, was no counsel, but a precept; it brooked no hesitation and no temporizing in obedience. He consoled himself with the thought that what appeared to others to be indecision and timidity was known to himself —and, he hoped, to Christ—by its real name: love. If love required passiveness, then he would be passive. The only important thing was to be sure of one's motives. And if anything, however slight a mote, dirtied them, then the only alternative was to refrain from acting.

There was a knock on the door. Father Kirsch turned from the window in his swivel chair and said, "Come in." The door opened and a good-looking young man in a rather shiny double-breasted blue suit entered. Father Kirsch took note of the stern expression in his eyes, the reddish hair cropped short in an almost military style, the strong regular features, and was oddly reminded of some painting he had once seen of Michael, the warrior angel. There was just that expression of dedicated militancy in this young man's face.

"Good afternoon, Father," the young man said. "I'm Christopher Gavin. The new teacher on the English faculty. I thought we should get acquainted."

"Happy to meet you, Chris," Father Kirsch said, rising and shaking his hand. He recalled now that someone had mentioned the name to him. "Won't you sit down?" He nodded at a chair beside the desk. "Cigarette?" He gestured toward a package on the desk blotter.

"No, thank you. I don't smoke."

Father Kirsch lit his own with a little silver lighter. "Well, it was awfully nice of you to drop in on me like this, Chris," he said. "I get few enough callers here in my cell."

"Are you here every day, Father?"

"That's right. It keeps me pretty busy too." He smiled at the young man. "But what about you? How do you like Webster so far, Chris?"

"Well enough. But of course it's not like the seminary," he said pointedly.

Father Kirsch laughed. He pushed his clean white hair back from his temples with his thin well-manicured hand and took a drag on the cigarette. "That's true enough," he said. "But then one doesn't want every place to be like a seminary. Were you in yourself?"

"No," Christopher said. "I had hoped to be, but my application was rejected. Poor health."

"I'm sorry to hear that. But you look well enough now. Are you——"

"No, I'm not going to try again," Christopher said, clipping off the words coolly.

Father Kirsch was aware of a note of resentment in the young man's voice. To change the subject he asked: "How did you happen to come to Webster, Chris?"

"I was really quite lucky," Gavin said. "After I was turned down—for the seminary—I couldn't find anything to do. Anything I *wanted* to do, that is. I hadn't really thought of anything—except being a priest." He smiled slightly for no apparent reason. "So when I couldn't do that I decided to be a teacher instead. I put in applications just about everywhere. Well, apparently somebody quit unexpectedly here, they had my name on file—and here I am."

"It's not a bad place to be," Father Kirsch said.

"No, it isn't," Christopher agreed. "I think I can do some good here."

"Yes, teaching offers a lot of opportunity that way."

"Oh, I didn't mean just through teaching."

"No?"

"No. Of course, one does do good that way, I suppose, though it seems to me rather pointless just to turn out intellectual sophisticates who have no beliefs."

"Very likely. But you see yourself molding beliefs as well?"

"That's it, Father, exactly." Christopher looked at the elderly priest with shining eyes. "I see a real need for it here—a real need for someone like me. These people are so aimless, so hollow. They need someone to tell them—to tell them——" He gestured vaguely as the words he meant to tell them failed him for the moment.

Father Kirsch watched the smoke spiral up from his cigarette. "Let me tell you something, Chris," he said gently. "You have a very fine ambition. I sincerely hope you can achieve it. But I'd advise you not to try to force anything down these people's throats. They won't take it. They'll only rebel against it and the net result will be just the opposite of what you intended."

Christopher's face hardened. He knew this type: the weak priest who liked to be a good fellow and wanted above all to avoid controversy. He had seen enough of *them*. So it was going as he had expected. He could count on no allies. But then, he wanted none. "I've heard that before, Father." He did not take the trouble to suppress the contempt in his voice. " 'Don't offend anyone.' But I can't help suspecting that sort of advice usually conceals lack of desire to make an effort. It is an effort, you know, and I don't think God would let it go unrewarded. And what do you have to propose as an alternative?"

The priest was surprised at the bitterness he had aroused in this young man. Quite by accident his words had uncovered something fanatic and a little frightening. He knew how others would have dealt with the situation, crushing Gavin on the spot with a word or a look, or else ordering him from the office. And yet he hesitated to do either. Bitterness was after all a sign of suffering, and if Gavin were in pain, what sort of response was it to slap him in the face? If he could be brought to understand that this bitterness of his was wrong and that by indulging it he only caused himself more anguish—that would be worth doing. But how to begin? What could he say that would deflect into healthy channels the crude energy embodied in this young man? He felt somehow futile, for there was no communication between them, and he did not know how to create it.

"What would you suggest?" Christopher repeated.

The priest flicked ashes from his cigarette into a china ash tray, a pretty, fragile thing a ladies' sodality had given him one Christmas. Suddenly it was as if he could see it with Gavin's eyes as a symbol of taste for comfort, domesticity, and the good life. He knew he deserved no such condemnation, and yet how could it appear otherwise to Gavin, given his bitterness? And if Gavin hated him, would it really make things better to hate Gavin in return? "Every man has a different way of reaching the same end," he said. He spoke almost absently, preoccupied as he was with trying to see things as Gavin saw them. "Perhaps yours isn't necessarily wrong. I only think it can be dangerous."

"And yours is eminently safe," Christopher commented. He saw now that the crisis had passed and he was in control, though something in the priest's manner, an air almost of inattention, perplexed him while at the same time it angered him still more. "What is your way, Father? To sit in this office?"

The challenge stung the priest at last. But what could he answer? He looked about at the half-empty bookcase, the sugary print of the Sacred Heart on the wall. Perhaps Gavin's attack was on firmer ground than his defense would be. "I wait for them to come to me. I do what they ask of me." He hesitated, then added with conviction: "God knows, I'm willing."

"You wait for them. But what if they're waiting for you?"

"It's not my job to run a conversion center." Father Kirsch spoke more firmly. Here at least he was sure of himself. "My job is with the Catholics first of all. If the others ask for help I give it to them."

"If they *ask*——"

"You don't have to be told to know. You can see it."

"That's very interesting." Christopher assumed a mockingly urbane expression, as if he had taken the remark seriously. "What have you seen in Mark Brodie, for example?"

"Brodie? What about him?"

"Certainly you know he's a Catholic."

"Yes, I do. What am I supposed to do about it?"

"What are you supposed to do——?"

"Christopher——" The priest gestured in frustration. He wanted desperately to make the young man understand, and yet he did not know how to begin. "Please, listen to me. I know my duties, and I do them. I know the limits of my job, too, and I do everything I can within them. You think you know my job better than I do. But you don't at all. It's easy enough for you to be sure about things, to see the mistakes—the fancied mistakes of the rest of us. But you're just a theorist, Chris. What do you know about Brodie? Do you know how to deal with a very pleasant, very intelligent man who's filled with hatred for the Church you represent and with pride in his own intellectual self-sufficiency? I've seen a lot of Brodies in my time. A few of them come back to the Church, most of them don't. But there isn't any panacea for them. And if you think there is—if you think that——" He had smoked his cigarette down to a tiny stub, and he crushed it out now with a nervous gesture. "Please try to understand," he started again.

Christopher watched him with a child's cold stare of evaluation. Then suddenly he smiled, a disarming grin that made his boyish face still younger. "I'm sorry, Father. I think *you* misunderstand *me*. I don't want to tell you your business. We both know I'm in no position to do that, and it's certainly the last thing I'd think of." His manner as he spoke was sincere and friendly, with just a touch of wistfulness to suggest that he had been hurt by the priest's suspicions. "As for Mark Brodie—why, I only wanted to know a little more about him. I had a theory about him—which you can confirm or disprove right here—and I thought that if I were right, then both of us together might find some way of helping him." He waited. Father Kirsch, his eyebrows lifted incredulously, said nothing. Christopher went on, still in the same friendly tone. "You see, I've heard— and you can tell me if it's true or not, Father—I've heard that when the Catholic partner to a mixed marriage loses his faith, it's very often because of pressure from the non-Catholic. That is true, isn't it, Father?"

"Very often," Father Kirsch said. He waited for what was to come next.

"Well, I'd thought, Father, that it might be the case with poor Brodie——"

"It's not."

"But isn't his wife——"

"Mrs. Brodie has no religious beliefs, as far as I know. But that isn't the problem with him."

"Are you absolutely sure, Father?"

The priest's head had begun to ache a little. He ran his fingers lightly over his temples. "I'm sure. It doesn't take any great perception. You can tell just by chatting with him, by seeing him."

"Oh, of course, Father. Just by seeing him." Christopher sat quietly for a moment, staring at the priest but not really looking at him. Then suddenly he rose. "Well, no doubt you're right, Father. Anyway it's been very nice talking with you. I hope I'll be seeing you again soon." He smiled, turned abruptly, and walked out, shutting the door gently behind him.

Father Kirsch stared at the door. He had a queasy, nervous feeling in his stomach, and the throbbing in his head warned him that he would have a full-scale headache soon. He felt tired and depressed by the whole incredible scene. If only he had known what to say, he reflected. He had wanted so to make Christopher understand. And yet—understand what? What was it he had wanted to tell him? Nothing that could be put into words, only love. What could he have done differently? He did not know. To have struck back at Gavin was unthinkable. And, short of striking back, what action was left to him, or what words? He wondered if it had always to be this way—that love was condemned to frustrated immobility, destined by its very nature to sit silent and abashed before violence and hatred. But he would have had it no other way. When, after all, had love suffered more willingly than in the agony on the cross? And if the cross were the model of love, who was he to claim to shape love in a pattern of his own design? Still— still Gavin frightened him. He did not know what was in the young man's mind, what insane plan might be forming behind those clear child's eyes, but he had a foreboding that it meant only turmoil and suffering. And if he could avert such evils, did he not have a duty to do so? But that would mean fighting Gavin, using his own weapons, a course from which the priest shrank in repugnance. He could see no alternative. Either one became as the enemy, or one consciously remained immobile in imitation of Love. Christopher had said he had a plan of action in regard to Brodie. What was it? But even if one knew, what could one do? Action of itself implied some falling off from the perfect immobility of love. To sit and wait—that was best. It was the only thing to do.

The priest hesitated. Nagging somewhere at the edge of his conscience was a suspicion he hardly dared put into words—that all his theorizing might be no more than rationalization of self-indulgence. He tried to put the thought out of his mind, but it would not go. Gavin, he reflected, seemed to have remarkable powers for creating disturbance. And so he sat a long time absorbed in his own ponderings, while outside his window the tennis players still traded shots now unwatched.

DONALD REINHART WAS NOT POPULAR WITH HIS FELLOW SOPHOmores, but on the other hand, he was not positively unpopular. They tolerated him, as they tolerated many things, in a spirit of uncomprehending amusement. Donald was a tall thin boy with lank blond hair, a long thin neck with a protuberant Adam's apple, and shy brown eyes that peered timidly out at the world through thick glasses. His clothes were moderately expensive and in collegiate good taste, but seemed somehow always to be just a bit too small for him, so that a bony wrist or ankle was forever forcing itself into sight. His behavior was as eccentric as his appearance. Donald was not an especially good student—in fact, some of his classmates were of the opinion that he was actually "thick"—but he was very definitely a thinker. He could be found at odd moments with an unread book lying open in front of him and a blank look on his face as he dreamily pondered some problem that could not possibly have been put into words so as to be intelligible to anyone else.

Donald himself was aware of his strangeness. He accepted it. Sometimes, he wondered vaguely what would become of him—

what he would do for a living, whom he would marry, if ever he did marry. But these were not the problems that usually occupied him. As for what those problems were—Donald was the last person in the world who could have said. All that he really knew was that they had to be settled—definitively, once and for all—before he could move on to anything else. He strove sometimes at least to formulate his questions. And though he recognized that his efforts were hardly successful, nonetheless it seemed at least nearest to the truth to say that, above all, he wanted to know why. Why: that was as precise as he could be. If his fellow sophomores had known his problem, it is not to be expected that they would have sympathized. Some things, after all, are beyond the powers of human nature. But, on the other hand, they might at least have understood the reason for the abstracted look in his weak eyes. Donald, naturally, did not tell them. Very likely, it was prudent of him.

Donald's fellow students were not consciously cruel to him—nor even unconsciously so, at least to any great degree. It was simply that, like most healthy people, they did not feel disposed to waste time on questions, especially such vague questions as Donald might have asked, had he had the wit to formulate them. It was precisely this impatience in them that had made them uneasy when, as freshmen, they had sat in Mr. Brodie's English classes and heard him throw out, not names and dates and similarly satisfying hard nuggets of fact, but rather speculations and queries—in fact, nothing less than questions. Donald's classmates knew the role they were to play, just as they knew equally well the role of their teacher. It was their function to absorb facts, and it was the teacher's duty to give them facts. Thus, Mr. Brodie's behavior had gone against their healthy sporting natures. Mr. Brodie asked questions, to which he was willing to admit he did not know the answers; this was a clear violation of the rules of the game. But for Donald, Mr. Brodie's freshman English classes had been revelation, illumination, rapture, and communion. In them he had found justification for his own habit of struggling with cosmic problems to which he could not even give a name. Mr. Brodie clearly was not sure of things either. And, in time, a relationship had sprung up, delightful for Donald, between him and his teacher. Mark Brodie had taken him under his wing, had listened to the stumbling exegeses he had attempted to give of his chaotic thoughts. He had even had Donald to his apartment several times, and the ungainly boy had begun to know the pleasures of being a protégé. But these pleasures were not without their bitterness too, for, while Mr. Brodie always listened to him and in fact encouraged him to speak, nonetheless their discussions ended as often as not with the teacher laughing at his pupil. "I'm all in favor of your asking questions, Don," he had said at the end of one evening, lolling comfortably in an easy chair while Donald sat in his usual tense position on the very edge of the sofa. "I'm all in favor of it. But I think I should warn you that I don't believe it can go any further than that." "You mean you don't think there are answers?" Donald had asked anxiously. "Oh, there may be," Mark Brodie had replied. "But I think it's rather plebeian always to want an answer." "But what point is there in it otherwise?" "Why, the fun, Don, the fun! All the fun lies in asking the questions."

The answer had surprised and hurt Donald. He had thought before that in Mr. Brodie he had found a kindred spirit. And yet his teacher now revealed a dilettantism which was foreign and even despicable to him. Donald asked his questions in deadly earnest, and Mr. Brodie did not; and it made all the difference to the boy. However, he still remained attached to Mr. Brodie. The teacher was his only hope, his only assurance that it was worthwhile asking questions for any reason. And through the long summer months he had waited impatiently for fall to come and the start of school, bringing with it a resumption of the conversations with Mr. Brodie that meant so much to him.

Fall and school had come, but at the same time there had arrived on the scene even more than Donald had bargained for. His sophomore English teacher was Christopher Gavin.

Those of Donald's classmates who had had Mr. Brodie last year and who now had Mr. Gavin infinitely preferred their sophomore to their freshman instructor. Mr. Gavin played the game according to the rules. There was no hedging with him. He made statements, and one could accept these statements as dogma—at least for the purposes of his examinations. One knew clearly where one stood. It might have been expected that this would not sit very well with a person of Donald Reinhart's wavering temperament. But this was not so. Almost from the first Donald was attracted to the new instructor, for if Mr. Brodie had held out the promise that asking questions could be a rewarding pastime, Mr. Gavin offered assurance that it could produce positive results—that, in fact, there were answers and that they mattered. Mr. Gavin conducted his classes very well. He forced nothing down anyone's throat. His procedure was to offer clear statements, in whose truth he evidently believed wholeheartedly, and with them a wealth of logical confirmation that made it all but impossible for anyone to disagree with him. He was always ready to listen to opposing views from his students, but once one of them had finished he would meticulously refute what had been said and then go on to reaffirm his own position. All this was quite agreeable to the students, who appreciated a teacher who made his opinions sufficiently clear so that they could be parroted on examinations. And his assurance and certainty filled Donald with a frightened joy, a sense of being on the brink of a remarkable discovery. He had quickly resolved to become acquainted with Mr. Gavin.

Christopher had one more class on Thursday afternoon after his interview with Father Kirsch. He was in a bad humor—the priest had made him angry, though he believed he had concealed it rather well. However, the classroom atmosphere, the prospect of being able to express his beliefs not only without contradiction but with the assurance that all he said was duly noted and accepted, soothed him, so that as he wound up his lecture to thirty-one sophomores he was feeling quite cheerful. They had been reading "The Rime of the Ancient Mariner" and it was now time for what Christopher regarded as his summing-up. He proposed with enthusiasm the thesis that the poem was a failure because its beauty served no useful purpose. "Beauty," he said, "is only an accident. It must adhere in some substance if it is to be acceptable. Art, after all, just like people, exists for a purpose, and that purpose must be a worthy one. Clearly, pleasure, divorced from everything else, is not a worthy purpose, and consequently in such a case intensity of pleasure, far from recommending a work of art, an action, a sensation, actually serves to condemn it. That, I am afraid, is why one must regard 'The Ancient Mariner' and anything else that goes under the delusory title of 'pure' art, as actually a mockery of what true art should be."

The class clearly approved this. A faint sigh of satisfaction passed through the room. For most it meant justification for disliking a poem they had repeatedly been told was good and consequently had loathed thoroughly. To some few the statement had a faintly alien and unfriendly sound, but they brushed away their qualms on the grounds that it was at least eminently clear and not a little novel. But to Donald Mr. Gavin's reasoning represented an unbearable temptation, almost sensuously seductive; for while he recognized it as a flat denial of everything Mr. Brodie held—and everything he had held too while he was under that teacher's domination—at the same time it offered such blessed certainty, such alluring escape into an area where everything lay just a stone's throw from some immutable and reassuring first principle.

The bell rang, ending class. Thirty young men and women stumbled out of their seats, laughing and talking, art and its problems banished once more to the limbo of the insignificant where, in the final analysis, all ideas really belonged. Donald stayed in his place. Christopher stood at the teacher's desk, packing some books and notes into a shabby brief case. He was aware of Donald's presence, but pretended not to notice the boy till, looking up as he snapped shut the catches on the brief case, he said, "Join me in a cup of coffee, Don? That is, if you're not busy with something else."

Donald's face brightened with pleasure, then flushed at once. "No, I'm not," he said. "I mean, I'd like to."

"Fine," Christopher said, walking to the classroom door.

Donald rose and followed him and the two walked down the long hallway together.

"It—it was very interesting, what you said in class," Donald said. This was the first time that he had ever spoken to Christopher outside of class. And the teacher's familiar—almost knowing—way of suggesting they have coffee together had flattered him, though at the same time it increased his normal shyness.

"Which part?" Christopher asked. They turned down the steps that led to the basement.

"About art—and pleasure. The reason for pleasure, I mean," Donald said.

"And for art too," Christopher corrected. "Pleasure is just a part of the art."

"Yes, that's right," Donald said. "What I meant was—it was interesting when you said that things exist for a purpose. That——"

He hesitated. "That's something I've wondered about sometimes."

"Wondered about?"

"Yes. I've wondered—sometimes—whether things did have a purpose."

They entered the basement cafeteria through swinging doors. It was a huge room, heavy with the odor of frying hamburgers and filled with the noise of conversation. There were not too many people there now, though some of Donald's classmates—Christopher's students—sat about at tables and raised questioning eyebrows when they saw the two enter. It was not that they resented Donald's familiarity with Mr. Gavin. They had outgrown that a long time ago, they told themselves. It only seemed a bit odd for anyone to talk with a teacher when it was not really necessary. But then, Donald had done the same last year with Mr. Brodie, and it was expected of him.

"Shall we sit here?" Christopher said, tossing his brief case onto a table against the wall near the door. "Coffee for you, Don?" he asked, turning toward the long gleaming counter.

"Oh, no!" Donald said desperately. "Please—let me buy it." There was something so intense in the request, as if the boy might actually cry if he were refused, that Christopher only nodded and sat down while Donald went for the coffee.

"Black for me, please," Christopher called after the long thin figure. Donald turned to nod with a smile of pure rapture. He came back quickly with two black coffees and sat down opposite Christopher. The teacher sipped his coffee, then blew on it, while Donald felt a spasm of wretchedness as if he actually thought for the moment that it was his fault the coffee was too hot.

"So you wonder if things have a purpose," Christopher remarked abruptly.

Donald blushed in surprise. "Yes, I did. I do, I mean. Beyond themselves, that is. Or beyond the people who use them, if you see . . . But I think what you said about pleasure would mean that things don't have a purpose just for people. I mean they don't exist just for us, but for something else."

"Yes, that's right," Christopher said.

"And if you knew that purpose, then everything would make sense. Really, everything would, wouldn't it?" Donald said.

"Yes."

Donald hesitated. He was on the very brink now, he knew. But he did not have the courage yet to go further. "But I wonder why things couldn't exist just for the pleasure they give people?" he said, backtracking.

"Then what do people exist for?" Christopher replied. "For the pleasure they get from things? That's horrible to think of—a tight little circle like that. I don't think it gives any meaning to life."

"No, it doesn't," Donald agreed with the fervent conviction of one who had stared that conclusion in the face and been repelled by it. "Still, if that's not the purpose—" he had to take the plunge now, "—then what is?"

Christopher looked at him with a very slight and gentle smile. "Do you believe in God?" he said almost in a whisper.

Donald stared at him in trembling fascination. He had heard stories about Mr. Gavin. That he was a Catholic, that he had been a priest—or was studying to be one. He had half-dreaded that Christopher might ask him that question and, though he did not fully realize it, he had half-desired it. "No," he replied in the same whisper Christopher had used. "No, I don't. At least—I'm not sure."

"Hello, Don," a drawling friendly voice said. They looked up and saw Mark Brodie standing by the table. "Hello, Chris," he said, smiling now at Christopher. "Mind if I join you?" Brodie sat down next to Donald, placing the cup of coffee he had been carrying in front of him. "What were you two so intent on just now?" he asked with a mild querying smile.

Donald colored, as if he had somehow been caught out in a betrayal of trust. Christopher smiled back at Brodie and said evenly, "We were talking about the purposes of things."

"The purposes of things," Brodie mused. He sipped his coffee. "That's awfully comprehensive for a cafeteria conversation. The subjects discussed down here aren't usually quite so weighty."

"But you'll agree that seriousness is never out of place?" Christopher replied pointedly.

The significance of the remark seemed to escape Brodie. "I'm afraid I have to confess to a certain frivolous inclination myself," he said lightly. "But Don knows about that. In fact, I believe I've rather disillusioned him sometimes."

"Oh, no, Mr. Brodie," the boy stammered, flushing an even deeper red.

"Actually, we were talking about the purpose of pleasure," Christopher said, sternly pulling the conversation back into line.

"Really? And what did you decide?"

"I don't think we reached a decision. But how do you feel about it, Mark? What do you think is the purpose of pleasure?"

Brodie's smile was ambiguous. "I've hardly ever thought of pleasure as the sort of thing you could say has a purpose. At any rate, not with any overtones of high seriousness. If one enjoys something —why, one enjoys it. I should think it's as simple as that. I don't see any necessity to push on further."

"But if pleasure exists for the individual, then what does the individual exist for?"

"You want me to say pleasure, don't you, Chris?" Brodie asked pleasantly.

Christopher scowled without being conscious of it. "I thought you might," he said.

"You're right—I *might*. And tomorrow I might say that an individual exists for the good of the state. And the next day I might say—well, for no discernible reason that's ever occurred to me."

"But don't you want to know?" Donald broke in urgently. He turned searching eyes on Brodie, who looked back at him with a grin. When he did not reply at once, Christopher prompted more quietly: "Yes, don't you want to know, Mark?"

"I suppose so," Brodie said. "In the same way I'd like to know how the force of gravity operates. I don't doubt for a minute that it would be very interesting. But I hardly think that the knowledge would affect my life very much."

"That's a foolish thing to say," Christopher blurted out angrily.

Brodie was unruffled. "Perhaps it is," he agreed. "Still, I'm not so sure. After all, many people do claim to know why they exist. As a matter of fact, I imagine that you can get any number of different answers to the question. Well then, how does this knowledge affect all these initiates into the secret of their own existence? Not very perceptibly, as far as I'm aware. They go on cheating and lusting and hating—most especially hating people who have a different answer from their own. Of course, now they can do all these things with the explanation that they're acting to serve the end of their existence. But that sort of self-justification doesn't really appeal to me."

"Because others have made mistakes, you're too fastidious to risk dirtying your hands by coming in contact with their mistakes?" Christopher questioned. "You'd rather maintain your superior position above and beyond all that, I suppose?"

Something in the tone or substance of Christopher's query struck Brodie unfavorably and he reddened with annoyance. "Put it that way if you like," he said rapidly. "But to my mind it's humility—a quality for which some God-fearing zealots seem to have remarkably little appreciation."

Christopher leaned back in his chair, satisfied. His face relaxed and his eyes, which had grown dark during the exchange, cleared. He had broken through Brodie's wall of imperturbability and he knew now that he could do it again. He drained his cup of coffee while Mark looked at him with both a lingering wariness and a growing embarrassment. Donald watched in confusion, uncertain what had happened.

"Humility," Christopher reflected rhetorically. "It certainly is a virtue to be admired. However, as you say, Mark, this is no place for such weighty matters. Besides," he said, glancing at his watch, "I have one or two things to take care of. You'll excuse me?" He rose.

"I'd better be getting along myself," Brodie said. He still felt rather chagrined at his outburst. He seemed to have given himself away, and in hopes of minimizing through a display of cordiality whatever advantage Gavin had won, he added: "You know, Chris, I feel ashamed of myself for not having asked you over to my place before. We English teachers ought to stick together. I wonder—would you care to drop by one of these evenings? I'm sure my wife would enjoy meeting you."

"That's very nice of you, Mark," Christopher said. "I'd certainly like to."

"What about tomorrow? Friday, end of the week, time for some relaxation, you know. Could you make it for dinner about seven?" Then, unable to suppress a surge of impish maliciousness: "I guarantee—we'll have fish."

Christopher only smiled. "Fine," he said. "Seven it is."

They nodded at each other with excessive cordiality, and Brodie hurried off, while Christopher stood at the table adjusting some books in his brief case. He continued this ritual until the other man was out of sight. Then, to Donald's surprise, he suddenly sat down again.

"Well, it's a relief to have *him* gone," Christopher said, smiling warmly across the table at the boy.

Donald gaped slightly in surprise. "I don't want to keep you, Mr. Gavin," he said anxiously. "If you have something else to do——"

"I just said that to see if I couldn't dislodge Brodie," the teacher replied with a laugh. "And it worked too. I'll have time to get at him later—especially now that I have this dinner invitation. But what I'm interested in at the moment, Donald—" he bent forward and spoke in a lowered voice that made the boy listen more intently to hear, "—is you." He stared, still smiling, into the boy's eyes, and Donald stared back, fascinated but uncomprehending.

"Do you—do you think you can help me?" he asked, not knowing quite what he meant by the question.

"I can help you, Donald," Christopher said without shifting his gaze. "I can help you in a way no one else can. I can help you to find something to believe in. I can help you to come to know God."

Donald looked almost frightened. "I don't know . . ." he began vaguely.

"No, of course you don't." Christopher chuckled softly. "You don't know anything. But believe me, Donald, that's a good beginning. At least you admit your ignorance. Not like him——" He nodded in the direction Brodie had gone. "You admit you need help. And that means you'll let me help you. Donald, you believe me, don't you— you believe I can help you?" His eyes held the boy's in a gaze that seemed to sound his soul.

Donald nodded slowly. "I know you can, Mr. Gavin," he said, almost in a whisper.

Christopher leaned back then and stretched, relaxing the intensity of the bond between them. "Then that's settled," he said with a grin. "From now on, we're partners, Donald—partners in helping you. Don't worry about a thing. You're in good hands. Leave it all to me."

The words seemed to flow out of him in a stream of elated triumph. Donald did not catch them all, but he knew their meaning clearly. They were words of comfort and encouragement, promising him an end of seeking and of responsibility. He listened in grateful relief, with only one troubling thought to disturb him: If Mr. Gavin should fail him, where would he turn? But even to hint of failure seemed somehow—he could use the word now that there was someone else who cared what happened to him—somehow disloyal. With a feeling of shamed repugnance he put the thought out of his mind and bent all his attention upon the teacher. Failure, he promised himself, was impossible.

CHRISTOPHER ROSE LIGHTLY FROM HIS KNEELING POSITION ON THE floor beneath the crucifix, kissed the Corpus dangling from the black wooden beads and slipped the rosary back into his pocket. He crossed the small room to the desk in a corner by the window and sat down on the hard straight-backed chair. His fingers drummed softly for a moment on the desk, then he got up again abruptly and began pacing the narrow space between the sofa-bed and the chair. His eyes examined the floor restlessly, rising now and again to the agonized figure of Christ on the wall, then dropping again impatiently.

He was dissatisfied somehow, something was disturbing him, buzzing at the back of his mind, though he could not lay his finger on what it was. It was unfair, he thought, that he should be troubled this way now, when his course of action was so unmistakably clear and pre-ordained. Of course, if it was God's will . . . But it was not, he knew. God did not treat his servants this way. Nor did this faint disturbance arise from within himself, he felt sure. The straight path was open to him, he saw his way and was ready to proceed along it. He found no fault in his own behavior or plans.

It must, then, be the others, he thought. Try as he might, he could not keep himself from the wasteful luxury of being angered by them—by Brodie, by Robbie Bond, and especially by the priest. Yes, the priest was the worst of the lot, he thought, the priest was his true adversary. That cowering timidity that could find its boldness only in thwarting the bold! He had seen enough of them to know all there was to know about them. Their little bird-eyes, sharp and cold, their soothing tones creaking with a weary triteness, their shock when one confronted them with their own hypocrisy and their retreat into conclave one with another, from which they emerged reheartened to utter the condemning cliché. That was how it had been when he had gone from one to the other, asking—begging even—to be allowed to enter the seminary. They had scented in him something alien and hostile to their genteel world of ladies' clubs, bazaars, and mild confessional remonstrances administered from the wisdom of a too-full stomach. This Kirsch was one of them. He had all the proper responses down pat, he deified his weakness and called on others to pay homage to it.

He stopped pacing suddenly. That was what they all did! he realized suddenly. Brodie with his disgusting cant about humility, Bond with his pretense of liberalism. They all seized upon their weaknesses and sang hosannas to them. They all turned the coin over, showed a false side, and called it reality. They built their belief in themselves precisely on that quality they lacked. The poor cheats, he thought, how he pitied them for it. They needed him to do the decent thing and open their eyes. It was only he who, loving them, could cut away their self-deception and make them see themselves.

This Brodie, now. Humility was it? Hardly. A monstrous pride really, urged on and fed by that wife (and how he longed to have at her!). Arrogance like that didn't spring from nothing, he knew. There was a cause—again the wife. As he had sat listening to Brodie spout his filthy nonsense in the cafeteria, he had imagined that he could almost hear her speaking through him. The poor devil. Well, thank God, he knew how it was. He knew where the root of it lay and soon he would be able to reach that root, to touch it, to snatch it out and thrust it in Brodie's face.

He would be very kind then, he thought. Brodie would imagine he loved her and that she loved him. In the end they could always fall back on love, find a streak of altruism in what they had done, object "I did it for someone else," and so expect to escape justice. The hypocrites. How he hated them and their lies.

They would call him cruel, he supposed. They would say he was heartless, inhuman, enjoyed making them suffer. Well, perhaps it was cruelty of a sort, as the world looked at it. But it was the cruelty of the just man, the inhumanity of God's agent. What he did, he did not for himself, but for God. Loving God, he would not love men more.

Only of course they would not see it that way. They never had. Always they had judged him by their own petty motives, found him callous, selfish, presumptuous. Presumption! That was what they accused him of. Because, deep down, they did not trust themselves, they called him presumptuous for trusting himself.

There was so much he had to do to enlighten them, to open their eyes, to make them see themselves for the poor wretched creatures they were. He had made a beginning with the boy, but Donald would not slake his thirst. He wanted a more meaningful victory—the priest, Brodie.

Abruptly he knelt again before the crucifix. "God," he murmured, "judge me. When have I presumed on You, when have I allowed myself to feel a pride You did not give me? I thank You for having singled me out from among so many to do Your will." He knelt with his eyes screwed shut in an ecstasy of concentration. "Work Your will on them through me. Grant them light. Grant them mercy. Grant them the purgation of suffering, God. Let them suffer as they have caused You and Your servants to suffer. Strip them of their comforts and deceptions, let them feel Your justice. Let justice be done. And grant strength to the instrument of Your justice."

Christopher rose. He rubbed his eyes and smiled. Tomorrow night at seven, dinner with the Brodies. He really felt much better now. He stood before the battered dresser, his hands resting on its surface. In the middle was set a small upright crucifix, while on either side were small votive lights—thick wax candles encircled by red glass. In the arrangement there was something reminiscent of an altar; except that in the very center, where the tabernacle should have been, hung a mirror.

JULIE BRODIE ABSENTLY STIRRED THE THREE DRINKS ON THE SINK with the handle of a spoon. From the living room she heard the voices of the two men, but she could not make out what they were saying. Not, however, that she was trying. She was absorbed in her own thoughts just now, trying to put some order into her first impressions of Christopher Gavin. It was a habit of hers—studying people, analyzing them to her own satisfaction. She admitted to herself that she was far from omniscient in such matters; in fact, accuracy did not even interest her. Instead, she had the artist's passion for the plausible, rather than the true. Her hobby lay in making up explanations for people—why they were the way they were, why they acted as they did. She did not care particularly if the pattern thus evolved were an accurate reflection of reality; rather, it was her concern to be sure that, whatever the facts of the case, her explanations were at least *possible*. Julie did this in all good will, as an exercise less in insight than in palliation. She was not aware that her hypotheses most often erred on the side of the too-charitable, tending as they did to excuse even the worst individual on the grounds of a bad environment, while frequently overlooking an assiduously cultivated nastiness or a carefully tended dishonesty. This habit of Julie's, with its attendant bias in favor of mercy over justice, had given her the outlook of a social worker. She possessed an almost reflex sympathy that made her fair game for anyone callous enough to play upon it.

Just now she was attempting to arrive at some conclusion in regard to Christopher. It would be inaccurate to say that he had won her sympathy (except for that most obvious variety evoked by his down-at-the-heels look and thinness), for he seemed too confident and self-assured to require that. But he had aroused her curiosity strongly. Julie herself had been taught from childhood that the only thing one could be sure of was not being sure. That had been the habit of thought of her parents, her teachers and now of her husband. Christopher Gavin represented an unexplained and unprecedented phenomenon in her life: a man who was sure of everything.

She had been agreeably surprised, too, by the fact that Christopher's assurance had made him in no way disagreeable or rude. Mark's occasional jeers at the doctrinaire attitude of Catholics had led her to expect of Christopher a belligerent assertiveness. But he had simply failed to display any such tendencies during the dinner the three of them had just finished. The evidence of certitude was there at all times to be sure—a quiet and indeed peaceful conviction that certain basic questions had been answered finally and required no further discussion—but she had seen no rudeness in him. Thus, on all counts, she found it virtually impossible to explain him to herself. And she felt an eagerness she could not explain to do just that.

Julie had stopped stirring the drinks some time ago. She realized now with a start that she had been standing motionless beside the sink for a minute or two and, shaking her head at her own foolishness, she placed the three glasses on an aluminum tray, shoved open the kitchen door with her shoulder, and carried them into the living room.

Mark was slouched comfortably in his easy chair and Christopher sat with his legs crossed on the sofa. They broke off their conversation as Julie entered the room. Christopher rose.

"Let me take that, Mrs. Brodie," he said smiling and reaching for the tray. "Please, sit down. I think you've waited on the two of us quite enough."

"Don't spoil her when I've just got her broken in," Mark said with a laugh.

Julie shot him a glance of mock anger and sat down at the other end of the sofa. "Thank you, Mr. Gavin," she said, smiling back at him and taking her glass from the tray as he offered it to her.

"What's this 'Mrs. Brodie–Mr. Gavin' business?" Mark asked, as he accepted his drink from Christopher. "Didn't I mention your first names when I introduced you two?"

Julie and Christopher smiled at each other in friendly embarrassment.

"I'm afraid I interrupted your conversation," Julie said. "What were you talking about—Chris?"

"Teaching," Christopher said. "As a neophyte, I need all the advice I can get."

"Chris is too modest," Mark said, grinning. "Besides, we weren't really talking about methods. We were getting involved in ultimates. The why and wherefore of teaching. Your conversations seem to have a way of ending up in ultimates, Chris."

"And have you decided yet why people teach?" Julie asked.

Christopher sipped his drink. "Mm," he said, swallowing hurriedly, "that's just it. I don't think Mark wants to decide."

"I teach because there's very little else I can do," Mark said. He looked suddenly at his wife. "Julie has heard all this before."

"Yes, I've heard it," Julie agreed without looking up.

"*Can* do, or *want* to do?" Christopher asked.

"Can or want, what's the difference?" Mark shook his glass. The ice made a clinking sound. "Some people can't do something if they don't want to do it. I'm that sort of person."

"I deny that a person can't do something unless he wants to," Christopher said. "For one thing, it lets out the possibility of most sorts of heroism. And yet people are heroic, sometimes at least."

"But suppose a man had been trained against heroism all his life. Suppose he had been taught that there's something vulgar or unworthy about it," Mark said. "If he had really absorbed all that training, really thought about it and made it a part of him—then I think he couldn't be a hero. Well, that in effect was what happened to me. Not in regard to heroism, of course—I hope. But in regard to ninety-nine and ninety-nine hundredths per cent of all the vast number of ways there are of making a living. You see, I'm that quaint thing known as a humanist." He chuckled. "Humanists are out of fashion these days. But, mind you, we don't complain. If anything, we prefer it that way, since we've been taught that it's somehow degrading to be *in* fashion. We are very much unequipped to deal with the world as it is. And, since as good humanists we've been taught not to make compromises, we resolutely turn our backs on the world and retire majestically to the college campus, where the compromises are at least fewer and less—less——"

"Disturbing to your equanimity," Julie suggested quietly.

"Yes, exactly," Mark laughed. "Granted, I may have to pass some kid because he's the son of a moneybags alumnus. Or I may have to keep my mouth shut in class about politics if the dean and I happen to be on opposite sides of the fence. Still, these things don't really touch me—they don't disturb me—and consequently I'm quite willing to put up with them."

"As long as they don't touch *you*," Christopher echoed. "What about the goals of teaching? It sounds suspiciously, Mark, as if you're identifying them with your own satisfaction and personal comfort."

Christopher was surprised to see that Julie had abruptly sat up very straight and was looking at him with an odd expression in her eyes. He could almost have imagined that it was admiration he saw there. Mark apparently did not notice.

"Let me tell you a story, Chris," he said. "I don't offer this by way of vindication—because I'm not at all sure that it vindicates me. So let's call it an exercise in elucidation. When I got out of college I was, like every other apple-cheeked kid, all atwitter to share my accumulated wisdom with the world. I was shrewd enough, I think, to know that the world didn't really want any part of me or my wisdom—but I was also naïve enough to think that once it had gotten a sample it would change its mind. So, what do you think I did? I went to work for a newspaper. A molder of minds, a shaper of public opinion—that was how I saw myself. Well, do you know what I found out? In six months I found out that I was all wrong—that newspapers don't really create public opinion, that they're created by it instead. And I was very rapidly becoming a creature of public opinion, something strapped together by a lot of Frankensteins—gouty old men with their shoes off, pimply secretaries on buses. I'll admit perhaps I'm wrong about newspapers and public opinion. It's a debatable point. Just like the chicken and the egg. But whichever came first, they're trapped now, they're utterly dependent on each other and can't possibly escape. And you know, the realization that I was becoming trapped too made me almost sick. I was frightened to death—really I was. So I sat down to take stock. I was still a kid, of course, but I could see that out there—in the big bad world—you're a victim, no matter who you are or what you do. You're always—what shall I say?—*bound up* with other people. You can't ever be sure that you do what you do because you want to do it. You can't even be sure that your ideas are your own. Well, God knows I didn't like one little bit of that. I'm not a spiritually gregarious person, I'm not an intellectual mixer—in fact I'm something of an intellectual party-poop. I'm not much interested in other people's ideas or emotions and I'm frightened right out of my skin to find them intruding on me."

"I understand you," Christopher said in a tone suggesting it might be time to move on to something else.

"So, as I say, I sat down, I looked at myself and I looked around me. And I put two and two together and got teaching. A minimum demand on your time and attention—and on your involvement, which is what I'm saying really appealed to me. So I quit the paper, scuttled on back to graduate school and landed here."

"And that is why Mark teaches," Julie said, taking a long swallow of her drink. There was something in her tone that made Christopher look sharply at her again in surprise.

Mark smiled, but the expression in his sleepy eyes was irritated and faintly unpleasant. "We're hovering just now on the brink of our perennial family crisis," he explained to Chris. "Would you like to shove us over?"

"You can hardly call it a crisis, Mark," Julie corrected. "Crises reach critical points. This never does."

Christopher assumed an expression of interest. Mark noticed and turned back to him with a laugh. "You see," he said, "I am a dilettante and Julie—Julie is a seeker. Of course, she's not quite sure what she's seeking—so if it comes to an argument, I almost always win."

"You could be a dilettante and I wouldn't mind," she said with an intensity that surprised both of her hearers. "But what's worst—what's wrong, positively wrong—is that you don't take anything seriously. You laugh at everything. And especially you laugh at seriousness."

"Yes, high seriousness," Mark said ironically. "And for that we turn to our honored guest." He had spoken lightly for some time, but during the exchange with his wife irritation had become apparent in his voice. Julie, on the contrary, despite her evident sincerity, had remained dispassionate. There had been no hint of acrimony when she spoke. Mark now faced Christopher again with a smile that, perhaps because of some odd play of light and shadow, looked disagreeably crooked. "Now it's your turn, Chris. I've said my disedifying say. But you haven't yet told us what brought you into teaching."

Christopher returned his smile, sizing him up all the while, keeping his thoughts well concealed behind his guileless blue eyes. Intuitively he knew that he had nothing to say to Brodie, but that—though he had not as much as suspected it five minutes before—his words could with great profit be directed at Julie. He did not need to look at her to know that she was watching him, and so as he spoke he kept his gaze fixed on Mark's heavy-lidded eyes, grown now a little bloodshot with the alcohol and the poor light.

"Why do I teach? Well, I don't want to give you a sermon. Let's just say I think that I know something worth teaching, something other people will be better for knowing too. Oh, I don't mean that's any credit to me. Many people know what I know and a great deal more. Probably any one of them would teach it a great deal better than I do. Still, for some reason not many of them try. So I do—because I believe it's something that should be done."

"I think that's splendid," Julie said involuntarily.

"Yes, it really is," Mark said, emptying his glass. "I'd give you an 'A' for that any time, Chris. Still, weren't you playing that tune in a different key yesterday? I notice you aren't passing judgment this evening. Granted, the implied contrast is very effective. But I didn't think you were one for nuances. Can't we make the difference between black and white a little more explicit, just in case there's someone nearsighted in the second balcony?"

"Mark!" Julie exclaimed.

"I don't believe in passing judgment on others," Christopher said.

Mark sobered suddenly and stared closely at him. Christopher returned the look.

"I don't know," Mark said thoughtfully. "I just don't know." It was almost as if he were talking to himself and not to the two other people in the room. "You say that so convincingly. I'd almost be ready to think you believed it."

"Mark, really," Julie said. "What are you thinking of? How can you?"

Christopher laughed suddenly, a clear musical laugh that had the effect of clearing the room of its accumulated ugly emotions. "Mark may be right," he said smiling. "They say we're all deceivers, and particularly when it comes to deceiving ourselves. I suppose we all have faulty vision about ourselves—our own motives. Well, perhaps we can argue it out some other time." He rose abruptly. "Thank you for the dinner, Julie. I really enjoyed it. Thank you, too, Mark. I'll give some thought to what you said."

Julie saw him to the door, flustered and embarrassed. "I'm awfully sorry," she said as he stood in the hall outside the apartment. She looked down in confusion, her gray eyes shielded by her long silken black lashes. A slight flush had risen to her cheeks and stood out against the paleness of her complexion. Christopher stood rather closer to her than he had intended and the scent of her perfume came to him, carrying with it the suggestion of something delicate and hidden. The realization struck him that she was very lovely.

"Nothing to be sorry about," he said, smiling. For some reason he wanted to take her hand. "Just two college teachers sounding off."

"Please—come again," Julie said, looking up at him with her large intense eyes.

Christopher hesitated for a moment. For the first time in longer than he could remember he felt confused. "Yes," he said. "Yes, I will." And as he walked away he retained the impression of her slim graceful figure outlined in the doorway.

When Julie returned to the living room she found that Mark had fixed himself another drink. He sat gloomily in his chair, staring between his knees at the floor.

She sat down opposite him on the couch where Christopher had sat. After looking at him in silence for a few moments, she asked, "Why did you do that, Mark?" There was no recrimination in her voice, only the invitation to him to explain, if he wished, so that she might understand.

Mark looked at the drink in his hand, held it up to the light. "I don't like him," he said after a pause. "Neither personally nor as a symbol. But that's a false dichotomy. Actually, Christopher is sort of a living symbol—the incarnation of a Platonic Idea—he's dogmatism on two legs and he makes me sick to my stomach."

Julie sighed and looked away from him.

"What's wrong?" Mark asked.

"It's just that I don't think you're right," she said. Then suddenly she corrected herself. "No—I think it's more than that. I think you're harming yourself with this terrible fear—that's really what it is—this fear of believing in anything. Why, I think if a man told you it was going to rain tomorrow, you'd call him dogmatic."

"And I'd probably be right."

"As if that were some sort of terrible condemnation. Like saying he carried the plague. What's wrong with being dogmatic, Mark, when all it means is that you believe in something?"

"Do you remember what I was telling Robbie the other day?" he asked. "I said I had the advantage of having been on both sides and knowing what both are like. Believe me, it makes a difference. You know, a born Catholic will ignore little slights and insults to his religion that put a convert into a genuine passion. I think that's partly because he doesn't know what they really mean, he doesn't understand the malice behind them, the threat to his whole way of life that can be implied in a wink or a sneer. Well, it's the same way on the other side too. Robbie gets upset when Gavin tells him he believes in God. But he gets upset in the same way and for the same reason he would if someone said a dirty word in his presence. It's something that just isn't done—gentlemen's agreement, you know. But I have the dubious privilege of knowing what's behind Chris's lofty sentiments, his heroic poses. It's just as if I could read his mind. And I don't like it."

"But that doesn't tell me why."

"Oh God—why? How do I know? There are so damn many reasons. Because nine Catholics out of ten are narrow-minded bigots hell-bent on persecuting everyone who doesn't share their bigotry. Because their favorite prayer is 'Give us this day our daily bread—but withhold it from everyone else.' Because in high school a Jesuit gave me a whipping under a crucifix. Because they tell me I'll go to hell. There are a few reasons for you."

"And because of our marriage—and your father."

Mark reddened and frowned. "I wish you wouldn't bring that business up so damned often. I've told you a hundred times you've got it all wrong."

"I know what you've told me, Mark. Perhaps you even believe it yourself. But if that's so I think you're simply deceiving yourself."

"All right—my father was opposed to our marriage. I married you anyway. What of it? What's that got to do with any of this?"

"Didn't you leave out something, Mark? Why was your father so opposed to our marriage? Wasn't it because I'm not a Catholic, and he thought marrying me would cause you to lose your faith?"

"Lose my faith—that's a laugh!" He chuckled, but it was a sound of anger, not of amusement. "As if I still believed any of that nonsense even then. Julie, don't you make the same mistake Pop made. I stopped believing all of that a long time before I married you."

"You don't have to convince me, Mark. I believe you."

"Then what the hell is it you're trying to say?"

"Your father had been worried for a long time before we married that you would leave the Church—that's so. He'd been so worried that you and he quarreled about it."

"Among other things," he muttered.

"Yes, among other things, I suppose. But I think, Mark, that whether it was the cause or just the symbol of all your other differences with your father, religion eventually came to be the focus for all of your conflicts."

"Well, you have me figured out, don't you?" His voice was heavy with irony.

She nodded. "I think so. All your rebellion and resentment against your father and against the things he stood for in your mind came to center on this one issue of religion. As you say, you were out of the Church before we married. But in your father's eyes— and in yours too, I believe—our marriage was the final act of breaking away—breaking away from the Church and from him and from everything in your past that you hated. It's hard to put into words, Mark, but I think that you have to hate the Church now—you really *have* to—because if you didn't you'd be admitting that all your grand symbolic acts of repudiation were pointless—and most of all you'd be admitting that your father was right after all."

"Oh, he'd love to have heard you say that. Pop always had to be right. Pop went to Mass every day and had a private chat with the

Holy Ghost, so he couldn't be wrong. The old—never mind!" He slammed his fist into the palm of his other hand.

"He didn't even come to the wedding."

"Pop come to a justice-of-the-peace wedding? Not on your life. Even if it was his own son—what the hell difference did that make? Pop knew all the answers—he listened to the priest up in the pulpit on Sunday, and no one was going to put anything over on him. Oh, why the hell do I waste my time thinking about the old man? All right—I suppose you've proved your point. The main reason I hate the Church is because it's Pop's Church. It's what he believed in, and it's what turned him into the dried-up hard-hearted old bastard he was. But what about it? It's as good a reason as any I've heard. For more than twenty years I lived with a flesh-and-blood argument for what's wrong with the Catholic Church. And now, incidentally, I've met another one—your friend Christopher Gavin. He should have been Pop's son, not me. Honestly, Julie, it's a strange feeling, but when I talk with Gavin it's as if I were talking with my own father. The old man must have been just like that when he was Christopher's age—he *must* have been."

"Mark, how can you? Do you think it's fair to transfer all your hostile feelings for your father to a man you hardly even know?"

"Hardly even know? But I do know him, that's just it—I do. It's as if I could read his mind. I know what Catholics are taught and I know the way they think. Believe me, it's as if I had a road map to their narrow, hate-filled little souls."

"You always say 'they.' 'They' do this, 'they' believe that. But they can't all be the same, you know. Not every Catholic can be 'hate-filled.' Look at poor little Father Kirsch."

"Yes—'poor little' Father Kirsch. Why is he poor and little? Because he's a misfit. He's too damn kind. The silly old booby really believes what they told him once in a careless moment about charity, tolerance, understanding, loving your neighbor. Well, you see what it's got him. He's in his sixties and he'll never even be a pastor, much less a monsignor or a bishop. They can't trust him. Sure, there are other Catholics like Kirsch. But they're a minority, and a persecuted minority at that."

"Mark, they never told you you had to believe in Catholics. Only in Catholicism."

"Say, that's very clever," Mark said with mock enthusiasm. "You really ought to write a book on apologetics. Where did you pick that up? Something Chris whispered in your ear?"

"No."

"Well, I'll tell you about that. That's what they always say when they get to the Renaissance popes. 'You mustn't confuse the Church with its members.' Very true. The only trouble is, they all do it. You know, they call themselves the Church Militant. And by God if you aren't as militant as the most militant of them, then you're through. Turn in your indelible seal of Confirmation, boy, you've had it. To be a Catholic, you can't just believe in Christ. You have to believe in the Knights of Columbus, too. There isn't any room for dissent with them. If Thomas the Apostle were alive today, your friend Chris would agitate to have him excommunicated as a doubter. And I damn well think he'd bring it off, too."

"Mark . . . Can't you understand what you're doing to yourself? When you talk like this you sound as if you really hated Chris and Catholicism and—and everyone who doesn't agree with you. And the longer you talk the worse it becomes. You're feeding this awful hatred that's so wrong."

"Yes, I think I do hate them," Mark said. "But at least I know it. And I *call* it hatred—not love, not Christian charity."

"What do you mean?"

"You think Gavin doesn't hate me? Believe me, he does. When you want to change a man completely so that he's no longer what he was before—so that he's something entirely different—and when you're willing to substitute for that destroying him completely—I think you can call that hatred. Well, that's what Christopher wants to do with me."

"Mark, he didn't act like that, he didn't say anything——"

"Oh, no, he was on his good behavior tonight. But you know, as a matter of fact I got the distinct impression that he lost interest in me this evening. I wouldn't say he gave up—he's not the sort of person to give up anything—he just stopped caring about me. I imagine as far as he's concerned I no longer exist. And I really think you've usurped my place in his affections, Julie."

"I? Mark——"

He chuckled and sipped a little of his drink. "Oh, I'm not hinting at an affair," he said. "Don't be upset. It's just that I think that you bring out his—oh, call it his apostolic appetite. I'm quite sure he hasn't any interest in women, as such. The boy's a born priest. I can't imagine why he hasn't become one. But, as I said, you're his cookie now and I'm quite sure he's out to effect a seduction—conversion, if you prefer."

"Now you're being silly."

"No, I'm not. You're ripe for a conversion, my sweet." Mark had talked himself into a better mood. He spoke now with his ordinary light cynicism. "Zen, Christian Science—anything at all. I'm constantly amazed that you didn't turn out a Communist somewhere along the line. You're in a positive sweat for something to believe in. It must be something you inherited."

"My parents never believed in anything."

"On the contrary—if you'll permit me to analyze your parents? My impression of them is that they were positively fanatic believers in disbelieving. I know—that's something you accuse me of. But I don't fit the part. I don't believe in disbelieving. I just don't especially care one way or another. What I get exercised about is having people try to force me to care. But as for your parents—well, my God, look at them. Your father a scholar in anthropology. I imagine he could have recited *The Golden Bough* by memory. And your mother—the emancipated woman. The 'new' poetry, Aldous Huxley, and bathtub gin. And I'll bet she really loved it—and believed in it. Don't tell me your parents didn't believe in anything!"

"They didn't," Julie said. Her eyes had a rather distant expression, as if she were looking within herself and seeing something that had happened long before. "They didn't believe in a thing. I was with my father when he died. He was so frightened. . . ."

Mark pursed his lips slightly and emptied his glass.

"Oh, they believed things," Julie went on. "But they didn't believe *in* them. You have to believe *in* a person. And there was never anyone for them. . . ." She was silent for a while. "You know, you're right, Mark. I do want to believe in something—in someone. Sometimes—when I'm alone here, just cleaning the apartment or reading a book—sometimes I feel so terribly frightened. There's nothing to frighten me—and that's it, that's what's the matter. There isn't anything. I want to believe in something, Mark."

He put his empty glass down on the coffee table. There was a slight frown on his face and when he spoke he sounded rather gruff. "Then you've come to the wrong person. I can't offer you anything to believe in. Except possibly myself." He did not look at her as he spoke.

She did not answer for a time. Then she said at last, "No. I wouldn't lie to you, Mark. That's not enough. There has to be something else. Human beings—are just human beings. And we can never get close enough to each other to have any real strength, to unite into something more important than the importance of any one of us."

"Oh, my God, this is just too damn weird!" Mark exclaimed, rising and beginning to pace the room. "Why the hell do you have to talk like somebody out of Dostoievski? This is just the sort of crap that gives me a pain. All this mystical gibberish. You want to be a part of some greater entity or some crap like that? What the hell, go join the Catholics then. They have their mystical body, and every individual Catholic is just a little bit of lint in God's right-hand pocket. If that's what you want, it's there waiting for you."

"But I don't believe in it."

"Believe? What difference does that make? You feel it—that's what's important. The belief will come after, if you really want it. And don't forget, Christopher is there just waiting to take care of you."

He stopped and stared at her. When she did not reply he picked up his glass with a snort and walked into the kitchen.

CHRISTOPHER HAD MADE A NEW DISCOVERY, HAD STUMBLED QUITE by accident or providence upon a new goal, and he spent the next few days mulling it over, weighing it, turning it this way and that to catch the gleams of light from its every facet, and in general preferring it immensely to his former ambition. The conversion of Julie Brodie had, as Mark supposed, become his new project. He had substituted her for her husband. Hence, he had changed his mind. But in Christopher, a change of mind did not mean quite the same thing as with most people. For with him a change of mind did not imply consciousness of change, nor certainly any admitting of one's former mistake in judgment or sense of proportion. Christopher changed his mind in the same detached and impersonal spirit with which a snake sloughs off his old skin. And, after the event, he was quite oblivious to the fact that any transformation had taken place. He was strongly stimulated and excited by his new plan, perhaps because Julie promised quicker and easier results than her husband. But Christopher was hardly one to shy away from a difficult task, and more probably his feeling of satisfaction arose from the anticipation of more rewarding results. Christopher had been granted a vision, a sudden intuitive illumination, as he had stood in the dim hallway looking into Julie Brodie's gray, clouded eyes. Her confused soul, he saw, was one from which something out of the ordinary could be expected. And he felt a considerable eagerness at the prospect of drawing out whatever it might be.

He gave little thought to Mark Brodie. Mark, in his mind, had been consigned—or rather, had consigned himself—to the fires and the torments. If questioned point-blank, Christopher would naturally have denied that he subscribed to the Calvinistic notion of election. But, perhaps without his knowledge, his thought ran along rather similar lines. If men were not predestined to salvation and damnation, they were, at least, predestined to profit from or reject his help. They were predestined to be for him or against him and since, to his way of thinking, the two things were virtually interchangeable with salvation and damnation, he was ordinarily quite certain of the eternal destination of any one of his acquaintances. God, he would have admitted, might perhaps interpose an amendment between the last breath and the personal judgment. But since he and God were almost always of one mind, the odds against it were rather high.

While his center of interest had shifted from one to the other of the Brodies, it remained constant in regard to Donald Reinhart. He had followed up his first conversation with the boy in the basement cafeteria and was slowly but firmly leading Donald to belief. This, indeed, was no easy project. Unlike many adolescents, Donald could hardly have been described as coltish, for he was quite lacking in anything suggestive of high spirits or whimsicality. But nonetheless he had a colt's habit of starting inexplicably at unseen dangers, invisible phantoms. There was in the boy an exasperating sincerity, a maddening intellectual honesty. He could not progress one step further unless all possible doubts had been settled. And, if any one of the stages in his past progress seemed on the point of shifting or slipping, he would insist on an immediate about-face to re-establish its firmness. Thus Christopher had often the feeling that the two of them were making some sort of absurd excursion together, on which it was a rule that for every one step forward there had to be two steps back. Nevertheless, he kept his exasperation hidden prudently, only letting a hint of it escape now and then in a faintly barbed comment or a slightly grim set of his mouth. All the same, he felt at times an immense frustration, as if they would never reach the point for which they had set out. But then, as so very often in his life, providence intervened, apparently with the intention of making his task with Donald easier; providence, in the form of love.

It was several weeks after the start of school. Late afternoon on a day in early fall—one of the fragile days when the air has a brittle warmth to it and the sunlight falls through thinned golden leaves which serve less as shade than as a filter for the light; one of those fall days on which no wind stirs, sounds are muted and the very stillness seems in its unnaturalness to convey a premonition of change, to evoke a feeling of urgency to get done what must be done before the winter comes.

Christopher had returned some books to the library and was walking toward his apartment across a broad park, the only hint of "campus" which Webster University could claim. He wore his usual shabby blue suit and his face expressed its ordinary alert pleasantness. One would have thought from the look of him that he was enjoying thoroughly the exquisite day, basking in it with the keen sensitivity to pleasure of a young man. However, he was actually quite oblivious to the weather, as ordinarily he was to most externals. He noticed *things* when it was convenient or necessary, but otherwise not at all, putting aside as irrelevant any pleasure they might have given him. At the moment, he was in fact rather more irritated than anything else: there had been no developments in the interesting case of Julie Brodie for some time now—not since the memorable evening of his dinner with her and her husband—and his conversations with Donald had lately been far from satisfying. He was eager for something to happen. Inactivity was fretting at him.

Absorbed in his thoughts he walked across the park, rather quickly as was his habit, until someone called him.

"Mr. Gavin!"

He turned and saw Donald hurrying after him along the concrete walk. He was rather surprised. It was unusual for the boy to seek him out, and out of character for him to shout. And, as Donald caught up to him, he thought there was something different about his manner—an unexpected excitement and a nervousness different somehow from the boy's ordinary shyness. There was even, he imagined, a certain hint of enthusiasm in Donald's appearance: his cheeks were flushed and one might have said that his eyes sparkled a bit behind their distorting lenses.

"Hello, Don," he said. "Rushing to make a class?"

"No, I'm through for the day, Mr. Gavin," Donald said. "Do you have another class?"

"No, I'm through, too. Just on my way home, in fact."

"Oh. Well, I don't want to keep you. That is——"

"I'm perfectly willing to be kept, Don. You wanted to talk to me about something? Did you look through those books on the Church I suggested?"

Donald blushed. "I'm afraid I didn't. Not yet. I had an exam coming up. But I will."

"I thought perhaps they'd given you some new ideas you wanted to talk over."

"No, it wasn't that."

Then what was it? Christopher asked himself. "Let's sit down, Don," he said, pointing to a green wooden bench next to the sidewalk. He tossed his worn brief case onto the bench and settled himself. Donald sat awkwardly next to him, crossing his long legs uncertainly, then uncrossing them.

"Now, what can I do for you?"

"Well, I wanted to tell you, Mr. Gavin . . ." And there Donald stuck, as he often did, stumped by the problem of organizing his disordered thoughts and, worse still, putting them into words. After a moment of inner turmoil, he said suddenly, "I wanted to know whether you were going to the Newman Club dance Saturday."

Christopher did not know at first whether to laugh or frown. But then he thought better of doing either. He had learned by experience that, whatever Donald was, it was not frivolous, and that even the most apparently pointless of his remarks or questions bore at least some tenuous relevance to his confused lines of thought. So, suppressing his first impulse, he said simply, "No, I wasn't planning to. Why do you ask?"

"I wish you could go—I wish you would," Donald said.

"It's nice of you to be concerned about my social life," Christopher said with an amused smile. "Still, I don't see any particular reason for me to go."

Summoning up all his reserves—for what purpose Christopher

did not quite fathom—Donald said resolutely, "I'm going to be there."

"Well, Don, I'm sure they'd be glad to have you. Still, you know, the Newman Club *is* for Catholic students. And I imagine the same thing holds true for their dances."

"Yes, but not if you've been invited," Donald said mysteriously.

"And you were invited?"

"Yes."

Christopher waited, but it was evident that Donald did not intend to go on and was expecting him to speak. Such moments had come before in their conversations, when Donald's inadequate powers of expression had carried him as far as they could toward explanation and he waited expectantly for Christopher to divine his meaning. Ordinarily, Christopher attempted to do so, but he felt that in this case he needed at least a bit more help. "Who invited you?" he inquired gently.

"That's just it," Donald replied desperately. "Mr. Gavin, I want you to meet her."

"Oh," Christopher said, light beginning to seep through. "You want me to meet her. What's her name, Don?"

Donald paused a moment, then said with a hint of unaccustomed pride, "Eileen. Eileen McGovern."

"McGovern—oh yes." Christopher remembered her now. "She's in my other sophomore class." The girl had made no very strong impression on him.

"Yes."

"You think a lot of her."

Donald turned to look at him and, something he almost never did, stared directly into Christopher's eyes. "Mr. Gavin," he said, "I've only known her two weeks. But—but—so help me, I think I would become a Catholic if—if—" But he could not go on beyond that point.

Christopher's mind, meanwhile, had begun racing. It was a tremendous windfall, a stroke of almost incredible good luck. He had never expected allies. But now—what more powerful ally could he ask for? Still, he thought he had best sound judicious and a bit reserved, lest Donald spook at overt enthusiasm.

"You're very lucky, Don," he said, "if you really have fallen in love with a good Catholic girl—and if she loves you. But you know there's got to be some better reason for you to enter the Church than that. You shouldn't take a step like that just to please someone else."

"I don't know," Donald said. It was not an expression of disagreement, but of uncertainty. "If I married, I'd feel—I'd feel as if I had to offer something better than just myself."

Christopher dismissed the remark impatiently. "You can't bargain with religion as bait," he said. "God isn't a dowry you throw in to make the contract a little more palatable."

"I didn't mean it that way." Donald sought helplessly for the words to explain.

"Most people do," Christopher said. "God doesn't want wedding-bed conversions any more than the deathbed ones." He spoke as if he were rejecting scornfully some unworthy gift that had been offered to him, a poor sop of conciliation to be put aside majestically.

"I was thinking of the Brodies," Donald said suddenly.

Christopher hesitated. "What about them?"

"I could see sometimes—when Mr. Brodie had me over—what it was like when there wasn't anything but themselves. Mrs. Brodie wants something else, but Mr. Brodie can't give it to her—or won't. I think she needs something to believe in."

Christopher felt a thin surge of annoyance, as if a clumsy interloper had blundered into an inviolable sanctuary of his own. It did not please him that someone else had stumbled upon what he regarded as a unique discovery.

Donald did not notice. He went on: "That's what I meant when I said I could become a Catholic if I married Eileen. It would be something we'd need—both of us."

"But what about God?" Christopher pursued ruthlessly, his irritation giving an unkind edge to his questioning. "Where does He enter in? You'd believe in Him because you needed to. The same way you'd keep a dog because you felt lonely. Something to fall back on." His lips almost curled in disgust as he spoke.

Donald stared down at the ground. The trees sighed, a few brown leaves fluttered down. A cloud crossed the sun and it seemed for a moment rather cold there on the bench. "I didn't mean it that way," Donald repeated unhappily. "I'd have to believe in Him—of course. And if I did believe in God—the God you believe in—then I'd love

Him. I couldn't help but love Him. But I don't think He would mind my needing Him, my relying on Him. We have to rely on Him, don't we?"

"But not as a convenience," Christopher said drily. "Not as a short cut to a happy marriage, good health, success in business. We have to love a stern God, a God Who could do without us."

"But can He?" Donald said. "If He created us, He must want us. And if He can never change—then He can never stop wanting us, can He?" He flushed deeply. "I know, that sounds—presumptuous, I suppose. And I didn't mean to be. It's only that—that if there is a God—why should we set up barriers between His loving us and our loving Him?"

"Then I suppose you think of the Church as a barrier?" Christopher said angrily. The boy was really infuriating, he thought. "Something standing between you and God?"

"No," Donald said. "No, I don't think of it that way, Mr. Gavin. If there is a God—then a church would be something to make it easier for us to love Him. We could use it to show Him we loved Him—and He could use it to show us how He wanted to be loved, I guess. That's what I think a church must be for."

"Always on your own terms," Christopher said contemptuously. "It all has to be on your own terms."

"But Mr. Gavin," Donald cried suddenly, "why does it have to be on *your* terms?"

Christopher started up angrily. Donald looked at him in fright and it required an effort for Christopher to refrain from striking out at the boy's ugly worried face. "I've tried to help you," he said. "I thought I might have earned a little gratitude, instead of insults."

"Mr. Gavin!" Donald exclaimed pleadingly. "I didn't mean——"

"I know. You didn't mean it the way it sounds. You never do. Well, you ought to think sometimes how the things you say *do* sound, Donald. So far today you've told me that you'd condescend to enter the Church if you thought it would help you get married, that you think God is under some sort of obligation to love you, that the Church is a convenience set up for your private gratification, and finally that I'm trying to force my own peculiar brand of Catholicism down your throat!"

"Please, Mr. Gavin——" Donald rose too. "I didn't mean to make you angry. You know—you know how I depend on you. I don't always see things clearly, but I try, really I do. If you'll only help me—"

"How much do you want to be helped?"

"It's all I do want. I promise—I'll try to understand—if you'll just help me."

Suddenly Christopher smiled. He had won, he saw, but he would not press his advantage any further now. A crisis had been passed, but there was still much to be done. It was enough for one day. He put his hand on Donald's shoulder. "I believe you, Don," he said. "And I'll help you. Now, about Eileen—"

"Will you meet her, Mr. Gavin?" Donald asked anxiously.

"Of course. I want very much to meet her. When is this Newman Club dance?"

"Saturday. In the gymnasium."

"Saturday in the gym. Fine. I'll see you there, Don," Christopher said.

"WELL, IF YOU WANTED MY OPINION," MARK BRODIE SAID, SETTING his cup of coffee back down on the table, "I'd say it was definitely an unhealthy business. Still I'm not in a position to do anything about it. After all, you're the head of the department, Robbie. My superior, and all that."

"Oh, well." Robbie Bond hemmed and coughed magnanimously. "Just a figure of speech, Mark. Just an administrative detail. You know I never think in terms of superiors or inferiors—anything like that. We're all on a common footing as far as I'm concerned." He smiled in self-satisfaction.

Mark felt impatience at Robbie's preening. Damned hard to keep him on the subject, he thought petulantly. He would have liked to have tackled him somewhere else than the cafeteria too, and at some time other than the lunch hour, when the place was excessively noisy and they were liable to interruption. Nevertheless, he managed to conceal his annoyance and press on, while Robbie spooned out the last of the chocolate gelatine he had bought for dessert. "Of course," he said. "We all know how you feel about that, Robbie, and we respect you for it. But just the same it's precisely because this is an administrative matter—and you're the head of the department—that I'm putting it up to you to do something about it."

Robbie smacked his lips, sighed, and sipped his coffee. "I suppose you're right, Mark. It's up to me to say something to him—if something has to be said."

"Certainly," Mark said. "No one else in the department has the authority to talk to Chris and tell him to tone down his proselytizing. And frankly I rather doubt that he'd listen to any of the rest of us."

"Still, you know it isn't the sort of thing I like to do." Robbie twisted the end of his necktie.

Again Mark found it difficult to conceal his annoyance. No fool like an old fool, he reflected, smiling commiseratingly at the older man, and Robbie was a prime specimen. Well, he'd bring him around yet. This idea of his was too good to let it founder on Robbie's scruples. A rap on his knuckles, he thought, might very well stop Gavin in his tracks. And, if it didn't, it would do no harm to have put him in the position of having defied the head of his department. That, in fact, could very well lead to interesting developments: renewed instructions from Robbie, renewed defiance from Christopher, and a little note from the dean's office informing him that his contract would be terminated as of the second semester. If only he could prime Robbie to the task.

"No, naturally it isn't," Mark agreed. "It isn't the sort of thing that anybody *likes* to do. But just the same it's something that should be done. I think you'll agree we can't have a teacher spouting a steady stream of sectarian propaganda in the classroom."

"Of course not!" Robbie exclaimed indignantly, rising to the phrase as to a battle cry. But then he hesitated for a moment and his brief enthusiasm seeped out of him. "But it's awfully hard to prove that he has been preaching propaganda to his classes."

"Proof isn't necessary!"

"Really, Mark!" Robbie said in shocked surprise.

Mark backtracked hastily. "What I mean is that we don't have to have evidence—times and places, statements from students—any of that."

Robbie recoiled visibly. "I should hope not," he said nervously.

"Things haven't gone that far. And I hope they never will. As it stands now, it's just a matter of a little chat between you and him—

a few suggestions which, heaven help us, I certainly hope he'll take." He paused for dramatic effect. "But you know, Robbie, that's only how things stand now. If we let this slide, close our eyes to it—then there may come a time when it won't be quite so easy."

"What do you mean?"

"Well, it's not too hard to see what might happen. A few student conversions and what do we have on our hands? A little Oxford Movement. Very nice, no doubt, but rather hard to explain to parents, for example. And rather hard to explain to ourselves too. We can see this thing coming, Robbie, and we have a chance to stop it. But if we don't—well, I for one might feel a little as if I'd fallen down in my duty."

"Yes, of course," Robbie repeated mechanically. "Duty." It was clear that he was being swayed, that his own aroused convictions were forcing him toward something his instincts naturally avoided. "I see your point. But all the same, no one else has mentioned this to me but you, Mark. Perhaps you're just imagining—getting apprehensive about a danger that isn't really there at all." He smiled hopefully.

"Didn't I tell you about the Reinhart boy?" Mark asked sharply, a little of his irritation showing in his voice despite his best efforts. "Chris has got him hooked, to all intents and purposes. Really, Robbie, it's quite a *cause célèbre* among the students. The talk of the campus. And you know what that can lead to. One year it's existentialism, the next it's Bermuda shorts. Lord only knows, it may be Catholicism with them this year. And that, I'm afraid, is a hell of a lot more serious than most of their fads."

"And he really is carrying on this way in the classroom?"

Mark hesitated a moment. But the exaggeration did not seem serious—the principle remained the same and it was worth it if it would stir up Robbie. "Of course he is," he said. "Where else? I'm not sure you understand that sort of mind—and that's all to your credit. But I can assure you that for a person like Chris, it's easy to confuse the teacher's platform with the pulpit—and with the very results we're beginning to get now."

Robbie Bond sighed unhappily. The case was clear and his duty plain. "Very well," he said. "I'll talk to him."

Mark smiled. "I knew you would, Robbie," he said. "In a case of duty like this. And you know," he added, assuming suddenly an intercessory air that he realized would not be lost on his hearer, "there's no need to be harsh with Chris. Just an explanation of what's expected of him, something to set him straight. I'm sure it's just a question of too much enthusiasm on his part. Once he understands what you're driving at—why, that will be the end of the trouble, I'm sure." (I doubt it, he thought. But that will be just as well.)

ROBBIE BOND SAT ONCE MORE AT HIS DESK IN THE ENGLISH DEPARTment office, waiting for Christopher to arrive. He could not help but recall with a sense of vague displeasure their first meeting here and the recollection made the prospect of the approaching interview only more distasteful. Still, it was something that had to be done. One could not permit a teacher to use his classroom as a pulpit for religious exhortations. And, after all, it mightn't go so badly. Robbie had an abiding faith in the ultimate reasonableness of all men, a conviction that once they were made aware of their mistakes and a proper course of action was pointed out to them, reformation would follow immediately. At any rate, they would be alone. He had asked Christopher to come late in the afternoon, when one could expect with confidence that no other members of the department would be there. Not, of course, that he anticipated a scene. But still, considering Christopher's temperamental eccentricities, it did no harm to take precautions. Besides, their being left alone put him more at ease too. Not liking what he had to do and feeling rather embarrassed over it, Robbie much preferred to be spared an audience, discreetly peeping out of the corners of their eyes at himself and Christopher.

The door opened and Christopher walked in. "Hello, Doctor," he said, smiling and crossing the room toward Robbie's desk.

"Hello, Chris." He got up and for no accountable reason shook the young man's hand, realizing even as he did it that it was an awkward action, excessively formal, and likely only to perplex Christopher.

Gavin, however, seemed to have noticed nothing odd. He settled himself into the chair by the desk, quite at ease, looking at Robbie with expectant but polite curiosity.

Robbie drew his large greasy pipe from the breast pocket of his conservatively tailored tweed jacket, produced his tobacco pouch, and began to fill the pipe. "Well, Chris, it's good to see you," he said with excessive heartiness. "It's a pity—but once school gets rolling, I almost never have a chance to sit down and have a good talk with the fellows in the department. It's really a shame."

"Yes, I imagine it is," Christopher agreed blandly.

"After all, a school—well, the Greek word for school means 'leisure' too, doesn't it? Time to think and time to talk over what you've been thinking about. I'm afraid we sometimes lose sight of that ideal here—in this country, I mean. Hurry, hurry, hurry—that's our society in a nutshell, isn't it? And I think some of that habit of rushing has rubbed off on our schools."

Christopher shifted his position and nodded. A slightly bored look had crept into his eyes. "That's very true, Doctor," he said. He turned over the brief case in his lap with an abstracted impatient movement, then put it down on the floor, leaning against his chair.

Robbie, meanwhile, was lighting his pipe, puffing out huge clouds of thick blue smoke that looked somehow as greasy as the instrument that had produced them. "Well, tell me, Chris," he said, between puffs, "tell me, how have you found these first few weeks? You like it here? Happy with teaching?"

Is that supposed to be a leading question? Christopher wondered. He had been rather curious about what Bond wanted ever since the department chairman had stopped him in the hall on his way to his first class that morning and asked him to drop in that afternoon— "If it's no trouble, of course. Some other day if you prefer, my boy." It was obvious that Dr. Bond would have preferred it to be some other day—any other day—or better still no other day. And Christopher was on the alert now for the first phrase that might give away the reason for this interview which Dr. Bond himself would clearly have liked to avoid. "Yes," he said, "I've been very happy, Doctor. I like to teach."

"That's fine, my boy," Robbie said. "I'm glad to hear you say that. It's a wonderful profession. Something I've dedicated my whole life to." His eyes clouded sentimentally at the thought of his own dedication. "And you must be able to imagine how happy it makes old hands like me to see young men like yourself coming along, eager—and qualified—to take the torch from us as we falter." Robbie paused. He puffed on his pipe, frowning suddenly. We must be getting there, Christopher thought. Dr. Bond turned his attention back to Christopher with an effort and said: "Eagerness—that's what you young men have. It's a fine thing—something I hope you'll never lose. Still——" His eyes shifted aside uncomfortably from Christopher's. "Still, there are dangers involved," he said enigmatically.

"I'm not sure I follow you, Doctor."

"Well, Chris, it's possible to be too eager, as we both know. One can want to do too much. Even to teach too much. It's possible for a man to want to teach his students everything he knows—everything he thinks is worth teaching. And of course that won't do. It only leads to confusion, to mental indigestion for the students." He laughed without conviction, hoping desperately that Christopher would co-operate now, say "Yes, I understand what you mean. I'm sorry if I've erred that way, and I promise it won't happen again."

To his despair, however, Christopher merely said, "Yes, probably you're right, Doctor." Christopher knew that there was a personal reference intended in Bond's remarks. He even suspected that Bond knew that he knew. But he could not yet make out quite what it was the other man was driving at, and he had no intention of exercising his powers of intuition to help him out of a situation that was manifestly embarrassing to him.

Robbie waited a moment. But Christopher said nothing else, so he plunged on miserably: "To come to the point, Chris—it's been brought to my attention that you've been perhaps a bit too zealous. Hardly a fault, of course. In a way, it's—it's almost praiseworthy. But still it is a failing in a teacher and it's something I'm sure we both want to correct, don't we?"

"If I've done something unsatisfactory, of course I want to correct it, Doctor," Christopher said coolly.

"I knew you would my boy."

"The only trouble is, I don't know what it is you're trying to say I should correct."

Robbie almost groaned aloud. Damn it, he thought with a bitterness unusual to him, why do I always have to get these jobs? The immense injustice of it all weighed heavily on him. "What I'm trying to say, Chris——" He gestured feebly. "Well, of course, it's not your fault. You can be sure I don't blame you for it. As I said, in a way it's almost something laudable. But still——"

"What is, Doctor?"

"Well, we—we all know that you have strong religious convictions. Now, please," he exclaimed quickly, as if to forestall some anticipated objection, "please don't think we hold that against you in any way. Naturally, I personally don't share your beliefs. But I certainly concede your right to hold them. And you can be sure that every man at Webster feels the same way. Your religion is your own business. We don't inquire into it—we simply don't want to know."

"I'm not ashamed of my religion, Doctor."

"No, no, of course you aren't," Robbie agreed hastily. "You have no reason to be. I sometimes think that if ever I went in for religion myself, why, it would almost certainly be the Roman Church I'd choose. But all the same—well, can't you see that it isn't proper for you to be trying to teach your religion to your students?"

Christopher did not bother to play a part with Robbie Bond, except perhaps for an occasional studied incomprehension that he thought might rattle the older man. It was as if he were too insignificant, too incapable of doing either good or evil, to merit the effort. So now he only said negligently: "Who told you that I had?"

"No one," Robbie said. He lied badly and Christopher began at once to speculate on the identity of his informant. "It's fairly common knowledge, Chris. That's one of the reasons I wanted to have this talk with you now—while it was still early enough for—well, still early enough."

"I'm inclined to think, Doctor, that you ought to be a little more suspicious of common knowledge," Christopher said acidly. "It's not the most reliable source of information in the world. And I'm afraid that in this case it's completely wrong. I've never tried to teach Catholicism to my students."

Robbie listened in disbelief. He had not really hoped for an outright apology, and he had steeled himself for an unpleasant argument. But he had been quite unprepared for a flat denial and he did not know what to do now, for he felt certain that Christopher was lying. "But," he said weakly, "but what about—well, what about the Reinhart boy? You can't deny that, can you?"

"It depends on what you ask me about him. Do I want him to become a Catholic? Yes. Have I been doing everything I could—within reasonable and proper limits—to convince him that it's what he should do? Yes. But have I been using my classroom lectures for that purpose? No. I haven't. That's all there is to it."

Robbie's resistance collapsed utterly. "Oh. I see," he murmured.

"I quite agree with you, Doctor, that it would be, to say the least, imprudent of me to attempt anything like that."

"Fine."

"And, under the circumstances, Doctor, I think you'll excuse me for being a bit—put out, shall we say—that you imagine I lack that rather fundamental prudence and sense of decorum."

"I'm sorry, Chris. Really, I must have misunderstood somehow——"

"Yes, I suppose you did. Or someone else did it for you. But it's not the misunderstanding I object to so much as your apparent eagerness to make it."

"Please, my boy, don't put that interpretation on it. You can be sure——"

"I'll tell you what I can be sure of, Doctor. I can be sure of being distrusted. I violate the code, I know, I don't conform to the rules of the club. Consequently, I'm the object of a constant and rather hostile suspicion. That's all right. I expect it. But I'd really much prefer it if you wouldn't accompany your suspicion with long stretches of rhetoric about my inalienable right to believe what I please."

"I wish you wouldn't take that attitude, Chris."

"Tell me then, Doctor, what attitude should I take?"

"That there isn't a man on this campus——"

"—Who wouldn't lay down his life for my freedom of belief. Perhaps so. Some men will lay down their lives for almost any ridiculous cliché. But on the other hand there apparently isn't a man on this campus—if I may take yourself, Doctor, as reasonably typical of the intellectual climate here—who wouldn't at the same time be ready to indulge in all sorts of nasty suspicions about me, my motives, and my behavior. As I said, Doctor, it's not so much what you believe about me that disturbs me, as the haste with which you seem to have come to believe it."

"We all make mistakes, my boy," Robbie said, squirming in his chair. "I can only ask you to try to be patient with them."

"Unfortunately, Doctor, you're asking me to display the very virtue you seem to lack yourself. After all, I can only call it impatience on your part to believe the worst about me before you had any better reason for your belief than just 'common knowledge.'" Christopher got up, taking his brief case from the floor, then paused as a second thought struck him. "You know, it's odd, Doctor, but I have the impression that you would have let almost anything else get by. Incompetence, absence from class, favoritism— I'm sure you would have decided to wait it out for a while, at least. But religion? That brought you up short, that put you on the track right away, without even bothering to find out if there was anything to be tracked. Correct me if I'm wrong, Doctor, but that *is* my impression. And that's why I find it rather difficult to stomach your talk about my freedom to believe."

Christopher turned and strode out. Robbie Bond, sweating and rumpled, sat for a while in the darkening room, then sighed, collected a few books and papers from his desk, and left.

"Mark, it was dreadful," Robbie said. "Absolutely dreadful. I don't know when I've had such a thoroughly shattering experience." He stared down at his drink, then lifted it to his lips and sipped rapidly.

Mark watched him in some apprehension. He had expected to hear something about the interview with Christopher, but the sight of a frantic Robbie rapping on his door, eyes rolling like something rescued from a burning stable, had unnerved him more than a little. He had hoped liquor might soothe Dr. Bond and had been plying him with it steadily during their conversation, with only mildly successful results. Fortunately, Mark reflected, Julie was out babysitting for neighbors down the hall and he could alternately pump and quiet Robbie without any worries from that quarter.

Robbie, indeed, required very little pumping. He had run on freely from the moment he all but burst in on Mark's sedate evening, and it was only now that his emotional torrent had begun to slacken a bit. "I'm just not cut out for that sort of thing," he said. "Dreadful," he reiterated. "And the worst of it was that he was justified, absolutely justified."

Mark had been surprised and intrigued by that statement the first time he heard it, but as yet Robbie had supplied no elaboration. Now, as Robbie applied himself to his drink again, he managed to put the question. "You said that before, but I'm afraid I don't quite understand. *How* is he justified? Objectively speaking, I mean. We both know that by his own lights Gavin is justified in whatever he does. But I think we're agreed that we can't quite accept him at his own evaluation. Therefore, I repeat: how is his conduct justified?"

The question halted Robbie for a moment and he seemed actually to be reflecting rationally before he spoke. "It wouldn't be," he said at last darkly. "It wouldn't be. If—mind you, Mark, *if*—his conduct had been as you described it to me. But it hasn't. It just simply hasn't!"

Mark frowned slightly, but Robbie did not notice. He continued: "You told me he'd been using his classes to try to make converts. That's a serious charge and it's something I couldn't condone. I wouldn't, not for a minute. But he hasn't been doing it, Mark, he just hasn't been doing it."

Mark's frown deepened. "How do you know?"

"He said so."

Mark positively scowled. "Then how does he account for Donald Reinhart?"

"Perfectly naturally, in a perfectly above-board manner. He admits he's been encouraging the boy to become a Catholic. But he hasn't done it in the classroom. It's just a private affair between them."

"An extracurricular activity? The Convert Club—Mr. Gavin, faculty advisor?"

"It's something private. Purely private." Robbie paused for a moment, but Mark said nothing more. He wanted Dr. Bond to commit himself a bit further before he chose the position that would be most advantageous to himself and his intentions.

"Now, don't think I'm blaming you for all this, Mark," Robbie said at last. "You misinformed me, but you were the victim of misinformation yourself." Mark did not contradict him. Actually, while he had not been misinformed, neither had he actually lied. Having heard from his students of Christopher's efforts with Donald, he had automatically concluded that Christopher was abusing his classroom privileges. He admitted the mistake now to himself, but felt no discomfort over it; Christopher's character, as he saw it, was such as to make the error a natural one, and he imagined that he might very well simply have anticipated something the young man had already planned but not yet put into effect. But meanwhile, Robbie was continuing: "It's the sort of mistake that we shouldn't have made. And I'm inclined—honestly inclined to think that we both owe him an apology."

Mark suddenly forced a laugh which caught Robbie by surprise. He looked at him in amazement. But Mark was only smiling at him. The position he should adopt had come to him quite suddenly. It was, when you thought of it, obvious. Simply renew the attack. "Robbie," he said with a good imitation of a chuckle. "Robbie—really! You're a very clever man, but I'm afraid you're also the most easily imposed-on one in the world."

"For heaven's sake, Mark, what do you mean?"

Mark rose and began pacing the room. "What do I mean?" he said. "Really, Robbie! All right, let's examine what you've just been saying to me. Apologize to Christopher, you say. We've done him a great injustice. And what injustice have we done him? Why, we accused him of trying to make converts in class, when actually all that he's been doing is to make converts outside class. Now, I ask you!"

"Well, what about it, Mark?" Robbie asked rather petulantly. "Granted, that's what I said. But what's wrong with it? It seems clear-cut to me. We've done Gavin an injustice and in all decency we owe him an apology."

Mark stopped in the middle of the room and spun around to face Robbie. "What difference does it make *where* he practices his damned convert head-hunting?"

Robbie blinked in surprise. "I'm not sure I follow," he said confusedly.

"Then I'll explain." Mark began pacing again. "You're basing your defense of Gavin on the premise that a teacher is a teacher only so long as he's standing in front of a class. Outside of the classroom, you seem to be saying, he suddenly ceases to be a teacher and can indulge in any sort of disreputable or corrupting behavior he likes. Am I right?"

"Of course not," Robbie said indignantly. "I don't believe anything of the kind."

"Well, that's a relief to me at any rate."

"Where does all that leave us?"

"I'll explain a little more," Mark said. "We're agreed then that a teacher's responsibility to his students doesn't end as soon as he steps outside the classroom?"

"Naturally."

"All right. Then I think we'll also agree that the question in this case is *whether* Christopher has neglected that responsibility and abused his privileges—not *where* he may have done so."

"Yes, I agree to that."

"And it's my contention that Christopher *has* abused his position as a teacher. He has used that position to attempt to make converts to his religion. And that I consider an abuse."

"An abuse?"

"Robbie, it's no secret that we teachers are regarded—by at least *some* of our students—as omniscient oracles. You know how suggestible these kids are. Hell, we both know that a teacher has to watch every word he says, every joke he makes, for fear some lunatic in the back row is going to take him literally, do something absolutely insane and then explain in all innocence that his teacher told him to."

Robbie shuddered slightly. "Yes, I know what you mean," he agreed uncomfortably.

"All right. Now, what I've been talking about is a question of prudence, due caution, all that. In this case, however, I think we are dealing with something more than imprudence. In fact, your talk with Christopher convinces me of it. He knows precisely what he's doing with the Reinhart boy—who is, I might add, one of the most impressionable students I've ever encountered—and it's even his fully planned intention to conduct himself as he has."

"Yes, I can agree to all that, Mark," Robbie said. "But you said that what he's doing is an *abuse*. I don't see how."

Mark sat down on the sofa next to him. "Robbie," he said in a tone of gentle patience, "this is something very serious. It isn't as if he were trying to persuade the boy to change the color of his neckties. He wants to make him a convert to a religion—to *his* religion, Catholicism. Don't you believe that's serious? Don't you think that for him, as a teacher—as a symbol of authority and wisdom to a high-strung impressionable boy—it's an abuse of his position to act in the way he has?"

Robbie pondered a moment, then said emphatically, "Yes, you're right, Mark. Of course it is."

Julie walked down the hall to the apartment. Her friends had returned earlier than she had expected, and she was relieved of her baby-sitting duties. She reached the door of her apartment, opened it, and stepped into the little hallway outside the living room.

She was surprised to hear Mark speaking. No one had been expected. She was about to go into the living room when some phrase of his made her stop, and she stood and listened in mounting surprise and disgust.

"Then that's settled," she heard Mark say. "We're both in agreement that Christopher's convert-making is going a little too far."

"Yes, we're agreed," Robbie's voice replied. "The only question is—what now? Really, Mark, I don't think I could face another session with him."

"Knowing him, Robbie, I don't blame you. But as a matter of fact I wouldn't suggest that you take any action now. I'm sure he's not the sort of person with whom persuasion would work anyway. No, I think the important thing is that we both feel the way we do about him and his activities. Action can wait until—well, until the propitious moment. I think Christopher himself will supply——"

Julie reached behind her, opened the door, and slammed it shut. Mark's voice stopped abruptly. She collected herself as best she could and entered the living room.

Mark and Robbie both looked at her in surprise and, she imagined, with guilt in their expressions as well. She in her turn feigned surprise at Robbie's presence and after greeting him cordially—something that required an effort on her part—she explained why she had come back earlier than expected. She could see that Robbie was watching Mark—for some signal, she knew, whether or not to resume their conversation. But Mark refused to notice and Robbie shortly rose and said good night. Mark saw him to the door and then returned. Julie was picking up their empty glasses.

"Quite a surprise, Robbie dropping in," Mark said blandly, lighting a cigarette.

"Did he have any particular reason?" Julie asked, keeping her eyes averted from his while she bent over the coffee table and emptied out an ash tray into one of the glasses.

"No, just a social call. You know how Robbie is," Mark said. Then, after a pause, in a tone of the utmost casualness: "Why do you ask?"

"I just wondered," Julie said. She walked toward the kitchen. "I have a little headache, Mark. I think I'll just wash these up and then go right to bed."

"I'm sorry, honey," Mark said. "Couple of aspirin and a good night's sleep will do the trick." He called after her as the door to the kitchen shut, "I'm going to stay up for a while. There's some reading I want to do."

THE GYMNASIUM SMELLED PERMANENTLY OF SWEAT, ROSIN, AND innumerable exotic preparations which had been rubbed into and swabbed onto its hardwood floor with the intention of preserving it. That floor, in fact, was something of a sore spot between the athletic office and the rest of the university. It was reputed to be of pecan wood, or some equally improbable substance, and to have cost a sum that would have represented a sizable chunk toward a new library, science laboratories, or some other foolish investment. The fabulous floor was jealously guarded by the athletic department, which muttered dire threats toward careless students who scuffed it, and repined bitterly when such nonessential functions as academic convocations or, final indignity, student dances, were held in the gymnasium. And, in fact, the athletic department might be thought to have been represented, symbolically at least, at the Newman Club dance by two malevolent janitors who brooded gargoyle-like over the floor from a vantage point in the tiered seats. Their presence served to put a certain desperate spirit into the dancers, who, under their surveillance, displayed remarkable lightness afoot upon the floor.

There was, of course, no way of disguising the gymnasium to resemble anything else but a gymnasium, even apart from the problem of the smell. But the Newman Club dance committee had done its best and, as Christopher entered through the big double doors of the gymnasium, even he was momentarily dazzled by the effect of colored paper streamers, balloons, card tables covered with immaculate white tablecloths and a brilliantly spotlighted band in evening dress playing Latin American music with practiced abandon on a small podium set to one side of the dance floor.

It was quite a chilly evening, but though the dance had just begun, the gymnasium was already overheated from the presence of some two hundred people, and it promised to become positively airless as the night wore on. Christopher had not cared for dances when he was in school—their frivolity annoyed him and he had often remarked, to anyone who would listen, that he had never in his life heard anything intelligent said at one. His feelings toward them had not softened, and he felt an automatic surge of patronizing disgust well up in him as soon as he entered the gymnasium. Still, he reminded himself, this was something that had to be done, and he began to look around the room, among the crowded tables and laughing couples, for Donald.

But his attention was caught first by the sight of Father Kirsch, standing by the bandstand, a happy smile on his face, his right foot tapping rhythmically with the music as he surveyed the dance floor. Christopher hesitated a moment, then a sudden whimsicality seized him: why not talk to him? he thought. It was as if a bit of the holiday spirit had infected him too, and as he threaded his way between the tables toward Father Kirsch there was even a faint smile on his lips.

The priest was turned away from him as he approached. The noise was really quite deafening where he stood and Christopher had almost to shout to attract his attention: "Good evening, Father!"

Father Kirsch turned. Christopher noted with amusement the surprise on his face, but the priest mastered it and said cordially, "Good evening, Chris."

"I don't suppose you expected to see me here, Father," Christopher said.

"I'm glad you could come," the priest said equivocally.

"Yes, but I imagine you're a little surprised to see me," Christopher pursued. The music stopped and he lowered his voice. "I shouldn't think I was expected."

Father Kirsch pursed his lips slightly. "I'm afraid I didn't give it much thought whether you'd come or not, Chris," he said.

"I didn't suppose you would," Christopher said in a satisfied tone.

The priest shrugged his shoulders wearily. "There's no reason for you to feel discriminated against, Chris," he said. "There's a lot of preparation involved in organizing a dance like this. One doesn't have time to wonder whether this or that individual is going to come."

Christopher seized upon the rebuke happily and set it aside for future reference. Then, taking a hint from the priest's remarks, he observed, "Yes, I imagine there is a good deal of work in getting this sort of thing ready. It's awfully nice that someone at least has time for it. I'm sure we couldn't have dances without your efforts, Father."

Father Kirsch sighed resignedly. "Are you with anyone, Chris?" he asked.

"I was looking for someone, Father. A boy named Donald Reinhart. He asked me to come especially—otherwise I'm afraid I might not have found the time."

"Reinhart? I'm afraid I don't know the name."

"No, you wouldn't, Father. He's not a Catholic, you see, and of course it's not your business to try to make Catholics of those who aren't. Nevertheless, I hope he may be one someday."

"*You* hope?"

"Yes, I've been talking with him about the Church, Father. He's a very fine boy and he wants the truth. I'm trying to give it to him. I honestly think there's great hope for him."

"Chris——" Father Kirsch began, then stopped.

"Yes, Father?"

"You're an intelligent person. I oughtn't to have to say anything."

"If you have something to say to me, Father, please do."

"It's this conversion business, Chris. It can be dangerous." The priest hesitated. Even now he had no wish to hurt Christopher. He would have preferred to give him encouragement, if only he had been involved in something he could honestly have encouraged. But he saw grave risks in Christopher's attempting to make converts. Although—was he not perhaps misjudging the boy? If only he could put it gently, so that Christopher might see things as he did. "The process of conversion—it's a very delicate thing. I don't believe you should let yourself get too deeply involved. It would be better if some time early in the game you let a priest take over."

"A priest—you perhaps?" A contemptuous smile played on Christopher's lips. "I'm not sure I'd feel at ease giving way to someone who thought of conversion as no more than a 'game'—your word, you know."

"Why do you insist on misunderstanding what I say?"

Christopher shrugged. "I think I understand you quite well."

"Do you?" To his surprise the priest found irritation mounting in him, and he spoke more sharply as a result. "Then understand this. I'm telling you to stop this conversion business now. If the boy is serious about the Church, send him to me or to some other priest. But above all I want you to stop thinking you can do a priest's work yourself." The conviction that he was right gave an unwontedly firm set to the priest's jaw.

"Excuse me, Father," Christopher said politely. "I think I see Donald now." He turned and walked away. The priest started after him, but the band began again and he was cut off by dancing couples. He stood looking in frustration after Christopher's ramrod figure.

Chris jostled his way deliberately across the crowded dance floor to the table at the far side where he had caught a glimpse of Donald. The boy saw him before he arrived and was already rising as he approached the table.

"Hello, Mr. Gavin." He smiled nervously. "I'm awfully glad you could come."

"I'm glad I could too," Christopher said.

"You know Eileen, of course." Donald turned to the girl sitting beside him.

Christopher looked closely at her as, covertly, he had done in class several times in the few days since Donald had first mentioned her to him. But neither there nor now did he find anything remarkable in Eileen McGovern's appearance. She was a mildly pretty girl with brown, conservatively bobbed hair and a rather too-large nose. The friendly smile she gave him suggested self-possession and intelligence.

"I'm glad to see you, Mr. Gavin," she said. She introduced him respectfully to the other young people at the table, friends of hers, obviously, and not of Donald. The introductions over, Christopher took the empty chair next to Eileen. "I've heard a lot from Donald about you, Eileen," he began, smiling and sitting down.

Eileen only laughed and asked, "Are you by yourself, Mr. Gavin?"

"I'm afraid so," Christopher said. "I haven't had the chance to make too many acquaintances here yet."

Donald was leaning forward with anxious pride to hear their conversation. Now he interrupted to ask, "Would either of you like something to drink? I mean, I think they're selling cokes over there—" he gestured to the other side of the room, "—if you think you'd like something."

"I'd like a coke please," Eileen said, smiling encouragingly at him.

"Same for me, Don," Christopher said, and Donald went off happily on his errand.

"He's a fine boy," Christopher said tentatively, looking at Eileen.

"Yes, I like him very much," she said. Her tone did not commit her to anything and Christopher felt rather dissatisfied.

"How did you happen to get to know each other?" he asked. "I know Donald's rather shy."

"We met in the library, of all places," Eileen said. "But then I suppose that's the most likely place of all to meet a shy person. I work there three afternoons a week and I gave Donald some help in finding some books he wanted. As a matter of fact," she added, "he was looking for some books you'd suggested."

"Really? Which ones?"

"On the Church," Eileen said. "Apparently you've mapped out quite a reading schedule for him."

There was a hint of flippancy in the remark that Christopher did not care for. He was about to reply when Donald returned, gingerly balancing three paper cups full of coke. He handed Eileen and Christopher theirs and then sat down again.

"Eileen tells me that I was accidentally instrumental in your meeting," Christopher said to him.

Donald blushed and smiled. He was evidently very happy, but very embarrassed at the same time. "Oh, you mean the books, Mr. Gavin," he said. "Yes, that's right. I guess in a way it was because of you that we met."

"And how are the books coming along?" Christopher asked.

"All right," Donald said. He hesitated a moment, then added, "But there's just so much you can get out of books."

Christopher's mouth hardened at what he took to be an insult. "That can be a dangerous attitude, Donald. Your intellect is a better guide than your emotions." He glanced at Eileen. "You oughtn't to put too much confidence in the efficacy of personal relationships."

"I think you misunderstood Don," Eileen said pleasantly. "After all, he *is* right—books and arguments can take you only so far. And I should imagine that there's a gap between that point and belief that can only be filled by grace. I'm sure that's what he was referring to—not personal relationships. Although of course they often play an important part too."

Christopher sucked in his breath sharply. "You seem to know a lot about conversions, Eileen," he said.

"My mother entered the Church just a year ago," she explained.

"That's fine," Christopher said. "I suppose you can take credit for that?"

"I'm not sure I understand, Mr. Gavin. It's not a matter of 'taking credit' is it?"

"I should hope so," he replied.

"But why?" she asked. "I should think an individual is just sort of—well, an instrument in another person's conversion. There's surely nothing he can do or say directly to bring it about."

"I hope you don't adopt that attitude toward Donald," Christopher said sharply.

Donald, who had been listening closely again, flushed deeply. Even Eileen seemed rather embarrassed by the remark. "I was hardly thinking about Don," she said. "Naturally, I'd like—— But that's his own affair. Certainly no one should try to rush him or force him into anything."

"Very likely. The only trouble, Eileen, is that that attitude leads to doing nothing at all," Christopher observed triumphantly. Eileen was evidently struck by the inappropriateness of his remarks, but Christopher pursued his point happily. "Donald has reached a very critical stage in his progress toward the Church. Certainly this is no time for anyone who feels the least interest in him to tell him in effect 'sink or swim.' We ought to help him all we can, not just leave him to help himself as best he can." Donald was evidently not quite certain how to react, but Christopher gave him a reassuring glance and he smiled timidly back.

Eileen looked curiously at the teacher. "But what about leaving it all up to his intellect?" she inquired. "You were just saying—"

"I'm sure I didn't rule out the help of his friends, Eileen," Christopher said. "I certainly don't want to give that impression. The point I'm making is simply that Donald's friends ought to give him *real* help. But of course there are some people who, with the best intentions, don't know how to do that. That's why I would caution Donald against relying too heavily on what I called personal relationships. I suggest that he exercise extreme selectivity in them—at this point, especially."

Eileen appeared both embarrassed and disgusted. Seeking to change the conversation, she looked around the room, then said, "It's a very nice dance, isn't it? Do you know Father Kirsch, Mr. Gavin? He's the one who really deserves credit for arranging all this."

"Yes, I know him," Christopher said. "He's a pleasant little priest. I suppose he's quite in his element planning dances."

Eileen's jaw dropped a little in shocked surprise, but she said nothing. She had been predisposed beforehand to like Mr. Gavin for the sake of Donald, who spoke of him to her in terms of admiration used for no one else, and even now, for the same reason, she remained grimly determined to find at least something agreeable in him. But the conversation lapsed at this point, for Christopher no longer showed any inclination to speak, Donald was his usual reticent self, and Eileen was too disturbed to draw either of them out. When one of the other girls at the table asked her to join her in a trip to the powder room, she agreed readily.

Christopher watched Donald look lovingly after her. He cleared his throat abruptly and moved over into Eileen's vacant seat next to the boy. "Enjoying yourself, Don?" he asked.

"Yes. Aren't you, Mr. Gavin?" Donald questioned anxiously.

"Oh, very much." Christopher idly traced circles on the tablecloth.

Donald was silent a moment, then with an effort said, "Mr. Gavin, I want to ask you something."

"Go ahead."

"What do you think of Eileen? I mean, do you like her? And do you—do you think she likes me?" There was a sudden burst of giddy laughter from a table nearby and Donald looked around, blushing furiously, as if he imagined it were directed at him.

Christopher looked at him with a slight sense of revulsion. My God, he thought, that I should have to waste my time with a puking adolescent. But the urge to dominate was stronger than his disgust, and he smiled at Donald.

"I'm hardly a judge of the female mind, Don," he said. "But I'd guess that Eileen likes you—in her own way." He was ready to elaborate, to explain that, like most girls her age, Eileen was only interested in testing her powers, snaring a boy—any boy—but to his vast annoyance he saw that Donald had absorbed only the first part of his remark and was basking in the confirmation that Eileen *did* like him. He was about to go on, unasked, but Donald interrupted before he could speak.

"But do *you* like *her?*" he asked.

Christopher took his time about answering. This would require care, he knew, and he chose his words carefully. "She's a nice girl," he said, "not extraordinary in any way." He was quietly pleased to see Donald's face fall a little. "She has some rather odd opinions—and I'm afraid I can't say I'm pleased at the way she insists on them."

"I guess everyone has opinions that they want to defend," Donald said, a surprising spark of aggressiveness flaring up in him. "You do yourself, Mr. Gavin. And I guess we all think other people are wrong if they just don't happen to agree with us."

Christopher's fingers stopped their doodling and clenched into a fist. "It's all very well to talk that way, Donald," he said coolly. "It sounds very tolerant, very broad-minded. But it also sounds suspiciously like the way you were thinking when we first met—and I'm disappointed to find you haven't progressed any further than that. I'd hoped that you'd grown out of playing with ideas and beliefs as if they were toys."

Donald gave him one frightened look, then dropped his eyes. Christopher smiled thinly and went on. "If you want my opinion—and I assume you do, since you asked me—I'd say you ought to exercise a good deal of caution in your relations with Eileen. I have no doubt that her intentions are good. Most people's are. But right now you require more than good intentions. You think you want to become a Catholic—perhaps—don't you?"

"Yes."

"But you're not sure, are you?"

"No."

"Well, then, I'll tell you something, Donald. It's quite possible that Eileen, all by herself, can either keep you out of the Church, or force you into it—but in either case it will be for the wrong reason. She may keep you out because, like many watery well-intentioned Catholics, she won't want to push you into anything, won't want to intrude on the privacy of your conscience—in short, will encourage you in your natural weakness and indecision. Or she may force you into it because, having decided that you'll do for a husband, she'll insist on your becoming a Catholic before she marries you. As I say, she may do either one. I'm not sure which, because I haven't seen enough of her. But——" He noticed Donald glance past him and he turned and saw Eileen returning.

He smiled ingratiatingly at her and stood up. "I'm afraid I took your seat." Christopher pulled out the chair for her.

Eileen sat down and turned smilingly to Donald. "Well, you two were having quite a discussion," she said. "What were you and Mr. Gavin talking about, Don?"

Donald fixed his eyes on the table. "Oh, nothing," he said.

"Nothing?" Eileen repeated uneasily.

Another bit of whimsy stirred Christopher and he interrupted. "Eileen, I'm awfully out of practice as a dancer. But if you wouldn't object——?"

Eileen looked surprised, but replied quickly, "No, of course not, Mr. Gavin, I'd love to." Then, with a return of her ordinary liveliness, "Don is such a sobersides—he thinks dancing is a spectator sport." But Donald could manage only a faint smile.

Christopher was a naturally graceful young man and danced quite well, though he had never made any particular effort to acquire the skill. He guided Eileen across the floor for some time without speaking and she, uncomfortable in his presence, at first made no attempt to start a conversation. She was, however, a naturally vivacious girl and she still desired to find something redeeming in Donald's friend. Therefore, she tried again with an innocuous subject. "It's a very good band, isn't it?" she asked.

"Yes, very nice," Christopher said.

"I only wish Don liked dancing more. I love it myself. But perhaps I can change him."

"Eileen, I'd suggest that you don't try to change him too much. It's a temptation, of course, to try to make him over in your own image. But that isn't necessarily always a kindness."

Eileen hesitated a moment, but Mr. Gavin, though he did make her ill at ease, held no terrors for her. "You don't like me very much, do you?" she queried directly.

Christopher laughed softly. "Of course I do."

Eileen ignored his disclaimer. "But I wonder why you don't? We've never met outside class before, I don't believe you can have heard anything too bad about me. And I don't think anyone else has ever found me so terribly disagreeable—at least, not on first acquaintance."

Christopher did not answer for a moment. When he spoke, he was no longer smiling. "If you'll pardon me, Eileen, I think you're displaying a certain feminine conceit. Women always like to imagine that they evoke violent reactions in the people who meet them. You're a sensible girl, and I'll be sensible with you. The fact of the matter is that I don't dislike you. I really feel rather indifferent toward you. But I *do* have a high regard for Donald."

"I'm afraid you've gone a little bit over my head, Mr. Gavin." Eileen's eyes flashed but she spoke with the utmost politeness. "I don't quite see why the fact that you like Donald should influence your attitude toward me unfavorably——"

"Not *unfavorably*," Christopher corrected mildly.

"—unless you happen to consider me a bad influence on him."

The music stopped, and there was a smattering of applause. The band began again, a waltz, and they glided smoothly among the laughing happy couples.

"Not necessarily a *bad* influence," Christopher said. "But a very strong influence. And this is a time when Donald—or someone interested in him—should be very careful of just what does influence him."

"And you, of course, are a good influence, Mr. Gavin?"

"I certainly hope so. I'm sure that if I thought I weren't, I'd let Donald alone."

"I doubt it," Eileen said quietly.

Christopher's eyes darkened faintly. "What do you mean?" he asked.

"I'm sorry, Mr. Gavin. I think I was wrong. I think if you did believe you were doing Don harm you'd let him alone. What I should have said is that I can't conceive of your ever thinking that. I can't imagine that you'd ever be unsure of yourself."

"Should I apologize for that, Eileen?" Christopher's tone was quite friendly, even a little bantering. But there was still something dangerous in his eyes. "Is there some peculiar virtue in feeling unsure of yourself? If there is, I'm afraid you lack it too—I hardly think you feel any qualms about influencing Donald."

"Then one of us is wrong, isn't he?" Eileen asked.

"Yes," Christopher said, "I'm afraid one of us is."

When the music stopped again, Christopher took Eileen back to the table. After she was seated he turned to Donald and said, "Well, I think I'd better be getting on now, Don. We teachers aren't used to late hours."

Donald looked at him in surprise. "Do you have to, Mr. Gavin?" he said. "I mean, it's still early. Really, couldn't you——?"

"No, I'm afraid not. Besides—" he glanced at Eileen, "—I'm sure I'd only be in the way. And I hate to interfere in anything important."

Donald reluctantly gave in and was about to accompany him at least as far as the door, but Christopher only laughed at the idea. "Eileen," he said, "it's been quite a pleasure meeting you outside class. I hope we can do it again."

"Do you, Mr. Gavin?" she asked with a coquetry whose irony was not lost on Christopher and angered him. "I certainly do. Good night."

Christopher walked away. He was still angry, but nonetheless he felt that he had done rather well. His remarks to Donald had been fairly well put, he thought, and he had caused Eileen to dislike him—perhaps enough to complain of him to Donald and thus unwittingly, if he had calculated correctly, turn him against herself. In any event, it was a good night's work and he was satisfied with himself.

He left the gymnasium. He was surprised at how much colder it had gotten—a chilly wind was sweeping across the parking lot in front of the building—but the fresh air was invigorating. Then abruptly he heard the gymnasium door open, emitting a snatch of Latin American music, then slam shut, and a voice call his name. He turned and, to his surprise, saw Father Kirsch come quickly down the steps toward him.

"Hello, Father," he said. He noticed with amusement that the little man was shivering in the wind. "You shouldn't have come out without your coat. It's cold here."

"You aren't wearing a coat either, Chris," the priest said.

"Oh, I'm used to that, Father. But I'm sure you aren't. I suppose in our cases it's the difference between—well, an alley cat and a house cat, if you see the analogy." They stood at the bottom of the steps. One of the towering arc lamps that lit the parking lot cast a pale and rather greenish light over their faces. Now and then a fragment of melody came from the gymnasium and the wind sighed coldly.

"Yes, I see the analogy," Father Kirsch said. "You're seldom very subtle, Chris."

"I seldom try to be, Father. Subtlety isn't one of the qualities I value very highly. I've always thought it rather effeminate."

"Then I won't be subtle either, Chris. Because I'd hate to have you think badly of me." Christopher was amused again—this time at the priest's feebly venomous sarcasm.

"Goodness, Father, I wouldn't do that," he said. "And I'd hate to have you catch cold either. So, if I'm not rushing you, what was it you had to say to me?"

"I wasn't very satisfied with our conversation earlier this evening, Chris."

"Really?"

"You told me you were trying to bring some boy into the Church. Well, I want to repeat to you, Chris, that I think you should be very cautious——"

"Cautious!" Christopher spat out the word. "Yes, I'd expect you to urge caution, Father. I imagine you've been practicing and urging caution all your life."

"Not all my life, Chris. And above all—not to everyone."

"Not to everyone? Then why to me?"

"Because I think you need it more than most people."

"That's rather weak, Father. I'd expected something more impressive than that."

"I can put it more strongly if you like."

"Please do."

"Then I'll be frank with you, Chris, and say that you're the last person I'd ever want to see make a convert. Because I don't believe you'd ever really bring anyone into the Church." Christopher raised an eyebrow, expressing mild interest. "Oh, you'd bring them into *a* church—but it would be your own private religion, on your own private terms. The thing you lack, Chris, is a sense—a sense of unity, I suppose. It's a very strange thing to me that you call yourself a Catholic—a member of a complex organization, a member of the Mystical Body—because I'm quite sure you haven't the faintest idea of what it means to be a member of anything. All things for you have their beginning and end with yourself. And that's why I believe that you could only make converts to yourself—not to the Church."

Christopher's face had gone rigid. "That's being quite frank, Father," he said stiffly, hardly moving his lips in the effort to control himself, to keep from striking out at the priest. "I'm sure then that you'll excuse my frankness if I say that I think you're a coward. There are a lot of them like you—a lot of whining little priests with their pious phrases and good intentions and a horror of anyone who tries to show them up for what they are and getting something done without your approval, your gracious permission." He felt himself growing incoherent, but the sheer pleasure his words gave him kept him from stopping, and they tumbled out in a wild bitter stream. "Yes, your priesthood—your precious holy priesthood—that's something reserved for the meek docile little men who are afraid of thinking for themselves. It's a closed circle, isn't it? No one else can get in. No one else can dare say he speaks for God unless he speaks in chorus with you. What do you know about the Church? How do you dare to tell me about the Church? Is a man like you qualified to judge me? I leave it to God to judge——"

"Shut up!" To the priest's surprise Christopher stopped. But this sudden silence was plainly less a response to the command than a deliberate lull in which Christopher was seeking to master the choking rage which had brought him to the brink of incoherence. Father Kirsch took advantage of the pause to speak as authoritatively as he could. "I think I understand something about you now, Christopher. It's taken me a while, but I think I have the key now."

"Do you?" Gavin growled. "Don't be too sure."

"How can I help but be sure? You've been telling me yourself."

"So damned clever, aren't you?"

"That story you told me in my office about the seminary—about your being turned down because of your health—that isn't true, is it?"

Christopher shrugged contemptuously. "Of course not. What of it?"

"But the seminary is the key just the same. You couldn't make it—they wouldn't let you in—and the result—" he gestured vaguely, "—is all this."

Surprise and suspicion mingled in Christopher's expression. "I don't know what you mean by 'all this.' But you're right, up to a point. They wouldn't accept me. I saw priest after priest, and still it was the same story—a flat no."

"I'm sorry."

Christopher hesitated, and the priest saw something like eagerness flicker in his cold eyes. His bitter words of a moment before seemed abruptly forgotten. "Do you think you could help me? If I could just get a recommendation from someone—something to give me a start."

The priest frowned and looked away. He knew what he had to say, and he knew too that it would only rekindle Christopher's rage. But there was no alternative, and honesty could be his only kindness. "You're asking the impossible——"

"I knew it!" The young man's face hardened again and his eyes flashed. "That's what I expected to hear. You're all alike."

"About something like this we have to be. How could I recommend you? That would mean I thought you had the qualifications for the priesthood." He took a deep breath and, not meeting Christopher's eyes, went on. "But I don't think that. It's the furthest thought from my mind. You aren't in any condition to help others. You need help yourself. Believe me, Christopher, you do. You're spiritually sick and, God help you, I think you're emotionally sick too. I don't know what the other priests you talked with told you, but I'm sure of one thing—that they all thought what I'm telling you now. For your own sake, listen to me——"

"God damn you," Christopher said. The blood had drained out of his face. His fists were clenched at his sides. "Damn you to hell."

A chill wind blew across the parking lot, and the priest was suddenly aware that there was sweat on his forehead. His hand shook slightly as he wiped it off. "I want to help you——" he began again.

"You want to. Oh yes, you want to terribly. But of course you can't. Or rather, you won't. That's the help you offer me—the kind that you can't give. Well, do you know what I think of your help? Do you know what I think of you?" Christopher's voice had been rising again until now he was almost shouting. "I think you're a lousy, stinking, overfed little hypocrite. You all are. You'd change your tune quickly enough if I just knuckled under, if I took my orders from you, if I were a good boy and didn't make any fuss. But I'm not going to do that, and you know it—you all know it—and so you band together to fight me, to deny me what I want, what I should have——"

"The priesthood?"

"Yes, the priesthood! What else? What the hell do you think I'm talking about?"

"Why do you want to be a priest?"

"To serve God and to make others serve Him."

"*Make* others?"

"Make them," he repeated. "Of course I want to make them. Oh, I know you wouldn't understand that. It's not important enough to you—what you say you believe in—to want to compel others to believe it too. But it's different with me. It matters to me whether or not others believe. And if they don't, then I'll make them, or I'll ruin myself and them trying."

"Then God help you and them both, because the only thing you want others to believe in is yourself, not God, and your only motive——" The priest hesitated, then forced himself to continue. "Your only motive is the most insanely diabolical pride I've ever seen."

Christopher looked him up and down slowly, and a smile that chilled the priest's heart spread over his face. "Then we know where we stand, Father."

The priest nodded wearily. Suddenly he felt as if he could say nothing more, even had he known what to say. "I suppose we do." Wanting now only to get away, he turned and went back up the steps.

"We know where we stand now, Father!" Christopher shouted again after him. The door to the gymnasium slammed shut and he was left alone. He inhaled the cold air hungrily. Then he began to laugh, a low warm chuckle, and he laughed all the way home.

IT WAS THE TUESDAY AFTER THE DANCE AND CHRISTOPHER HAD taught his last class for the day. It had rained all morning, a sullen late-October rain out of leaden skies, stripping brown leaves from the trees and spreading them matted and pasty on the sodden ground. The rain had stopped in the early afternoon, but it remained overcast and damply cold. Christopher paused for a moment outside the classroom building to slip on a soiled and spotted raincoat, then began to walk in the direction of his apartment house. He had not gone far when suddenly he saw coming toward him along the wet leaf-strewn concrete walk Julie Brodie.

Christopher was surprised—first at seeing her, then at his own reaction. For he discovered that he was pleased to see her, and pleased not alone at the unexpected opportunity of pushing forward the project he had first set himself during the dinner at the Brodies' apartment, but pleased also at her trim figure in an immaculate white mackintosh, pleased at her dainty precise steps as she avoided puddles and clotted heaps of leaves, pleased at the way the wind blew at her black hair. It was something for him to wonder at, and he was still wondering when they drew near enough for her to smile shyly and say, "Hello, Chris. How are you?"

"I'm fine, Julie," he said. She stopped and he did, too. "How are you?"

"Just fine." She looked embarrassed. "Have you seen Mark?" she asked.

"No, I'm afraid I haven't." Christopher too felt a certain embarrassment. For once the words did not come easily and he found to his chagrin that he had nothing to say.

"I was looking for him," Julie explained vaguely. "Are you going home?"

"Yes. I'm through for the day."

"Oh." She hesitated a moment, then: "Do you mind if I walk along with you?"

Christopher's eyes widened. "No," he said. "No, of course not."

They walked side by side in silence across the university's central park. Up ahead of them a group of freshmen in T shirts and khakis were playing a furious game of touch football, shouting and sloshing around in the puddles like puppies. As they drew near, two of the boys raced out from the group while another faded back and threw a long wobbly forward pass. The football went astray and one of the boys, lunging for it, almost collided with them.

Christopher scowled at the boy, who grinned back, hastily said "Sorry," and ran after the ball.

He was about to make a caustic remark when Julie suddenly turned and, smiling after the boy, said: "They're cute, aren't they? So grown-up sometimes, and other times just like little boys."

"My difficulty is that I'm expected to make them act grown-up all the time," Christopher said drily. "As you can see, it's not always an easy job."

There was a pause. Then, in a surprisingly different tone, Julie said, "Chris, I wasn't telling the truth before. I didn't really come to find Mark at all."

"No?" He listened with interest and—he could not deny it—that same unfamiliar pleasure he had felt before. He wanted to urge her to go on, and yet he was afraid to for fear—for fear she might not say what he hoped to hear, though he could not have explained what that was.

"No. I came because I wanted to see you. I even called the

registrar's office to check on your schedule so I'd know when and where to find you."

Christopher did not know what to say. He realized somehow that she had said what he wanted, but what his reply should be—he could only mumble stupidly, "Did you?" He cursed himself silently for his awkwardness.

"You see, I wanted to tell you something."

"What is it, Julie?"

"It's—— Well, it sounds so awfully silly—so melodramatic. But I wanted to warn you of something."

Christopher felt vaguely disappointed, and at the same time angry with himself for being disappointed. "Warn me of what?" he asked, almost sharply.

"Before I tell you, I want to explain—I thought for a long time about whether I should do this or not. I suppose in a way it's being disloyal. But still it wouldn't be fair not to tell you—and I think, believe me, it's for Mark's good too that I tell you."

Christopher frowned. "For Mark?" he said. "What's Mark got to do with it?"

Julie blushed. "I'm telling this so badly!" she exclaimed. "I did want to make it all clear. Please—" she gestured toward a wooden bench by the walk, "—could we sit down?"

"Yes, certainly."

The bench was damp but their raincoats protected them. They sat silently for a moment, while Julie looked down at the ground, trying to collect her thoughts. At last she lifted her eyes to Christopher's and he felt a momentary confusion before their clear direct gaze.

"I'm sorry to be so silly," she said smiling. "Please put up with me, Chris."

"Yes, of course, Julie. But perhaps if you'd begin at the beginning——"

"Well, there's hardly anything to tell. One evening last week I was out of the apartment for a little while. When I came back, I found that Robbie had dropped by and was with Mark. They didn't hear me come in and I couldn't help overhearing——" She stopped herself suddenly and made a gesture of impatience. "No, I want to be honest about this. Actually, I deliberately listened to what they were saying. I don't know why—it was just an impulse,

I was surprised that Robbie was there. Anyway, they were talking about you, Chris."

"Were they?" Christopher was following her story closely now. "What were they saying?"

"You understand, don't you, that I hate telling you this—that I feel like a spy or something? It's only that I think you should be told——"

"Of course, Julie."

"I didn't hear much—and I don't really know what they were talking about exactly. But they were saying something about your making converts. It seemed as if they wanted to stop you and as if they were just waiting for an opportunity to—well, I don't know what. But it seemed as if they were planning to wait for a chance to make you lose your job."

Christopher laughed suddenly and Julie looked at him in confusion. "Please, Chris, why are you laughing?"

"I'm sorry," he said. "It's not at you—or at what you've told me. Not exactly, anyway. But I think I know what it is they were talking about and what they were cooking up. Would you like to hear?"

"I don't know," she said anxiously. "I'm not sure it would be right."

"Oh, it's nothing so very terrible," he said. "And you might find it interesting." He glanced covertly at her to see if there were any sign of protest on her face, but discovering only indecision he went on rapidly. "It all centers around a student of mine—a former student of Mark's. A boy named Donald Reinhart—do you know him?"

"Yes. Mark had him to the apartment several times last year. But I haven't seen him this year."

"That's understandable enough. You see, to put it bluntly, Donald has more or less dropped Mark in favor of me. And I'm afraid that's what's at the bottom of things. Of course, you shouldn't think badly of Mark for it."

"You mean he's jealous of you? But that's so silly."

"Really, Julie, I wouldn't want you to think any the worse of Mark because of it. It's a perfectly natural reaction under the circumstances. And he has the best intentions, I'm sure. It's just that—

well, no doubt he feels very strongly about the matter and he's reacting rather—imprudently, I suppose you'd say."

"But to make all this trouble over something so small. It just isn't like Mark," she protested.

"Well, of course the whole affair is magnified in his eyes. And then there is another aspect to it that I haven't mentioned."

"Another aspect?"

"Julie, I'll admit I'm rather reluctant to talk about this. I can understand Mark's feeling a little—well, jealous, if you want to call it that. But this other thing—I have to confess I don't quite understand Mark's position there and consequently I'm afraid I might misjudge him."

"What is it?"

"Well, it's this business of religion. You see, Donald has expressed an interest in my Church—in Catholicism—and naturally, I want to help him in any way I can. For some reason, that seems to—to anger Mark terribly. Of course, I'm certain he believes he's acting rightly."

"What has he done?"

"Well, I'm not sure. And, Julie, really—I don't want to speculate. It isn't fair to him. But you see, Robbie came to me the other day and as much as implied that I've been preaching my religion in the classroom. Now, I don't know where he got that idea. But if you heard him talking with Mark about it——" Christopher gestured vaguely, an unhappy expression on his face. "But of course we can't draw any conclusions from that."

Julie's appearance had undergone a transformation. Her face was pale and her eyes very large. "I wouldn't have believed it possible," she exclaimed. "I knew Mark didn't like your religion, even that he was bitter about it. But that he should take his resentment out in a spiteful personal way like this—it just makes me sick with shame, Chris. I don't know how to apologize."

"You don't have to, Julie. And I don't think Mark should have put you in a position where you would feel that you did."

"If only it made sense—if there were some rational reason—but his feeling toward you is just one more manifestation of his hatred for the entire Church."

"And why does he hate the Church?"

"I wish I could explain that—but it doesn't make any sense either when you try to put it into words. It's all tied up with his feelings about his father. The two of them never got along—don't ask me why—and as Mark grew older his hostility toward his father came to center on religion. I suppose there were a lot of reasons why Mark left the Church, but I think the main one was that he knew it was a way of hurting his father. And all the bitterness between the two of them has gotten mixed up with his bitterness toward religion—and toward you now. But I never dreamed he'd try to go as far as hurting you. I can't understand it. What right does he have? What right can he *think* he has——?"

"Prejudice is a terrible thing, Julie. People like you and myself who don't share it will always find it impossible to understand other people's actions under its influence. You know, in this case it's not so much the injury to myself that troubles me, but what Mark's scheming could mean for Donald. The boy is sincere. He wants desperately to find something to believe in——"

"—And to deny him that chance!" she whispered. "It's terrible."

"It is." Christopher paused a moment, thinking quickly. Then he said, "Julie, if you'll excuse me, there's something else I want to say. Perhaps I haven't any right to—please, stop me if I don't. It's just that—— Well, it's an impression I have that you are being denied that chance—to believe in something—too."

"I'm not sure——"

"Julie, I know Mark is your husband, and he must love you and he must want what he thinks is best for you. But you see how seriously he can be blinded by prejudice in this matter of religion. I only suggest—perhaps it's foolish of me—that Mark may be keeping you from religious faith, too."

"Chris, I don't know what to say——" She looked bewildered.

"No, of course you don't," he interrupted quickly and gently. "I suppose I shouldn't have mentioned it. I only thought that—— Julie, we all have to believe in something. For your own sake, please, give that some thought."

"I will," she said slowly. "I will."

"That's all I ask. And, Julie, remember—if I can ever help, please tell me. Because I do want to."

"Yes, I'll remember, Chris," she said.

They parted then. Julie went her way thoughtful and disturbed. But there was something positively jaunty in Christopher's stride, and he whistled a little tune.

THE COLD MIST DRIFTING DOWN THROUGH BARE BRANCHES, HAZING the street lamps, slicking the sidewalks, falling noisily onto the big black umbrella and seeping over its edges, provided just the proper contrast to heighten the sense of warmth and intimacy for Donald and Eileen. Few things can more effectively create a feeling of closeness between two people than walking together under one umbrella in the rain. And so Donald and Eileen found it. They had drawn close together so they would both be under the umbrella and she had taken his arm lightly. An occasional car passed them, but otherwise it was quite still and they seemed to have to themselves the side street by which Donald was taking Eileen back to her dormitory after an evening at the movies. Nor did either of them seem to have much to say, but rather both appeared lost in their thoughts—though in Donald's case, at least, the thoughts were almost wholly of Eileen. He felt an unusual pride and sense of protectiveness with her walking by his side, and he could not help but reflect with pleased surprise that only a few weeks ago he had been a stranger to both sensations. It was amazing, he thought, that this experience (he had not yet attempted to give it a name) should have befallen him, of all people. It was amazing that it really was possible to be happy. And, as the thought occurred to him, he wanted to tell Eileen of it—as he had found himself lately wanting to tell her of all the thoughts he had, of all the doubts and hesitations and the few faint stirrings of an alien courage.

"Eileen," he said softly.

She looked up at him with a smile. "Yes, Don?"

"I wanted to tell you—I suppose it sounds silly—but I just wanted to tell you I'm happy." The hesitation was almost gone from his speech when he spoke to her. He felt, without even thinking of it, sure of being understood and sure that he did not have to fear ridicule or a rebuff.

"I'm glad you are," she said, pressing his arm reassuringly.

"Are you happy too?" Their footfalls were muted as they passed down the long corridor of glistening bare trees. A few blocks back a trolley bell rang and one could have imagined it was a buoy at sea.

"Yes," she said, "I'm happy."

"I don't suppose," Donald said thoughtfully, "it's anything unusual for you to be. But for me—well, I don't want you to think I'm always unhappy. But I guess I haven't ever really been *very* happy before."

"Poor Donald," Eileen murmured. "What makes you happy now?"

"A lot of things," he answered. "I guess that's what surprises me mostly—that so many things should happen all at once to make me happy—after such a long while when there wasn't much of anything at all."

"What are some of the things?" she asked. They had slowed down now to the point where they were barely moving ahead at all.

"Most of all," Donald said, "knowing you." He caught his breath, not in fright, but seized suddenly with a pleasurable excitement that quickened his heart.

"How does that make you happy?" Eileen said softly.

"Well, it's hard to say," Donald replied, then caught himself and laughed, but freely and healthily, not out of pained embarrassment. "You know what I mean," he chuckled while she smiled up at him. "There are so many reasons. Since I've known you, I feel for the first time as if the reasons for everything didn't matter so much. . . . No, that's not quite right. I guess what I mean is that I feel as if there were good reasons for everything—especially my being what and who I am—but as if for that very reason it didn't matter so much whether I personally happen to be able to figure out the reasons for things. I mean, I feel as if I could trust in things' being all right without having to know myself why and how they're all right. What I mean——" He stopped suddenly and chuckled again. "Boy, I really get tangled up, don't I?" he said. "Does any of what I said make any sense?"

"Not much," she replied laughing. "But I think I understand anyway."

"There!" Donald exclaimed. "That's part of what I mean too. It's not even so important that I make myself understood—not so important if I don't always make good sense—because you understand what I mean just the same." He was silent for a moment, then added: "It's wonderful to be with you, Eileen. You don't know what it means to me to be able to talk with someone like you—or Mr. Gavin."

"Mr. Gavin," Eileen echoed. There was something peculiarly flat in her tone and she looked away from Donald now, drawing up her coat collar and shivering a little.

"What's wrong?" Donald asked.

"It's getting cold." A chill gust of wind shook the trees and sent a shower of water spattering down onto the umbrella.

Donald looked at her in perplexity. He had for a moment had a warm and reassuring sense of understanding, but it had vanished suddenly and he felt once more unsure of himself and hesitant. "Eileen," he said, "I noticed after you met Mr. Gavin at the dance last week—I mean after he left us—you didn't say anything about him."

"You shouldn't expect me to talk about people behind their backs, Don," Eileen said abruptly. She seemed annoyed, but Donald suspected that somehow she was only pretending, in order to conceal—what?

"I didn't mean that, Eileen," he replied gently. "I only wondered—well, you didn't mention him at all. You haven't said anything about him since."

"Has Mr. Gavin had anything to say about me?"

"No."

"Then why should I be expected to have anything to say about him?" She pulled away from him slightly to avoid a puddle gleaming darkly in the middle of the sidewalk.

"Eileen, didn't you—you and Mr. Gavin, I mean—didn't you get along together?"

She was silent for a moment. Then, without acknowledging his question, she asked: "Why do you talk so much about Mr. Gavin, Donald? Why does he mean so much to you?"

"Because—well——" Donald fumbled for words. "I don't know. It's hard to explain."

"Because you think you may want to come into the Church?"

"Yes, it's that—partly."

"Then why do you depend so much on Mr. Gavin? He isn't the only one who could help you. I think it must be bad for you to depend entirely on just one person."

"There's more to it than just that. Eileen, you don't know, you can't understand——" Donald spread his hands out hopelessly.

"You just told me I do understand you."

Donald gestured vaguely again. "I have the feeling I'm walking on the edge of something—no, it's more like I'd just escaped from something, but I could fall back any time, slip back so easily, if—if he let go my hand. Do you know what I mean?"

"Donald, you'll have to let go of his hand some time. You can't hold someone's hand all your life."

"I know. But once in my life—why shouldn't I once in my life?"

"Is it only once?"

Donald hesitated. "No," he said. "No, I guess not. I guess that almost all my life I've felt I had to depend on somebody else. But all right, supposing that's so? Then this will be the last time in my life. If I can take this step with his help, just this first step . . ."

"Shouldn't this be the one step you should take without anybody's help, Don?"

"God, Eileen, how could I? There's so much I'm frightened of and not sure of and don't understand. But when I turn to Mr. Gavin, he has answers. Alone? I could never do it alone, Eileen."

"Then perhaps if you looked for help from more than just one person——"

"I do, Eileen," he exclaimed. "Of course. Don't you know you help me? Haven't we talked—and even if I don't bring up all my doubts with you—well, you can't have any idea how it helps me just to know you, to know what sort of person you are, what believing in something has done for you."

"I'm sorry, Donald," Eileen said, lowering her eyes. "Perhaps I shouldn't have said all I said. I know I haven't any real right to."

"But you have. Of course you have."

She continued without seeming to have heard him. "It's only that I guess I've got to the point where I feel a little jealous when I have to share your interest with someone else."

"Jealous?" he repeated, not quite understanding.

"Jealous of Mr. Gavin." She laughed in embarrassment. "Does that make any sense to you?"

"I don't know," Donald said softly. Their voices had dropped again and they walked slowly once more, close together and looking into each other's eyes. "I'm not sure that anybody has ever felt jealous about me before. My parents dying when I was little and my sister getting married . . . Well, I owe her a lot. But I don't know that she's ever thought much about me. I'm sure she's never been jealous about me. Eileen, do you think you could——? What I mean is——" They had stopped walking altogether. Staring at her solemnly, he said, "Eileen, I love you."

"Donald." She came close to him and suddenly he found himself with his arms about her, kissing her. They were interrupted by the umbrella clattering to the sidewalk. Eileen stepped away from him a few inches and stood smiling up at him.

"We'll get soaked if you don't pick up the umbrella," she said.

"Oh," Donald said. It was all he could think of to say. He stooped and retrieved the umbrella. Eileen took his arm again and they continued on up the street while the mist fell softly.

It was an enchanted period for Donald, a time of emotions and sensations he had really never believed existed but all of which he found now to be verified in his own case. It seemed impossible that anything could ever be seriously wrong anywhere. Everyone he knew seemed somehow to have changed overnight, to have become amiable and witty, generous and thoughtful—and most especially so toward him. He found their kindness and their good wishes beaming out at him in every gesture, every glance of their eyes, and, although he did not realize it, he smiled frequently himself without any perceptible reason. Eileen filled his thoughts. He woke in the morning and went to bed at night with her name running through his mind. He recognized the fact that he was manifesting in their purest form all the classic symptoms of young love, but the thought somehow made him, not chagrined, but only happier than ever. Problems melted away for him as if they had never existed—or rather he found that situations which once would have seemed to him problems no longer caused him concern, but submitted meekly to his control.

All problems, that is, except one. He was in doubt as to how to bring Eileen and Mr. Gavin into some satisfactory sort of relationship. It was not that either maligned the other; it was just that, after her one outburst, Eileen had not returned to the subject of the teacher, while for his part Mr. Gavin had not so much as once mentioned Eileen to Donald. The boy wanted painfully to ask him why, to try to draw him out on the subject—for Donald had a pathetic faith in the ultimate reasonableness and maturity of other people, their ability to work out sane and healthy solutions to dilemmas. Such a faith was essential to him. For if others dealt as ineffectually with their problems as he felt he did with his own, then the world was reduced to a state of moral anarchy in which the only motive forces came from whim, accidental collisions, and sheer inertia.

Donald had not yet, however, steeled himself for the task of questioning Mr. Gavin directly about his feelings toward Eileen, chiefly because he feared to annoy the teacher. But also he had not yet reached the point where he felt at ease in asking questions of Mr. Gavin on any matter. Questions were as likely as not to alienate Christopher, he had found. It was almost as if, unlikely as it seemed, Mr. Gavin thought of questions only as means of trapping or being trapped, feints in an unmistakably hostile dialectical game. Most of Christopher's thought, in fact, had a hint of warfare about it, Donald could not help noticing. His conversation seemed seldom spontaneous, but had the planned and calculated appearance of a campaign. It proceeded, sometimes deviously, sometimes not, but almost always with a didactic and sermonizing self-consciousness. And it was for this reason, among others, that Donald, despite his dependence (attachment might not have been too strong a word, considering the boy's present state of mind), despite his feeling for Mr. Gavin, still was far from at ease when he was with the teacher.

For their periodic discussions of Donald's progress in belief, they had worked out an arrangement whereby Christopher visited the boy's dormitory room once a week at least, usually on a Wednesday evening. The procedure was an unorthodox one yet suited to an unorthodox situation.

Donald shared his room with another sophomore named Harvey Wecter. Superficially, the two boys seemed alike in temperament: both were solemn and rather humorless young men, more or less self-consciously serious-minded and, at least in the estimation of their less thoughtful classmates, rather pretentiously intellectual. The resemblance, however, was one more of appearance than reality; and the mutual discovery of this fact had begun definitely to sour the boys' relationship in the few months they had been rooming together. Harvey Wecter was undeniably and unabashedly an aspiring intellectual. His tastes leaned heavily toward cool jazz, Dylan Thomas, and the beat poets. He was an habitué of small dusty movie houses that specialized in rereleases of *I Am a Fugitive from a Chain Gang* and *The Cabinet of Dr. Caligari*. He made it a point to keep an esoteric Penguin or Pelican crammed into the pockets of his carefully tailored shapeless jackets. And one of his choicest memories was of an evening spent in a New York theater watching the latest Samuel Becket. In freshman year he had taken Donald for a kindred spirit—and Donald, similarly, had imagined that Harvey's undoubted high seriousness was of the sort he would find congenial. The result had been their agreement to room together as sophomores. But it had taken only a few weeks of close association for them to discover that they simply did not share the same interests. Harvey had at first found Donald's preoccupation with religion a novelty and hence interesting—but that stage had quickly passed and he now regarded it simply as a bore. For his part, it was hard for Donald to understand how his roommate could be so excessively solemn over matters that were, to him, of little more than trifling importance. Their relations at the moment were polite but distant, although recently a slight scorn had crept into Harvey's voice, especially when making some reference to Donald's growing interest in questions of religion, or to his frequent sessions with Mr. Gavin. For, as it happened, Christopher too had become a cause of tacit disagreement between the roommates. It was, in fact, a question of allegiance. For Harvey, like Donald, had been one of Mr. Brodie's boys as a freshman, and had retained his enthusiasm for that teacher this year; while Donald only too clearly had abandoned Mr. Brodie for a rival who was intellectually, if not personally (and a certain understanding regarding the antipathy between the two teachers had, as if by magic, become current among their students) hostile to Mr. Brodie.

Harvey therefore made it a point of honor to absent himself conspicuously from Christopher's sessions with Donald, although the latter had on several occasions invited him in all sincerity to stay. This evening, however, Donald was immersed in a book as Harvey prepared to abandon the room for the library, and he made no effort to delay or prevent his leaving. It was perhaps for that very reason, then, that Harvey hesitated, watching Donald, hunched at the desk, pore over one of the two large red volumes stamped in gold *The Teaching of the Catholic Church,* and then finally spoke.

"What is it you're reading about, Don?"

"The sacrament of penance," Donald replied without looking up. He underscored several lines heavily with the pencil he held.

"Oh." Harvey, dressed in a baggy black sweater, khakis, and scuffed white bucks, sat down on the edge of his bed and lit a cigarette, flicking the match vaguely in the direction of Donald's bed across the room. He stared for a while at Donald out of his sleepy gray eyes, then leaned back and looked at the Toulouse-Lautrec prints he had hung over his bed. "That's very interesting," he said, blowing smoke toward the ceiling.

Donald scraped his chair back from the desk, walked to the window, and opened it several inches. A gust of cold air swept into the room. "Lets the smoke get out," he said, returning to his desk and to the book. He ran his fingers through his long hair, then bent over the page again.

"I've always thought," Harvey remarked, sitting up again and knocking ashes onto the shabby little scatter rug beside the bed, "that it was remarkable that the Christian church should anticipate psychonanalysis by so many centuries through the institution of the confessional."

"It isn't so remarkable," Donald replied.

"I'm afraid it's only hindsight that enables you to believe that, Don," Harvey said. "Of course, in view of what we know today——"

"I didn't mean that," Donald said. "What I meant was that—well, you see, Harvey, if this church *was* really established by a divine person—by God, as they say it was—well then it's just silly to say it's surprising that anything he set up was ahead of its time or has worked better than we would have thought it would, or—well, anything like that." He had turned toward Harvey and remained staring at him now that he had finished.

"Oh, of course," Harvey said, pursing his lips. He took another drag on his cigarette and returned Donald's stare. "You really are convinced by what you read in those books, aren't you, Don?"

Donald lowered his eyes. "I don't know," he said. "Sometimes I think so. But it's all so new to me. There's so much I don't understand."

Harvey chuckled. "That's right, so much you don't understand," he said. "So much nobody understands. I've always thought that was one of the charming things about religion. You don't have to understand anything. You just have to believe."

"It's not that easy," Donald replied. His roommate raised his eyebrows skeptically. "Tell me something, Harvey," Donald said suddenly. "Why—why are you so afraid of believing in anything? Why won't you even believe that there might just possibly be something to believe in?"

Harvey laughed again, although Donald saw nothing amusing in his question. "I'm not afraid of anything," Harvey said, smiling and getting up. He walked aimlessly over to the window and stared at the darkness. After a moment he tossed his cigarette outside and, shivering, shut the window sharply. "It's just that all of these things you believe in," he said, turning back to Donald, "or think you may believe in—they've been exploded so often. Why, even if there were a god—if he isn't just a name for natural powers made up by our ancestors thousands of years ago in hopes they could placate the thunder and the lightning and tame the river and bring the rains when they needed them—even if there is something somewhere corresponding to your idea of God—well, what do we know about him, what *can* we know about him?"

"I'm not sure."

"No, and nobody else really is, either." Harvey walked back to his bed and sat down again. "Oh, those books you have," he added, pointing, "they sound as if they're sure. But how can they be?"

"I don't know," Donald said. "If there is a god, wouldn't he want us to know about him?"

"Then he's done a pretty bad job of it," Harvey said. "There must be thousands of religious sects, and every one of them has it's own idea of god, and every one is sure that its god is the only god. Well, who's to know which one is right—if any one of them is right and if there is anything to be right about."

Donald gestured vaguely. "I'm not sure," he said.

"And the god Christianity proposes——" Harvey continued, without heeding Donald. "I've always found him particularly unattractive. A god who'd come down from his heaven and become like us and even die for us——" He shrugged.

"Yes," Donald said. "I know. It would be frightening to be loved as much as that."

Harvey stood up impatiently. "That's not what I meant," he said. "I think that sort of god would be—well, vulgar. To want so badly for us to love him—I couldn't put up with a god like that." He strolled over to his own desk and half leaned, half sat on it.

"I suppose that's something we don't understand anymore," Donald said, looking at the floor and concentrating. "What it means to want something that way. Our idea of wanting is to want things for ourselves. But to want a thing, not just because to have it would fulfill us, but because it would fulfill the thing we wanted too—that would mean you wanted a thing because you loved it, instead of loving a thing because you wanted it."

Harvey had stood with his arms folded, watching Donald, and now he suddenly clapped his hands down behind him on the edge of the desk. "Really, Don!" he exclaimed, half amused and half annoyed. "I think you've been reading those books of yours too long."

Donald smiled faintly, recognizing that he had failed once again to put his muddled thoughts into intelligible order. "I guess I don't make myself very clear," he said.

"Not very."

"But you don't make yourself very clear either, Harvey," he added. "I don't understand how you can reject something without having studied it, without even having made an effort to understand it—and you know you haven't."

"No, I haven't," Harvey said, "but other people have, and they reject religious belief. And I'm willing to accept their conclusions, for now. When I get a chance, I'll examine the arguments on both sides myself, but I don't expect that my mind will be changed."

"Not unless you're at least willing for it to be."

"Which is to say: not unless I want it to be. As you do yours. Well, I don't exclude the possibility of that happening. Religion serves purposes—otherwise it wouldn't have survived this long. And it might some day come to serve purposes of mine. In which case, I suppose I'd have to become what you'd call a religious person."

Donald's face screwed up in disgust. "That wouldn't be religion," he said.

Harvey smiled. "Isn't that precisely where we disagree?" he asked. "You think the man is made to serve the religion. I think the religion is made to serve the man. But please don't imagine I have anything vulgar in mind. I hope I wouldn't be one of your pious people for whom church on Sunday is only as necessary—and for just the same reason—as the country club on Saturday. No, I was thinking of something different. I suppose religion could give one a certain feeling of stability, a sense of emotional well-being. As I say, if I ever feel I need that, I won't hold back from accepting it in religion."

"But religion isn't what you feel. It's what you believe."

Harvey shrugged. "We go around in a circle," he said.

Someone knocked at the door. Harvey looked toward it without enthusiasm. "Mr. Gavin, I suppose," he remarked, lifting a fawn-colored overcoat off the foot of his bed and squirming into it.

"You don't *have* to leave," Donald said.

Harvey did not answer and, after looking at him for a moment, Donald went to the door and let in Christopher. As the teacher slipped out of his frayed gray coat Harvey nodded hello and went out. Christopher paid him no attention beyond a nod in return. Making himself at home at Harvey's desk, he began to thumb through the books he had brought with him. Donald, however, continued to stare after his roommate, lost in thought, till at last Christopher looked up.

"Well, Donald," he said.

The boy abruptly recalled himself to the present situation. "I'm sorry, Mr. Gavin," he said. "I was thinking."

Christopher leaned back and assumed the wearied look of one

who knew what to expect. "And this time," he said, "about what?"

"Harvey."

"What about him?"

"It sounds silly." He gestured and lapsed into silence.

Christopher tapped his foot impatiently. "Nevertheless, you'll tell me eventually. So you might as well do it now."

Donald hesitated. Then he said, "I feel sorry for him."

"Why?"

"He doesn't understand—not the first thing—what it would mean to believe."

Christopher was unimpressed. "I wouldn't waste sympathy on him," he said. "Of course he doesn't understand. He doesn't want to."

Donald looked vaguely disturbed. "I know he doesn't," he said. "But that doesn't mean that people who do believe should just—just sort of abandon him, does it?"

"You have to draw the line somewhere," Christopher said, eyeing the boy coldly. "There's such a thing as conserving your energy. Granted, I don't sympathize with these fat-cat priests who sit on their behinds and don't stir themselves because it's too much trouble—but I do believe in saving my efforts for occasions and people who will profit from them."

"I wasn't thinking so much of efforts, Mr. Gavin," Donald said. "Just—just of sympathy."

"Sympathy is useless," Christopher said. "I don't believe in it. If I can help someone, I do. If I can't, I don't give him any more thought. If I can't because he doesn't want me to——" He paused a moment. "Well, whatever I feel, I wouldn't call it sympathy."

"You can feel that way, Mr. Gavin, because you've never had any doubts yourself. But if you had—if you knew what it's like not to be able to believe——"

"Precisely. The sympathetic fallacy. You imagine you know what someone else is feeling. But you don't. The fact is, most people don't feel anything at all. They react—like animals—but they don't feel. They're too shallow and stupid to feel. No, Donald, believe me—there's no point wasting your time with them. Deal with the elite, convert them—and their example will bring the sheep into line."

"I don't believe you can think of me as one of the elite, Mr. Gavin," Donald said.

Christopher looked at the boy without enthusiasm. "You underestimate yourself, Donald," he said noncommittally.

"No, really, Mr. Gavin," Donald insisted. "I've been thinking about this lately. And I can't understand why you should give so much time to me."

"One soul, Donald, is worth more than——"

"But do you really believe that, Mr. Gavin?"

"Of course I do."

"Then what about——"

"Not Harvey again?"

"Yes, Harvey—and Mr. Brodie, and Dr. Bond, and all the other people you speak about as if—as if somehow they really didn't matter."

"The fact that nothing is more precious than a human soul doesn't mean that all souls are equally precious."

"Not even to God?"

"Are the souls of sinners so very precious to God?"

"But if he died for them——"

"He made a Hell for them too. Don't try to be too ingenious in interpreting God's motives. You can't escape from the facts."

"Don't you believe God loves all men?"

"Love. What do you understand about that sort of love?" Strangely, Christopher echoed the words Donald had spoken a few minutes before. But spoken by him they had a dead sound, like the wooden clapper used at Good Friday services. "We only use the word because we haven't a better one. When we speak of God's love, we don't know what we're speaking of."

"It's something greater than we can imagine."

"It's something *different* from what we can imagine. The distinction is not just in quantity, but in kind. A love that knows the value of suffering and death, that uses them freely as instruments for molding its objects—that's not the sentimental sort of love most people mean. But that's God's love, and to accept Him we must accept His love as it is, not as we'd like it to be."

"But that's only half of it. There's kindness in it too, isn't there?"

"Too many people emphasize the kindness and forget the——"

"The cruelty."

Christopher shrugged. "The cruelty," he agreed. "Again, it's a question of names. God's cruelty is kindness and His kindness cruelty—and both together make up His love. It's only that most people are too sentimental to admit that there is anything but kindness, pure and undiluted, as we understand it. Their idea of God's kindness is a sort of omnipotent Society for the Prevention of Cruelty to Animals. Mercy and justice, Donald—they're both in God. But the only thing we ever think of is mercy. Most of us forget about justice, or we don't believe it exists, or we try to persuade ourselves that somehow it will be suspended for us. But it won't."

"Are you glad of that, Mr. Gavin?"

"It doesn't matter whether I'm glad or not."

Donald paused fearfully, then licked his lips and persisted: "But are you?"

Christopher hesitated only a moment. "Yes. 'Blessed are they who hunger and thirst after justice.' Sometimes I think to myself when I hear that some vicious fool has died who's hated God all his life—I think to myself: 'Well, now he knows what a mistake he made. Now he's tasting the justice he thought would never touch him.' Yes, I'm glad of justice, Donald. If I didn't believe in justice, I don't know how I'd find life tolerable."

"But how do you know any more about God's justice than I do about his love? Isn't 'justice' just our way of giving an approximation for something we can't really understand?"

"Whatever justice is, it's giving everyone what's due to him. That's enough for me to know."

"Don't you want to know what—what God's mercy is too?"

"Justice is enough. I only ask justice for myself. And I hope others will receive no more than justice too."

"Mr. Gavin!"

"What? Does that shock you?"

"Yes. Shouldn't you—shouldn't you wish mercy for others?"

Christopher did not answer for a while. When he spoke at last, he ignored the question entirely. "This is an awfully long interrogation, Donald," he said.

"I didn't mean it to be—an interrogation, I mean. It's just that I've been reading and thinking."

"And talking?"

"Talking?"

Christopher smiled, but there was no warmth in it. "To Eileen," he said.

Despite himself Donald blushed, tongue-tied for the moment. He had hoped Mr. Gavin would mention her sometime, say something at least. But now, at such a time—he did not understand. "No," he mumbled. "We don't talk about these things."

Christopher stared at him, still smiling. "Not at all?" he said.

"No. I mean, well—not very often. I mean—when I'm with her, I don't feel I have to. Everything seems clear, it all makes good sense."

"Good sense," Christopher repeated. "And is this some of Eileen's good sense you've been talking to me?"

"No, Mr. Gavin, I told you——"

"You told me *you* don't talk about these things. But perhaps she does."

"You don't understand. You——"

"Donald!" Christopher's voice snapped out like a whip. The boy raised his eyes once in fright to the teacher's, then dropped them. "I've let you do a good deal of talking this evening—not because any of it was very clever or even very true, but just because I was curious about what was in your mind and I wanted you to tell me. Well, now you have, and I'm afraid I can't say I like it." Christopher rose and began to walk back and forth in the narrow space between the two sets of beds and desks. "We've talked together a good deal before this, Donald," he continued, "and I think I know your ideas when I hear them—just as I know other people's when I hear you mouthing them. And in this case I can assure you I have no trouble recognizing the sort of sentimental silliness I've been afraid Eileen would fill you full of."

"It isn't true, Mr. Gavin."

"It is, Donald. I'm willing to admit it's possible you may not realize yourself what's been happening. But there it is. Whether you like it or not, whether you want it or not, you've been influenced by this girl. And believe me, not for the good."

"Mr. Gavin, how can I make you understand?"

"How can *I* make *you* understand? How blunt do I have to be, Donald? All right, I'll give it to you straight. You'd better break off with this girl, you'd better never see her again, if you want——" For the first time he faltered.

"What?" Donald whispered breathlessly.

Christopher did not finish the sentence, but turned abruptly away from the boy. "Take my advice, Donald," he said in an oddly hoarse voice. "Take my advice. Please."

Please. The word echoed hollowly up from an abyss, like a cry shouted forlornly, desperately by a creature fallen into a pit. Please. It swelled and boomed, piercing his ears, filling his skull, pushing outward from the inside on his skull, drowning him in overpowering waves of vibrating sound. He felt his head spinning, his body spinning, whirling through space, spiraling down and down and down like a dead leaf toward the source of the sound. And it frightened him. He did not want to see the source. He did not want to see the anguished creature that made that sound. He tried to struggle against it, his hands went up to break his fall, to try to tear apart the fibrous curtain and get away, get the sound out of his skull, get back to . . .

Donald sat up suddenly in his bed, his senses sharpened to an almost unbearable keenness. It was as if he had reached the crisis of his life, when all inessentials were cleared out of his consciousness, the trivia lopped away, and he was free to concentrate all his powers of mind and body on the one essential purpose, the one all-important object. But there was nothing. The room was still and cold and dark. The sound of Harvey's heavy regular breathing came to him from a few yards away. At the window he could see heavy flakes of snow falling quietly, muffling sound. The moment of epiphany passed unfulfilled, and his energies seeped and receded slowly out of him as the rhythmic thud of his heart grew calmer and softer. He got quietly out of bed and went to the window. The snow lay thick and wet over the street outside. It had been falling for some time. A few flakes blew into the room through the narrowly open window. Donald closed it a few more inches and shivered a little. Somewhere in the distance a clock struck three. His sleeping roommate shifted his position with a rustling of covers. Donald, bleary-eyed and fatigued now, shuffled back to bed and climbed in, pulling the blanket up to his chin.

But sleep did not return. His mind, robbed of the alertness it had had for a moment, nonetheless clung doggedly to consciousness, feeling a vague disturbance somewhere, seeking to locate it, identify it, analyze it. What had he been dreaming about? A sound. A word. Please. Mr. Gavin's word. It was the first time he had ever heard the teacher speak like that, had ever heard him ask—beg— for something. It frightened him. He did not know what he wanted. There had been something so much like anguish when he spoke, so much like torment . . . Let him try then to fit it together, to see the pattern. That had never been his strength before, yet he had to go on making the effort, go on trying to understand. Now especially. Now when so much depended on it. So many things were moving relentlessly toward a simultaneous climax in his life. So many persons making their demands increasingly persistent, increasingly uncompromising. Mr. Gavin. Eileen. Even—his sleep-muddled brain felt incapable of thinking except in parallelisms— even God. What did they all want? Eileen . . . she wanted nothing for herself. What she wanted was for him. He loved Eileen; he was sure of that. And she loved him. That was simple, that was incontrovertible. But what about his other relationships? Mr. Gavin. What did he want? The teacher wanted to control him, to direct him. To what? To God. Away from whom? Eileen. But was the dichotomy a real one? Wearily he pushed his flagging thoughts on, marshalled his minimal powers of coherency. God and Mr. Gavin— that was the alignment as the teacher saw it. Arrayed against Eileen; with himself in the middle. But what about God? The teacher presumed to speak for Him—and yet, when he did, it was not with same voice that he had heard sounding in these books he had been studying, it was not with the same voice of mercy and love and gentleness. It was with a harsh voice, a cruel voice of command—and tonight it had been with a voice of entreaty choked out of anguished depths of unnatural, unhealthy pain. There was something wrong about the teacher, he thought with a shudder at his own boldness, there was something sick about him. And in a sense, if they could be said to be paired somehow, it was he and not Mr. Gavin who was the strong and stable and sane one. And yet, where did that leave him? If he were the strong one, what became of Mr. Gavin's religion; how could the religion be true if its spokesmen were weak even by the standards of a foolish adolescent boy? Say that the teacher's religion did not correspond to the religion he had found in the books. Yet was not the living example more meaningful than the ideal that existed only on paper? If Mr. Gavin was wrong, he was still somehow the product of the ideal Catholicism Donald had read so much about. Somewhere it must have started with his religion molding him into what he was—and if now he molded the religion to suit himself, that did not absolve his Church of its progenital role. He was its offspring, for which it could not disclaim responsibility. And yet there were large assumptions involved here, ones which he was not yet prepared to make. He knew he could not presume to judge in these matters himself. The possibility remained—and remained strongly—that the teacher was right. After all, he spoke with such confidence, such assurance —and so much of what he said, no, all of it, made sense. One denied it, rebelled against it, because of one's own sentimentality. . . . He *had* to trust the teacher. He could not hope to go on alone. Who would he ask for help, who would he turn to with his doubts and problems? Eileen? He knew instinctively that, however much they might love one another, she could not help him intellectually, she could not clarify his muddled thinking by the sheer force of her presence. He had to depend on the teacher to help him. But if he did—what became of Eileen? If Mr. Gavin was right and she was actually keeping him from the truth . . . And even if that were not so the fact that his allegiance to her might incense the teacher and drive him away . . . Try to think of God. What would he want? But whose god? Did he exist; and if he did, did he care about any of these things, did he care whether Donald Reinhart lived or died, or whether one silly boy believed in him or not? And if he cared, if the things one read in the books were true, then how could it possibly have been made so hard to believe, so hard even to know what to believe? How could it be that the people like Mr. Gavin, who said they knew this omnipotent power of love best, were themselves least filled with love? And if Mr. Gavin was wrong and if he did not really know God at all, after all the years and years he had spent in seeking him out—then how could anyone hope to know this God? And most of all, of all people how could he, Donald Reinhart?

Donald lay a long while with his eyes shut, thinking about these things, while the snow continued to fall outside. Then, finally, he dropped again into a troubled sleep.

CHRISTOPHER SHUFFLED AWKWARDLY ALONG THE SIDEWALK through the slushy snow. It had stopped falling during the morning and was already turning grimy on the city streets and melting into dirty pools. He walked with his head down, frowning. It was a relief for him to be through with his classes at last, for now he could give vent to the ill temper that had been gnawing at him all day. However, it was difficult for him to find an object in proportion to his annoyance—or if not to find one, at any rate to admit the existence of the one that seemed most obvious. It had been, he thought, poor strategy for him to say the things he had said to Donald. The boy obviously had not reacted well. It had been foolish of him to speak so bluntly about Eileen, without having first set the scene more carefully for what he had to say. Therefore, he was angry with himself. But there was another reason for him to be angry too, and though he did not admit it he had nonetheless a dim awareness of it, an awareness which had been souring his disposition all day. He knew without conceding as much that he had somehow given himself away the night before, destroyed both for Donald and for himself the illusion of his disinterestedness. At the time he had not thought of what he was doing; later, when he considered his action, he tried to convince himself that it was only a further instance of his devotion to God and to the cause of spreading His kingdom. But he could not easily conceal from himself the strange emotions that had come welling up in him when he appealed to the boy for his allegiance, he could not forget completely the sense of passionate desperation, the base willingness to acknowledge his dependence on Donald for—for something he could not give a name to; for acknowledgement of his wisdom and virtue, for acquiescence to his will, as much as anything else. Christopher had for a long time taken satisfaction in his own self-sufficiency, the adequacy of himself unto himself. The suggestion now that his self-sufficiency might, for whatever obscure reason, be only an illusion, had unnerved him more than he was willing to admit.

He passed through the dirty glass doors of his apartment building, checked his box for mail and found none, and was about to push the button for the rickety elevator when he saw hung on the door a crudely lettered sign: "Out of Order." Disgustedly he walked the four flights to his apartment and tramped down the hall, reaching for the key in his pocket. He had just gotten to the door when he heard his phone begin to ring. Angrily he fumbled at the lock, finally got the door open and picked up the phone from its small stand.

"Hello," he grunted.

"Chris?" came the thin voice. "This is Julie."

"Julie," he repeated. He still stood in the doorway, forgetting for the moment even to close the door.

"Yes. How have you been, Chris?"

"Oh, fine. Just fine, thanks." He reached behind him and shut the door cautiously, as if he were afraid that slamming it might somehow break off their conversation. "How have you been, Julie?"

"Fine." There was a pause. Then she said: "Chris, I'd like to see you if I could. If it isn't too much trouble."

He leaned against the door, and a faintly cunning look crossed his face. "No, of course it isn't," he said. "But could I ask you why? Does it have anything to do with——"

"Please, Chris, I'd rather tell you when I see you," she said. "Could you come over here?"

"Certainly." He paused, then asked, "Is Mark there?"

"He's giving make-up examinations this afternoon. He won't be here till much later."

"I'll be over in just a little while, Julie," he said.

"I'll be expecting you."

He hung up the receiver slowly. Perhaps then he was getting results? One never knew. He had done little enough himself to draw her out, but after all it was in the hands of God, and one could not predict or control His ways. He walked over to his dresser and stood looking for a moment at the crucifix. But oddly there seemed to be nothing to say and he turned and went out.

The first thing he noticed about Julie was how young she looked. In her blue dress with her hair fastened loosely with a ribbon and hanging down to her shoulders, she might have been a girl from one of his classes—only more graceful, more quiet, more thoughtful. He felt with pleasure her hands lightly at his shoulders as she took his overcoat and was amazed at the slimness of her body as she led the way into the little living room. She took a place on the sofa and he hesitated for a moment, about to sit next to her, until some prompting of an obscure propriety moved him to sit down instead in Mark's easy chair.

Then unaccountably he found that much as he wanted to speak, no words came to him. He noticed with surprised annoyance that his mouth was dry and there was a faint agitation in the pit of his stomach—the symptoms of a fearful excitement he had not experienced since adolescence.

Fortunately, Julie came to his rescue. "You wonder, I suppose, why I asked you to come, Chris," she said.

"Yes, I do. Of course it's flattering——" He smiled and was relieved to see her smile, too. "And it's pleasant for me to see you. Still, as you say, I do wonder."

"I don't want to be too melodramatic about it, Chris," she said. "Above all, I don't want to make it sound as if I'd made up my mind about anything. So I'll just say that I've been thinking about what you said to me the last time we talked—that you'd like to help me if you could. I think now possibly you can."

"What I said still holds good," he declared, leaning forward to emphasize his words. "Anything I can do."

"Chris, I'd like to know more about your religion."

"Julie, that's wonderful!" he exclaimed. "If I'd only known . . ."

"Please, Chris," she said, flushing, "I want to *know* more. That's all. I don't mean to commit myself to anything else."

Christopher checked himself. "Of course," he said. "I understand exactly."

"You must wonder why I'm telling you this."

He paused a moment, then replied, "Not really. I think I can guess. As you said—you don't want to commit yourself, and you think talking to a priest would. On the other hand, what you're looking for—what you want to *know* about the Church—is more than you can find out just by reading a few history books. So you want someone you can talk to, ask questions of—perhaps even take a little advice from. Isn't that it?"

She smiled slightly. "I couldn't have put it better myself," she said. "Apparently I'm not such a unique case if you have me pegged as thoroughly as all that."

"I should think everyone in your position feels much the same way," Christopher said. Suddenly he was acutely conscious that he was staring very deeply into her eyes. "But there are certain unique elements——" He trailed off.

She lowered her eyes. "Yes, there are."

"Julie, what—what is it that made you decide—well, to go this far at least?"

She gestured nervously. "It's so hard to say." Rising, she walked to the window, which was steamed over on its bottom panes, and stared out at the gray sky, the gray buildings, and the gray streets. "For me this is sort of an act of desperation. If nothing comes of this . . ." She did not finish.

Christopher rose and without thinking crossed to the window too, where he stood behind her. "Something will," he said. "If only you'll co-operate—with God."

She let her forehead rest on the cool glass of the window. He was unaccountably aware of the whorls of fine hair behind her ears, like black silk against the white skin. He felt a strange urge to touch her hair.

"I hope so," she said, closing her eyes. "I hope you're right, Chris. Because if you're not, then Mark must be. And I can't bear to believe that—that it's all just meaningless, that there's meaning in things only because *we* put it there."

"Yes," he said stupidly, gaping down at her, the blood pounding in his ears, his mind and body filled with strange new desires. His breath was short, his mouth dry. He wanted to reach out, to feel her skin beneath his fingers.

Abruptly, she moved away from the window and walked back across the room. Christopher leaned against the wall, a weakness in his knees suddenly.

"I suppose it sounds strange," Julie said, still not looking at him, "but I really haven't any respect for human beings. It frightens—disgusts—me to think that we are the universe's ultimate achievement, the most intelligent, highly developed, complex beings in existence. Even if there is nothing—no one—better than us, we have to imagine there is, or else, you know, we couldn't create any art or perform any good acts." She faced him now. "We have to have an ideal, something to model ourselves on. The minute we begin only to imitate each other, we begin to go to bad, to make mistakes, to do evil." She hesitated. "Do I make any sense, Chris?"

"Yes. Yes, of course you do."

"You asked why I decided to go—this far. I suppose that's why. I want to find out if when we create beauty—when we *live* beautifully—if there's any reason for it. I want to know if the beauty we can achieve is the imitation of some beauty that really exists somewhere—or whether we're just deceiving ourselves with dreams we might as well wake up from." She sat down abruptly and smiled at him. "I'm sorry—I do go on."

"It's good that you do," Christopher said cautiously. He was not yet sure that he had himself in control. "It helps us both to understand."

"To understand what?"

"You," he said. He walked slowly to the chair and sat down again, relieved to find himself calm once more. "I have to know what you're looking for if I'm to help you find it. And you—you have to come to know yourself, understand your thoughts and beliefs, better than you ever have before in your life. It's not only God you'll be finding out about for the first time. In a very real sense, it's yourself as well."

"It must be easier to know God," she said, smiling but still serious. "Knowing oneself—who can do that?"

"And yet you have to."

"You've done it, haven't you, Chris?"

"Yes."

"I suppose that's really the reason I asked you to help me. I feel as if somehow—*you* can."

"I'll try, Julie."

She was silent again for a moment as a shadow of sadness passed over her face. "Poor Mark," she said. "I know I'm being disloyal to him."

"Not really," he said.

She looked displeased at the facile remark. "But I am."

He retreated easily. "You have to get used to a hierarchy of loyalties," he said. "God comes first."

"If there is a God."

"If there is, you owe it to Him to find out."

She sighed. "It would hurt Mark if he knew."

"He has no right to be hurt."

"That doesn't stop me from feeling sorry for him." She unconsciously traced the flowered pattern on the arm of Mark's chair—the chair in which Christopher sat. "Besides, he won't be hurt for a common reason—out of pride—just because I wouldn't take his word for things about religion. No, the trouble is that—that he wants us each to be everything to the other."

"Then he's asking the impossible," Christopher said.

"He wants me to find my meaning in life in him—just as he finds his in me."

"You mean he wants you to be little gods to each other," Christopher said, his voice rising. "Please excuse me, Julie, and please understand what I mean when I say this—but I think that's horrible."

She looked down and said slowly, "Haven't I already told you how horrible I find it?"

"I'm sorry."

"But it means something to Mark. It has to—it's all there is for him to believe in. And when he knows that I've rejected it, that I've gone outside the two of us to find a meaning for my life—it's then he'll be hurt."

"Then it will be hurt pride after all," Christopher said. She winced a little. "You see things so clearly."
"One has to."
"One has to," she repeated.

Christopher sat in shirt sleeves on the edge of his bed. It was time for him to go out and buy his dinner, but he did not want to leave just yet. He preferred to sit there in the darkening room, the patch of light on the floor before him fading dimmer and dimmer, and for a while longer hug to himself his wonderful secret, before he had to mingle with other people and draw away some of his attention from it. He held his rosary in his hands, idly twitching the beads through his fingers but not saying the prayers. From outside came the occasional harsh jingle of chains on the tires of automobiles and a churning, sloshing sound as they sped through the slush in the streets. The radiator knocked and hissed now and then, steaming up the window and overheating the room.

He was still agitated—stimulated, one might say—by his immense good luck. Julie had committed herself, and for him that was the only thing needed. He was confident of ultimate success; in fact, the possibility of failure did not even enter his mind. The prospect of her conversion excited him, too, as Donald's had never done. She was, he felt, someone worth saving—or, if that seemed to imply that Donald somehow was not, someone worth being saved by him. Donald's was a dull plodding spirit (now, after what had just happened, he could afford disparagement of the boy without its implicitly reflecting on himself as well; something which had not been the case before). But Julie, on the contrary, had a rare intelligence—or less intelligence, perhaps, than immense sensitivity —one might say also sensibility—which made her conversion indeed a choice accomplishment.

The situation gained an incomparable piquancy, too, from the fact that she was married to Mark Brodie. It was as if things had been providentially arranged to give him the extra pleasure of having this to throw in Brodie's teeth. This and Donald, he thought, relenting suddenly toward the boy as he saw him fitting into the pattern in his own uniquely awkward and hesitant way. Julie and Donald—Brodie had lost them both, though as yet he knew of only one loss. He felt for a moment an almost irresistible urge to tell

Brodie at once and he only just suppressed a giggle of glee at the thought of what the other man would do and say and—feel. Of course, it would be for Brodie's good when the blow did finally fall. It might serve to shock him out of his complacency. What was it Julie had said? Mark wanted to make the two of them all in all to each other, to exclude other men and women and even God from their relationship. Julie was to be his sole prop and he, hers. But if she were removed, would not Brodie be thrown back inevitably on God? Julie, he thought to himself, had all this time been the unwitting accomplice to Brodie's escape from God. It was she who had made it possible for him to find a meaning, even if only a false one, in his life. Brodie had made her into a shield between himself and God. But he, Christopher, was going to snatch that shield from him now and force him to see God face to face. He was going to take Julie away from Brodie.

And that, he thought, seized by a sudden tremor of delight, that was the most exquisite, finely wrought piece in the whole complex machinery. It had, he felt, a master's touch to it—and, his fingers tightening around the rosary for a moment, he knew Whom to thank for that. Of all fine touches, it was the finest that he should fall in love with Julie Brodie.

For of course he knew that he was in love with her. He had never before known, he thought, what precisely the word meant. But now, in a matter of a handful of meetings, a few hours' talk, it had become clear to him what it was to love: to want something so badly that beside it nothing (with always the exception of God, he noted mechanically) mattered. That was how he wanted Julie, with her fine skin, her gray eyes, her thick lustrous hair—he had to have her, he thought, unconsciously straining the rosary till it almost snapped.

He recognized vaguely that to others his motives would have seemed devious and unpleasant. But they were clear and satisfactory in his own eyes. First, he wanted to convert Julie. Almost inevitably, then, it would be necessary that she and Mark separate. Secondly, he wanted to bring Brodie back into the Church a chastened and wiser man. But to conquer his pride and force him to acknowledge his need for God, it would be necessary that he lose Julie. Thirdly, he wanted Julie for himself. There was nothing wrong in that. Brodie would have married her outside the Church

—hence, since he was a Catholic and still bound by the Church's laws, whether or not he acknowledged them, there was no real marriage at all; the marriage simply did not exist. Legally, there was no bar to his desiring her, and morally—it was clearly best for both Julie and Brodie that they be separated. He smiled in satisfaction, as if at some dazzled jury he had just persuaded. His motives were unimpeachable.

Christopher got up and walked over to the window. A faint salmon flush tinged the overcast western sky, but everywhere else it was gray. There was a pleasing element of surprise in it all too, he thought—surprise that he should ever fall in love. Through the years when he had been preparing himself to enter the seminary, counting on the priesthood as his life, he had taken pains to school himself against such an involvement; a task simplified by the fact that his desires were not strong, but instead easily governed. Then, when they had told him (he still ground his teeth when he thought of it)—lacking in true spirituality, emotionally unfit for the priesthood . . . The habits acquired over years were not easily lost. And in his case there was no desire to lose them, nor any compelling reason to do so. He had been accustomed to ignore women. But from the first it had been impossible for him to be unconscious of Julie—the way she looked, the very sound of her voice, he recalled vividly now, even the gentle, somehow wistful odor of the perfume she used. His face felt suddenly hot and he put his forehead up against the cold window pane. It was the same pose she had struck that afternoon. He desired her immensely. He would have her. He had to have her.

He became aware slowly of a pain in his hand. It was caused by the cross dangling at the end of the rosary, which he was crushing into his palm. He looked at his hand in surprise, then smiled to himself and slipped the rosary into his pocket. It was time for him to eat, and snatching up his coat he went out.

Julie moved mechanically about the little kitchen, preparing dinner with automatic gestures. She was thinking of other things as she performed her routine duties, cleaning vegetables and fruit, putting things into the stove. She had always made a particular effort to do her homemaking well. Her reason was not, however, simply housewifely pride, the desire to match or excel her neighbors, but rather a desire to please Mark. His awareness of his domestic surroundings was almost nil, she realized, but nonetheless she felt sure that he would be acutely conscious not merely of any slatternliness, but of any falling off from the extreme care she had always exercised in preparing his meals, cleaning their apartment, keeping his clothes in order and performing her other tasks. She recognized that Mark was a spoiled man, who indulged himself and expected others to do the same. And, as was usually her way, she had not attempted to evaluate or pass judgment on this trait of his, but had simply acknowledged it, accepted it, and tried to cater to it as best she could.

But now, unaccountably in these last few minutes, she had become suddenly aware of this aspect of their relationship. It had become clear to her that she had sacrificed much to accommodate Mark's wishes and whims. However, the matter did not present itself to her in quite that light, for, far from indulging in recriminations, Julie was overwhelmed with a sense of guilt and of dishonesty. She felt—she knew—that somehow she had in the most essential way failed Mark, had committed an abysmal betrayal of her husband. And yet she knew also that if she had not done so, she would have betrayed herself in an even worse way—and perhaps would have betrayed God as well, if there were a god. She could not help but be obsessed with a feeling of hypocrisy as she prepared the dinner—she was so careful, so scrupulous to please Mark in small things like this, but in a matter of the utmost importance she had already been disloyal to him. Of course she recognized that someone else might have asked whether he had any right to require such loyalty. Supposing the answer were no, then her obligation to offer it disappeared at once. But such a solution, she knew, solved nothing, for she had never acted out of obligation, in fact did not even inquire into its existence. Whatever she did for Mark was done simply out of love.

That, then, was where her failure lay—in love. And she saw now that her analysis of a moment before—the argument that if she did not betray Mark, she would betray herself in a worse way, and a problematical god as well—had been too facile. It was true enough. But its truth in no way effected the central fact, that she had betrayed Mark and failed in her love for him. Mark's rights or absence of rights in the matter had no bearing on the case. She had entered an area where law could satisfy only the too-formal or hopelessly superficial mind. And hers was neither.

She had felt this way, in miniature, only once before, when she had gone to warn Christopher of the conversation she had overheard between Mark and Robbie. The situations were similar, she saw, but different too, and in a significant way. On the first occasion, she had acted to preserve a third person, Christopher, from possible injury, and whatever one might say of her betrayal of Mark, at least the onus of selfishness could not be placed on her. But now, this second time, she had betrayed him simply for her own sake.

Or had she? Was there not possibly a third person involved here as well? she thought suddenly. Was not God involved, if He existed? But to say that He was, led to immense and startling conclusions. What after all could one think of a god who lent himself as the third party in a triangle of this sort? What sort of god was it to whom one owed love and loyalty as one did to a husband or a wife, but whose claims outweighed those of a marriage partner and who would be hurt—simply, literally *hurt*—if one denied him love and loyalty? It was frightening to think of such things. Asking the questions required an effort that left one little energy for seeking an answer as well.

Seeking an answer. She would have to do that, incapable of it as she felt now. But she would not—and in all her confusion and fear, the thought was the only one that gave her security, as if she felt herself standing on a firm rock in the midst of tossing waves—she would not have to search for them alone. There was Christopher to help her. She admired him immensely. She did not think that she understood him thoroughly yet, but she hoped that someday she might be enough like him to know how and why he thought and acted as he did. There was about him, she thought, an immense purity and simplicity in all things. Not just in externals, of course; externals did not seem to involve or affect Christopher. But rather there was purity and simplicity in his motives, his actions. He had about him an air of conviction and of consequent purposefulness. He seemed to know at all times not only what he was doing, but why he was doing it. He saw meanings in things, and most especially in himself. And that was what she wanted, passionately and desperately. To find a meaning for herself. If only Mark would understand and help—but his life was devoted to a denial of meanings, or at least a refusal to search for them, on the ground that they could not be found. But if she succeeded, if with Christopher's help she found in religion something to answer her questions and soothe her fears—then perhaps, just perhaps, she might be able to return to Mark and slowly, haltingly help him to find what she had found.

Her face was radiant at the thought. But then suddenly a new concern struck her. What was she to do here and now? What was she to tell Mark? How could she explain—— But perhaps it would not be necessary. If she could keep it a secret for a while that she was investigating Catholicism—until she was certain one way or the other—it would spare both him and herself some of the suffering. No. She frowned at the thought. She was rationalizing. To conceal would be to deceive. To add deception to her betrayal. She could not do that to him. And yet, how could she tell him? He would be hurt terribly. It was fear that made her hesitate, she knew, but fear of hurting him, not of angering him. And yet she thought also that it would be better to hurt him than to deceive him. Instinctively, she saw in the decision facing her a test—of her honesty, her loyalty, her love.

She had a puritan facility for marking out tests and trials and torturing herself over the adequacy of her performance in meeting them. The trait had been hers for as long as she could remember. Perhaps it had originally been some sort of reaction against her doggedly unconventional parents, who had insisted almost frantically that they would recognize nothing and no one but themselves as a norm for their behavior. And yet, she reflected now, the trait could also well enough have been inherited, for one could see clearly at this distance that the compulsion for self-testing had motivated her parents too. They had made unconventionality the standard against which they measured and tested themselves. Absolute unconventionality, she thought, did not exist, for it implied a norm of conventionality, just as immorality implied a morality; and the assertion of absolute freedom was an illusion, for it always implied freedom *from* something that continued to exist. For herself, she had never even attempted to make the acts of denial and defiance that occupied so much of her parents' time. She had no inclination that way. On the contrary, she had been busied from the time when she was a very young girl in building up walls of defense—or, perhaps more accurately, foundations on which to rest her life. She felt she had to be able to believe in something—even if it were nothing. Even if the final answer to all her questions were a negation, a denial that anything in life or the universe made sense, had a meaning, that at least would be a belief one could hold. If she could hold it. If she could believe that or anything else firmly, unshakably, certainly. But she could not. No matter how far she pursued any given line of thought, it had been her experience that it was always possible to ask at least one more question that could not be answered. And if it was possible, then it was necessary, for she refused to deceive herself that she had gotten a final answer when she had not.

Mark, she knew, suspected her discontent. His references to it had grown frequent since Christopher's arrival on the scene, for he seemed somehow already to blame Christopher for disturbing her. And yet there were curious blind spots in his understanding of her state of mind. Or were they really so curious when one thought of them? The blind spots existed perhaps only where Mark refused to see something, not where he was unable, for if he had wanted he would have been able enough to see the whole situation. His refusal to understand or even admit much of the truth was, she knew, essential to him. For if he were to learn of what she was doing, of where she was turning for help, he would be crushed. His idea of their living only for each other was—little as he was willing to admit it—a substitute for the god who was absent from both their lives. And for her to turn now away from this relationship, to reject it as unsatisfactory by her actions as she had done by her words, would seem to Mark the ultimate reproach to his love and to himself.

How then could she tell him? And yet how could she not? If she told him, he would imagine a betrayal; if she did not, she would feel herself tainted, however slightly, with real betrayal. How could she——

The front door opened and he came in. She froze where she stood by the sink, listening to him move about, taking off his overcoat, tossing his galoshes into the closet. Then the kitchen door opened.

"Hello, honey," he said, crossing to her and kissing her on the cheek.

"Hello, dear." He looked very tired. "Did you have a good day?"

"So-so." He dropped heavily into a rickety chair at the dinette table. But then he looked up and smiled tenderly at her. "How about you?"

"So-so," she said brightly, smiling back at him. And something died inside her as she spoke.

PERHAPS IN THE WEEKS THAT FOLLOWED MARK MIGHT HAVE noticed a change in his wife, a hint of withdrawal that was at once hostile and apologetic. Yet such things were for him not unexpected. It would not have been the first time that Julie had shown an alienation of spirit which, he feared sometimes, might arise from something corroded and unstable at the very fundament of their life together. He *might* perhaps have noticed such a change now. But he did not. For Mark was preoccupied with other problems, other grievances, which were coming increasingly to focus themselves on the wavering figure of Donald Reinhart. Donald somehow had begun to symbolize and epitomize for him the whole contest (consciously, he scorned the word, but unawares it came oftener and oftener into his mind when he sought to describe the relationship) between himself and Christopher. When the boy had transferred his protégé-ship from himself to the younger man, he had at first dismissed the fact as inconsequential, had even with Julie made a few ironic remarks indicating relief at being released from an unsought and growingly undesirable relationship. "Donald is looking for idols, not friends," he had explained. "Toward the end, it was becoming rather tedious trying to live up to the ideals of an adolescent." "You didn't try very hard," Julie had replied quietly. But Mark had said nothing. He did not want to quarrel. He was too pleased and relieved at being rid of Donald.

But lately all that had begun to change, and his early jubilation, as of one delivered from an onerous burden, had subsided to none-too-gracious acceptance of the *fait accompli*. And this attitude, more recently still, had begun to degenerate into outright resentment. Brodie sought to regard his mental state objectively and felt he had succeeded. With a generous gesture (intellectually speaking) he acknowledged that he was not altogether free from personal motives in the case (and one could not, after all, ask so much of any man). To begin with, his pride was touched by Donald's defection, and that he should have transferred his allegiance to Gavin of all people magnified enormously this resentment. Moreover, he felt a genuine affection for the boy, a fatherly interest such as he might have experienced had he had a son of his own (as of course he did not, he and Julie having agreed that children could wait for another raise or two). But to Mark's mind it seemed clear that the consideration which weighed most heavily with him was the altruistic and abstract one that truth was being violated and that it was his duty to do something about it. He felt certain that Donald's conversion was imminent and he regarded the impending event as an intellectual seduction. His horror of the Church was unfeigned and violent. Here, too, he admitted the play of emotion upon his attitude. But all the same he believed that emotion exerted only a minor influence and that it was true intellectual conviction which chiefly motivated him. The Church, to put it plainly, was a fraud. Of course if that had been all it was, he would not have been so violently opposed to the espousal of its doctrines by Donald or by anyone else. Most men, he thought, found it necessary to fortify themselves against life with some comforting fraud, some self-deception which like a benign tumor was useless but did not harm. The Church, however, was another matter, as far as he was concerned. It was a malignancy. One could not tolerate it. In the temporal order it sought indiscriminately to amass power of all sorts, with the ultimate goal of bringing into being (if it did not already exist) some sort of aristocracy of celibacy. It strove by devious methods to dominate in government, business, entertainment, and to force even those who rejected it to conform to its standards—both in regard to behavior and, more seriously, in regard to thought. And all the while it posed behind the pale face of the pious hypocrite. But even more insidious was its effect on the private lives, the minds, the spirits, of its members. It sought to establish a joyless conformity, Mark told himself, enjoining nerveless resignation to injustice and cruelty. And thus it actively discouraged men from seeking to help themselves and each other.

With these ideas swarming in his mind, he found it impossible to watch with equanimity as Donald was drawn by Christopher farther and farther into the web. The thought of what was going on preyed upon his mind. It gnawed at him. He felt a duty to act, to rescue Donald before in his blindness he had gone too far. He felt a duty to thwart Christopher. And yet he formed no plan, and in fact it would have been almost impossible for him to do so. He and Donald met seldom these days, and then only briefly, passing in halls between classes. And the thought of asking Donald to his apartment specifically for the purpose of dissuading him from whatever it was Christopher was trying to persuade him to do, had been up to now repellent to him. It seemed too much to compromise his dignity, to put him in a position analogous to that of a rejected lover pleading to be returned to grace. His pride would hardly allow him to go that far. Moreover, even had he been granted fortuitously an interview with Donald, he had planned nothing yet to say. And yet something had to be said. The conviction of duty and the sense of urgency grew upon him day by day, till at length he felt almost a compulsion to act.

It was a cold clear afternoon in December. The sky was a harsh bright blue. Mark had returned a book to the library, a novel by a Frenchman about whom he had been curious. He came down from the second-floor circulation desk, brushed past a few knots of students in the first-floor lobby, and pushed through the heavy glass revolving doors. Emerging outside he almost collided with a tall figure, its arms filled with books. He frowned at the boy, then paused in surprise.

"Why, Donald!" he exclaimed. "I didn't even see it was you."

Donald looked at him in surprise. Clearly he had not seen either that it was Mr. Brodie. Mark imagined he hardly looked pleased.

"I'm sorry, Mr. Brodie," he stammered. "I wasn't looking where I was going." He stood there awkwardly, holding his books, his eyes averted from Mark's. Someone else came through the revolving door and almost ran into him.

"You'd better get inside with those," Mark said. "Here, let me help." Over Donald's murmured protest he took three books from the stack of six or seven the boy was carrying. Then he led the way back through the revolving door.

Inside, Mark was seized suddenly by the conviction that he was behaving foolishly. It seemed to him almost as if he were going through the motions of a heavy-handed student flirtation. He felt an unaccustomed embarrassment as the idea assailed him that the students hanging about in the lobby were staring at him and Donald, joking about them. But with an angry effort he suppressed the notion. Surprising, the nonsense one thinks, he reflected. He looked about for some place where he might have a private conversation with the boy—for he had decided at once not to let the opportunity so luckily handed him escape unused. His eyes were drawn to a leatherette sofa in a corner beside the broad flight of stairs leading to the second floor. He turned to Donald now and, to his annoyance, found the boy hanging back.

"Thank you, Mr. Brodie," he mumbled. "I can take the books now."

He half-reached for them, but Mark kept them. Clearly, the boy wanted to go, and he was disgusted with himself for not letting him. It came perilously close to compromising his dignity. But he had set his mind now on talking with Donald and he intended above all else to have his way. He smiled with an effort and said, "Are you in a hurry, Don? I'd like to talk with you for a minute. We don't see much of each other these days."

The boy looked miserable. What the hell had Gavin been filling him full of to make him act like this? "I am in sort of a hurry, Mr. Brodie——"

Mark managed to keep the smile on his face. "But not as much of a hurry as all that." Hating himself and Donald, too, he took the boy by the arm and guided him, unresisting, to the sofa.

When they were seated Mark unaccountably found himself for the moment at a loss for words. Donald of course said nothing, but kept his eyes turned aside. At last, to break the silence, the teacher repeated, "We don't see much of each other these days, do we, Don?"

Donald automatically went on the defensive. "I have a lot of studying to do this year." He sat rigidly, out from the back of the sofa, awkwardly holding the stack of books in his lap.

Mark leaned back, assuming an attitude of amiable calm. "I suppose so," he said. Idly he picked up one of the books he had tossed down beside him. It was a history of the Catholic Church. He looked up and saw Donald blushing, though his eyes were once more averted. He glanced at the backs of the other books he had been carrying. They were works of Catholic apologetics.

"This is what you've been studying?"

"Some of it."

A scowl grew on Mark's face. "Why do you waste your time on this crap?" he blurted out suddenly.

"Please, Mr. Brodie——"

"Please what?"

"You haven't any right to say that, just—just——" Donald hesitated, then stopped altogether. Mark looked at him in curiosity. It was hardly like Donald to insist on his rights. And he wondered also what the boy had been about to say.

He changed his tone now to one of wheedling affability. "You were going to say something else. 'I haven't a right to say that, just because——' why?"

"Because you envy me." He said it so low that Mark was not sure at first that he had heard correctly. Then he laughed, though he felt more anger than amusement at the boy's effrontery. The only extenuating circumstance was that he was obviously parroting something he had heard from someone else—from Gavin. But what exactly had he been told? He could guess, but he wanted to hear it from Donald.

"Envy you, Donald? Why?"

"Because you hate to see me gaining what you've lost."

"And what is that?"

The boy's face was a fiery red. He was sweating under his heavy tan overcoat with its foolish little belt in the back. "Faith," he said.

Mark laughed out loud, but checked himself when several girls passing by looked curiously their way. He took out a cigarette and tapped its end on his thumbnail. "I don't envy you, Donald," he said, lighting the cigarette. "I pity you. I hate to see someone else walking with his eyes closed into what it cost me so many years and so much pain to escape."

For the first time Donald looked directly at him. "Mr. Brodie, please. Can't you see I don't want to talk about it with you?"

"We were friends, Donald—once. Then why do you feel now that you can't discuss this with me?"

"Mr. Gavin——"

Mark's scornful laugh interrupted him. "That's splendid. That's quite enough. You needn't go any further, Donald. Mr. Gavin. That answers my question."

Donald lowered his eyes again. "It won't do you any good to say things about him."

It was not so much what the boy said that struck Mark like a blow in the face. It was the tone. He could almost have imagined that Donald hated him, so contemptuously did he speak, warning him in a tone of ironic scorn not to stoop to the slander which was only too much expected of him. He was amazed at how thoroughly Gavin had carried out his indoctrination. But blotting out that impression almost before it became articulate thought was his rising anger, against Christopher and against Donald as well. He had sought to help the boy, had abased himself, gone out of his way—and insults were the thanks he got. Well, Donald should be made to know that he was no prize, that people sought him out in a spirit of charity, not because of any personal charm of his. Perhaps the unaccustomed luxury of having two persons sue for his favor had gone to his head. If so, it would be his pleasure to disabuse Donald of any tendency toward conceit.

Mark took the time of a drag on his cigarette to gain control of his anger and channel it to its most effectively venomous outlet. Then he said deliberately, "You're a fool, Donald."

For the second time, he boy looked up. "It won't do any good to call me names either," he said. But his voice lacked conviction and there was something very like fear in his eyes. It was plain that Donald was still Donald, that he could be hurt with almost ridiculous ease. Mark smiled contemptuously.

"Why should I bother?" he said. "What the hell do you think you matter to me that I should take the trouble? Don't flatter yourself,

Donald. Nobody gives two pins for you. No, not even your precious Mr. Gavin."

The boy said nothing. Mark indulged himself and went on. "Let me tell you a thing or two about Gavin. Don't worry—I'm not going to call him names. I'd just like to suggest an interpretation of his motives that probably hasn't occurred to you yet. You might find it interesting."

"I don't want to hear," Donald protested.

"Of course not," Mark said. "Of course you don't. You're too far along the road to being a true believer, and they never want to hear anything if it's the truth. They'll always shut their ears if you threaten to tell them something that's true. How could they believe in their gimcrack Church otherwise? But all the same, Donald, I think I'll tell you a little truth anyway, just for old times' sake."

"Why can't you leave me alone?"

"I promise you—I will. Just as soon as we finish this chat. Then you can go running off to your Mr. Gavin. But before you do, I just want you to know that he doesn't give a damn for you. He wants to make a convert—that's what they call it, you know—but whether it's you or somebody else doesn't matter at all to him."

"You don't know what you're talking about. No one has ever done more for me than Mr. Gavin."

"We could get into quite a semantic haggle over whether it should be 'for' you or 'to' you," Mark said smiling. "But that's irrelevant. As for our friend Chris—perhaps you're right. Maybe no one ever has shown more interest in you than he, God help you. I wouldn't know. That isn't the point. The question is—why?"

Donald had locked his fingers in front of him. He stared at them now as his knuckles grew white. "Because—because he wants to help me save my soul. What better way could he prove that he likes me—that he's interested in me?"

"You keep missing the distinction," Mark said. He tossed his cigarette onto the cracked stained marble floor and ground it out with his shoe. "'Interested,' yes. 'Likes,' no. He just wants someone he can dominate, someone he can make over in his own image. He calls it converting you to his God. But it's really converting you to himself. Why does he bother? I couldn't tell you—except that he must somewhere somehow have gotten one god-awful feeling of inferiority—of deficiency, that he's got to keep making up for over and over again. Or rather, that poor boobies like you have got to keep making up for. Tell me, Donald, how does it feel to be a human sacrifice?"

He had seen as he spoke that his words were producing an effect on the boy, though whether it were rebellion or shocked recognition that he was speaking the truth, he could not say. Donald had grown paler and paler, his jaw had clenched and his breath came in audible little puffs. "You couldn't understand him," Donald said now in a low voice. "You couldn't possibly know what he's like." It was impossible to tell whether the boy were indignant at fancied effrontery, or shocked and horrified at having caught a glimpse of the reality of his relations with Gavin.

But Mark quite suddenly did not care to know. In moments of such tension as this it had often happened that he somehow stepped outside himself and surveyed the scene in which he had become embroiled with a cool and ironic objectivity. This happened now, quite without his willing it, and it was borne home upon him suddenly that his interview with Donald was growing increasingly ludicrous and degrading—to say nothing of the patent impropriety which had been present from the very beginning. Besides, the conversation had begun to weary him. He shrugged. "Very likely I don't know what he's like," he said. "I'm afraid though that I don't feel any sense of loss."

Donald got up abruptly. He reached for the books lying beside Mark, grasped them precariously in one hand, then dropped them with a crash to the floor. Mark stooped over, picked them up calmly, handed them back.

Donald blushed deeply again. "Why couldn't you have left me alone?"

Mark looked up at the tall thin boy. Oddly, he felt a little sad. "It's a fair question," he said. "I wish I had a fair answer. I suppose there's something of Gavin in me. I suppose I wouldn't be talking with you like this if there weren't."

Donald turned on his heel and walked away toward the steps. Mark did not bother to watch him. The sense of sadness persisted and deepened. There had been something so decent about Donald once, something so sincere when he had first met him. Could Gavin have accomplished so much in so short a time? The memory drifted into his mind of those evenings the boy had spent at his apartment the year before, of the conversations they had had, of the times Donald had asked to be given something to believe in. What had he given him? All he had—nothing. And it had driven him straight into Gavin's arms. It was his habit to laugh off ultimates. But others did not, and some of them depended on him to help them toward an accommodation with eternity. Donald was one, and Julie the other. Had he failed them? But again his knack of objectifying came into play and the drift of his thoughts was spread out suddenly for him to survey at a little distance. They made a rather foolish tableau, he thought. He shook himself and got up, taking another cigarette from his pocket. Well, if he had driven Donald into Gavin's camp— what of it? If that was the sort of mumbo jumbo that appealed to the boy, let him have it to his heart's content. And anyone else who shared his tastes. It hardly affected him, Mark Brodie. He lit his cigarette and walked jauntily out of the building.

Donald half-ran up the steps to the second floor. He had to see Eileen. It was absolutely imperative. What exactly he would say to her, why he had to see her, he did not know. But his mind was reeling, his shattered nerves were jagged and raw. He needed help —help that even Mr. Gavin could not give; he needed to be soothed.

She was one of three girls behind the circulation desk when he entered the room where she worked. She smiled at him as he came in, but went on methodically stamping dates in the backs of a pile of books a graduate student was withdrawing from the library. Donald waited in an agony of impatience till she had finished, then moved forward to the long counter which ran the width of the room. There was a shallow space behind the counter where the girls stood, then a drab gray wall. Through an open door one caught a glimpse of the beginning of the stacks, row on seemingly endless row of books.

Eileen was smiling at him. Her smiles for him had always a faint hint of amusement as if, try as she might, she found it impossible to take him quite seriously. Donald usually felt faintly wounded at this look of hers, but today he hardly noticed that it was there.

"Eileen, I've got to talk with you," he said in an urgent whisper. She reached out and took the armload of books from him, almost without his noticing, and set it down on the desk.

"What about, Don?" she asked. Flipping through the books he had returned she asked, "Are any of these overdue?"

"We can't talk here," he said, glancing quickly at the other girls, who were busy helping other people returning books or taking them out of the library.

"Oh, Don—don't be so silly."

"Eileen, please——"

There was something in his tone that made her look at him again, this time without the smile. "There isn't any place."

"In there." He nodded toward the open door beyond which were the stacks. She hesitated. "Please, you've got to."

Eileen excused herself to the other girls. They nodded. They knew Donald and knew Eileen's relationship with him. Although they put him down as an eccentric, they conceded Eileen her right to choose him if she liked.

Back in the stacks Donald drew her into a narrow cubbyhole between two shelves full of books. He did not bother to conceal the physical relief he felt as he leaned back against one of the crowded shelves and closed his eyes. The emotional strain he had been under had worn him out physically.

"Donald, what is it?" Eileen said, concerned for him and yet annoyed at his strange behavior. "I can't stay away long. The other girls——"

"Please, Eileen," he said, "I need you." Their surroundings made them speak unconsciously in whispers.

"Then tell me what's wrong, Don."

"Mr. Brodie."

"What about him?"

"I met him coming into the library."

Eileen was mystified. Donald's apparent reluctance to make sense got on her nerves. "Am I going to have to get this out of you question by question?" she asked. "Why don't you just tell me what happened?"

"Don't you start on me too, Eileen," Donald half-whimpered. "For heaven's sake, I should think you'd——"

"All right, Donald. Please, tell me what happened."

"Mr. Brodie stopped me. We talked."

Again he paused. Resignedly, Eileen prompted him. "What did you say to each other?"

"It was awful. First—first he started out pretending he was my friend. But then—it was just like I knew it would be."

"What?"

"He wanted to talk me out of entering the Church. And when he saw he wasn't going to get anywhere, he started to talk about Mr. Gavin, to revile him. It all happened the way I knew it would." Donald clearly felt that he had told his tale. He looked expectantly now at the girl, waiting for a response. But what was the response he expected? Eileen wondered.

"Is that all?" she asked.

"Isn't it enough?"

"Donald, don't be silly. What else did you expect? I suppose Mr. Brodie thought he was doing what was right, and you can't blame him for that."

"But he attacked Mr. Gavin, he tried to make me distrust him."

"Don, you're so naïve. What else did you think he'd do?"

"Oh, I knew what he'd do, all right. Mr. Gavin had told me that."

She flared up suddenly, as if his words has been a spark firing something dangerous inside her. "Mr. Gavin told you," she repeated. "So when Mr. Gavin attacks Mr. Brodie, it's perfectly all right. But when Mr. Brodie attacks Mr. Gavin, you've got to come cry on someone's shoulder."

"Eileen!" he exclaimed. He stared at her in genuine shock.

"Keep quiet," she whispered. One of the other girls passed by their cubbyhole on her way deeper into the stacks. She glanced out of the corner of her eye at them, then looked away quickly when she saw they were watching her.

"How can you say that, Eileen?" Donald pursued when the girl was out of earshot. "It's so unfair."

"I'm sorry, Donald." She gestured with her rather too large hands. She was finding it particularly difficult to communicate with him this afternoon. "I'm tired. It's been a long day. I'm a little on edge. I may not say things as nicely as I'd like to say them." She hesitated, then added, "But I mean them when I say them, all the same."

"You don't understand, Eileen," Donald said. "Mr. Brodie said that Mr. Gavin doesn't care about me as an individual, he doesn't care what becomes of me. He said he's just interested in dominating someone, and I happen to be the person he's chosen."

"And probably he's right," Eileen said in a low voice that was no whisper.

Donald could not even muster a reply. But his face spoke eloquently. Eileen looked helplessly at him. "Please, Don," she said. "This isn't the time for us to talk. Just forget for now that I said anything. We'll discuss it all later." She turned to go. But Donald suddenly, to the surprise of them both, grasped her by the wrist and held her back. They looked at each other in amazement.

"I'm sorry, Eileen," he said. He let go of her wrist. Surprisingly, he did not appear as flustered as she. It was as if he were gaining strength as their conversation wore on, while she was losing it.

"I'm sorry," he said again. "I don't want you to go though. I want you to explain what you meant."

Eileen blushed. "I meant what I said," she replied, "and nothing more. I just happen to think Mr. Brodie may be right. I think probably Mr. Gavin does want to dominate you, and I'm not sure at all that he's interested in your welfare."

Donald nodded. He said nothing.

"Don, please—I know how you feel about him. I don't want to say anything against him."

"Of course not." The heavy tone of irony did not conceal the tremble in his voice. He seemed suddenly on the brink of tears. His momentary strength had gone.

"Don, won't you ever grow up?" she pleaded. "Are you always going to let people make you cry just because of what they say to you? Are you always going to have to run to someone else to wipe your nose and dry your eyes when you're hurt?"

"Eileen, please, don't say those things to me. Not *you*——"

"Why not me? Oh, I know, I'm one of the people you depend on. But I don't want it that way, Don. It isn't good for you. That's why I'm saying these things. And if Mr. Gavin would say the same things——"

"Mr. Gavin again. Why does everyone have to talk about him?" He turned away and faced the books behind him. Suddenly his shoulders began shaking a little and she knew he was crying. "You're going to say I have to choose between you. I know you are."

"Don." She put her hands on his shoulders and pressed her cheek up against the back of his neck. "Poor Don. Not yet. I won't make you choose yet."

CHRISTOPHER STOOD AT HIS DESK, STOWING BOOKS HAPHAZARDLY into his brief case. It was time to go home. He felt tired and disagreeable. There was a throbbing in his temples that was less an ache than a constant dull and annoying pressure. He seldom had headaches, but when he did they were severe. This was the way they usually started—fatigue, a throbbing sense of pressure in his temples—and he sourly anticipated a wretched evening. Across the English department office by a window Robbie Bond was seated, listening distractedly to a student who had been stringing out some protracted petition or complaint for almost three quarters of an hour. Robbie did not look up—but then, he seldom did get much attention from that quarter these days, Chris reflected. It was obvious that Dr. Bond was at more of a loss than ever how to deal with him, and that his solution was therefore not to deal with him at all, at least so far as that was possible. Robbie confined himself strictly to civilities and went so far out of his way to avoid discussion with him on any topic, either alone or in the presence of others, that Chris actually found his behavior rather amusing. Mark Brodie was not there at the moment. He, thought Chris, at least did not try to avoid him altogether, as Robbie did. But when they met, Mark's air of casualness and business-as-usual showed signs of strain that suggested he actually felt no more at ease with him than did Dr. Bond. Christopher smiled inwardly at that thought. It was somehow strangely gratifying to know that he had gotten under the skin even of the imperturbable Brodie.

There were one or two other teachers in the office, young men like himself, but they did not pay him any attention either as he prepared to leave. Christopher had earned a reputation as a fanatic and most of his fellow faculty members displayed little enthusiasm for associating with him—though they were without exception formally polite, with the sort of insincere placating good manners that he sneered at to himself. He snapped the brief case shut, adjusted a woolen scarf around his neck, buttoned his shabby overcoat and, without nodding to anyone, swung jauntily out of the office.

But he was rather far from feeling true jauntiness. His head was beginning to hurt, a dull grating pain, and he wished he were home already where he could gulp some aspirin and lie down on his bed in the dark. He walked painfully down the three flights of steps to the street floor.

He was surprised suddenly to see a figure standing by the door to the street. In the dim light from a dirty window by the door he saw it was a woman and his heart leaped as the thought flashed into his mind: Julie! But his eagerness faded as quickly as it had come. It was Eileen McGovern standing there in the shadows.

If it had been possible, he would have ignored her. But there were only the two of them there. He nodded curtly. "Hello, Eileen."

"Hello, Mr. Gavin." She paused. "I've been waiting here for you," she said.

He had no wish to speak to the girl. His head hurt and he was tired. He had nothing to say to her. "I'm afraid my office hours are over now. See me some other time, Eileen."

"What I wanted to see you about is something private," she said. "Nothing to do with school."

He shrugged. "As you like." He pushed open the door. Eileen followed him outside. It was late in the winter afternoon, about four-thirty. Dusk was beginning to fall. There was a damp cold in the air, as if it were going to snow. With his free hand Christopher pulled his scarf more tightly about his neck. He always felt badly in the late afternoon. In the morning he was fine and in the evening he bounced back again. But he was at his lowest ebb at this time of day. He could muster only a dull resentment against the girl walking beside him now.

"You did say there was something you wanted to see me about, didn't you?" he prompted at last.

She did not speak at once. Then she said: "It's an odd thing—now that we're together it's hard for me to remember what exactly I wanted to say."

Christopher snorted slightly. With exaggerated distinctness he said, "I have a headache, Eileen. I'm tired and would like nothing so much as to go home and go to bed. Couldn't you come back tomorrow——or whenever you manage to remember what you wanted to say to me?"

"There's really no point in your treating me like a fool, Mr. Gavin," Eileen said quietly. "I know I'm not one, so it doesn't intimidate me. And I think Donald knows it too, so it's going to take something more than telling him I'm stupid to discourage him from seeing me."

"What Donald does is no concern of mine," Christopher said automatically.

"Really, Mr. Gavin!" Eileen seemed genuinely disappointed in him. He had the distinct impression she expected him to damn himself out of his own mouth.

"Donald is perfectly free," he added. "If he wants to see you, there's nothing I could do about it, even if I wanted to."

"I want to talk seriously with you, Mr. Gavin," she said gravely. "I don't want just to play games."

"I'm quite ready to talk seriously," Christopher said. "I had the impression I was. But I do wonder if we're going to get anywhere so long as you can't remember what you want to say to me."

"I know what I want to say well enough. I was just trying to find some nice, pleasant words to say it with. But I suppose that isn't necessary with you."

Christopher chuckled. "I don't stand on ceremony," he said.

"I want to ask you a question, Mr. Gavin. What are you trying to do to Donald? And why?"

They walked slowly, close together. One might have taken them for a young couple in love.

He smiled drily. "Why should I bother giving you an answer?" he said. "You have an answer of your own already. Why don't you tell me instead? What *am* I trying to do to Donald?"

"Tie him to you in every possible way," she said. "Make him believe what you tell him to believe and do what you tell him to do."

He would have liked to have been able to summon a strong and violent reaction. But he was too tired even to bother to deny what she said. He did not feel like wasting his energy on her. "Is that so very different from what you want to do?" he asked.

"What I want to do?"

"You love Donald, don't you?"

She hesitated. The thought passed automatically through his mind: These fools who can't make up their minds what they feel and what they want! "I don't know," she said. "Perhaps I do."

"For the sake of argument—" he explained. "Suppose you do love him. Love means desire. The end of desire is possession. Possession means to add things to oneself—in a sense, to make them over into oneself."

"Things."

"And people. Your loving Donald simply means you want to make him over in your image. And if I want to do the same thing, it's because I love him too."

"That's what you call love, Mr. Gavin?"

The way in which she spoke, the tone almost of pity, drew a twinge of anger from him. What business did she have pitying him? He hated her pity. He did not need it. He rejected it scornfully. "That's what I call love. I know it isn't the stupid sentimental feeling *you* call love. But if you knew yourself, knew your own feelings—if you had the honesty to do that—you'd admit that I'm right. What a lot of damned nonsense people talk about love," he added.

"And you think we love people the same way we love things?"

"The mistake is in assuming that the emotion changes with its object. The emotion is a constant. The circumstances may change, but it doesn't. Love is always the same. It aims at possession—and assimilation."

"Do you think it's a good thing for Donald to—to be loved this way by you?"

"Why not?"

"Don't you think he's already too weak—too unable to stand up to what you call assimilation? You could destroy his personality——"

"In order to remake it. Is that wrong? I want Donald to know what is true and to act accordingly."

"But you think that only you can tell him what the truth is."

Eileen felt a frightened fascination in contemplating this strange man's mind as he revealed it. And he in his weariness was no longer quite conscious of what he was saying—or rather, did not bother to check the introspective working of his mind or stop the flow of dogmatizing it had produced. He took an actual pleasure in this conversation now. He enjoyed taking out the ideas he had cherished to himself for so long and turning them over proudly one by one for inspection. "No, I don't think that," he replied. "It's just that I'm the only one who has ever bothered to tell him what the truth is. The rest of you, you good Catholics, have always been too busy, or too indifferent—or too polite. You wouldn't want to risk offending anyone. So you leave people like Donald to find their own way themselves. You leave them alone. You wouldn't want to intrude on their right to be confused and miserable all their lives. And when someone else does try to help them, you accuse him of being authoritarian, trying to run other people's lives."

"But, Mr. Gavin, in the Church—you must know—there are people whose job it is to do what you're trying to do. That's the responsibility of a priest."

"How many times have I heard that as an excuse for doing nothing? How many people like Donald are ever in their lives going to come near a priest? And supposing they did—how many priests would bother to help them?"

"It's their job."

"It's a privilege—bringing people to truth—not a job. And you have to earn a privilege—and work at earning it. And if the priests don't, someone else will have to."

"You?" He did not answer. She paused. A question had come into her mind that she hardly dared to ask; and yet for these few moments she could ask anything, it seemed. Strangely, she and this man had gained an unsought, unexpected intimacy. Tacitly, they had discarded pretense and spoke only as they thought and felt. "Why haven't you become a priest?" she asked.

A look of anger crossed his face, not at her, but at some memory her question had conjured up for him. "I wanted to be a priest," he said. "I should have been one. But they wouldn't have me."

"Why not?"

"Shall I tell you what they told me—or the real reason? Well then, both. The excuse was that I lacked humility. I wouldn't have been willing to submit myself to superiors. Of course, they were probably right about that—I wouldn't obey someone I didn't respect, and I couldn't respect one of these miserable compromisers. Still—still——" he gestured vaguely. "It was only an excuse for them."

"And what was the real reason?"

He paused. When he spoke again it was in a lowered voice, as if he were sharing with her a treasured secret. "They were afraid of me. They were afraid I'd show them up, make them look inferior, unworthy of their vocations. You see, they envied me my vocation. They envied me so much that they've tried to deprive me of it. They're still trying, but they won't succeed." The cold air had given his usually pale cheeks a ruddy color. His eyes sparkled with the excitement of what he said. He had forgotten about his weariness and in his absorption he looked very young, very wholesome. There was something immensely frightening about him, Eileen thought.

"But what about Donald?" she said, anxious now to change the subject.

"I've told you what I feel," Christopher answered. "Now what about you?"

"I don't understand."

He frowned impatiently. "Do you love him?"

"Not in the way you described love."

"Well, in any way? I'd hardly expect you to concede that my definition of love is correct. But applying your own definition, whatever it is—do you love him?"

"I'm not sure I'd tell you if I knew. But I don't know. I'm not sure. I want to help him."

He dismissed her words with a contemptuous gesture. "Help him. What does that mean? You don't know. Just as you don't know if you love him. I hate that. It's stupid—the way you people can't make up your minds, don't know what you think, or believe, or feel. People shy away from certainty. They're afraid to commit themselves, afraid they may be wrong—or even that they may be right, if it should happen to offend some fool."

"No one can be certain of everything, Mr. Gavin."

"Is that a reason for being certain about nothing?" He had begun to walk more quickly, as the annoyance mounted in him. Eileen found it rather difficult to keep up with him. "And you think you want to help Donald. For heaven's sake, how? You want just to substitute your doubts for his? The boy needs something to believe in—and what do you have to offer him except confusion and hesitation?"

Eileen in her turn had begun to grow annoyed. She did not like Christopher, nor his boorish behavior and insulting words. Whatever it was she had hoped to accomplish by this interview, it was only too evident to her now that it had been a chimera. She had given Gavin an opportunity to unburden himself of some of his fanaticism and ill temper—and that was all. Her common sense asserted itself now and she said: "I think we've wasted enough of each other's time, Mr. Gavin. You don't understand me any more than I understand you, so there isn't much sense in our talking any more."

"Why don't you answer my question?" Christopher persisted. "What do you have to offer Donald?" They had stopped and stood close together on a corner.

"Like you—only myself," she said. "But at least I won't tell him it's God." She turned away and began to walk back toward school.

The blood rushed into Christopher's face. His body twitched forward slightly as if he were going to follow her, and he called after her, "I'll fight you for him and I'll win!"

He waited, but she did not turn around or answer. Then, angry still but justified, he swung about and walked away.

"That's very good," Christopher said, shutting with a snap the little pocket catechism covered in gray paper. "You learn quickly." He smiled across the room at Julie, sitting on his couch which, for the occasion, had blossomed suddenly with three shabby but still brightly colored throw pillows.

She smiled back rather wistfully. "I learn," she said. "But do I believe?" She rose and stretched a little, then went over to the window and pulled up the shade. Great gray rows of clouds, stretching from horizon to horizon, were moving pompously out of the west, where the setting sun threw a pinkish light over them.

"The belief will come in time, Julie." He sat forward anxiously in the straight chair by the battered bureau.

She lifted her shoulders slightly. "Can you promise me that?" she said. Her tone had a hint of teasing to it, but Christopher in his earnestness did not notice.

"I can't promise it," he said unhappily. "All I can do is to pray, and to ask you to pray too—that you may have the grace to believe."

"Shall I pray to someone I don't know exists to make me able to believe in something I'm not sure is true?"

Her words hurt him more than she could guess. The worst pain of all for him was to hear her joking about it, to have her hint that, at bottom, she took none of it quite seriously. "But you believe sometimes, don't you—at least, that there is a God?"

"Sometimes I—I *feel* there must be," she said, turning now to him, all trace of joking gone. "But that isn't believing, is it, Chris?"

"No," he admitted. "It may help you to believe—but you have to be convinced, to know and to understand the truth, to see why it is the truth and why nothing else could possibly be true."

She shook her head a little, as if it were all too much for her, and turned away again toward the window. "I ought to go soon," she said without making any movement to leave.

"You said Mark wouldn't be home for dinner."

"He was going to eat at school and stay for a meeting of the literary society. But you can't ever tell—he might change his mind. And if he were home already—you can stay out shopping for groceries just so long," she said, gesturing at a brown paper bag set in the corner.

"He hasn't guessed anything yet?" Christopher asked, smiling a little craftily.

Julie winced at his words and his expression. "No," she said, lowering her eyes.

Her reaction did not escape him and he rose, concerned. "What's wrong?" he asked, crossing to her.

"Nothing," she said. "It's just that— Oh, nothing!"

"Please, Julie."

She did not answer at once, but instead looked up and smiled at him. She had a thousand different smiles, he thought, all of them enigmatic and delightful.

"You're a funny boy, Chris," she said. "About some things you're so sensitive. I don't think anyone could trick you into believing he was honest if he weren't. You can actually sense honesty and dishonesty, I think. But when it comes to other things—I think you must have a hide like a rhinoceros." She still smiled, and he smiled back at her now.

"Why do you say that?" he asked. "What have I missed now that I should have seen?"

"The way you talk about Mark and me," she said. Then, seeing the questioning expression in his eyes, she laid her hand on his arm.

"I know you don't mean any harm—it's just that—well, you seem to think I enjoy deceiving him."

Christopher was rather taken aback, both because it had never occurred to him that she did *not,* like himself, enjoy it, and because he saw at once that he had come close to a serious blunder by not perceiving her true state of mind. Naturally, he reflected now, she would have some feeling of guilt, and he at once set about mending his fences.

"Of course I don't think that, Julie," he said. "I know you're not the sort of person who'd take pleasure from deceiving someone else —even when, as it is in this case, it's in the best interests of you both."

"If I could be sure it is in our best interests . . ." Her voice trailed off. After a pause she said, "I think you enjoy deceiving Mark, Chris."

"I?" He suspected something mischievous in her look and held back from committing himself too deeply either to denial or acquiescence. "What do you mean?"

"Of course, I wouldn't blame you. Mark has been simply horrid to you. Perhaps all of this—" her vague gesture encompassed herself and him and the room, "—would seem an appropriate way of getting back at him."

"Julie!" He was genuinely horrified. What had put such ideas in her head? If she should come to believe what she was saying, all he had hoped and worked for would be irretrievably lost. "How can you think that?" With a movement that he hoped would appear unpremeditated, he took her hands in his.

"I'm sorry, Chris. I didn't mean it." She seemed genuinely abashed at having upset him so. "I know you wouldn't do something like that. But one gets so used to acting out of petty spite and meanness and to seeing others act that way that he automatically assumes everyone has the same nasty little motives."

"I understand."

"That's just it—you don't." She looked into his eyes now and, to his immense gratification, her expression was one of deep admiration. "You aren't like the rest of us, Chris. You don't act out of spite— but only out of principle."

"Anyway, I try to," he said.

"If only I could." She freed her hands gently and walked back to the couch. She did not sit down, however, but remained standing there.

"You do, Julie, as much as anyone I know."

"Thank you, Chris. But you know as well as I do that if that were true, I'd have told Mark about this a long time ago."

No, he thought, we can't have that. He would be delighted to have Mark find out—but all in good time. For if it came too soon, Mark might still be able to reverse the course of events. "There's no sense in telling him now," he said. "You'd only cause him pain—and give him a weapon with which to hurt you in return. Better wait until you've made up your mind. At least you'll save him an agony of suspense that way."

"Oh, Chris—you don't understand again."

And, in fact, he did not. He raised his eyebrows questioningly and waited for her to go on.

"You take me at face value," she said. "When I say I want to tell Mark what I'm doing because I want to be honest with him, you believe me."

"You don't want to tell him?" He began to feel a faint annoyance. Did people always have to indulge in introspection, unpeeling layer upon layer of motive like an immense head of lettuce? The foolishness of it disgusted him, even when it was Julie who did it.

"Oh yes, I want to tell him," she replied. "But honesty has nothing to do with it. You see, I know that if I tell him, he'll try to hurt me. And that would be my justification—I'd have an excuse then for going on. Mark himself would give me a clear conscience."

He hardly saw what she was driving at. Self-analysis, even his own, held little interest for him. He shrugged his shoulders. "I don't understand why you need 'justification' for trying to find out the truth."

Julie had picked up the catechism and was turning it over in her hands. She stopped now and looked at it. "This little book—it's a repudiation of everything he stands for, everything he believes in."

"He has no right——"

But she broke in quickly. "—To stop me from believing? I know, Chris, you've told me that before."

"It's true."

"Perhaps. But still we're man and wife. Hasn't he a right to my loyalty? And if the price of loyalty is not to believe this—" she held out the catechism, "—then what right do I have to believe?"

"When there is an apparent conflict of rights, one of them is only illusory."

"That's just a formula, Chris," she said. "But how do you apply it here and now? Whose right is an illusion—mine or Mark's?"

"I don't understand how you can even ask the question. The principle is clear—"

"You forget, Chris," she said with a little smile, "we don't all live by principles as you do."

"Then you ought to begin." His voice rose slightly in anger and frustration. "Mark's right is limited only to what is reasonable. When he asks you to share his unbelief, he goes far beyond what is reasonable."

"Am I supposed to give him only a 'reasonable' amount of love?" she asked quietly.

He hesitated. He knew it would be dangerous to go too far too quickly. Julie's code was to him incomprehensible, but clearly it was for her no less binding on that account. To force the issue now might be disastrous. He said in a suddenly gentle voice, "Julie, you must learn that there is no conflict between love and principle. There can't be any. I hope eventually I can help you see that—but all I can do now is pray that you will."

To his surprise, she moved suddenly to him and took his hands, as he had done hers. "Poor Chris," she said. "You work so hard for me—and I make it so difficult for you."

He smiled quietly at her. "I do what I want to do," he said.

"Why do you bother with me?" she asked. There was something almost coquettish in her manner that both amused and pleased Christopher.

"Say, because I love you."

"'Those Christians—how they love one another!'" she remarked musingly.

Christopher felt almost like correcting her, telling her that it was not that sort of love he had meant. But it was certainly too soon for that, he knew. Instead, he said, "Do you love Mark, Julie?"

"That's your great charm, Chris—you're direct, you come right to the point." She let his hands go and walked back to the window.

Dusk was falling now and she shut the shade abruptly, at the same time switching on an old table lamp set on a rickety low table.

"Do you?" he repeated, sitting down on the couch.

"As a Christian would?"

"As a wife would."

"We depend on each other. I try not to disappoint his dependence on me. I suppose that's love."

"Would you ever leave Mark?"

"I don't understand why you ask, Chris."

"I wonder what you would do—if you had to choose between Mark and God."

"It would depend," she said seriously. "I wouldn't leave Mark so long as he was weak and needed me—no matter what he did to try to force me. But if he did something—something that would make me want to leave and that was done out of strength instead of weakness, then——" She paused.

"Then you would leave him?"

"How can *you* ask me that, Chris? Certainly your Church wouldn't be in favor of wives leaving their husbands."

Christopher shrugged casually. "In the eyes of my Church," he said, "you aren't really married." He watched closely to see the effect of his words.

Julie looked at him in surprise. Then, unexpectedly, she laughed. But her laughter was rather strained, Chris thought. "Mark never told me that," she said.

"It isn't likely he would."

She looked more intently and rather anxiously at him. "Really, Chris, what do you mean? It isn't a very good joke."

"It wasn't meant to be a joke. I'm sorry if I upset you, Julie. Forget about it. It's not important right now."

"No, tell me what you meant," she persisted.

With pleasure, he thought, happy at the chance to plant in the back of her mind an idea that might well take root and flower prodigiously, if it were tended carefully by an interested party—like himself. "You weren't married by a priest, of course?"

"I was willing—if Mark had wanted it. He wouldn't hear of it though."

"It wouldn't have been in character," he said, half to himself. Then he added, "I'm no expert in canon law, Julie, but it's a simple

"But it must be embarrassing for you."

"Embarrassing?"

"Your neighbors."

"Oh." He smiled. "Not that it's any of their business—I'd just tell them you're a student whom I'm tutoring."

"Chris, don't be silly!"

Strangely enough, she was easily flattered and even the most banal compliment, he knew, was not lost upon her. In anyone else the trait would have disgusted him, but in her it was only another element of her charm. She had gotten into her coat but still stood with her back half to him, looking at him over her shoulder, smiling, her lips parted.

"Julie——" He reached out, but did not touch her.

Something in his look disturbed her and the smile left her face. She turned fully toward him now. "What is it, Chris?"

It seemed a long time before he answered. "Forget what I said, Julie, about you and Mark not being married. Just forget I mentioned it." But it was quite the reverse that he hoped.

application of a principle. Baptized Catholics can't contract valid marriages outside the Church. If a Catholic isn't married by a priest, he isn't married at all. In the eyes of the Church you'd be quite free to leave Mark."

While he spoke she had moved across the room to the dresser, where she stood now toying with the crucifix. "I suppose your Church would want me to?" she said.

There was again a hint of something dangerous in her tone. He had gone far enough for now along those lines. "The Church wouldn't take a position on it," he said. "It would only want you to do what was right to do—in the particular circumstances." He paused, then added, "I'm sorry I brought it up, Julie. Perhaps it makes the Church seem harsh to you."

"That wouldn't matter," she replied. "If it were—if it is—all it says it is, then it would have a right, even a duty, to make rules like that. It's just—it takes you a little by surprise to hear something like that."

"Of course," he said. "I'm glad to hear you talking so sensibly about it, though. I'm glad you can see that the Church could conceivably have a right to make that sort of rule. Most people get so angry at the thought of a church laying down any sort of rules for them, that they don't even bother to inquire whether it has a right to do it."

"No—that's what I want," she said. "If I were to believe in a religion, I would want it to be a religion that's sure of itself, that insists on its members' believing this and not believing that, doing this and not doing that. If a church isn't sure that what it teaches is true, why should anyone else be?"

Christopher laughed in satisfaction at her remark. "Why indeed?" he asked. "You have remarkable insight, Julie."

She did not reply, but looked instead at her watch and said again, "Really, I have to go, Chris." And almost before he could rise she had crossed the room and removed her cloth coat from its hanger on the back of the door to the hall.

Christopher reluctantly helped her into it. "Will you be able to come here again next time?" he asked.

"I think so," she said. "I hope so—it really isn't safe for you to come to our apartment. But I do hate to impose on you like this."

"Don't be silly, Julie. There's no question of your imposing."

MARK LEANED BACK IN THE PLASTIC-COVERED LOUNGE CHAIR and blew out a long cloud of smoke. He cocked his head slightly to one side, as if to hear better the hoarse adolescent voice which drifted down to him from the other end of the long room, now softly, now loudly, as the unpracticed speaker struggled unsuccessfully to control it. He wondered if he might risk closing his eyes—it would perhaps look as if he were concentrating more closely—but decided against it as being too hazardous. After all, faculty members did have to present an at least moderately convincing appearance of interest when attending the meetings of the student Literary Society. Robbie insisted on few things, but that was one of them. And it could not be retorted that he himself violated his own rules, for Mark could see him from where he sat, seated at a prominent spot at the long table, giving every sign of respectful attention to the boy who was painfully reading his way through a paper on—what was it? Mark forced himself to listen for a moment to what the boy was saying—on Dylan Thomas and the Romantic Spirit. Poor Dylan Thomas, he ruminated. To have become the property of the Eternal Student so soon—it hardly seemed fair. Though of course there did seem to be an ironic reverse logic in the transformation of Thomas, of all people, into a subject for the preciosities of a campus aesthete.

Mark felt tempted almost to bitterness at the cruel fate which had condemned him to waste his evening this way. But he resisted it, for his presence here represented nothing more than simple justice. Robbie was moderator of the Literary Society, as befitted the head of the department, but he invariably insisted that some other member of the English faculty accompany him to its meetings —"To show the students we're interested," he had explained during a departmental meeting. The distasteful biweekly assignment was filled in rotation by the staff and Mark's turn had come up again, as it did periodically. Well, make the best of it, he thought, crushing out his cigarette in an ash tray by the chair he had chosen in a distant corner. The other fellows have to go through this too.

Though, of course, he reminded himself, not really all of them. Chris Gavin had never to his knowledge taken a turn at chaperoning the Literary Society. But one could hardly blame Chris for that—it had simply happened that no one had ever asked him, he thought, lighting another cigarette to relieve his boredom. Not "simply happened" either, though. Rather, happened by more or less conscious design and mutual though tacit agreement on the part of all concerned. Chris's failure to participate in this particular responsibility of the department members only fitted the general pattern of his relations with his fellow teachers and his role within the department. He was in these areas as in so many others a "loner," Mark thought, both by his own choice and, once they had come in contact with his acid personality, by the choice of his associates. Associates was hardly the word in fact, for his fellow teachers were at pains to keep association with him to a minimum. It was for this reason that Chris had never been asked to join Robbie at one of the Literary Society meetings. And it was for this reason that he had seldom, and with sharply decreasing frequency after his first few weeks at the university, been asked to share any other duties with the other members of the department, or been consulted on matters of policy, or been drawn beyond the necessary requirements of mere everyday politeness into social relations with his fellow teachers.

In this approach to the "problem" of Christopher, the way was led by Robbie. Since the time of the incident over alleged classroom proselytizing, Dr. Bond had gone out of his way to avoid questioning Chris about anything. His efforts seemed to Mark to be in fact quite conspicuous. It was as if he had closed his eyes to Chris or anything he might choose to do. Robbie for his part simply did not want to know what he might be up to, as if on the theory that unknown evil was no evil at all. It was an approach that Mark found distasteful, particularly when it meant tolerating an affront such as he took Christopher Gavin to be. Nevertheless, he realized that it would be folly to attempt to rouse Robbie against Chris again, unless Gavin could be caught red-handed in some truly heinous crime. The earlier fiasco had undoubtedly made Dr. Bond gun-shy and it would take a considerable stimulus to move him to renewed action so soon. And as for what he might do himself, Mark thought—it was little enough. He might speak against Chris to other teachers as often as he liked (and in fact he did), but as far as taking any effective action went, as far as approaching the administration, say, was concerned—well, without the head of the department leading the way, to appearances at least—he would be wasting his time, he knew, and perhaps even putting himself in danger.

So Mark waited and fumed. Much as he was waiting and fuming for this intolerable evening to be over. But still he had his hopes. He believed he knew Christopher, and from what he knew he believed he could count on his eventually committing some supreme act of *hubris* that would compromise his position and make it possible for his antagonists to silence him once and for all. But in the meantime, he reflected dourly, it was a question of waiting, and he always had been bad at waiting.

Still, patience did inevitably have its reward—as in the present instance. For it seemed that, contrary to what one might have believed in a moment of tortured fantasy, the expositor of Dylan Thomas was actually drawing to a close, in a burst of "one might say's" and "it seems assured's." And at last the paper did end and was rewarded with a smattering of applause, in which Mark dutifully joined. Then came a few words from the president of the society, a stocky boy with short-cropped brown hair combed unaccountably forward, and finally with a scraping of chairs and stretching of cramped limbs nearing the point of atrophy, the meeting itself actually came to a close.

Mark rose with the rest and, his foot painfully asleep, hobbled over to a half-open window to get some air and wait for Robbie. Dr. Bond had become the center of a little knot of English majors anxious to make their mark as intellectuals with the head of the department. Mark stood looking out the window onto the dark street, where nothing moved under the dim lamps except a few scraps of paper blown by the cold January wind. He wished absently that Robbie would hurry and disengage himself, and drive him home.

"Mr. Brodie."

Mark turned wearily at the sound of the adolescent voice. Apparently he was to get his share of it, as well as Robbie. It was Harvey Wecter. Harvey had been in his class last year and had fancied himself, Mark knew, rather a disciple of his. However, there was something about the boy—not alone his affected intellectualism, but a certain insinuating and faintly patronizing manner of his— which Mark had found distasteful and which had moved him to keep Harvey at a distance. This year, he knew obscurely, the boy was rooming with Donald. He was also, Mark recalled now, one of Chris's students.

"Hello, Harvey," he said. "How are you?" He surveyed without enthusiasm the angular slouching figure in khakis, flannel jacket, and sweater.

"Fine, thank you, Mr. Brodie. And you?"

"Just fine."

"And Mrs. Brodie?"

"Fine," he said shortly.

"It was an interesting paper, didn't you think?"

"Terribly."

Harvey smiled knowingly. "You don't sound as if you quite meant that, Mr. Brodie."

"Why would I say it if I didn't?"

Harvey laughed, too loudly, and a couple of other boys turned to look. I didn't say anything funny, Mark thought. I suppose he just wants to butter me up.

"Oh, of course, of course," Harvey burbled as if at some choice joke. "Why would you indeed?"

Mark was growing tired of this line of conversation. "And how have you been lately, Harvey?" he asked desperately.

"Oh, pretty well," the boy said. "Still—it's not like last year."

"No?"

"My English class, I mean."

Mark's attention perked up slightly. After all, Gavin did teach him. "In what way exactly, Harvey?" he asked.

"Well, Mr. Gavin——" The boy shrugged. "He has his eccentricities."

Mark knew that he ought not to tolerate such talk from a student about another teacher. More important still, he should not encourage it. But the temptation to draw out Harvey on this interesting theme was too strong to be resisted. He fell. "What sort of eccentricities?"

"I wouldn't want to seem to be complaining——"

"Of course not, Harvey."

"—But on the other hand I might be able to tell you some things you'd be interested to hear, Mr. Brodie. After all, I know you don't quite get along with Mr. Gavin."

How the hell did he know? Probably from Donald. But of course it didn't matter much. A school, he knew, had its own unique subterranean machinery for spreading gossip—truth and falsehood mixed indiscriminately. His quarrel with Gavin, Mark reflected, was probably common knowledge among the students already, and from a dozen different sources. Still, one had to keep up appearances. "I think you've been misinformed on that score, Harvey," he said. The phrase sounded to his ears both unbearably pompous and incriminatingly equivocal.

Harvey only smiled back at him with the look of one who is willing to go along with a joke but wants it clearly understood that he is as thoroughly in on it as anyone else. "Oh, have I, Mr. Brodie?" he said.

Mark would have been happy to drive his fist into the smirk confronting him. "You said you had something to tell me?" he asked.

"About what goes on in Mr. Gavin's class."

"Well?" Mark noticed uncomfortably that they had lowered their voices conspiratorially. Harvey had drawn closer, and it was not hard to imagine that he might in a minute begin running his fingers confidentially up and down the lapels of Mark's jacket while he spoke.

"You may have heard already," Harvey said softly. "It's about the reading list he's assigned."

"Reading list?"

"Yes. A required reading list. Books we *have* to read and give detailed reports on."

Disgusted, Mark took a step backward. "He has a right to assign you reading if he wants," he said. "Really, Harvey, I'm not interested in your gripes over being worked too hard."

"But you haven't heard it all, Mr. Brodie." The boy's tone expressed injury.

"Well, go ahead."

"It's the books he's put on the list——"

"What about them?"

"It just seems to me that they're rather strange books to *require* us to read."

"What are they?"

"Catholic books."

"Catholic books?"

"Yes. Almost all of them. Things by Newman and Chesterton and Belloc—people like that. And most of the books are things defending the Catholic Church. Why, even in poetry—if you read this list you'd think the only English poets are Hopkins and Coventry Patmore and Francis Thompson. I mean really, Mr. Brodie, some of the books are just plain outright propaganda for his Church— that's the sort of thing we have to read."

Mark did not answer at first. The best news always comes as a surprise, he thought, and this was certainly some of the very best. Give him enough rope—well, Gavin had hung himself this time. When he spoke, it was not to Harvey at all.

"Robbie!" he called down the room.

The crowd of students around Dr. Bond had thinned out. He looked up now and saw Mark beckoning to him. Relieved at the excuse, he detached himself from the remaining hangers-on and made his way to where Mark and Harvey stood.

"Thanks for saving me, Mark," he said, lighting the habitual pipe which had gone cold in his mouth. Then he noticed Harvey. "Hello—" he groped for the name, "—Harvey."

The boy shuffled his feet uneasily. It was plain that Mark's action in calling Robbie had caught him by surprise. He wondered if he was about to be given a dressing-down for his impertinence in criticizing one teacher to another. The idea of approaching Mr. Brodie had occurred to him only on the spur of the moment as a means of currying favor and perhaps causing Mr. Gavin some inconvenience—and he was apprehensive now that it might have more serious and unpleasant results than he had suspected. "Hello, Dr. Bond," he murmured.

"Robbie," Mark said. "Harvey has been telling me some things I think you might find very interesting."

"Oh?" Dr. Bond looked apprehensively from Mark to the boy. There was something vaguely unsettling in Brodie's manner, a dangerous hint of things to come.

"About a mutual acquaintance. In fact, another member of the department."

Harvey and Dr. Bond eyed each other worriedly. Each seemed to the other a potential threat due to be activated momentarily. Aware of their mutual nervousness, Mark paused a moment to savor the situation, then turned the screw a notch tighter. "Chris Gavin," he said. "Harvey was just giving me a report on him."

"Really?"

"Tell Dr. Bond what you told me, Harvey," Mark prompted with the air of a tutor bringing forward his prize pupil.

"Well——" Harvey began. But he was sure now that it would be an indiscretion of the first rank to repeat what he had told Mr. Brodie. And so abruptly he declared, "What I said before wasn't meant as a complaint, you understand. I just thought you'd be interested to hear, that was all." His eyes turned from Mark to Robbie and back again.

"And so I was, Harvey," Mark said. "And so will Dr. Bond be. But if you don't want to tell him yourself——" He paused. It was clear that the boy was beyond speech by now. "—Then I suppose I'd better."

"Mark, please," Robbie said. "Don't overdo it."

"Far from my intention. Well then, to be plain and blunt, Harvey was telling me about Chris's reading list."

"Reading list?"

"Required reading list."

"What about it?"

"It's a rather unusual one, Robbie, in that all the authors are

Catholic authors and all the books are works of Catholic apologetics."

"Most of them," Harvey mumbled. But neither of the teachers paid him any attention now.

"It's hard to believe," Robbie said—though it was plain to Mark that he believed it only too well.

"If it were anyone else—yes. But with Chris . . ."

"Even so—can we get a copy of this list?"

For the first time, Mark was apprehensive. He glanced questioningly at Harvey. "Do you have the list?" he asked.

"It's in my room," the boy said.

Robbie spoke. "Would you mind getting it for us, uh——?"

"Harvey," Mark said.

"—Harvey?" Robbie finished.

"Yes, sir." The boy detached himself from the two teachers with relief.

"We'll be right here," Mark called after him. Lowering his voice, he turned back to Robbie. "Well, what do you think of that?" he asked. "Has Gavin finally gone far enough for you?"

"We don't want to be hasty, Mark."

With a snort of impatience Mark walked to the long table and dropped into one of the chairs there. The room was empty now. "I'd say we'd been the reverse of hasty, Robbie—letting it get this far."

"How far? We don't know anything for certain yet."

"We will as soon as Harvey gets back."

"The boy could be mistaken—or lying."

"He's not a fool. You know what he told me is true."

Robbie nodded reluctantly. "I suppose so," he said. He chewed the stem of his pipe in silence for a moment. Then suddenly he burst out, "Why would he do it?" The question was less one of anger or bewilderment than of injured complaint. He had a gift for personalizing misfortune and seeing in it a malevolence aimed directly at him. Mark imagined that this latest misdemeanor of Chris's seemed to him more in the nature of a personal betrayal than anything else.

"Given Christopher, and given the circumstances, it's hardly surprising."

"What do you mean?"

"After all, Robbie, we both know he has some sort of religious mania. He's apparently obsessed with the idea of evangelizing and proselytizing for his religion. From his point of view a classroom full of young people must be a golden opportunity, a chance too good to be missed. And this business of the reading list is almost inevitable. He can't tamper with the curriculum, but there's nothing to stop him from assigning outside reading. We all do it—why shouldn't he too? Or at least, I imagine that's what he thinks, and what he's planned as his defense."

"Defense?"

"When and if he was found out."

Robbie knocked his pipe out in an empty wastepaper basket. "I don't like this, Mark," he said.

"I should hope not."

"You don't understand."

"Perhaps I do." Mark stared sullenly at him.

"I hate this constant quarreling, this intramural sniping."

"Naturally. That's why you ought to take a firm stand on this, Robbie, and have it over with once and for all."

"What do you suggest?"

Mark took a deep breath. "I'd go to the dean."

"No, I couldn't——"

"This isn't the first time you've had trouble with Chris. And you can go just so far within the department. Sooner or later either he has to play it your way—or he has to be gotten rid of."

"But is it that serious?"

"I think so. Both in itself and when you take into consideration what it may lead to. I suppose the next step would be to start assigning catechism lessons."

"You're exaggerating."

"Not so much. I think that's the spirit of the thing. You know, I warned you before, Robbie—our own little Oxford Movement. Well, it seems to me we've gone at least one giant step closer to that."

"Here it is, Dr. Bond." Harvey, slightly out of breath, stood in the doorway, a mimeographed sheet in his hand.

Mark crossed to him and took the list. "Thank you, Harvey," he said absently, running his eyes down the column of titles.

"You can go," Robbie said to the boy. Harvey nodded hurriedly at them and disappeared.

"Is it bad?" Robbie asked as Mark walked back to him, still absorbed in the list.

"See for yourself."

Robbie took the paper fearfully. After a moment, he groaned and lowered himself slowly into a chair. "Terrible," he murmured. "Simply terrible. Chesterton, Belloc, *The Seven Storey Mountain*. I don't see how it could *be* any worse."

Mark smiled grimly. "It couldn't."

Nervously Robbie took a tobacco pouch from his coat pocket and began to fill his pipe. "I don't understand it," he complained. "I've always treated him decently—more so than he deserves. Why would he do a thing like this to me? Hasn't he any sense of gratitude?"

Mark waved his hand as if to put the question aside. "What's important now is to do something about it—about him. As I said, I think the dean——"

"No!" Robbie interrupted. "No, I can't agree with you, Mark."

"What other way is there?"

"Honestly, in some ways you're just like *him*." Robbie gestured toward the mimeographed sheet which he had put on the table. A few grains of tobacco fell on it from his pipe. "You see everything in black and white. When you act, you act by extremes."

"Should we just pass this over in silence?" Mark asked in a voice heavy with sarcasm.

"No, of course not," Robbie said. He seemed more confident now than he had a moment before, as his plan, whatever it might be, grew and took shape in his mind. He could even afford to adopt a faintly pedantic tone as he added, "But there are ways of doing things—decorum—a right way and a wrong way. After all, it's not as if he were some sort of criminal——"

"That depends."

"No, he still has his rights. And there's no sense or justice in condemning him out of hand. He may have an explanation for all this. That boy may not have told us everything, or he may not have understood the purpose of this reading list. Or perhaps it's simply an honest mistake on Chris's part—after all, he's not an experienced teacher. And he might be quite willing to listen to reason, perhaps even glad if we called it to his attention——" Dr. Bond ignored

Mark's laugh. "At any rate, we have to hear what he has to say. He must be given his chance to explain himself."

"And so?"

"I simply think that the best thing to do is to sit down and discuss things with him quietly and calmly and rationally without making threats or talking of going to the dean or anything else. Let's first just try to understand his point of view, and then see if we can persuade him that he's made a mistake, and then——"

"Then we go to the dean."

"Then the problem may simply have disappeared."

"You want to talk to him?"

"Yes." Robbie lit his pipe now, blowing out great clouds of smoke.

"You remember what happened the last time."

Robbie choked slightly and coughed. Clearing his throat, he said: "I had something a little different in mind this time."

"Oh?"

"I thought, Mark, that since you take such an interest in the matter, you might like to sit in on the discussion. And after all, it is a departmental affair."

"Reinforcements," he could not help saying.

Robbie looked unhappy. "If you want to put it that way."

"Sorry, Robbie." He had no desire to alienate Dr. Bond at this stage of the game. "All right, if you want me, I'll be glad to be there."

"Thank you, Mark." Robbie rose to go.

"There's one thing though——"

"What?"

"If this doesn't work, if Gavin doesn't co-operate—*then* we go to the dean. We have to, Robbie."

"Yes. But heaven forbid!"

Heaven might, Mark reflected, but heaven might not have too much to say about it.

Harvey returned rather nervously to his room. He could not help wondering what exactly he had done—the way in which Mr. Brodie and Dr. Bond behaved had confused and frightened him. He would have liked to put the matter out of his mind.

Donald was sitting at his desk reading as he came into the room.

He had not been there before, Harvey recalled. The boy hung up his coat and lay down on his bed.

"Harvey," Donald said from the desk, "have you seen my reading list?"

He started slightly. "Reading list?"

"The one Mr. Gavin gave us. I thought I had it right here on my desk. But then I went out for a while to get a coke—and when I came back it wasn't here."

He remembered now. He had seen the list on his roommate's desk as soon as he had come into the room before, and in his haste to complete his errand, had snatched it up and hurried off with it. But it would not do under the circumstances to explain that to Donald.

"I wouldn't know anything about it, Don," he said.

Donald shook his head in annoyance. "Darn it. That's the second one I've lost. This one wasn't even mine. I had to borrow it from Eileen after I misplaced my own copy."

"Too bad," Harvey said. "I think mine is in my desk drawer if you want to take a look at it."

"Thanks." Donald rose.

"Sure thing, Don." He bit his lip nervously. Best just to forget about the whole business, he decided. He rolled over on his side, turned on the lamp on the table next to his bed, took up a book and began to read.

THE WIND SWIRLED A FEW DEAD LEAVES UP INTO THE AIR IN the middle of the empty tennis court. They spun as if they were whirling about an invisible funnel, until the wind whipped them contemptuously up against the high wire fence and into a little heap in a corner. It was a cold sight and even seen from indoors it made Father Kirsch shiver and shift his gaze to the bright blue sky as if he were looking for a hint of warmth. But even the sky looked icy blue and he turned back to his desk still shivering.

He had been trying now for the better part of an hour to review and rethink some notes on the virtue of charity which he wanted to use that evening in a lecture—part of a course in Christian doctrine he was conducting for Catholic students. But so far he had accomplished little or nothing. The notes were hopelessly inadequate (he had been meaning for some time to revise and expand these and the others he had used in the courses of past years), crabbed and cryptic to the point of unintelligibility. It was clear that they would once again be of little help and that he would end, as usual, by extemporizing in platitudes on his theme. But even if he had been able to make sense of the notes, he thought, his real problem would have remained. They would have continued to be inadequate, to fall far short of what he really wanted to say. What could one say on a theme like charity? How little the virtue was understood today. What a mean, self-seeking notion of love the world had. He wanted so much to tell them . . . But he knew too how it would be. His voice would drone dully over the faint sound of jukebox music coming from another part of the student-union building, while before him the apathetic young people would yawn and drowse, feeling that by attendance alone they fulfilled their duty or kept the promise made to parents (a few boys came, he knew, simply because girls in whom they were interested did so too). It was just as well his words were inadequate, for adequacy on such a theme would be a shameful waste on such an audience. But at once he regretted that thought. It was unfair, patently an attempt to shift blame for his failures onto the shoulders of others. If the students were apathetic, that was his fault, not theirs. The theme sought—demanded—a dynamic treatment. And he could give it only his own hesitance and inadequacy. After all, what did he know of love that he should presume to advise anyone else on the subject? His own love was such a feeble thing. And lately all of his doubts had redoubled in intensity. In recent weeks—(no, he corrected himself sharply; it was necessary that he be frank about this) —since, then, he had last met Christopher Gavin, he had begun to question his previous assumptions about charity. Everything he had believed before counseled him to bear with Gavin patiently, suffer him to go his way unhindered, refrain from any action against him. And yet this pattern of response was so clearly not enough. Gavin was unprecedented in the priest's life, his challenge altogether new. And in response Father Kirsch had begun to suspect that passiveness and meekness were not enough for this situation, and that before Gavin was through action would be necessary. As if in anticipation of that event, the priest had already begun to remind himself that what he had heard so often was indeed true—that charity might sometimes be betrayed rather than served by a failure to fight.

His thoughts were interrupted by a knock on the door. He called, "Come in," and Eileen McGovern entered.

"Hello, Eileen." Father Kirsch smiled. He liked the girl. There was something essentially wholesome, sane, and common-sensical about her that he found refreshing and reassuring in the sometimes giddily rarefied intellectual and social atmosphere of the university. But today her manner hinted at concern. She sat nervously on the edge of the chair he offered her, forgetting even to take off her heavy tan coat.

"How have you been, Eileen? I haven't seen much of you lately?"

"I was busy studying for the midyears, Father."

"How did you do?"

"Pretty well," she said absently. At any rate, he thought, it was not bad marks that had brought her to see him. Nor, if he interpreted correctly her preoccupied air, was it merely a social visit. What then?

"I've always thought myself," he said, "that sophomore year is the hardest of all four in college. The really inadequate students automatically disappear in first year. But the weeding out among sophomores is more careful, more searching. And not only do the teachers evaluate the students, but the students are called on to perform some self-evaluation."

"I suppose it is an important year," she said. Then she added, more meaningfully, "In a lot of ways."

"How do you mean?"

"Well—*personally*, Father. That evaluation you mentioned—it seems to me that in a lot of cases it has to be an evaluation not just of a student as a student, but of a student as a person. We can postpone growing up for a long time, I suppose, but it begins catching up with even the most delayed of us about now."

Father Kirsch lit a cigarette casually. It was clear that she had something to tell him, or ask him. They always did when they were this roundabout. And he felt always a little frightened when these conversations reached this stage, for soon, he knew, the appeal would come for help or advice or consolation. And he would be brought face to face again with his own insufficiency. "I don't think anyone would accuse you of being immature, Eileen."

She smiled a little. "Would I come to you if I weren't, Father?"

"Perhaps it's a sign of maturity to know when to ask for help."

She seemed struck by that. "I hadn't thought of it that way," she admitted.

He made a gesture signifying that it was not an important

point. Now, he thought. I have to do it now. "What sort of help do you need, Eileen?"

She lowered her eyes for a moment. When she raised them again to his she seemed at last to have made up her mind to speak. "Advice, Father," she said. She went on then. It was about Donald Reinhart. Did the priest know him? Yes? Oh, from the dance. Perhaps he knew also that they had been seeing each other regularly for several months? Then he might be able to guess her problem. Donald wasn't a Catholic, of course. But he had fallen under the influence of Mr. Gavin. In fact, he was apparently taking instructions from him—if you could do that with anyone but a priest. She felt that was none of her business. But what did concern her was how Mr. Gavin's influence affected her relations with Donald. Of course, she didn't want to seem to be passing judgment on the teacher—she couldn't, naturally. But just to state the facts—it was plain that Mr. Gavin required, and Donald gave, an unflagging and unquestioning allegiance. In regard to what? In regard to everything. Or rather, in regard to his spiritual life. Donald was required apparently to place his spiritual life absolutely under Mr. Gavin's direction. But since Mr. Gavin was at pains to make it clear to Donald how every element in his experience played its own unique and important role in his spiritual development—since that was so, Mr. Gavin had taken it upon himself to direct Donald's activity in almost every sphere. Donald was frighteningly dependent on him, both intellectually and emotionally. But where did she come into the picture? Well, she had a certain interest in Donald, a certain desire for his welfare, a certain wish to play a certain part in his life. But that was out of the question—it was absolutely impossible, so long as Mr. Gavin retained his hold over Donald. Mr. Gavin would tolerate no rivals for the boy's allegiance, and he had made it clear that she was regarded as a rival. She had no desire to take part in some sort of unnatural contest over Donald. That was simply not to her taste—and besides, it promised no good results for any of them. So her problem was, then—simply, what should she do? Just let things take their normal course, break off entirely her relationship with Donald—or insist that he make some sort of choice, between herself and Mr. Gavin, and then act accordingly?

The priest passed his fingers lightly over his temples and rubbed the corners of his eyes. "Anyway, the first solution is out of the question," he said. "You can't let things take their 'normal' course—because in the 'normal' course of things, the whole situation will only become more abnormal."

She nodded. "I know."

He stubbed out his cigarette in the ash tray on his desk and lit another with his little silver lighter. "This will sound a little beside the point, Eileen—still, it would help me to know. Why do you come to me with this problem? Don't misunderstand me—I'm glad that you have come. But I'm not so sure I know why."

Eileen looked rather surprised. "I hadn't thought, Father. It seemed the natural thing. Because, I suppose, because of Donald—I mean, because he's thinking of becoming a Catholic and Mr. Gavin is trying to bring him into the Church. And I can't help but think that what I do will have some effect on that. There's more at stake that just my personal wishes."

The priest could not help but smile a little. "But you do have personal wishes, don't you?"

Eileen smiled too, a little uncertainly. "Yes, I suppose I do."

"Perhaps I could be of more help if I knew what they were."

"I'm not certain——"

"Do you love the boy, Eileen?"

She hesitated. "I don't know. I think I do."

"What about Chris Gavin? What do you think is his interest in the matter?" The priest felt faintly guilty at having asked. He knew he was hoping that Eileen would confirm his preconceived suspicions.

Eileen again hesitated, weighing her words carefully. "I don't really understand Mr. Gavin, Father. He speaks of loving Donald too. But when he uses the word, it means something different from what you and I would mean. I honestly think he isn't interested in Donald as a person, but as a symbol of—well, of conquest."

She had put her finger on it, the priest thought. Conquest. That summed up Christopher's program in a nutshell. Life for him was a battlefield, and personal relationships a series of skirmishes to be won or lost. Even religion fitted itself ultimately into this pattern. God became a sort of commander-in-chief. The spiritual life was a form of precision drill. And private victories in one's relationships with others underwent a sublimation by being directed, nominally at least, to the glory of God. From this point of view hatred could be called love and love a form of weakness. It was frightening, Father Kirsch thought. The sort of mind that embraced this position could tolerate no doubt or hesitation. Truth was not only one; it was at all times obvious. Neither the end of one's activity, nor the form that activity should take, need ever be in doubt. It was an attitude wholly alien to the priest's way of thinking, an abomination, an evil to be stamped out. And in Christopher's case he felt a special urgency. The priest hated to acknowledge the fact, but he knew beyond any doubt or evasion that he thoroughly disliked Gavin. Even apart from their grave differences of theory and method, there was between them a personal antipathy that had grown each time they had met. The priest found Gavin aggravating and thoroughly repellent. He hoped that he still had at least the minimal degree of Christian love for the teacher, but he could no longer pretend to himself that he liked him.

He hesitated, while Eileen eyed him curiously, waiting for him to speak. What was he to tell the girl? It was a terrible burden she was volunteering to assume, and yet she gave the impression of being quite aware of what she was about. Certainly, then, there could be no injustice to her in granting her wish. As for the boy— it was vitally important that he be removed from Gavin's influence before it was too late. Nothing but disaster could result from this "conversion" which would be a mockery of the real thing. Because Christopher was incapable of bringing the boy to healthy religious belief, it was essential that he be stopped in whatever it was he was trying to do before he had accomplished some irremediable harm. And as for Gavin himself—— No, the priest thought deliberately, he deserves no consideration. Christopher Gavin was simply the enemy, and the first essential was that he be defeated, not sympathized with. He had for so long hesitated and even failed entirely to act, because action seemed a contradiction of charity. But that attitude merely sentimentalized charity, he saw now. There were times when action was necessary, and to fail to act was to fail in charity. Eileen's single-minded determination shamed him. It all was so clear—what was he waiting for? Gavin was to be stopped, and it was he who had to do it. He felt a thin quiver of satisfaction somewhere deep inside him as he said:

"Eileen, tell the boy that he has to choose between you and Gavin." Her look of approval reassured him and encouraged him to go on. "Tell him—warn him that he will lose his soul, not save it, by handing himself over to Gavin. And tell him that if he wants to become a Catholic, he can come to me for help."

The girl's eyes shone. "Yes, Father." It was what she had hoped to hear.

The priest leaned back in his chair. He had acted now, acted rightly, and he should have been at peace. But something disturbed him. That pleasure he had felt in striking out at the enemy—at Gavin—seemed somehow out of place; satisfaction in these circumstances was inappropriate. That strange joy had unsettled him by revealing to him something within him (he did not know its name) of whose presence he had been unaware, as one is sometimes made uneasy when at night a flash of lightning reveals, or seems to reveal, a strange and ominous object in a familiar landscape. God grant that I'm right, he thought involuntarily.

It *was* what she had hoped to hear, Eileen reflected as she walked in the direction of the library, where she had still to put in several hours' work that afternoon. Her instructions from the priest had been clear and to the point, and she had no longer to be in doubt as to what it was she must do. And yet some small shred of indecision remained to nag at the back of her mind—a doubt whose essence, she could now no longer conceal from herself, lay not in what she should do, but in why she wanted to do it. And bound up in this question, she had begun to realize, was the larger question of what direction her relationship with Donald was taking. The wind, cold and piercing, blew suddenly and shook the bare branches of the trees overhead.

Her relationship with Donald. It had begun, she knew, in curiosity and—yes—even in a certain amusement on her part at the gangling, awkward, inarticulate boy who seemed so earnest and yet so unable to express himself. But that stage had passed quickly and given way to—what should she call it?—sympathy at least. She had wanted, genuinely and sincerely, to help him. She had begun to draw him out, had accepted his first shy invitations to join him at movies and concerts and on long walks which rambled almost as much as his conversation. She made no pretense of understanding what it was—in so many words—that Donald wanted. Not even he could explain that, and the effort to understand, or to pretend that one understood, seemed to her merely fatuous. And more than fatuous, pointless, for she knew surely and instinctively that what Donald wanted and needed was at bottom an emotional thing, a feeling that when the sense of his own inadequacy became too oppressive he could turn and find something—someone—on whom he could depend. And with this realization, it had all become very simple for her: she would be that one.

But only briefly had her decision been satisfactory. She had hardly made it before a new name began to be introduced into Donald's conversations—Christopher Gavin. Her first reaction had been gladness that she was to have an ally in giving aid to Donald. But then had come their first meeting, at the Newman Club dance, and her illusions on that score had vanished. An alliance with Christopher Gavin, she had discovered, was out of the question, for the teacher did not think in terms of allies, but only of rivals.

Eileen had accepted this new turn of affairs with equanimity. If it was rivalry Christopher Gavin desired, it was rivalry he would get, and the more she had learned of the teacher's dealings with Donald, the more convinced she had become that it was imperative for the boy's well-being that Christopher's influence over him be challenged and broken. This, then, had been her intention for almost three months now. She had not, of course, gone about the operation crudely. Instead of arguing Donald out of his attachment to the teacher, she had hoped to lead him gently away from it, through the force of her own personality. The plan, if so her vaguely formed intentions could be called, had seemed simple enough and likely of success. And yet, for reasons she could hardly understand, success had been denied. For Donald, so malleable, so easily persuaded in other things, had here unaccountably balked. His dependence on Mr. Gavin had not weakened in intensity with the passing of time; on the contrary, it had grown steadily and inexorably stronger. This was a development she had not foreseen and was hard put to understand. She knew the boy did not like the teacher; from his point of view to have liked Mr. Gavin would have been comparable to liking a thunderbolt or some other elemental force of nature. Rather—and here too, she felt, the analogy held good—Donald stood in awe of the teacher. To him, she knew, Christopher Gavin represented something—he could hardly have said what—that compelled and coerced him with an iron grip on his spirit. Donald was afraid of him, and the thing he feared most was to be rejected and cast aside by the teacher. Whatever Christopher Gavin represented to the boy, it was something he had absolutely to have; his very survival depended on it.

So her own simple and common-sense plan for winning Donald away from Gavin had foundered and sunk out of sight. It had disappeared once and for all somewhere in the midst of Donald's frenzied words to her in the library after his meeting with Mark Brodie. And with it had gone—what, precisely? There, she knew, was where she had begun. With that question she was brought full circle to her first query: where was her relationship with Donald taking her? Where had it taken her so far?

During the months when she had told herself confidently that it was only a question of time before her influence won out finally over Mr. Gavin's, it had been easy to believe that she was in love with Donald. Why else, after all, would she have gone to so much trouble to coax and soothe the boy? Why else, indeed—unless, of course, it was simply that the spirit of competition had been aroused in her and that she had enjoyed her struggle with Gavin? No; she shook her head to put the thought out of her mind. She *did* love Donald. And yet, what had she said when Father Kirsch had asked her that question? "I'm not sure." And had she not been grateful that the priest had not pressed her on the point into some absolute commitment which for unknown reasons she felt reluctant to make?

But that scene in the library had not changed everything, she reminded herself almost desperately. Had it not, in fact, prompted her to her boldest action of all—her meeting with Christopher Gavin and their strange walk in the snow? Surely if she needed proof that she loved Donald, that must be it. Only, what did it prove? If she chose that scene as the ultimate gauge of her feelings, then she had to be honest in acknowledging all of its implications. She had left the teacher, she remembered, shaken and frightened by what she had seen in him—something perverted and unhealthy to which even now she could not give a name. And paramount among her thoughts had been the reflection that if *this* was what Donald wanted, that very fact spoke volumes about the boy himself. The aura of spiritual depravity was new and unfamiliar to her; she had scarcely recognized it for what it was in Christopher. But if it was this that held such sway over Donald, that so attracted and appealed to him, then that could mean only there was something sick and rotting in his heart as well, something from which instinctively she shrank.

Where then had all her plans of helping Donald gone? The question had to be faced. The answer came easily—perhaps too much so. Her plan, now ratified by the priest (for she had had, she knew, quite clearly in mind what it was she wanted him to tell her)—her plan to force the boy into choosing once and for all between herself and Gavin, was the culmination of all she had hoped to do for Donald. It was the dose that would either cure or—or kill. It was the sensible thing for her to do. It would be best for them both to have it out once and for all, now before things had gone too far.

But was not that simply too pat? If she could face the desperate alternatives—cure or kill—without a qualm, what did that indicate of her true feelings for Donald? She frowned unconsciously, walking down the block to the library entrance. Might it not be—just possibly—that she was acting to save herself, instead of Donald?

She stopped at the steps leading up to the library. No, she told herself; no that was *not* it at all. She *did* love him, she wanted to help him. And this plan of hers was the best way—the genuinely sensible way—of doing so. Hadn't the priest told her, hadn't she his assurance that what she was doing was right? What more did she need? Nothing, Eileen thought determinedly. I know what I have to do, and I'll do it. But as she started up the steps, a new doubt nagged relentlessly at her mind: she was going to make Donald choose between Gavin and herself; but which one of them—really —did she want him to choose?

MARK TROTTED UP THE STAIRS TO ROBBIE'S SECOND-FLOOR FLAT whistling a little to himself. He was rather looking forward to what was coming. The opportunity to cross swords in earnest with Christopher was one he had long hoped for. He would have preferred, of course, to have it out with him somewhere else. The office would have given it the proper touch of formality. But it had been Robbie's idea to have the meeting on a Saturday afternoon in his apartment —"Make it a little more relaxed all around," he had explained—and Mark was inclined to give him his way in small things. He would soon enough be called on to assert himself—never an easy task for Dr. Bond—and it was, Mark realized, better not to scare him off at the very beginning by insisting on incidentals.

Mark rang at the door. Robbie let him in, took his coat, then ushered him into the living room.

"Hello, Mark."

Brodie gaped just slightly. They were not alone. He recovered himself quickly. "Hello, Harry," he said. "Hello, Paul."

Harrison Tyler and Paul Hughes sat together on Robbie's sofa. Both of them were from the department, Mark's seniors and, he knew, Robbie's most trusted advisors and mentors. Together, the three of them pretty well ran the department—if their activity could be called "running" anything. They were, Mark knew, three of a kind—indecisive, strongly convinced only that it was somehow improper to have strong convictions about anything, virtually incapable of taking action without being prodded. Mark knew without being told why Tyler and Harrison were there. He sought Dr. Bond's eyes, but in vain. Robbie kept his glance lowered in embarrassment.

"I asked Harry and Paul up here to sit in on our talk with Chris," he said needlessly. "Didn't think you'd mind, Mark."

"Mind? Of course not."

It was a typical maneuver on Robbie's part. He was determined to be fair to Gavin at all costs. And he had grown to doubt that Mark shared this intention. Moreover, he dreaded being made the fulcrum in a test of strength between the two younger men. Harry Tyler and Paul Hughes, then, were his equalizers. They contributed impartiality to the coming interview, and they served also to insulate him against any rude shocks. Mark was disgusted. Robbie would turn it into a tea party yet if he had his way.

"Drink, Mark?" Harrison Tyler rose and walked over to a table in the corner on which glasses, bottles, and ice were set out. Tyler was an introverted man who attempted to make up for his lack of assurance by a display of efficiency and businesslike snap. But he was uncertain of himself and shy. He blushed easily.

"Thanks, Harry. Just a little one."

He sat down opposite Paul Hughes who, in contrast with the meticulous Tyler, was a large uncombed man with careless manners and a booming voice. But like his companion he was unsure of himself and easily disconcerted. He smiled now—too largely, Mark observed—and said, "Robbie tells me we're going to have to set young Gavin straight on a few things."

"I'm afraid so," Mark said. He did not wish to commit himself until he was sure whether or not the other two knew that his interest in the case differed from theirs.

"Pretty funny business if you ask me," Hughes said. "The boy needs a good talking to."

"Deplorable business," Harry Tyler added, handing him his drink now. "I suppose you've heard about it all from Robbie, Mark?"

Then they did not know. But that too was like Robbie. Dr. Bond probably was afraid they would have been prejudiced against *him* if he had said anything. "Robbie and I found out at the same time—didn't we, Robbie?"

Dr. Bond had walked nervously over to the window and stood there watching his three guests apprehensively. "Yes, that's right," he agreed.

Mark sipped his drink. Tyler made them too weak. "By the way, have Harry and Paul seen that reading list?"

Robbie took a folded paper out of his coat pocket, then thrust it back in.

"We saw it," Hughes said. "I don't know what he could have been thinking of."

"It's such a blatant, simple-minded thing to do. Deplorable," Tyler said again, smacking his lips primly over the word.

It might be better than he had expected, Mark thought. They seemed already to see things his way. "It's the fanatic mind at work," he said. "I'm pretty well acquainted with Catholics, you know. I'm familiar with their habit of one-track thinking. This is just a typical manifestation."

"Perhaps we should hear what he has to say," Robbie remarked weakly. Clearly he did not like the drift of the conversation.

"That's very true," Hughes said. "Precisely because it is such a simple-minded thing on the face of it, there must be some more complex explanation for it than we've suggested so far."

Mark was about to reply, but Tyler beat him to it. "An excellent point, Paul," he said. "Mark's explanation is plausible, but hardly the only one possible."

"Here he comes." Robbie had glanced out the window. He turned back to them with a look almost of fear.

For some reason, they found nothing to say. They listened in silence to the downstairs door of the converted brownstone open and slam shut and then the sound of Christopher's quick firm steps climbing the stairs. Mark lit a cigarette and deliberately slouched a little. He did not wish to admit either to himself or Gavin the tension he was feeling.

The bell rang. Robbie let the young teacher in.

Christopher strode into the room and hesitated only briefly at the sight of the three men waiting there for him before he stepped forward to shake their hands. He must certainly, Mark reflected, have been expecting trouble ever since he received Robbie's summons, and the only question in his mind would have been concerning the form it would take, not its eventual appearance. Still, Mark had to admire the composure with which he greeted Tyler and Hughes and now himself, smiling a slight and enigmatic smile that might very well have passed for one of friendship.

"Good to see you, Mark," Chris said. "We don't get together often enough."

Mark could only smile foolishly and mumble a fatuous "Yes." He was nonplussed at the quality of the performance.

Christopher sat down in a wing chair across from the sofa. Tyler busied himself fixing a drink. Robbie came in from hanging up the young man's coat and looked around uncertainly.

"It was good of you to ask me over, Doctor," Chris said to him, taking his glass from Tyler. "I see my colleagues in the department much too seldom. But really, you know, it's simply for lack of opportunity."

A pattern began to emerge, Mark thought. It was Gavin's design to make the whole scene as painful as possible. Not a bad idea, either. If he could make Robbie and the other two feel guilty, it would be just like them to apologize themselves and forget why they had met in the first place. Well, that was why he was there—to see that didn't happen.

"One has to *make* one's opportunities, Chris," Mark said. And before Gavin could reply he added: "Particularly when it's a matter of business—as it is now."

"Business?" Christopher asked.

"I thought I made it clear——" Robbie fumbled.

"I'm sorry. I must have misunderstood."

Mark caught Tyler and Hughes looking at each other—already—in embarrassment. "Business and pleasure both, Chris," he said. "But business first—right, Robbie?"

Dr. Bond had retrieved his own drink from the coffee table. He stood in the center of the room nervously clicking the ice in the glass. Christopher looked at him. "Before you begin, Doctor," he said, "I'd like to be set straight on something. I admit it's awfully foolish and you'll have to excuse me. Still, I'd like to have quite clear the nature of this session. Because you know, I can't get it out of my head that—" with a gesture he indicated Tyler, Hughes and Mark, "—that somehow or other I'm to be judged for something. I have the feeling—as silly as it may seem—that I'm almost in a court of law here."

"Now, my boy," Tyler interrupted, blushing profusely. "Put your mind at ease. We just want to talk over a few things, that's all."

"No need for alarm," Hughes added with a loud and inappropriate laugh.

"One would almost think you were suffering from guilt feelings," Mark said with a smile.

Christopher smiled back. "And if I were in a court here, you know," he said, "I'd have the distinct feeling that you were the prosecuting attorney, Mark."

"Oh, for heaven's sake, that's enough talk about courts and guilt and all that nonsense," Robbie exclaimed. "Harry's right. We just want to have a friendly talk with you, Chris. I asked the other fellows to sit in because I value their opinions—and I hope you will too."

"What are we to discuss?" Chris said. He crossed his legs and sipped his drink.

"It's been brought to my attention——" Robbie began. "Well—I mean to say. Well, the long and short of it is, Chris, that we've all seen a copy of this." He pulled the reading list from his pocket and held it out to him.

He took the paper negligently and glanced over it. For a moment his eyes widened, as if something had surprised him. But then he handed it back and looked slowly from Robbie to Tyler to Hughes—and at last at Mark, where his eyes came to rest. "I know what it is," he said. "What about it?"

There was a general sharp intake of breath and then a general babble of voices as Robbie, Tyler, and Hughes all sought at the same time to express their surprise and disapproval. The other two gradually giving way, Robbie at length made himself heard. "Chris, really! I find it hard to believe that you don't realize—that you don't appreciate—— Well, there are some things that are done, you know, and some things that just aren't."

"Oh, crap!" Christopher said. The expletive brought the others up short and gained him a measure of their attention. "What sort of sense does that make? None. If I'm going to be brought to trial for heresy, it seems to me I at least have the right to demand that you use a little common sense in your arguments."

"How about this one then, Chris?" Mark said. "'Corrupting the young.'"

"That has a familiar ring," Gavin chuckled. "I think Socrates would have recognized it."

"Don't flatter yourself," Mark said. "You're no martyr."

"What about you gentlemen?" Christopher turned to Tyler and Hughes. "I haven't heard from you yet."

"This is a serious business, my boy," Tyler said. "I think you're taking it a little too lightly."

Christopher bowed just slightly. "Excuse me," he said. It was impossible to tell if he were mocking the other man or not.

Tyler, thrown slightly off his stride, continued, his face growing redder and redder as he spoke, till at the end he fairly shone. "It seems to me, my boy, that Mark is right. You have been guilty of 'corrupting the young'—though not in any morally evil sense, of course. But by circulating this reading list, so heavily weighted as it is on the side of your own sectarian religious commitments, and by requiring that the books it contains be read, you exert an improper influence over the minds of your students. Students who, as we all know, are at a most delicately impressionable stage. I would suggest to you, my boy, that you have gone far beyond your rights as a teacher. In fact——"

"How did I exert an 'improper influence'?" Christopher asked suddenly. "I only said they had to read the books, not that they had to believe them."

"At their age, how are they to discriminate, evaluate——?" Tyler replied.

"When else will they be given the chance, if not now?" Christopher said. "When else will they be brought into contact with the truth? Certainly it's been carefully screened out of the rest of the courses in this department."

Mark watched with satisfaction as Robbie, Tyler, and Hughes stiffened at his words. Foolish of him to worry, he thought; one had only to let Chris talk—he would damn himself. But now Hughes was speaking, his big voice booming as he hunched forward earnestly, rumpling his hair with one hand and sloshing the drink he held absent-mindedly in the other.

"Hell, Chris," he said, "that's pretty strong talk. Anyway, who are you to decide what is and what isn't the truth? I think there are a few older fellows here who wouldn't be quite as presumptuous as you and say they knew what is and what isn't true—about much of anything."

"And what relevance does that have to what we're talking about?" Gavin asked. He shrugged disgustedly. "All right. Tell me, Paul—do you think it's even possible for an individual to arrive at the truth?"

"I don't like to hear about *the* truth," Hughes replied. "Truths aren't constant things. They're always changing—just like the world which produces them and which they reflect. There's no such thing as *the* truth. There may be individual limited truths—but we have to re-evaluate them constantly so that we'll know when and how they've changed."

"Oh my God!" Chris exclaimed, slamming down his drink and bouncing out of his chair.

"Gentlemen, please——" Robbie interjected.

But Gavin, striding back from the window to which his first impetus had carried him, waved him aside and confronted the irritated Hughes. "Paul, how am I supposed to talk with you?" he demanded. "Your mind is closed to anything I can say before I even open my mouth. If you don't even admit the possibility——"

"You asked me what I thought and I told you," Hughes interrupted. "I haven't heard you say anything yet to refute it."

"Here?" Christopher yelped. "Now? Did Dreyfus manage to circumcise his court?"

"If no one minds, I think I might shed a little light on this confusion," Mark said. He had watched the scene in quiet amusement and spoke now almost with reluctance, but yet with the feeling that matters had to move on.

"Please, Mark!" Robbie threw up his hands and retired to the window himself. "If you can do anything——"

"Oh, I'm sure he can, Doctor," Chris said. "I'm sure the prosecutor can do a great deal. After all, I dare say he's masterminded this whole operation."

"That's unfair, my boy," Tyler said.

"Never mind, Harry," Mark said. "Chris is a little upset now—we needn't take everything he says quite seriously."

"Thank you!" Gavin snapped out, dropping angrily back into his chair.

Mark smiled and lit a cigarette. Christopher had let his temper run away with him a little too far this time, he reflected. All the better—he no longer stood a chance with Tyler and Hughes. Still, the discussion had not been quite relevant up to now. "I think we're getting rather off the subject," he said. "I don't believe we need to go back to fundamental philosophies to settle the matter at issue here. After all, it seems to me the question is one of simple everyday practical prudence—which Christopher has violated."

"Exactly," Tyler approved.

"And not for the first time either," Mark continued. He saw Tyler and Hughes look up in surprise. Glancing quickly at Robbie, he knew from his apprehensive expression that the matter of Donald Reinhart had not been broached to them. "As it happens," he said, "Christopher's activities have had the effect of bringing at least one of his students almost to the point of conversion to Catholicism."

"And other people too," Christopher said. The full significance of his quietly, almost satisfiedly, venomous tone escaped Mark.

"I had no idea," Hughes exclaimed. "This is really serious." He turned abruptly to Christopher, demanding, "Well, what have you got to say?"

Gavin, once more in control of himself, only sipped his drink. "I doubt that you'd understand," he replied.

"The question is, where do we go from here, Robbie?" Mark's voice carried a hint of command.

Dr. Bond stirred irresolutely. He had been mopping his damp face with a handkerchief and gestured vaguely with it now. "I think," he said, "I think the thing to do—that is, if you and Paul agree, Harry—the thing to do is to ask Christopher for a guarantee that all of this sort of thing will stop."

"At once and once and for all," Hughes amended, and Christopher murmured, "Amen."

"I certainly agree with that," Tyler said. "And you, Mark?"

Brodie looked evenly at Christopher. "Of course," he said.

The eyes of the other three men turned to Gavin. He finished his drink calmly and set it down beside him. "May I?" he asked, looking around at them with an air of elaborate politeness.

"Go on," Tyler said.

"Then you'll excuse me if I say that I think this whole scene has been a farce." Christopher's voice was quiet, his tone urbane. Mark was impressed once more by his resources and self-command. "No one here has shown the least interest in hearing any explanation I might have to offer. Your minds were made up before I walked in that door. Nothing I could have said would have made the least difference. You decided to issue an ultimatum and you did it—'Shut up and conform.' The rights and wrongs in the matter never interested you at all."

"I think you're being a little presumptuous, Chris," Mark said quietly. "You seem to think we owe you the right to debate your position with us. But we'd only be betraying our own principles if we did so. As far as we're concerned—and I think I speak for all of us—an ultimatum is the only response we can make to what you've done. And in making it we feel we're amply justified."

"The thing that bothers me—" Chris said without looking at Mark, "—the thing that really rankles is that you should all follow *his* lead." And he nodded now at Brodie. "If he could show any reasonable pretense of disinterestedness——"

"The *argumentum ad hominem* now?" Mark said.

"Tell me, Mark, what is it with you?" Christopher said, staring with sudden intentness at him. "What are you so afraid of?"

Brodie laughed. "Oh, really!" he exclaimed.

"I don't expect an answer of course," Christopher said, leaning back. "Still, it would be interesting to know. After all—" he added, turning to the other three men, "—when one is as frightened of something whose truth one denies as Brodie is of the Catholic Church, it would at least be interesting to know why."

"If you think you're going to irritate me by harping on that word *frightened*——"

"If I had to guess—and I don't suppose anyone is asking me— I'd say it was a fear of admitting failure. After all, none of us likes to admit a mistake—that we've done something absolutely and earth-shakingly stupid. And when one has devoted so much of one's energy to the most absolutely stupid mistake of all—well, I can see how it might be a frightening thing to look the fact in the face."

Robbie, Tyler, and Hughes squirmed in embarrassment and dismay. The exchange between Gavin and Brodie, both verbal and on some more subtle level of communication, confused and worried them, like a vague pain whose point of origin could not be determinded but which nevertheless unbalanced and frayed the whole delicate physical mechanism. They wished for their own comfort to interrupt and yet felt somehow that it was obscurely better to let the two men say these inexplicable things to each other.

Mark was frowning now, unconsciously. "You think you know so much," he said. "You think you can sit in judgment. Well, I'll tell you something. I don't accept your standards. I set my own standards and I judge myself by them."

"Do you?" Christopher said. "I doubt it. I don't think you'd be so frightened if you did."

"I believe none of what you stand for," Mark replied. "I have consciously and sincerely rejected it. It is no longer part of me. It exercises no influence at all over me."

Christopher smiled. "But negatively——? It makes you hate me, doesn't it?"

"You do that yourself."

"I'm flattered—but I doubt it. You don't see me as an individual. You only see in me—as you yourself just put it—what I 'stand for.'"

"Don't underrate yourself. You have your unique points."

"But what is it I stand for?"

Mark's face was distorted—with anger, with hatred—as he replied. "The whole idea of—of judgment. The idea that you hold the one and only truth by which we—all the rest of us—must be judged. Who are you that you have the right——? Humility—you wouldn't have any idea what the word means."

"Humility. It's amusing to hear you speak of that, Mark. I wouldn't have said it was your great virtue."

"I have the humility at least to admit that I haven't somehow been given a magic key to all truth and all goodness. And I have the humility not to sit in judgment on others."

"Except for me."

"You—you don't deserve any consideration. If we pass judgment on you, it's only what you'd like to do to the rest of us."

"And so you wage a preventive war. Convenient. Only, what are you trying to prevent?"

"Any more of this." Robbie Bond unexpectedly broke in, shaking the reading list at Christopher. He, Tyler, and Hughes had followed the conversation with mounting indignation as the insolence in

Gavin's tone grew more pronounced, till even the mild Dr. Bond had found it necessary to express himself.

"That—what does that mean?" Christopher said, glancing contemptuously at the paper in Robbie's hand. "I'll tell you—the only reason you're upset about that is because it's a symbol and it's frightened you."

"You flatter yourself, Gavin," Hughes said, lurching up angrily and striding to the window.

"I don't really think so. After all, this is just the occasion, the particular weapon with which you've decided to bring me down. If it hadn't been this, it would have been something else."

"Then you admit—you knew exactly what you were doing!" Tyler exclaimed, blushing with outrage.

"Don't be naïve. Of course I knew what I was doing—just as you did. I've been challenging you—all of you. I've been deliberately ignoring the rules of the game (and I know how much they mean to you) precisely for this purpose—to make myself a living contrast between you—you especially, Mark—and—" he smiled, "—what I 'stand for.' I'm sure you'll take it as only another instance of my insufferable attitude if I say I've succeeded."

"Nobody's denying you that, you poor simpleton," Hughes exploded. "You're a contrast all right."

"But why?" Dr. Bond asked helplessly. "What is the point——?"

"Ask Mark."

"He's a missionary, Robbie," Brodie said with a scowl. "A modern apostle, dropped right in our laps to show up our materialism and secularism and pragmatism and agnosticism and atheism and general what-the-hellism in the pure clear light of eternal unchanging verity." He spat out a shred of tobacco.

"Bravo," Chrispopher said. "So I'm under no illusions when I'm discussing these matters with you, gentlemen. You understand me no better than a stone wall would and you haven't any impartiality toward me or my religion. In that at least we're alike—you start from the premise that I couldn't possibly be right, just as I start from the proven evidence that you are not."

"You actually think of us as your enemies," Tyler said in surprise.

"How else? After all, you are." Christopher rose suddenly. "But we're just wasting time this way," he said. "We haven't anything to say to each other. I might at least talk to Mark—he understands the vocabulary—but he's closed his ears, so that it's useless. Therefore, I'll just ask you for my coat, Doctor——"

Robbie hesitated. When he spoke his tone was plaintive. "But, Christopher—you haven't yet heard what we want to say to you."

"I haven't?"

"You see, it's either stop this sort of thing—" and once more he gestured faintly with the piece of paper, "—or I'll have to go to the dean and ask him—ask him to ask for your resignation."

"I think that was generally understood, Doctor," Christopher replied, nodding his head in a faintly patronizing manner. "And I thought I had made my answer clear. However, in case you're in any doubt, I repeat that I don't intend to stop anything I've been doing and that you can take any action you like about it. Now may I have my coat?"

Robbie's face had gone as red as Tyler's as Christopher spoke and now without a word he walked out of the room. Christopher nodded gravely at Tyler and Hughes. Turning at last to Mark he paused, winked broadly and then followed Robbie out. A moment later they heard the door slam and the sound of his footsteps going quickly down the stairs. Robbie came back into the room.

"Incredible," he murmured. He sat down in the chair Gavin had vacated and then suddenly got up again as if he had been stung.

"It isn't catching, Robbie," Mark said.

Dr. Bond reseated himself with a look of embarrassment. "I apologize to you," he said. "I had no idea."

"Hardly your fault, Robbie," Tyler replied in a strained voice. Throughout the scene he had held his ice-filled glass in his hand and it was now reduced to tepid water.

Hughes still glowered from the window. "Sheer impertinence," he said. "What that sort needs best is a good punch. I have to congratulate you, Mark, on your patience. I'm afraid if he'd said some of that to me——"

Mark felt himself the master of the situation once more. He blew a smoke ring. "He has a martyr mentality. He'd thrive on anything that smacked of persecution. So why give him the satisfaction? But I don't think there's any point in concerning ourselves with all that. The question is, what now?"

"Robbie made that clear enough," Hughes said. "The dean. That fellow's a lunatic. We have to get rid of him."

"I agree," Tyler said. "It's intolerable he should remain here a day longer than necessary."

Robbie drew himself up and said with as much firmness as he could muster, "I shall see the dean Monday."

Mark smiled slightly. "You'll probably think me a bit of a Machiavelli," he said, "but I've had some dealings with our friend before and I had a suspicion how this might turn out. So—" he reached into his coat pocket and drew out a folded sheet of paper, "—I thought that if Robbie were going to see the dean, it might be more effective if he had something like this." He extended the paper and Robbie took it. "Of course," he added to Tyler and Hughes, "I had no idea you'd be here this afternoon. That simplifies matters a good deal."

"A petition!" Dr. Bond exclaimed. "For Christopher's dismissal. Mark, I hardly know——"

"I'll sign that," Hughes growled, coming away from the window. "And if you want any more signatures, I can get them for you."

"I hope you worded it strongly enough, Mark," Tyler said, reaching for his pen.

Dr. Bond watched them, a bit bewildered. "Well, Robbie?" Mark prompted.

"It seems—everything happens so suddenly," Dr. Bond said. "Perhaps in a sense we have prejudged——"

"In matters of self-defense, Robbie, one has to act first and think later."

Dr. Bond sighed just slightly. "I suppose so," he said as he took out his pen.

EILEEN POKED LISTLESSLY AT HER GLASS OF BEER. SHE HAD NEVER liked liquor, and beer was particularly distasteful to her. Tonight of all nights it tasted especially sour on her tongue. For tonight she had to tell Donald. . . . The raucous sound of the piano and violin and boys' hoarse voices singing college songs rose to drown out her thoughts. Across the table on the other side of the booth Donald craned his neck to see the musicians and smiled slightly. The music was awful, but he liked any music, she knew. She wished in a way that she did not know—that she knew nothing about him. For after all, when one knew what another person liked and disliked, one became inevitably involved in making choices to please or displease him, and thus an emotional relationship was established. And tonight, for some reason, she, who had never feared involvement or been nagged by scruples—she might have wished herself free of all emotional relationships. For not only did she have to hurt Donald, but she was uncertain whether the thought of doing so caused her any real pain—and it was this fact, the discovery of a previously unknown capacity for callousness, that worried and fretted at her.

Donald drummed his fingers on the table in time to the music and hummed along with the singers. He took a mouthful of his beer and smiled at Eileen. He was at home here, she thought, and that would have been impossible only a short while before. The fact that he could now feel himself one with these other young people around them in booths like their own—that was something she had done for him, she knew. And as yet, she realized instinctively, it was something fragile, something requiring protection, an assurance and a happiness in him that had come lately and might leave without warning. And she was going to put all that in jeopardy—almost without feeling any remorse.

That was the worst part of it, she thought again. Without feeling sorry about it, perhaps. If only she knew what she really felt. Was uncertainty the price one paid for becoming involved with a person like Donald? Had his recovery been somehow achieved at the expense of her well-being? In some ways, the evidence seemed to her irrefutable. So now perhaps she had simply grown tired of him, had found that his novelty had worn off, and all the things she had said to Father Kirsch had been no more than rationalization and justification. After all, she thought a trifle petulantly, he had no *right* to make demands—there was no obligation on her part. Except that which she had assumed herself, and a self-assumed obligation, she saw now, was the hardest of all to slough off.

And did she, after all, want to? She did not know. In a way it still seemed she loved him. But he was so horribly exasperating. He was so dependent—on herself, on Christopher Gavin, on anyone who would consent to lift the burden of responsibility and decision-making from his shoulders. How could she love a person like that? And yet, how could she not, if love were in any way related to the need for it? And where did that leave her? Where she had already been. The only solution was not to consult her feelings, to act before she had given a name to her motive and to do that for which she felt herself to have extorted permission from Father Kirsch—force Donald to make the one decision that would be the hardest of all for him. Of course, there was nothing else *to* do. It would have to be done eventually—it was better for them both that it be done now. But still, the very eagerness with which she had contemplated doing it seemed to her in this brief moment of retrospect virtually blood-thirsty. What had happened to her? she asked as the music and the singing roared to an end. It must be some sort of infection that he had conveyed to her—the curse of introspection. She shuddered. The experience was a novel one for her and a little frightening. It came as a far from pleasant shock to meet oneself and find a stranger.

Clapping and whistling filled the big dimly lit cellar room as the musicians bowed, grinning and hamming it up. The place catered to the college crowd and on a weekend night like this there was almost no one else there but students. The waitresses, sour-faced with aching feet, moved rapidly in the narrow space between tables and booths, bringing bottles of beer and carrying away empties. There was a constant hum of conversation, frequent loud laughter, and a heavy pall of cigarette and pipe smoke. New people—mostly couples, but occasionally groups of either sex—were arriving constantly and yet no one seemed to leave. Ordinarily it was the sort of environment in which Eileen thrived. But this evening she found it both stifling and depressing. She would have liked to have been somewhere—anywhere—else. The music began again. Vienna waltzes. No singing this time at least. It was a little more quiet.

"It's great, isn't it?"

She looked up in surprise. Donald was smiling in his gentle way at her. "What is?" she asked, hiding her confusion.

"This," he said, indicating the room with a gesture.

"Really?" Then, in a spirit which she felt immediately to be one almost of maliciousness, she added, "I didn't know you were so social-minded, Don."

He only laughed. "Neither did I," he said. "I guess I'm not really —or I wasn't until——" He reached over and to her surprise took her hand. It was unlike him to make such a gesture of affection in public. "So much has changed since I met you, Eileen."

So much indeed, she thought, for both of us. Was it possible they had somehow exchanged personalities? she wondered. Surely it was Donald's febrile, spinsterish conscience that had descended unannounced upon her.

"Has it, Don?" she asked. The words sounded wrong to her. So awfully coy, as if she were trying to lead him on, draw him out, get him to commit himself. What did she want from him, an engagement ring? That was a good question, she reflected a shade bitterly. When you came right down to it, it was *the* question. She wished she knew.

"Things have changed more than you can imagine, Eileen. At least, they've changed—*inside* me, you might say. It's as if I'm beginning to—to see things differently, to feel everything differently. I know, I don't make much sense. But, well—you know how I used to be. Don't you see a difference?"

"Yes," she said, "I see a difference."

He grinned jubilantly. "It's what you've done for me, Eileen. You and Mr. Gavin."

He was not unaware, she knew, of the possible ill effect that particular juxtaposition might have on her. But it was as if the new carefree Donald were a bit of a gambler, and willing to take the risk—or perhaps this was even a fledgling gesture toward dominance, an attempt to wring from her tacitly or otherwise the concession that Mr. Gavin might come and go in his life unchallenged by her. If so, the effort had disappointing but not altogether disheartening results. She simply failed to react in a way perceptible to him.

Inwardly, however, his words had stirred a turmoil, which her outward stoicism was the deliberate product of an effort to conceal. So that was really how matters stood. She and Mr. Gavin were co-redeemers to Donald Reinhart. The fact dismayed her, both because of the relationship established between herself and Christopher and—more unsettling to her—between herself and Donald. Was not that ultimately what frightened her—the realization that she and Donald had gone so far together and stood now on the brink of some ultimate emotional involvement? It wasn't, she thought with a perhaps incongruous sense that injustice was being done her, it wasn't the way she had planned it. But she had not really planned it at all—that was what had gotten her into this mess. She had let herself drift, carried along by her sympathy for Donald and her curiosity about him, and perhaps, to a degree she was only dimly beginning to imagine, by her dislike of Mr. Gavin and her desire to thwart him. Poor reasons, she saw now with sickening clarity, for going so far.

But were there other reasons? Was there, most important of all, the possibility that love was among them? If only she knew. She could not think clearly—or rather, she could not feel clearly. Her mind functioned well enough, but her emotions were a confused welter of unnamed and unexplained motives. Her mind tried to sort them out, but it was like reaching down into a dark writhing mass and trying to pick up things which only slipped away between one's fingers. At least she had her plan. And it remained valid—and in a sense sanctioned by Father Kirsch's consent. She might apply it without fear, for it was designed for a good end, quite apart from her intentions in putting it into action. To have known her motives would have been a dividend, desirable to be sure, but nonetheless essentially irrelevant to the purposes of the plan. The ends at which it aimed were purely good, and she might therefore act without troubling herself further. Beyond this point she refused to think. That even the good ends of her good plan might somehow be tainted was a suspicion she would not admit.

But to act. She must act. "Mr. Gavin and I?" she repeated.

"That's right," Donald said, a little less certainly. "Without the two of you—I don't know what I'd do."

"Suppose you had to choose between us?" she said without preamble.

Donald blinked. He tried to smile but did not quite succeed. "I know you and he don't get along, Eileen," he said. "But I'm sure—at least, I hope—it won't ever come to that."

She felt a surge almost of fright. "It has," she said.

There was a loud applause as the musicians finished once more. Donald did not join in this time. His face looked suddenly pale and drawn. With both hands he gripped his glass. "Are you joking?"

"Don't you think it's a serious matter, Don?" She felt slightly disgusted with herself that only now, almost for the first time in the evening, did she use his name, after she had regained a position from which she could safely patronize.

"Very serious. That's why I don't understand——"

"It's for your own good——" The words were dry like dust on her tongue. "Don, I can't stand things the way they are now. I don't want to have Mr. Gavin for a rival. It's not healthy—it's not normal."

"Eileen, I've never been happier than——"

"Then there's something wrong with your happiness. It's sick somehow, Don. Don't you see that?"

"I'm not strong. I never claimed I was."

"And so you carry weakness to an extreme by depending for everything on *two* people. Don, it can't go on. I want you to be a happy normal person. That's all. But if I can't have you that way, then—then——"

"You don't understand what Mr. Gavin has done for me, Eileen," Donald broke in as if to forestall her going further. "He's given me something to believe in. It's through him that I'm beginning for the first time in my life to know God just a little. The first time, Eileen—you don't know what that is. The first time I've ever known that there was any real meaning in life—"

"I'm a Catholic like he is. I know the things he's teaching you. And I know that anyone else could teach them to you. You don't need him."

"I *do*. Who else would give me the confidence, who else could I depend on?"

"What sort of religion is that, Don? You depend on one man, one single man, to bring you to God—as if he were the only one who could."

"But who else has ever bothered to try?"

"I don't pretend to understand everything about Mr. Gavin, but I do understand this—there's something wrong with him. It isn't just because he loves God or he loves you that he's doing this. It's because somehow he has to. You're important to him, Don, only not for yourself—but as a conquest. Really. That's how he looks on you. It's an awful thing to say, but I think he wants you to serve him and not God."

"Eileen, you don't understand. You've never had to stand alone—"

"When have you? Your whole life is just spent trying to avoid standing alone. Only that's got to stop. It's got to stop now. And it's got to stop by your breaking off from Mr. Gavin."

"Please—I can't."

"I told you once, Don, that I wasn't going to make you choose between us—*then*. But now I am. So choose—you have to choose."

She waited. The laughter and talk and clink of glasses bubbled up around them. Donald lowered his eyes to the table top. He did not speak. "All right," she said. She got up suddenly.

"Eileen!—I don't know."

"Tell me when you do," she said. "But don't wait too long." She pulled on her coat and walked away. Out in the street the cold night air seemed to revive her. The scene just over seemed almost dream-like. She shuddered a little as she thought of it. Had she been hoping he would choose Gavin?

Donald pushed through the swinging glass doors on his floor and walked down the hall, his head hung low in dejection. It was still early on Saturday night. Most of the occupants of the dormitory rooms were out. The few who had stayed in were playing radios or phonographs. Through the open door of one room he caught a glimpse of a bridge game in progress among four boys in shirt sleeves. The hall smelled of soap and dirty laundry, human bodies and books. In the distance someone was crooning a popular song.

"Reinhart." Donald started. It was the voice of the corridor prefect. A graduate student, he leaned in the doorway, looking a little curiously at Donald.

"Yes, what is it?" Donald tried to pull himself together. He was aware now that his appearance must betray his feelings.

"Call for you," the prefect said, fishing a slip of paper out of the pocket of his khakis. "That's the number."

Donald took the paper. He recognized the number as Mr. Gavin's. The teacher had given it to him some time ago and he had devoutly memorized it, though he had never yet used it.

"Anything the matter?" The prefect had a drawling, sympathetic voice. He scratched his close-cropped head and looked closely at Donald.

"Nothing," he said. He moved away. "Thanks for giving me the message. Thanks."

The phone booth was on the landing of the stairs at the other end of the hall. When he got there, he found another boy already occupying the booth, slouched contentedly down in it, the door open and his legs stretched out, as he talked animatedly to a girl. When Donald came up the boy straightened and shut the door.

The delay gave him time to think. He wondered what Mr. Gavin wanted. He would almost—though he hardly dared admit it to himself—have wished that the teacher had not called. He was too shaken, too confused, by what Eileen had said—he did not know what to say to Mr. Gavin. He would have liked to have been left alone. Should he tell the teacher what she had said? But what would be the use? He could already imagine the reaction that would bring. And above all he needed to think uninterruptedly, to see the thing in all its dimensions, without external influence being applied. He had to decide what was right—how to act, what to say in reply, what she had really meant, what he could do to change her mind, whether it were even allowed for him to make the choice she had demanded of him.

The boy hung up and left the booth. Donald entered it, closing the door tightly, though there was no one there to hear him. It was only as he was actually dialing the number that he thought to wonder at Mr. Gavin's having called him. It had never happened before. He felt some apprehension as the phone at the other end of the line rang once, twice. . . .

"Hello." It was Mr. Gavin's voice, businesslike, a little abrupt.

"This is Donald, Mr. Gavin. I got your message."

"Oh yes, Donald. Good to hear from you." There was no warmth in the voice. "There are a few things I wanted to tell you."

"About what, Mr. Gavin?"

"They're out to get me again."

"Please——?"

"Brodie and Bond. They want my head. Brodie especially. They're going to get me fired."

"Mr. Gavin!"

The teacher's laughter was strained and unexplained in Donald's ear. "It's not the end of the world, Donald. There are other jobs."

"But what about——?" He stopped.

"You?"

"Yes."

"We'll have to talk about that. I imagine something can be worked out. After all, there's no reason why I have to leave the city. But I didn't call to discuss that."

"Yes?"

"Do you know what the gimmick is, Donald—what it is they're going to use to get rid of me?"

"What, Mr. Gavin?"

"The reading list."

Reading list? Donald's head was swimming. It meant nothing to him. He knew of no reading list. "Yes?"

"And do you know where they got a copy, who it was that called their attention to the list and put them onto the scent?"

"Who?"

"Eileen." There was a pause. The teacher had aroused himself with a cumulative wrath. His breath came in quick pants over the phone. "Did you hear me, Donald? I said Eileen is the one who betrayed me. She called the list to their attention. There's no mistake—I saw her name on it. She and Brodie worked hand in glove and they're going to get me fired. She and Brodie."

The intricacies of it escaped Donald. He did not understand exactly what the teacher was telling him. Something about a list—it made no sense to him. It was only clear that he was accusing Eileen of betraying him to Mr. Brodie. So Mr. Brodie had had his revenge. And Eileen was his instrument. Eileen.

"It was her copy," Mr. Gavin's voice quivered with anger. "She had signed it herself. I saw it with my own eyes."

"You saw it——"

"And do you know why I'm telling you this, Donald? Do you know why?"

The boy did not answer. He had put his head back against the metal wall of the booth and taken the receiver a few inches away from his ear. The voice came through thin and disembodied, like crackling paper.

"Donald, we've reached a turning point. You're going to give her up—you hear me?—you're going to give her up, or else I'm through with you. You understand me? Give her up or I'm through with you."

Donald nodded. He understood. "Yes, I see," he said. The voice crackled thinly again, but he did not make out the words. He hung the phone up.

He walked back up the hall to his room and opened the door with his key. It was dark. Harvey was spending the weekend out of the city with friends. He closed the door and turned on the lamp on his desk. It cast only a dim light over the room, hardly penetrating to the corners. He hung his coat over the back of his chair, but it slid off onto the floor. Still with his jacket and tie on and without removing his shoes he tossed himself onto his bed and lay on his back staring at the ceiling. The white paint there was cracked and flaking in one patch. The cracks looked like the lines on the palm of a man's hand. He closed his eyes, but the lids were dry and burning and irritated his eyeballs. He stared once more at the ceiling. If only he could think. But the channels of thought seemed somehow broken, the automatic processes somehow would not occur. He could not think, for there was only one thought in his mind and it crowded out all other thoughts. It had to end. Somehow. He could not stand it.

MARK FELT A FAINT TWINGE OF CONSCIENCE AS HE POURED THE bourbon over the ice. He had already had two at Robbie's, and now another one at home—still, he told himself, he had earned it. The ice chinked merrily in the glass and he splashed in a few drops of water from the tap, quickly but ceremoniously, like a priest adding water to the wine. He took a rather large mouthful. The liquor was suave and soothing. He added a little more bourbon, splashed in some more water. He turned to leave the kitchen, then snapped his fingers at his forgetfulness. Julie's ginger ale. He scooped up ice cubes from the sink, where he had emptied a tray, tossed them in a glass. From the cupboard he took a ginger-ale bottle of thick green glass, unscrewed the metal screw-on top. He poured too generously, and a little of the frothy golden liquid sloshed onto the sink top. He picked up both glasses and carried them gingerly into the living room. Perhaps he shouldn't have had this one, deserve it or no. Well, what the hell. A hard afternoon. Anyway, it was by way of being a celebration. And you needed liquor for a proper celebration. Even the Catholics would tell you that. No Mass without the wine—

no Communion banquet without the wine-blood. Damn nonsense he was thinking.

"Here you are, honey," he said. "Whoop!" A little of the ginger ale spilled onto the rug. Julie took the glass and looked at him with a slight smile.

He sat down in his easy chair across from where she sat on the sofa. Funny, he always felt embarrassed when he got tight in front of her. But at the same time, he always felt irresistibly silly. Unexplained desires to giggle swept over him. She never said anything either. A swell girl about that—about that, like everything else. He smiled back at her.

"Cheers," he said, raising his glass and drinking.

"Cheers," she repeated, sipping her ginger ale. "You must have had quite a party over at Robbie's."

"No party," he said. He was anxious to tell her about it—yet apprehensive too. She was funny when it came to Gavin. Yet he was eager, for he wanted desperately to tell her of his triumph.

"I thought it was going to be strictly business," she said. "A meeting of the department."

"Not the whole department." He put the drink down on the table beside him and leaned back, relaxing at last. He took out a cigarette and lit it. "Just Robbie and myself. And Harry Tyler and Paul Hughes."

"Just the four of you?"

"And Chris Gavin."

She started, but only slightly, almost imperceptibly, so that if Mark had not been looking for a reaction, he would not have seen it. As it was, he noticed and wondered what it meant. "I didn't know that Chris was being let in on the inner councils these days," she said.

He smiled, but his heart shrank within him as he paused before committing himself. But he could not delay forever, and he said: "He's not." It was that simple, he knew. The inevitable chain of question-and-answer had been set in motion, ending—where he did not know, and for some reason he was afraid to know. But soon he would see.

"Then why were Robbie and you and the others consulting him?"

"I wouldn't exactly call it that."

"Mark, I know you're getting at something. Can't you just tell me what it is?"

"Well——" He puffed out a big cloud of smoke. "You might say we had it out today with Mr. Gavin."

"Had it out——?"

"I think we've just about seen the last of him."

"Mark——!"

Her tone brought him forward to the edge of his chair. "What is it, Julie?"

"Mark, just tell me what happened. From the beginning. Please. Tell me exactly what you're talking about."

He looked curiously at her, trying to guess what she was thinking. She had always been sympathetic to Gavin, he knew, but this seemed like something more. If only he could know what was going through her mind. They said you did when you had been married as long as the two of them, but somehow Julie's mind had always remained a mystery to him, a concealed world whose secrets he could divine only darkly and incompletely. "I don't understand," he began.

"Please, Mark!"

He shrugged. Her tone left no room for refusal. "To make it short —we found conclusive evidence that Gavin has been using his classes to spread Catholic propaganda—almost to force it down the students' throats as part of the curriculum. We asked him to stop. He refused. So tomorrow Robbie goes to the dean. And that will be curtains for Mr. Gavin."

She got up abruptly and walked into the kitchen. Dumbfounded, he sat looking after her. In a moment the clatter of dishes and pots and pans began, the sounds of dinner being got ready.

"What the hell——" he exclaimed. He rose and strode into the kitchen. He had heard correctly. She was busy at her usual routine, dragging out dishes and pots, opening and slamming the refrigerator door. "Julie." She did not look at him. "*Julie!*"

"What is it? What do you want?" She turned on him with a sudden—fierceness was the only word that occurred to him. It was as if she were accusing him, challenging him.

"What do *I* want?" he repeated. "I want to know what the devil you think you're doing."

"Getting dinner." She turned away from him.

"Julie, stop it!"

"What do you want me to do?" Now it was less accusation than appeal in her voice and in her face as she turned again to look at him. "What else can I do? Do you want me to talk to you, to tell you what I think?"

"Why shouldn't you?"

"All right," she said. "But first—" stooping to one of the cupboards below the sink where he never went, "—to understand how I feel there are some things you should know." She pulled out the small book bound in stiff gray cardboard and handed it to him.

He took it slowly from her. It carried him back so many, many years to when he, a schoolboy in knickers, had stuffed books like this one into his satchel as he hurried to be on time for hated class in the drab arid parochial school, or when at night—night after night—he had pored relentlessly and desperately over the pages in their alternating dark and light type, driving his memory to master the sterile formulas. "Why did God make you?" "God made me to know Him, love Him and serve Him in this world and be happy with Him forever in the next." He took the catechism from her and turned it over wonderingly in his hand. It was as if a phantom of his memory had somehow been excised from his mind and given substance and were being now inexplicably handed back to him.

"Where did you get this?" he asked. His voice was quiet. He wanted simply to know.

"Christopher gave it to me."

The dizziness and tipsiness had left him. His head ached from the alcohol now, his tongue felt swollen and fuzzy and his eyeballs ached as if something were pushing on them from behind.

"Christopher gave it to you?"

"Yes."

He hesitated, then suddenly shrugged and tossed the book with assumed casualness onto the kitchen table. "Well, what about it?" he said, forcing a smile. "It's just a book." He waited breathlessly for her to reply. When her words came they chilled as if a sword of ice had been thrust into his stomach.

"Mark, I think I want to become a Catholic."

"Julie——" He did not know what to say. He was aware suddenly that the smile was still on his face and it required conscious effort to relax the muscles that held it there, fixed and foolish.

"I suppose we'd better sit down and talk about it," she said simply. She walked past him toward the door.

Then suddenly the anger struck him and he was shaken for a moment by blind rage at whoever had worked this bad joke on him. He stepped after her, fumbled savagely at her arm, gripping it at last above the elbow, and swung her around violently so that she almost lost her balance.

"Mark!" She was frightened now and the sight of her fear encouraged him with a feeling of power.

"Sit and talk!" he growled between his teeth, squeezing with his fist until the thumb and middle finger almost met on the other side of her arm. "What the hell do you think we have to talk about?"

"Mark, please——" With her free hand she tried to pry his fingers loose. Her face was contorted with pain.

"Who do you think you are? What right have you got to do this to me—what right?"

With a violent twist she pulled her arm loose and retreated back against the doorway. "Stop it, Mark."

Something in her eyes, an expression of fright as if she were looking at some dangerous animal, made him pause. The look warned him that he had come perilously close to losing control of himself. He turned away abruptly and leaned on the sink, gripping its edge in his hands. "I'm not sorry," he said. "I'm not sorry. You may think you have an advantage, but you don't because I'm not sorry."

"Mark, don't talk about 'having an advantage.' Please. Can't we just discuss this?"

"Discuss—you keep talking about discuss. You know what I have to say, and I'm not interested in what you have to say. So what do we discuss?"

"You asked before what right I have. I ask you the same thing. What right do you have to act like this?"

"My right as your husband. My right to expect that you love me, that you do as I say—that you love me."

"You have a strange idea of love, Mark."

"Perhaps I do. But at least I have an idea of it."

"And I don't, is that it? Because I'm not ready to sacrifice myself for you—body and *soul*—I don't love you?"

"Julie——" He turned to her now. "Julie, it was always just the two of us—that was the way it was supposed to be. Just the two of us—you depending on me and I on you. And now——"

"And now I find that isn't enough, that—" she hesitated only a moment before pronouncing the word, "—God has to enter the picture. Are you jealous of God, Mark?"

"I've never asked for anything more than you. You've always been enough for me, Julie."

"I don't believe that. You may want to tell yourself it's so—but I doubt that it is."

"Julie, I don't believe in God, I don't believe in eternal life, I don't believe God died for me because He loves me. And God knows if He did, I don't give a damn. You understand me? I don't care about Him. He's nothing to me. If He died for me, I didn't ask Him to. I ask nothing of Him, and He should ask nothing of me. Above all, I don't love Him, and I don't want Him to love me. The only person I love is you, Julie, and the only person I want to love me is you."

"I can't love you like that," she said. "I don't. If you think I ever have, then you've deceived yourself. You're asking too much of me. To try to find the whole meaning for my life in another human being—I wouldn't begin to try. What would be the point? How could you satisfy me completely? How could I satisfy you?"

"You have."

She gestured impatiently. "You say that. But if you're sincere, then you're terribly deceived. How much happiness do you find in loving me?"

"As much as I ask or expect."

"But as much as you want? That's what counts, Mark—don't you realize that? You must see it—you must know that neither of us could ever come close—not in a million years—to satisfying the immense capacity we have for loving and being loved. And yet we love each other, Mark—as much as two people can, we love each other. So if loving you as much as I do, I still feel that I won't be happy unless I can love someone else more—and being loved by you, I still feel a need to be loved more by someone else—then how can we really say that we satisfy each other? And how can we say that we don't need God, either to love Him or to be loved by Him?"

"'To know Him, love Him and serve Him in this world, and be happy with Him forever in the next,'" Mark recited bitterly. He picked up the catechism once more. "It's all here, isn't it? All the answers. That's what they tell you. Well, I know it all by heart, and somehow I don't think they're such good answers—and perhaps they aren't even such good questions, because they don't bother to ask the embarrassing ones."

"Perhaps," she said. "But if these aren't the right questions and the right answers, I don't know what are. The Church at least says it knows the answers. I'm willing to give it the benefit of the doubt."

"You don't say things like that to your great and good spiritual advisor Gavin, do you? I hardly think he'd care much for 'the benefit of the doubt.'"

"It's as far as I've gone so far, Mark. If I'm lucky, I may find a way out of the doubt eventually."

"Oh, you can if you want to. Just keep telling yourself 'believe, believe' and one morning you'll wake up and you will believe. You can believe in anything if only you want to badly enough."

"Why do you have to say that, Mark? What makes you hate the Church so much?"

"I'm a teacher. It's part of my job to hate everything that's false and dishonest."

"Forgive me—I don't believe you're that altruistic."

"Well, what is there so lovable about the Church? Tell me that. A lot of superstition and mumbo jumbo, all mixed up with stained-glass windows and incense. Oh, it suits your potato-eating Irish and your Spiks and your Polacks just off the boat. A little bit of the old country and all that. I admit, for them it serves a need—a social prop to fall back on amid the terrors of the New World. But for the next generation—what's the point? Let the priests get fat on somebody else for a change, that's the way I feel about it."

"That doesn't explain *why* you feel the way you do."

"To be specific then, what do I owe to the Church? What has it done for me? Given me a few useless educational references and a whole flock of superstitious prejudices to overcome. My parents were typical examples. For people like them—fresh out of the old country—the parish church was just a way of defending themselves against a lot of pressures they didn't understand and were afraid of. And believe me, the priests were happy to keep them under their wing too—keep them ignorant, keep them from thinking for themselves. God, those Sunday sermons! You would have thought our little parish was the last bastion of virtue in the country, standing off the forces of hell itself. Well, the priests knew what they were doing all right. I have to admit that. My parents swallowed it all and begged for more. My poor mother—even on her deathbed she was in a sweat for fear the priest wouldn't come in time—she, who never did a mean bad thing in all her life. Well, they raise you in fear, make you live in fear, and even have you die in fear—it's a terrific system. So in due time my father sent me to the parish school and then the Jesuit high school and then—after I finally managed to convince Pop I didn't want to be a priest—off to the nearest Jesuit college. Now there was an education for you. Narrow-minded, bigoted—do you know, they had names for a lot of different courses—English, history, biology, Latin—but they were all the same thing, every damn one of them was a religion course. They never turned off the propaganda for a minute. And when you've heard the same drivel over and over all your life, you reach a point where you don't even recognize it for what it is, you don't even know they're feeding you full of the party line. That is, most people don't. But they do run a risk, you know, even if it's only a slight one. They aren't very subtle and if someone once wakes up to what they're doing—why then that's it. The balloon is popped. You can't be deceived any more."

"And how did you happen to wake up, Mark?"

He smiled. "I just looked around me. I read a little and I talked a little. I found out how these infallible teachers of mine were valued outside the charmed circle—outside the Church—and that was all I needed. It was a little painful at first. But it would have been more painful if it hadn't happened when it did. It was when I was in graduate school—around the time I met you. People would ask me where I'd been to college, and I'd tell them, and——" He laughed, but rather weakly. He could not put his heart in it, for he remembered now too clearly, felt the sting of contempt, disdain. "Well, there were three general reactions—a sort of courteous distaste, an immediate desire to start a debate, and just sheer outright scorn—laughter. You can't imagine how effective a dose of laughter can be in making you see things clearly."

"Do you really believe it does? I think it might have the opposite effect."

"Don't misunderstand me," he said quickly. "If the cause had been worth it, I wouldn't have let a little laughter bother me."

"I wonder," she said. "You're a proud man, Mark. Were you any different then?"

He saw angrily that it would do no good to talk to her now. And his anger was increased by his own sense of being here on weak ground. He could not escape the sharp remembrance of his feelings then—the shame and anxiety, the embarrassment at the gibes of fellow students or professors, the wish, sometimes suppressed as shameful, at other times flaunted despairingly, that he could be like them, share their ideas, their intellectuality. And as a background to all this there was the constant conflict with his father. The old man had given only grudging consent to the idea of his leaving home to attend the graduate school of a famous non-Catholic university, and Mark was barely gone before he began to nag him about the practice of his religion. And not without reason. Even at home Mark had been at pains to annoy his father by demonstrating his laxity in conspicuous ways—missing Sunday Mass frequently, going to confession only at widely spaced intervals, taking a patronizing and slightly contemptuous attitude whenever the subject of religion came up. This behavior had infuriated the old man, and when Mark's letters home as a graduate student made it plain that he was becoming even more irregular in the practice of his faith, the elder Brodie's replies grew truculently bitter. And then Julie had entered the picture. Mark knew very soon that he was in love with her, and he knew too that this would be the occasion of his formal break with the Church—and very possibly with his father as well. It was not that Julie insisted on his taking either of these steps; far from it, she was too gentle to relish such hostility as existed between Mark and his father. As for his Catholicism, though she had no belief of her own, she seemed somehow saddened at the thought that he was losing his. No, Julie had never forced him into anything. What he had done had been his own idea entirely. He remembered the occasion on which he formally sealed his loss of faith. He had planned it thoroughly. It was a Sunday morning and he went to Mass (for the first time in two months) and at Communion time he walked to the railing and knelt and took the Host, keeping his eyes open and watching the little wafer approach his mouth between the priest's fingers until he was almost cross-eyed. And then he walked back to his pew and knelt there, thinking as deliberately as he could, concentrating as hard as possible: "It's only a piece of bread." When the Mass was over he walked out of the church. He had not returned since. He telephoned his father that same afternoon to tell him he was going to marry Julie outside the Church. The old man's rage was titanic, but Mark's own cold anger matched it in malice and intensity. Separated by six hundred miles and by an intellectual and spiritual infinity, father and son spoke words of hatred to each other. When Mark hung up the receiver he was drenched with sweat. It was the last time they communicated. The old man died four years later, and at his specific and tyrannical insistence Mark was told nothing of his last illness until it was over.

He shook his head angrily, trying to clear it of these thoughts that were so clearly extraneous. "Unfortunately you began this conversation with the assumption that I can't possibly be right—or even sincere. I wish I'd known as much at the start. I would have saved myself some time."

"No—I'm glad you said what you did. It helps me to understand you a little more."

"I'm surprised you're interested."

"Mark, don't be childish. If you're going to feel sorry for yourself——"

"Don't start passing judgment on me!" he shouted suddenly. "You're in no position. After what you've done——"

"And what have I done that is so awful, Mark? So far I haven't done anything."

"'So far.' Is that meant to be a threat?"

She gestured helplessly. "You don't want to understand."

"I understand well enough."

"All I want to do, Mark, is to save my soul. You have no right to refuse me that."

"So good of you to keep reminding me where my rights begin and end. But perhaps I know of a right or two you've forgotten."

He paused, but she did not prompt him, so that he had to go on unasked, his temper rising. "I have a right to ask you not to insult me and flout my wishes—my most serious wishes. And if you do so, I have a right—to take certain steps."

"I don't know any steps you can take, Mark. But if you were to want me to leave——" Her chin trembled a little and for the first time it struck him that she was deeply hurt. But he had no time to think of that now, for her words had suddenly brought him out of the realm of rhetoric into that of desperate cold fact. That she might leave—it was odd, but somehow that idea, perhaps most obvious of all under the circumstances, had never yet occurred to him. He shuddered at the thought. And yet he did not want to show too much of what he felt.

"I suppose you'd like the opportunity," he said.

"No, but if you forced me——"

"And you wouldn't *like* to be forced?"

"Mark—I can't talk to you!" she cried. Bursting into tears, she turned away and left the room. A moment later he heard the door of the bedroom slam shut.

So she wanted only an excuse to leave him. It had gone that far. Remarkable, he thought, without emotion for the moment. Remarkable that so much had happened to which he had been quite absolutely blind. One had to hand it to Christopher Gavin. Whatever it was ultimately that he was trying to do, he seemed to have a knack for getting it done.

CHRISTOPHER CLIMBED WITHOUT HASTE THE STEPS TO THE THIRD floor of the men's dormitory. He was rather tired. It had been a busy, demanding day. But the climax was still to come, and he had to be sparing now of his strength so that in the scene with Donald he would be fully alert and would make no false steps. For he felt that the coming interview was important—that, in fact, it might be crucial as far as winning or losing the boy was concerned. He might almost have wished, so important it seemed, that he had not made that phone call earlier. That had been done in a burst of anger and had been less thought out than he would have wished. Still, it appeared to him now that it had in all likelihood been the right thing to do and that he could have hit on no better stratagem no matter how many pains he might have taken to plan his actions. If he knew Donald, the boy would by this time be positively frantic. Left alone for an interval to brood over what he had been told, Christopher reflected, he would have worked himself into a state of mental and emotional collapse—at which point one would be able to do as one pleased with him. So at least the teacher imagined, and he looked forward anxiously to the coming scene to prove him right.

He did not wish to admit that this trip to Donald's dormitory, unannounced at ten o'clock at night, had been tinged at all with anxiety. But still it was difficult to deny that it was so. Of course the explanation was that much of the success or failure of his efforts depended on what happened this evening with Donald. The boy (the *foolish* boy, he could not help thinking) represented half of an ambition of which Julie Brodie was the other half. And it was Donald who appeared the more attainable of the two. If he were lost, then—— But he would not even consider the possibility. Donald would surrender to him. God would see to that. After all, did He not have to? The injustice otherwise would be monstrous, inconceivable. This was his first effort, his first experiment in putting into practice the plans he had perfected over such a long time and for whose fulfillment he had prepared himself so carefully, so meticulously. When the conspiracy had become evident to him, the unspoken agreement among the priests that he was not to be allowed to become one of them, he had for a time not known where to turn, what to do, how to find a meaning in his life when the meaning he had assigned it was suddenly, flatly denied. He had no vocation, they told him. As if they knew. They, with their petty, jealous little souls, they had determined to thwart and frustrate him, to deny him the priesthood, because—as he and they knew—his living of it would have been always a constant reproach to their own cowardice, their eagerness to compromise, their failure to sacrifice comfort and convenience and good name in the service of God. But one advantage they did have—the power to block his way, and this they had determined to exercise coldly and calculatedly. What was his response to be? For a time, he had thought that there could be no response and that because the fight was unequal he would at length have to succumb. But slowly, he had begun to see things in a new light. He had realized that God had reserved him for a special task. Perhaps, had he become one of *them*, it would have been the start of his subtle corruption. Instead, he was set aside for a unique role, called to a unique ministry, a double function of both drawing others to God and at the same time standing forth a living rebuke to the hypocrites who pretended to serve Him.

This insight into God's plan had given him new vigor and enthusiasm. Now he knew what God wanted of him and he was ready to do it. His preparations for a teaching career, begun after he had been refused entrance to the seminary, fitted in providentially. The intervention of a Higher Power was too obvious to be denied. As a teacher he could do so much to combat error, and his position would gain him the respect and confidence and obedience of those whom it was in God's plan to bring into the Church.

And Donald had been the first. The boy had fallen aptly into his hands without its even being necessary to shake the tree. In the months since, he had wished sometimes that he might have begun with someone else—someone nobler, more intelligent, whose conversion would have been more satisfying. Julie, say. But still, he reminded himself, the choice did rest with God, Who had His own reasons for deciding as He did.

So it had been Donald whom he would win for God, because it was Donald whom God wanted.

Only, the boy had hesitated so! He had hung poised, longing but not consenting, like an animal sniffing the ground in interminable caution before moving forward a pace. But the teacher had borne it all, and had controlled his impatience as best he could, had coaxed and humored the boy, until—until now, this evening, this moment, when at last the time of decision had come beyond which Donald could delay no longer. Donald was to be tested tonight—but, he realized dimly, so too in a sense was he himself.

Christopher reached the third-floor landing and paused for a moment. Now, he thought, now is the time for You to help me. I'm doing this for You. At least do something in return.

He pushed through the swinging doors. The hall was empty for the moment. It was too early for those who had gone out for the evening to be coming back. He walked down the corridor. There were lights on behind the transoms of a few rooms, but the doors were shut and the sound of radio or phonograph music came through faintly. The door of the prefect's room was open, but the young man was sitting at his desk, his back to the hallway, and did not turn around as he passed by.

He reached the door to Donald's room. The light was on but there was no sound inside. He knocked. No one answered. He knocked again. No sound. He tried the door. It was unlocked and he went in.

He halted suddenly, his hand still on the doorknob. Donald lay on his back in the middle of the floor. The straight chair from his desk was overturned beside him. He was fully dressed, but his necktie, instead of being at his collar, was knotted around his throat. Christopher glanced at the thick exposed water pipe which ran just below the ceiling. One end of a second necktie was still tied about it. The other end dangled down loosely, having come undone from the tie around Donald's throat.

Christopher came alive suddenly. He rushed to the inert form on the floor and knelt down beside it. Donald's usually pale face was comically crimson and distorted. His mouth was open and a gasping sound came out as he struggled for air.

The fool. Christopher got up and went quickly to the door. He shut it noiselessly and walked back to where the boy lay. Suddenly, as he stood there, he caught sight of something on the floor, half-hidden under Donald's body. He stooped down and picked up two sheets of paper, torn from a desk calendar. They were covered on one side with Donald's scrawl. He read the first:

I'm sorry to cause trouble by doing this, but I don't know what else to do. If anyone wants to know why I had to do this, ask Eileen or Mr. Brodie. They gave me no alternative.

Then the second:

Or you could ask Mr. Gavin. He knows as much as anyone. I suppose they all meant well toward me—at least, I want to think so—but just meaning well isn't enough.

Christopher hesitated. Then he put the second sheet of paper into his pocket and dropped the first. It fluttered down beside Donald. The boy's breathing had begun to come more evenly. Christopher bent over and loosened the knot at his throat slightly, but not enough so that it would be conspicuous. He wasn't even clever enough to kill himself properly, he reflected contemptuously. He went to the door and opened it. There was still no one in the hall. He slipped out, shut the door softly behind him and hurried to the exit close by. Once through the swinging doors he raced down the steps three at a time until he was out of the building.

Christopher leaned back in the phone booth and listened to the telephone ring at the other end of the line. He opened the door slightly to admit the noises of the drugstore, thinking they might help mask his voice.

"Hello," the corridor prefect answered a bit peevishly. He probably did not like to be interrupted while he was studying.

Christopher pitched his voice an octave lower. "Donald Reinhart, please," he said.

"Just a minute."

He could see in his mind's eye the young man setting the receiver down and rising, walking to the doorway, into the corridor, down the hall to Donald's room, knocking, opening the door. He hung up. There was no likelihood they would have time for an unidentified caller just now.

He left the drugstore and walked in the direction of his apartment building. He felt glad at having made the call. It gave him an excellent conscience.

THE DOOR SLAMMED SHUT BEHIND HIM AND HE FELT A POSitive relief to be inside the building, away from the cold late-winter wind outside which blew a sleety rain down out of the low clouds. Christopher paused a moment at the foot of the steps to turn down his collar and take off his shabby old hat, which he shook vigorously before starting upstairs to the English department office. He felt a slight thrill of excitement as he climbed the steps, with just enough fear in it to make it piquant and particularly pleasurable. He was eager to hear what had happened—for they had kept it out of the newspapers—to find out whether his plans had all gone smoothly. Certainly they should have. His ingenuity, he thought, had been remarkable. But there was always the possibility that something might somewhere have gone wrong. At any rate, he wanted and needed to know.

He wanted to know so badly that he was coming this morning to the English department, before the start of class. He seldom went there these days—he had no desire to see anyone there, and it was evident that none of his fellow faculty members wanted to see him. But this morning was different. Whatever had happened to Donald

Reinhart would, he knew, almost certainly be in circulation in the room at the head of the stairs he was climbing, and so it was there that he went.

He walked in briskly and went over to his desk, which he had not visited in more than a week. On the way he caught Harry Tyler looking at him. He smiled and nodded. Tyler blushed and grinned weakly back, then looked away.

He knew. That was clear enough from the look of him, Christopher reflected. He knew what had happened to Donald—but what else did he know? What exactly had happened? It was maddening to be there, with Tyler not ten yards away from him, and yet to be unable to walk over to him and question him directly. But above all, of course, he had to maintain the pretense that he himself knew nothing, suspected nothing. As far as everyone else was aware there was no way in which he could have known what had taken place. Whatever happened, he could not afford to let anyone even imagine differently.

So now he had to wait. He hoisted his brief case onto the desk and began taking the books out, as if with a purpose, so that he would not give the impression of simply standing there expecting to be told something he had come to hear. He had suddenly the awful fear that perhaps they would not tell him, that they would think he of all people should not be told. But of course that was nonsense, he reflected almost at once. Donald was one of his students. Surely he would be told something, sooner or later, by someone. Still, it began to look as if this were not the place after all. Besides Tyler there were three or four other teachers in the room, but they were ignoring him almost ostentatiously, correcting papers, studying notes, browsing through books, studiously keeping their eyes turned aside from his. He had suddenly the temptation to slam his fist down on the desk top and demand of them that they stop their pretending and tell him what they knew. But of course he could not, it would be suicidal, he had simply to wait—to wait.

Then suddenly Robbie Bond came in. He saw Christopher almost at once and, like Tyler, he blushed. Gavin watched him go to his desk, fuss with some papers—clearly, he was no more interested in them than he himself with the books he had taken from his brief case. Christopher sat tensely, watching Bond out of the corner of his eye. He felt that here at last was his source of information. But he was taking so long, so horribly long.

Abruptly Robbie turned away from his desk and went over to Tyler, who had opened a book and begun to read. He bent over the other man and the two of them spoke together in whispers. Once Tyler looked his way, and Christopher knew then that they were talking about him—and Donald Reinhart. Expectancy grew and throbbed in him until it was almost unbearable.

Robbie straightened up and looked at him. Their eyes met for a moment. Then Dr. Bond lowered his and walked toward him.

"Good morning, Chris," he said. He held the bowl of his pipe in his right hand, rather stiffly at the level of his stomach, and played nervously with it.

"Morning," Cristopher said. He had to control himself, to remember that when last he had seen Robbie, it had been in the midst of a bitter quarrel. He could not afford to encourage him—even though he desperately wanted to draw him out. And the situation was doubly difficult, for Robbie would need drawing out, he knew. After all, if as calculated he had actually managed to implicate Mark Brodie while getting himself off unscathed—Dr. Bond would hardly be in a mood to be very talkative about it.

"Nasty morning, isn't it?"

On another occasion he would have been amused at Robbie's embarrassment. Now, however, he was suffering with him. "Yes, it is."

With ill-becoming informality, Robbie sat down on the edge of the desk. "Chris, there's something I wanted to tell you," he said.

He held his breath. "Yes, what is it?"

"It's about one of the students in one of your classes—this boy Donald Reinhart. I think you've been rather close to him?"

"What about him?"

"He tried to kill himself Saturday night—tried to hang himself in his room. Luckily, the hall prefect found him——"

"Donald did what——?" The tone of shock sounded convincing to him, and Robbie seemed to accept it as genuine.

"Now don't be alarmed, Chris. Really, it's just as I told you. He didn't do himself much harm. They found him in there on the floor—— Well, what I mean to say is that they bundled him right off to the hospital and I understand that physically he's none the worse for wear."

Christopher had risen as he spoke. He stood now with his eyes fixed on Dr. Bond's. "But why would he have done such a thing? I just don't understand—— Was there any indication—did he say anything, leave a note?" He paused, watching the other man intently.

Robbie began to say something, then stammered. "I—that is——" His eyes dropped. "I don't know. What I mean is, I don't think so."

Christopher exhaled silently in relief. So, the plan had worked. Watching Robbie Bond, there was not the slightest doubt in his mind about that. "Nothing at all?" he said, enjoying the knowledge that his words must be like the turn of a knife to Robbie. "I just don't understand. I know Donald well—he's a hypersensitive boy certainly—but I can't imagine he would have done a thing like that unless he had really been driven to it by something—or someone. He hasn't said anything—in the hospital, I mean?"

"No. At least, I suppose not. I imagine they think it's better not to press him for explanations just now."

"Of course. He must have been pressured enough before. I haven't seen Donald to speak to in several days. If only I'd known there was something wrong——" He stopped suddenly, as if he had just thought of something. "Has Mark been told?"

Robbie started slightly. "Why do you ask?"

"I know how close he's always been to Donald. Of course, he was friendly with the boy even last year. I'm sure he'd want to know. And perhaps he'd be able to explain——" He gestured.

"I think Mark was notified." Robbie did not elaborate. But his very reticence gave one room to hope for the worst—or best, depending on one's point of view.

Christopher sat for a moment in thought. He had found out what he had come for, and further time spent here seemed to him now only wasted. There were other matters that needed attending to—notably, the matter of Julie Brodie. If Mark were being blamed for Donald's suicide attempt, and if Julie knew—the possibilities were, at the very least, intriguing; at most, there was at least a chance of pulling off what he had before hardly dared to put into words, even with himself. He flicked imaginary dust off the sleeve of his water-soaked overcoat, which he had not bothered to remove, and said:

"I suppose nothing has changed since we talked last, Doctor?"

"Pardon?" The drift of the question at first escaped Robbie. Then he understood, and was suddenly flustered. "Oh, you mean about—that is——"

"You still plan to see the dean about me?"

"I don't think anything has happened to change that." Robbie's voice was a little hoarse. He did not look at Christopher when he spoke.

Gavin shrugged. "Probably not," he said. "At any rate, that's all I wanted to know." He stood up abruptly and buckled shut the worn brief case. "The books belong to the department," he said, indicating the pile on the desk. "I borrowed them. I don't believe I have anything else that doesn't belong to me. If I find that I do, I'll send it along later."

Robbie looked in round-eyed wonderment at him. "I don't understand," he said. "What are you talking about?"

"Really, Doctor, if you take my advice, you'll begin to think through the consequences of your actions before you perform them. If you had in this case, it would be quite clear what I'm talking about."

"You aren't just—just leaving!"

"Well, seriously, what did you expect?" Christopher's smile was not unfriendly. Now, at the very end of it, he felt as much contempt as ever for Dr. Bond, but no very strong dislike. And the good news he had just heard had created in him so tolerant a mood, that even the contempt did not weigh very strongly. "You've wanted to get rid of me from the very beginning, and now the perfect instrument has been put into your hands—I certainly concede you that, I'd be a fool not to. Well, it happens—and you might certainly have expected this, Doctor—that I'd just as soon not sit around and wait to be fired."

"But—your classes——"

"Oh, I'm sure you can arrange something, Doctor. It will be no more difficult than if I'd phoned in sick this morning. And you'd have the same problem in a few days anyway, once I'd been fired. I should think you'd actually prefer it this way. After all, the dean will probably be grateful to you for saving him the trouble of seeing me."

"But I didn't expect——" The maneuver had clearly caught Dr.

Bond quite unprepared. He was a man who liked things to be done with decorum and a proper consideration for appearances. He paused now and, surprisingly, shrugged his shoulders. "But then, I've seldom expected the things you've done. I suppose it's only appropriate we continue the tradition."

Christopher laughed. "Exactly!" The other men in the room looked up curiously. He glanced around at them. "Gentlemen, it's been my pleasure," he said with a grin, and bowed. Then he walked out of the room, a slightly derisive smile still twisting the corners of his mouth.

Robbie Bond watched him go, shaking his head slightly. His glance met that of Harry Tyler, who raised his eyebrows and pursed his lips sympathetically. "Well," Robbie said to no one in particular, "it *was* an experience."

Christopher hurried down the steps. He had no very clear plan, but it was evident that he had first to get in touch with Julie. A phone call, perhaps. Or even a trip to her apartment. But that might be too dangerous. Mark might be there. He swung around to the last landing, hardly looking where he was going, and almost collided with a slight figure in a white raincoat.

"Julie!"

"Chris—oh, I'm so glad to see you."

Without thinking he took her hand in his and she made no protest. "This is an unexpected pleasure," he said.

"I was looking for you, Chris. You have no idea how much I've wanted to talk with you—to see you." There was something almost desperate in the way she spoke and in the look in her eyes. She stood so close that he could smell the damp odor from her raincoat and the faintly sweet scent of her hair. "Mark knows about what I've been studying. He knows—I want to become a Catholic."

"Mark knows——"

"I told him."

His heart leaped with joy. "That's wonderful," he exclaimed squeezing her hand.

"Is it? I don't know." She passed her free hand over her eyes, as if with confusion and fatigue. "Chris, it's been just sheer hell since I told him. And then, this other thing——"

"Donald Reinhart?"

"Yes." She shuddered slightly. "Do you know the police have been to our apartment to see Mark? And the dean? And Robbie, and I don't know who else. Chris, how did Mark get involved?"

He looked closely at her, then said evenly: "Mark has got me fired from my job here. The boy must have found out about it, and along with some other things, it was enough to drive him to—what he did."

"I thought so."

"One shouldn't blame Mark too much. There was no way for him to know——"

"He wouldn't have cared," she said with sudden bitterness. "All he wanted was to hurt you. He would have done anything—no matter what effect it had."

It required a conscious effort for him to suppress his elation so that she would not see it. Her words had an incalculable sweetness for his ears. It was as if she had surrendered herself to him. "We can't stay here," he said, taking her arm and guiding her gently down the steps. "Let's go some place where we can talk."

"But your classes, Chris——"

"Oh." He laughed, and it was a relief to give vent to his feelings. "I no longer have any classes. They were going to get rid of me as fast as they could, so I thought I'd save them the trouble and quit. That's what I've just been doing." He gestured in the direction of the English department.

"Chris, I want you to know—I think what Mark and the others have done to you is the most despicable thing I've ever heard of."

He only smiled. "God sees to it that everything is really in our best interests—even if we don't understand how. So—" he slipped his hand a little farther under her arm, "—they've probably only done me a favor."

For as long as Christopher could remember he had felt an unusual lightheartedness on those rare occasions when by some quirk of fate he found himself with nothing pressing to occupy his time or attention at the very moment when all the rest of the world was beginning its day-long drudgery. It probably dated back to his days as a schoolboy, when because of ill health or a school holiday he had had the day off—and yet had only to look out his window to see the rest of humanity settling down to its workaday existence.

The experience had always had for him a pleasurable and exhilarating effect. And this was as true now as ever as he and Julie sat over cups of coffee in a booth in a hamburger stand a few blocks from the university.

He watched her curiously, wondering what was going on now in her mind. She had hardly spoken all the way here, and her silence still continued. Under other circumstances, it might have worried him. But his holiday mood would not admit any note of real seriousness. In fact, interested as he might have been in her thoughts, he was even more taken up with admiring the fine delicacy of her features. Much too good, he reflected, for a coarse person like Brodie. He stirred the hot coffee and leaned back against the mottled red plastic of the booth. "What are you thinking, Julie?"

She hesitated. "Do you really want to know?"

"Yes, of course."

"I was just going back over these last few days—with Mark. It all seems so unreal. You live with someone for so long, and yet you still know so little about him when—when it comes to a crisis. Do you know what he did when he found out about the note that poor boy had written?"

"You don't have to tell me."

"Thank you." She managed to smile at him. "Probably that's why I want to. I feel with you, Chris, as if I can sort things out for myself—without any pressures or any insistence from you. One can't talk with most people that way. They want to hear—only what they want to hear."

"I'm glad you feel that way with me," he said. The description did not strike him as inaccurate. He had never been given to reflecting on what sort of person he was. Rather, he knew more or less instinctively that he was the sort of person whom the moment demanded, and might at the next moment be another sort of person—yet always really the same person, for the multiform guises he assumed were only means to the ends set forth by his inviolable self, the diamond-hard core of personality at the center of layer upon layer of masquerade.

"When Mark heard about—" she gestured, "—*it*, he got drunk. He's been drunk ever since. He was drunk when the police came, and Robbie, and the dean. I suppose he's still drunk. You have no idea," she said quite calmly, "how much contempt I have for him.

At a time like that, he was so weak——" She kept her voice pitched low, but it quivered with intensity of feeling. "How can I have any respect for him, when his only response was to get drunk?"

Christopher shrugged. "No one is blaming you, Julie. You don't have to feel as if you need to defend yourself."

She was silent again for a while, staring into her coffee cup. Then abruptly she said, "Do you know what his one justification was?"

"No."

"He blamed *you!*" She looked at him, as if waiting for some reaction. But he was momentarily too surprised to act the required part. Did Brodie know something? There was danger here.

"He kept saying," she went on when he did not reply, "that he didn't know how, but he was sure that at bottom it was all your fault somehow."

He felt a wave of relief pass over him. "I suppose it would be doubly hard for Mark to admit his own responsibility in this case. After all, he was genuinely interested in the Reinhart boy. And then to have this happen despite his good intentions——"

"You're too charitable, Chris," she said. "Mark hadn't any good intentions in regard to that boy. The only reason he was interested in him was because he represented a way of hurting you. In his eagerness to do that, he just stopped caring whether or not he hurt the boy too."

It seemed impossible to mistake the drift of her words. He could not be wrong. She was asking for the justification he so desperately wanted to give her. And yet his heart seemed to twitch in frightened little movements of apprehension as he asked, "Do you want to leave him, Julie?"

He knew at once that he had blundered. A look of dismay and fear spread over her face. "Leave him?" she said, staring incredulously at him.

"You said——" he began almost irritably, but then stopped himself. That would not do. It would be even worse folly to reproach her.

But she had picked up his train of thought, and he could see from her expression that it had given her a sudden frightening insight into herself. It was as if she were saying, "If *that* is the way I seem to him——" "I'm sorry, Chris," she said. "You must have misunderstood. I know, a lot has happened in these few days. I don't think it will ever be the same again between Mark and me.

But as for leaving him——" She shook her head as if she could only with difficulty grasp the meaning of the words.

Desperately he sought for something to rescue the situation. Then the idea came to him. He forced a smile. "I'm afraid *you* misunderstood *me,* Julie," he said. He tried to get the proper note of resignation to injustice into his voice, and fancied he had succeeded rather well. "Of course I didn't mean—what you seem to have thought—that you should leave Mark permanently."

She looked at him now, and he was relieved to see anxiety in her eyes. "Chris, I'm sorry——"

"No, don't apologize. It was a natural mistake. I suppose I shouldn't have sprung it on you the way I did. What I meant to say —excuse me if I seem to be butting in——"

"Please, go on, Chris. I need someone to tell me——" Suddenly she put her hands over her eyes and began to cry. The counterman looked up curiously at them from a frying hamburger. Christopher smiled and winked at him. The man nodded vaguely and turned back to the sizzling meat.

"Julie," he said in a low sympathetic voice. "Poor Julie. You want me to tell you what I think you should do? All right. It's very simple. Just leave Mark—not permanently, of course I don't mean that—but just for a few days, just until he's had time to think things over and come to his senses. As it is, he's only making life miserable for you. And you—well, I think your being there as a target for his anger and resentment and shame is bad for him too. He's got to learn to live with all that's happened."

"It's just——" She fought to gain control of her voice. "It's just that I feel as if he needs me especially right now."

"He *thinks* he needs you. But does he really? Isn't it actually doing him more harm than good to have you there? Julie, as long as you're around, he'll take out all his hatred on you. But with you gone, he'll have to face himself—and the sooner he does that, the better."

"He wouldn't understand——"

"No, not right away. But eventually he will, and he'll thank you. Besides, what am I suggesting after all? Not that you take a cruise around the world." He smiled encouragingly at her. "No, just that you get away from him for a day or two, so that you can both get a little perspective on—on what your lives are going to be like from now on. Listen, I'm absolutely convinced of this—Mark has got your conversion and what happened to Donald all mixed up in his mind. As far as he's concerned, the two things go together somehow. Well, how is he ever going to face either thing sensibly as long as that's so? What he's got to do is to separate the two things, face each one by itself and learn to live with it. And as long as you're there, he's not going to be able to do that."

He could tell that his words were having their effect and he felt he had won, but he went on still like a card player piling up unnecessary points, for the sheer pleasure of scoring them. "Julie, Mark needs help, but it's not the kind of help you can give him. He needs to have someone reason with him and explain why you're doing what you're doing, why you're going to enter the Church. I can do that—if you'll let me."

She looked at him with a direct and surprisingly calm gaze. "Why do you take this much trouble for me, Chris? Why do you concern yourself with me so?"

"Because——" For a wild moment his heart pounded crazily and the truth danced fantastically to the very tip of his tongue. But on the edge of the abyss he held back, and caution prompted him. "Because I want to help you to save your soul," he said. Confused, he lowered his eyes for an instant, then forced himself to raise them again.

"Thank you," she said.

To his surprise he felt suddenly awkward. He laughed, a little hoarsely. "My pleasure."

She smiled, then with an unexpected movement reached out and took his hand. "Chris, I owe you so much."

His heart was racing. He desired her immensely. "Not really," he mumbled in confusion.

"All right," she said. "I'll do what you suggest. If I leave him it can't be any worse than it has been. Anything is worth trying."

"You won't regret it," he insisted.

Suddenly a frown passed over her face and she let go his hand. "Only—Chris, how can I go back there now?"

"Go back?"

"To the apartment. I have to pack, get some money. But I can't face him, knowing—what I'm going to do."

He thought a moment, then grinned. "No need to," he said. "I'll get him out of the apartment for you. Then you can go and do your packing and be gone before he's back."

"How will you do it?"

He nodded toward the phone booth in the back of the restaurant. "Give him a call and ask him over to my place," he said.

"You mean—play a trick on Mark?"

"Not a trick. I'll be there to meet him. If I'm going to have a talk with him, there's no time like the present."

"But, Chris, do you think——"

"I think we'll have a good deal to talk about," he said. He looked soberly at her, though inwardly he somehow felt like laughing. "I haven't given up on Mark. I suppose there's not much chance of it —but you know, I still want to help him."

MARK BRODIE WAITED IN THE DIMLY LIT HALLWAY FOR THE rattletrap elevator which his push of the button had set in clanking motion several floors up. He drew a last angry drag on the butt of his cigarette and dropped it into one of the little pools of water which had dripped onto the floor at his feet from his waterlogged overcoat. He fumbled in his shirt pocket for the pack, then decided against taking another one. It would have seemed as if he were nervous, and he did not want to give that impression, especially to himself. There was a bitter morning-after taste in his mouth, overlaid by the stale flavor of not-quite-fresh instant coffee. The elevator groaned to a halt in front of him. He pulled back the frosted-glass door, wedged it in place with his foot, jerked open the grating, and stepped inside. He pushed the button and the ancient elevator heaved upward again. The taste in his mouth sickened him slightly. He wanted another cigarette. Hell, he thought, if I want one I'll have one. He reached for the pack once more, took out a cigarette and lit it petulantly. *He* hadn't anything to be nervous about, and he was damned if he'd let Gavin have the satisfaction of making it seem he was.

He had to admit, though, as the elevator rose slowly, that he had no very clear notion of why he had come here, and that he felt—if not nervousness—at least a nagging curiosity about just what would happen in the next few minutes. But he could hardly have refused to come when Gavin had asked him—to have done so would have been to admit that he was afraid of something—and since the moment he had hung up the phone back in his own apartment, he had been busily engaged in convincing himself that the coming interview was actually something he had himself desired. And, as a matter of fact, that was true to a certain extent. Ever since Saturday night, when he had first heard what Donald had done, it had been apparent that the whole thing—the dramatic action, one might even call it—would be subtly incomplete until he and Gavin had confronted each other face to face. And, in the intervening day since then, the intuition had grown within him, had reached in fact the proportions of a genuine conviction, that if he were to have the final explanation for what had happened, it would have to come from Gavin. For he *knew,* as certainly as he knew anything, he felt with an absolute conviction, that Gavin was at the very heart of the thing. He had, however, been thinking more in terms of reasoning his way to the heart of the mystery, of piecing together the scraps of information which he had, patching the pattern with conjecture, and in this purely intellectual manner determining at his leisure and when his mind had cleared just where Gavin stood in relation to what had happened. The idea of going to the very source and questioning the one person—exclusive of Donald Reinhart—who could tell him that, had simply not occurred to him. Or perhaps it had, and he had merely dismissed it as too monstrous, too sickening. For he had no wish to *see* Gavin. He had admitted as much to himself before the phone call. Somehow everything that had happened had filled him with—not anger, not contempt, not outrage—but loathing for the man, so that he had felt an almost physical aversion at the very thought of being in his presence.

But then, this morning, the phone had rung and it had been Gavin, breezy and cryptic, asking him to drop by later because, as he had explained, he thought they should have "a little talk about matters of mutual interest." For a brief wild moment the idea had flared up in him to refuse, to tell Gavin to go to hell and slam down the phone. The temptation had been strong. But stronger still had been the awareness that to do so would have been to admit weakness. And so he had merely said, as cryptically as Gavin, he hoped, that he would come when he got the chance, and then set down the receiver firmly but slowly. It had taken genuine self-control for him to wait out the forty-five minutes he had set himself before leaving the apartment. On the one hand, he did not want to see Gavin; but on the other, if see him he must, he was desperately anxious to have it over. The self-imposed delay (he refused, of course, to give Gavin the satisfaction of thinking he was at his beck and call) had been intolerable. The emptiness of the apartment had made him nervous too. Julie had been gone when he woke up, and in the first blurred moments after he had dragged himself out of bed and stumbled around the apartment he had even—it made him furious now to think of it—thrown open the bedroom closet to see if her clothes and suitcase were still there. They were. He had sat down on the edge of the bed and lit a cigarette from the pack on the night table. His hand had shaken a little and he had watched it with angry chagrin.

The elevator jerked to a stop. Repeating in reverse the clumsy routine of opening the doors, he stepped into the hallway. A child was crying in one of the apartments. He walked down the hall to Gavin's door. He knocked at once, refusing to allow himself the weak luxury of hesitation.

"Come in." Gavin's voice came from inside. Mark reached for the knob, then stopped. Damn him, let him open the door. He knocked again. He heard the muffled sound of a chair scraping, footsteps. Then the door opened.

"It's not locked," Gavin said, standing aside for him. Mark walked in without replying. "Let me have your coat." He slipped it off and Gavin hung it in the closet by the door. "Nasty day," Christopher said.

Silence seemed somehow foolish, a hint of childish stubbornness. "Yes, it is."

"Sit down, won't you?"

Mark walked into the bare little room, and sat on the sofa. Gavin followed him and took the chair by the desk, the one he had heard pushed back. He noticed the open book on the desk. Black cover and red-dyed edges. A missal, he supposed; it might even have been a breviary. The cheap crucifix on the wall and another on top of the bureau were unnecessarily stark symbols of pain. There was something about the whole place that disgusted him—an air of self-conscious asceticism. He would have liked to have looked in the refrigerator in the tiny kitchen. A carton of milk, half a loaf of stale bread, an opened tin of tuna fish, a few apples. Probably Gavin would have liked him to have looked, too. No doubt it was something he took pride in. Now that he was here, he wished almost that he had not come. Whatever Gavin wanted, it was sure to be something that would contribute to his own immense self-satisfaction. Better then to have it over quickly, not let him enjoy himself too much.

"What was it you wanted to see me about?" Mark asked abruptly.

Gavin smiled, one of his sincere, boyish smiles. Mark hated him for that. Surely by this time he might have dispensed with pretense. "It was a shame what happened—about Donald," he said. Clearly, he had no intention of being denied any of the pleasures of the protracted interview he had planned.

"Is that all you wanted to say to me?"

Gavin made a deprecating gesture. "Probably not all, Mark." After a pause, he glanced at his wrist watch and said, "I suppose you're in a hurry to get back to school."

"Hardly."

"Oh? Didn't you go in today?"

"You could have guessed that."

"I could have. But I prefer to be certain about things." Another pause, then: "This business must have shaken you up pretty badly?"

"Damn you," Mark growled, "what the hell sort of game is this? For God's sake, don't play at being *my* sympathetic friend."

Gavin merely shrugged.

"Anyway—" Mark went on, inconsequentially, in his anger, "—what about you? I don't see you at school." He hated the sound of that, the note of schoolboy tit-for-tat. Still, the sally served at least the purpose of getting information. Why, he had begun to wonder, *wasn't* Gavin in school?

"Oh, that. Well, as a matter of fact, I quit this morning," Chris said. "Let me get you an ash tray," he said, nodding at the smoldering cigarette Mark held. He rose and went into the kitchen, returning a moment later with a smudged saucer which he handed the other man. Brodie watched him in astonishment.

"You quit—why?" he demanded.

"Certainly you know as well as I, Mark," he said. "I was going to be fired as soon as Robbie got to the dean. You'd taken good care to see to that, hadn't you?" He smiled at Brodie. "Although I must say it took you an awfully long time. I'd begun to think I'd overrated you."

Mark ignored the gibe. "Is that the only reason? What about the boy?"

"Donald? Oh, I suppose he was another reason. Although I hear we owe that to you too, don't we? At least, I understand that was the substance of his note."

Mark crushed out his cigarette in a spasm of anger and disgust, directed both at himself and at Gavin. "None of it would have happened if it hadn't been for you," he said in a low voice without looking at the other man.

"That's true enough—but it's no great contribution to fixing the blame, is it? And after all, in our unbiased free pursuit of truth—which is what you've always been so anxious for—we do have to fix the blame." He drummed his fingers softly on the desk.

The realization dawned slowly on Mark that he was being judged. Gavin had finally achieved that, and he felt almost helpless to protest against it. "If you'd let Donald alone," he said desperately, seeking any turn of thought that might reverse their positions, "he would have been all right."

"But he didn't want to be let alone—by me. Only by you. Only by objective unbiased you. But you couldn't stand that. Your nasty dogmatism wouldn't suffer that to happen. You had to pry and poke, insinuate and scheme until finally—" Gavin's voice rose ominously, "—finally he went up to his room and knotted two neckties together and tried to kill himself. My only regret is that you couldn't be there to see your achievement."

Brodie had a rancid taste in his mouth, as if he had vomited. He ran his dry tongue over his dry lips. "What about that girl?" he said.

"What girl?"

"The one he mentioned in his note. I know her. A good Catholic girl—one of your accomplices. I can see your hand at work there—through her."

"Don't be stupid. The girl was on *your* side. She was just as jealous of me as you were. Don't think I don't know what happened. I saw that book list you and Robbie were waving around. It had her name on it. I know she's the one who gave it to you."

Mark shook his head in confusion. "She didn't give it to me," he said. "I don't know what you're talking about."

Gavin looked strangely at him. "She didn't give it to you?" he repeated suspiciously.

"No."

"Then who——"

"I have no intention of telling you that."

"It doesn't matter," Gavin said. He fell silent. Mark watched him curiously. Something had upset the mechanical precision of his mind and shaken his assurance for a moment. "It doesn't matter," he said again, half to himself. "She would have done it if she'd thought of it. Her moral responsibility is just the same."

Something seemed to click into place in Mark's mind. Gavin's words began to make a sickening sense. "Did you tell Donald——" he began, then hesitated. The idea was almost too appalling, even when applied to the man sitting across the room from him. Still, from Gavin's point of view, it would have been so pervertedly logical. "Did you tell him that the girl gave me the list in order to get revenge on you?"

Gavin's fingers danced more rapidly on the desk top. He glanced out the window, then looked back at Mark. "What do you take me for?" he said. "That would have been one of *your* tricks, Mark. Granted, I thought you'd gotten the list from her—and I'm still not so sure you didn't. But as for telling Donald that—well, I'd just as soon leave touches like that to you."

In a way, Mark was almost relieved. It was as if he had come to the brink of a moral chaos, then been pulled back at the last moment. "I owe you an apology," he said.

Christopher snorted contemptuously. "Always the sportsman," he said. "Always the decent fellow. I've seen a lot of how you decent fellows work while I've been here. You always play by the rules— except when you seem to be losing. Then suddenly the rules don't matter so much any more."

Mark's anger revived suddenly as the words sank home. "I don't think anyone has found *you* very concerned about the rules," he said.

"At least I never gave any guarantee that I was going to play by them. How could I? With you and the good Dr. Bond and everyone else in this citadel of intellectual honesty determined from the moment I came here that I'd never even have a hearing—"

"Oh, come off it. Martyrdom doesn't suit you."

"Exactly. If I'd let myself *be* martyred—quietly and inoffensively —everything would have been quite acceptable. You people tolerate corpses, because they don't hit back. But someone who fights for what he believes—that's a different story with you. That's when the sportsman's code disappears from view. You want to know something, Mark? You people make me sick with all your mouthing about freedom of speech, free inquiry, the right to this and the right to that. And you know who makes me sickest of all? You do. You haven't even the excuse of ignorance that a poor fool like Robbie Bond can dredge up to defend himself with."

"You just can't forget I was a Catholic, can you?" Mark said. "'Once a Catholic, always a Catholic'—that's a favorite phrase with you people. I have an old aunt—daily communicant, Sunday night Benediction and all that—I see her at family reunions. And I know the pious old biddy goes around to everyone in the room behind my back, whispering that same damned phrase, 'Once a Catholic, always a Catholic.' I think the old fool has me confused with Martin Luther." He noticed with annoyance that despite his effort to keep his tone light and cynical, his voice had risen unaccountably as he spoke. The thought of that old woman whispering about him had always angered him. And he saw now to his further annoyance that Christopher too had caught the sound of anger in his voice.

"What are you getting so worked up about, Mark?" he said with exaggerated gentleness. "You don't mean to tell me that some old woman's opinion matters to you—free-thinking, emancipated *you?* Or—but I suppose it couldn't be . . . ?" He paused as if hesitant to go on. "It's not possible you're worried that she might be right?"

Mark held his temper. "What I hate about you," he said, "—all you good Catholics—is your damned smug superiority. You people are so absolutely righteous. You can't even conceive of the possibility that anyone is sincere who doesn't believe as you do. You know, as many times as I've talked to you, I don't believe you've understood a half-dozen sentences I've said."

"Don't flatter yourself too much, Mark."

"I'm not. I don't mean it that way. You see—" he chuckled, and enjoyed the vexed look that flitted at once across Christopher's face, "—you don't understand me even now. And you know why? Because you start with the basic assumption that I don't mean a word of what I'm saying. Oh, I can see it," he said, leaning forward with a smile and shaking his finger at Gavin. "This very moment you're trying to 'see through me.' You're not listening to what I'm saying. You think I'm trying to hide something, and you want to find out what it is. Well, I know it's not worth the effort—you won't believe me—but let me put the truth into words for you just once more, just for the record: I really believe what I'm saying, and—pardon the cliché, but I know you'll be hunting for an equivocation otherwise—I'm saying what I believe."

"Do you believe in God?" Gavin shot out.

The question startled Mark. "What?"

"I'm willing to take you at your own evaluation—you're a truth seeker and a truth speaker. Fine. Then tell me, unambiguously—do you believe in God?"

Mark frowned in irritation. Gavin had caught him off balance. "That depends," he said.

Gavin smiled insinuatingly. "Oh, I love your slogans," he said. "You believe what you say and you say what you believe. That certainly does sound fine. Until someone asks you what you *do* believe."

Mark scowled. "I'm giving you an answer," he said. "Or at least I'm trying to. But of course it's not so easy—with you convinced you know all the answers."

"Excuse me." Gavin's tone was one of exaggerated apology. "It's just that I thought you got off to rather a poor start. But don't let me rush you."

Mark paused. Then he began again: "When I say it depends, I mean—it depends on what you mean by 'god.' I believe in something—some*one*, if you prefer—responsible for all this, the world, the universe. Something that was here before it all began and that will be here when we've blown it up, or when it's simply fallen apart from sheer exhaustion. Something that put the initial jolt of energy into things, and will receive it back when the whole affair comes to an end. But I don't believe it—or he—takes any interest in what's going on in the meantime. I don't believe in a god who watches us all the time as if we were in a fishbowl, and sends us little presents when we're good or paddles our behinds when we're bad. I certainly don't believe in *your* god, because if I did I'd have to hate him. And I'd rather leave the hating to people like you."

"Why would you have to hate Him?"

"Can't you guess? Aren't *you* his servant?"

"Yes."

"How could I do anything but hate a god whom *you* served?" Mark looked calmly at Gavin. In the corner of the younger man's mouth there was just the hint of a smile. Or a sneer. "Does that answer your question?"

"Amply," Gavin said.

"Then let me ask you one—what sort of god do you believe in?"

Gavin nodded at the crucifix on the wall. "That one," he said.

"Why do you think he hung there?"

"Because He was put there—by men like——" He seemed to hesitate.

"Like me?"

"I think so."

"And did he hang there three hours damning me for it?"

"No."

"Then why——" For some reason he could not explain his voice shook a little as he asked his last question. "Why do you?"

"You do that yourself."

"You don't answer the question!" His shout was half complaint, half exultation.

Gavin brought his fist down on the desk. "Damn you!" he cried, springing up. For a moment Mark thought the other man might actually attack him. But after standing for a moment with clenched fists, glaring at him, Gavin instead turned abruptly and stalked into the kitchen. He heard the sound of water running from the tap, the clink of a glass. A moment later he strode back into the room, wiping his mouth with the back of his hand. He went back to the desk, but did not sit down.

"There's something I meant to tell you, Mark," he said, looking down at the book on the desk. "It almost slipped my mind. I'm glad I remembered it. It's about Julie." He turned his head and looked expectantly at Mark. There was something almost reptilian in his attentiveness.

"Julie." The word was wrung out of him. A cold fear pierced his heart at the sight of the merriment that crinkled the corners of Gavin's eyes.

"Julie," Chris repeated, lingering over the name. "You know, I didn't ask you over here just for the pleasure of your company—great as that is. Actually, you see, it was a little plan we worked out together."

"A plan?"

"I'm afraid she hadn't any desire to see you again, Mark. But of course she did have to get a few things together—out of your apartment. So it was necessary to get you out of the way. But I dare say she's through by now, so my telling you doesn't matter." He shook his head, in a gesture that seemed to mock sympathy. "You understand of course—she's left you. She's coming with me."

"You filthy bastard!" Mark started up. Gavin's body tensed. "I'm not going to hit you," he sneered.

"I wouldn't advise it."

His heart was pounding, his breath labored. "I suppose," he said, "this represents your final triumph. The moment of victory."

Gavin sniggered. "There are still a few technicalities to take care of," he said. "But I suppose you might call it that."

"I have to give you credit," Mark said. "I've never known anyone who could angle for a soul quite as well as you."

Gavin smiled. "Well, to be absolutely frank about it," he said, "in this case I hope there's something more than a soul involved. You see, I hope—I rather expect, in fact—that eventually Julie will marry me. It's quite kosher according to canon law, you know."

Brodie lunged forward and swung almost blindly. There was an immense satisfaction as he felt Gavin's jaw against his knuckles and saw him tumble back over his chair onto the floor. He hesitated a moment, trembling with rage. Then with an effort he turned away. Somehow he got his coat out of the closet, found his way out of the room. He was at the elevator door before he quite realized what he was doing. He pushed the button, heard the machinery clank into action. He leaned back against the wall, his body still shaking.

Then, out of the corner of his eye, he saw a movement down the hall. He turned. Christopher Gavin was leaning in his doorway, supporting himself against the door frame, watching him. Neither man moved, neither spoke. They stood looking at each other in silence for moments, minutes—an eternity. Till at last the elevator came, Mark pulled open the two doors and stepped inside. It was not until the elevator had started down, groaning and creaking as if it were in pain, that he began to cry.

THE PRIEST HAD KNOWN THAT INEVITABLY THE MESSAGE WOULD come. He had no wish really that it should not. So when the housekeeper had rung him up to tell him that Eileen was waiting to see him in the rectory parlor, he felt neither surprise nor regret. He would merely have wished to have had more time to work out this confusion which teased and puzzled him. That in fact was why he had stayed away from the university today—in the hope that the girl's visit might be delayed until he had been able to find an answer to this thing which troubled him. But her need had been too great, and it had brought her after class along the gray streets slicked over by a cold driving rain to the rectory, in order that she might see him and, by doing so, in some way ease her pain. And so it was perhaps selfish of him, he thought now, to have hoped for a postponement of the interview. Still he felt that if he could first have solved this problem which troubled him, he then might have been able to be of more help to her. But when the housekeeper had called him, he had merely said into the receiver, "Ask her to wait a minute, please. I'll be right down." He hung up the phone and sat at his desk, a wool-lined gray jacket around his shoulders against the chill that seemed habitual to the ancient rectory.

He had spent almost the whole day there, puzzling and praying over his problem, but he had come to nothing even approximating a solution. The difficulty was a simple one: He felt beyond any shadow of a doubt that there was something gravely wrong in what he had done; but he could not for the life of him see what it was. Over and over he had reviewed his actions, and as often as he had done so he had failed to put his finger on what was wrong in them. The crucial moment, he knew, had been his last interview with Eileen, when he had told her to force this unhappy Reinhart boy into a choice between Gavin and herself. That had certainly been the turning point, and it had marked for him a major departure. He, who had always been known for his vacillation and his inability to make decisions, had then reached and enunciated a decision which was to have enormous consequences for many others besides himself. Basically it had been a decision of war, a command to commence belligerent action against Christopher Gavin. And by that very fact it was a revolutionary change from his previous notions of what charity required of him. He who had turned the other cheek so often had begun in that moment to fight back against the evil in the world. And now, as the smoke and dust cleared from the first skirmish of his war, it was apparent that the results of his action had so far been disastrous.

All right. Granted that was true; what did it prove? It failed abysmally, after all, to tell him what the cause was of this gnawing sense of having done wrong. It was not, surely, the mere fact that events had turned out so badly. The disaster might account well enough for his regret and chagrin, but not for his sense of guilt. To feel guilty for a catastrophe he had not desired and could not have foreseen would be a giving in to weakness. Nor was the source of his discomfort in the advice he had given Eileen. He remained as convinced now as he had been then—even more so, in fact—that Christopher's neurotic influence over the boy had to be ended. And the means of achieving this which had offered itself and which he had taken—Eileen's ultimatum—was fair and acceptable. That being so, what was it then that troubled him? Perhaps, he speculated, it was the recurrence of his old trouble, that dread of taking positive action which had plagued him for so long. It was unlikely, after all, that he could slough off so easily the habit of a lifetime. True enough, and yet that answer failed to satisfy. He felt instinctively that there was some further cause of his discontent. For under the impact of events since Christopher Gavin's arrival, he had been forced almost against his will to acknowledge that his old reluctance to act, though assumed to be an offshoot of charity, had in fact been the product of mere sentimentality. It had taken a Gavin to teach him that charity could demand forceful action, but now that he had learned the lesson, he would not soon forget it. No, there was no question of a relapse into the hesitation which had been his former rule of life. There was no question of regret over the decision to fight Gavin. But what then? That left him where he had begun, unable to find fault with what he had done, yet depressingly aware that in its very heart it was all somehow wrong.

Suddenly he remembered Eileen. Foolish of him—he had been rambling on and keeping her waiting. He shook his head in annoyance and, slipping off the jacket, left the room.

On the way downstairs Father Kirsch tried to imagine what this interview would be like. He had no illusions that it would be a pleasant scene. The girl must be hating herself now, and for that reason she would be hating him, too, as the one whose advice had led her to this calamity. His own sense of having done wrong would not allow him the luxury of disputing with her. Certainly, in any event she could say nothing he had not already thought himself. And if the saying of it were of some relief to her, he would be glad that he could be of at least that much help. It was really more than he could ask that he should be able to do anything at all, and it was with a sense of gratitude that he entered the parlor.

"Father——" She rose as he came in. "I'm sorry if you're not feeling well."

He was surprised at her appearance. He had expected to find her haggard and wan. But instead she looked quite her ordinary, scrubbed, common-sensical self. It was his romanticizing, he realized, that had betrayed him into expecting something quite different from the reality. Still, there remained the question of what she would say. Would there be a surprise in that too?

"It wasn't my health that kept me away from the university," he remarked simply.

She seemed, however, scarcely to have heard him. "I did want to see you though. I felt I had to see you."

"I suppose so." She had taken the straight chair in front of the little desk which stood before the front window. Apparently she expected him to sit behind the desk in the approved priest-layman relationship of rectory visits. But the small symbol of authority seemed to him in this instance to be merely fatuous, and he chose instead an armchair against the wall. She sat down too, moving her chair a little to face him.

"You heard about—about Don?" she asked.

He reached under his cassock for his cigarettes and found that, annoyingly, he had forgotten them. "Yes," he replied. He wanted a cigarette desperately; his gums fairly ached for one.

"And about the note he left?"

That was something new. A student had called to tell him what had happened, but there had been no mention of a note. He had simply concluded automatically to a relation between the boy's suicide attempt and his last talk with Eileen. But there was a note, too. He wondered just how bad that made things. "No, I didn't know about the note."

"I have a copy." She fumbled in her purse while he reflected in surprise that she was much calmer than he had expected. "I guess they weren't going to tell me at first. But finally someone read it to me over the phone. I asked them to let me take it down and they did." She pulled out a slip of paper. "Here."

He glanced over the paper. Her name—and Mark Brodie's! He felt a shameful gladness at seeing another name there. It meant at least that the responsibility for what had happened was divided and did not rest entirely on Eileen—and, through her, on him. He handed the pencil-scrawled note back to her. "I'm sorry, Eileen."

"Father——" She hesitated. Then suddenly she spoke with intensity in a tone of anguish she had not used till now. "What can I do to make up for it?"

He almost started at the question. He had expected recriminations, and instead he heard only a plea for help. He felt suddenly an immense disgust with himself. He thought the girl had come to blame him. But she only asked him to help her. He wanted to ask her foregiveness, but that, he knew, would be a luxury, a form of self-indulgence. He had been asked for help. It was his duty now to give it, or at least to try. "Make up for it?" he repeated. "You haven't anything to make up for, Eileen. You only did what you thought was right—what would be best for Donald." The words sounded false. What comfort could there be for her in hearing that? It was not a mere mistake in judgment that tormented her now. It was regret that she had ever had the temerity to dabble in another person's life, the inevitable human regret at the inadequacy of one's charity toward others—magnified and distorted in her case by the catastrophe for which she felt herself to blame. And suddenly a realization began to dawn on him, as if the key to the puzzle that had teased him all this time had been handed to him at last. But his thoughts were interrupted by Eileen's voice.

"I wasn't really thinking of him, Father." She spoke slowly and quietly. "I was only thinking of myself. I wasn't willing that he love me on his own terms—only mine would do. All those things I told you were just arguments to justify me in hurting him, without admitting to myself that I *was* hurting him."

At last. That was it. He let out his breath in what was both a sigh of relief and a faint moan of repentance. At last he knew where the evil of his actions lay. Eileen had shown him. It was so simple after all. But of course these greatly simple things were sometimes the hardest of all to grasp. Like Eileen he had failed in his love. He had deliberately put love aside and had acted in his own interests without consulting those of love. With painful clarity he remembered that odd surge of pleasure he had felt when he had told Eileen to take the action which had set off this unhappy chain of events. He recognized that pleasure now as the joy of revenge. Through this girl and through the boy he had been striking back at Christopher Gavin. He had not thought of Eileen or the boy or of anything else. He had thought only of his quarrel with Gavin, and he had used others as his instruments in waging that quarrel. All his arguments about the need for opposing and thwarting Christopher held good, of course. Even now he had no inclination to question them. But at the moment of crisis, in the concrete situation, they had turned out to be irrelevant. All the arguments in the world could not have made up for his failure in charity—his failure to love Eileen and the boy and even—or rather, above all—Gavin.

It was curious, he reflected, how he had veered between the extremes. Only a short while ago he had been all sentiment and sweetness, and the result had been that ineffectuality which, in his foolishness, he had prized so long as a sign of purity. And then, when at last he had steeled himself to act, he had done so coldly and cruelly, striking out in anger and quite forgetting charity. He felt disgust with himself, though at the same time he experienced an immense gratitude for the mercy which had granted him this moment of insight. He had been a man of extremes, and in the one case charity without action had lapsed into sentimentality, while in the other action without charity had been utterly unhumane. In this moment of vision he saw beyond any doubt that the way he would have to travel lay in combining love with action, so that action might bring his love to others, while love purified and made perfect his action.

The girl was speaking again. "Father, I just wanted to think so well of myself that I was ready to cause him any amount of suffering if it would help to shield me."

"You didn't know what you were doing. You certainly didn't realize how—how it would end. And more than that, I know you didn't really understand what your motives were."

"A person knows what he wants to know, Father. I know now why I acted the way I did. I was hoping I could make Donald the one to break off whatever there was between us. I could have known that then, but I put it out of my mind, because I didn't want to know, because it might have stopped me from doing what I wanted to do."

"It's so hard to act out of love always." The priest tried to organize his thoughts so that she could share some of the light which had begun to flow in upon him. The ancient radiator by the window hissed faintly. The room with its impersonal gray walls seemed suddenly close. He rose and opened the window a crack. Outside the cold rain was still falling as it had done all day from a dull, heavy sky. "Even when we think we're acting out of love—" his breath steamed up the window as he spoke, not looking at her, "—we don't really know. Men kill each other, and they say they do it for the love of a woman, and sometimes they've said they did it for the love of God. But how can we ever really forget ourselves in what we do? We always act because we think that somehow the action will help us get what we want. That's the way we all are, Eileen."

"But that *can't* be the way we should be."

He hesitated. "No. You're right." He turned back to her. "To be selfish—what could be worse than that? We are made in the image and likeness of God—and what could be less like God than to think always of ourselves? You know, what you said about your acting without thinking of that boy, but only of yourself—that's true of me too, Eileen."

"You, Father?"

"Yes. Because in the same way you used him for your purposes, I used you and him for mine—to help me score some sort of cheap victory over Christopher Gavin. So you see—" he sat down again in his chair, "—I'm as much to blame as you. You ask me how you can make up for it—well, I ask the same of you. How can I make up for it?"

But she seemed hardly to have heard what he said. Her mind had fastened instead on one name, and she repeated it now. "Mr. Gavin."

"What about him?"

"It's his fault, Father," she said with sudden bitterness. "He's the one to blame for what happened—to all of us. If it hadn't been for him, Donald would have been different, and I could have loved him without any trouble, and you wouldn't——"

"Eileen!" She stopped in surprise. "Don't go on. Don't you see what you're doing?"

"I hate him. I see what he's done to me and to Donald, and I hate him for it."

The priest groaned softly and rocked his head back and forth. "Eileen, Eileen—are you going to make that mistake again?"

"What mistake?"

"The mistake of hating. Or even of just simply failing to love. The mistake of not loving when you should love."

"Love? How can I love him?"

"How can you afford not to?" Her look expressed astonishment. He wanted desperately to make himself clear, and so he spoke slowly, mustering his thoughts as well as he could. "Do you know what I'm beginning to think, Eileen, about those times when the wicked seem to be doing well and we—we *good* people come off second best? I'm beginning to think we haven't any reason to blame God or accuse Him of injustice. Because probably if you examine the case closely enough, you'll find that all God has been presented with is the bad—them—and the not quite so bad—us. I think we're mistaken if we assume that God *has* to choose the lesser of two evils. Where the alternatives are only a greater and a lesser evil, why should God choose? And if He doesn't, then it stands to reason that the greater evil, because it's more vigorous, more self-possessed, more certain of what it wants, the greater evil just sweeps the field. Take this case. What you and I did was right—but only *half* right. It was the right thing to do—I really believe that. But we did it for all the wrong reasons. And so our right actions turned out wrongly. Well, why should we be surprised? Why should God be on our side if the best we can say is that we don't hate our enemies quite as much as they hate us? Why should He be on my side if that's the best I can say about myself in regard to Christopher Gavin? God isn't impatient. I think He isn't in any hurry to choose sides. He can afford to wait till he finds those people who are fighting their fight out of love for their enemies, and not out of hatred or selfishness or fear or habit. When He finds them, He'll take their side. But before then we can't expect Him to commit Himself. We can't blame Him for not helping us, if we only want Him to help us destroy our enemies, instead of loving them. When you and I can kneel down and ask God to help us love Gavin, then perhaps God will help us. But until that time—well, I think it's almost blasphemous to ask God for anything else." He stopped then. He had been exhilarated as he spoke. But the feeling was replaced now by anxiety, as he watched Eileen frowning over his words.

"What's the expression they use in the Gospel, Father?" she said at last. "A 'hard saying'? That's what that is to me—a hard saying."

"Of course it is."

"I'm not used to loving my enemies, Father. I guess I'm not used to loving anyone really. Except myself. If someone hits me, I want to hit back. If I see something I want, I start after it—without asking myself whether someone else wants it too. These things you tell me—they sound fine. But how do I *do* them? How do I begin loving someone?"

"Have you tried, Eileen?"

"No."

"Then begin. Begin to ask God to help you. And forget about having God on your side. I wish I hadn't used that phrase. Because really the purpose of love—God forgive me for talking this way. I don't know anything about love, but if I don't try to think about it, I never will—the whole point of love, I think, is to put an end to *sides* and have only one side, God's side. Begin to ask God for that—and keep beginning, over and over, as many times as you have to."

"Father, I don't want to hate anyone. I wish I could love."

"If you want to, then you've already begun. It's a beginning."

"A beginning," she echoed uncertainly.

"And I think beginnings are all we can ask for."

"Yes." She nodded. Then, after a moment's thought: "But what do I do now?"

"What do you do——?"

"About Donald."

The priest passed his hand wearily over his eyes. "I don't know, Eileen. I asked you this before, and you weren't sure. Perhaps you know now. Do you love him? Not the way we've been talking about, but the way you'd love a man you wanted to marry."

She shook her head in a gesture of self-disgust. "Love him, Father—after what I've done to him?"

"I understand," he said quietly. "But is that your final answer? Don't think that because you've hurt him, Eileen, you can't love him. If that were true, who could say he loves anyone?"

She lowered her head. After a moment, without looking up, she said, "Father, after what happened I didn't want to admit it, not even to myself. It seemed too hypocritical. But if you say it's possible, then I think I can say yes, I do love him."

The priest smiled tenderly at her, though it was a smile she did not see. "I don't think you have to worry about hypocrisy now."

"But what shall I *do*, Father?" She looked up in desperation.

"God knows, if I had an easy answer that was a real answer, I'd tell you. I haven't any, though. All I can say is—perhaps someday, maybe sooner than you think, you can go to him and tell him you love him and then——"

"Then it will be up to him."

"I think it should be, don't you?"

"Yes."

"And in the meantime—— Well, what can I suggest. Only that you try to do what I've told you. That you try to love Christopher Gavin, as I shall be trying. Even—that you pray for him."

Suddenly she smiled, and the priest's heart lifted to see that it was her old smile. "I can do that now, Father," she said. "I guess really I can't afford not to love him—and to pray for him."

"I guess not," he said. "I guess none of us can."

MARK TURNED THE KEY IN THE LOCK WITH INFINITE CAUTION, AS if it were made of glass and might snap off. He closed the door to his apartment carefully behind him, took off his coat slowly and opened the closet door softly and slowly. All the way home he had held himself in check with an exhausting effort of will. He would *not* let himself go to pieces, he would hang on to his self-control, the fragile thread that bound his self-mastery. What he would do—what he *should* do—was not clear to him. But what was clear was that he had to move slowly, carefully, to avoid—whatever it might be he had to avoid. He reached for the coat hanger. Suddenly, though, his hands shook, his fingers fumbled at the wire, and the hanger clattered to the closet floor. He hesitated only a moment, trembling over it, before he threw his coat down and turned with a groan to half-run into the bedroom.

He flung open the closet door. Empty. Cleaned out. Even her suitcase, which had stood for months gathering dust in the back of the closet, had disappeared. He sat down heavily on the edge of the bed. After a moment he put his head between his hands and closed his eyes.

She had left him, as Gavin said. Had he seriously thought it was a lie? No, not seriously. But the thought had been there, somewhere in the back of his mind, and it had been all that had sustained him during the bus ride home. The faint hope that Gavin's malice might have prompted him to go that far—to lie about *that*. It was a curious thing on which to base one's hope—the evil in another person. But it had been all he had. Certainly there was nothing to hope for from the way Julie had acted. Her frigid silence, her look of disgusted aversion when he had come near her—what else had he expected? Hadn't he driven her to it?

He groaned softly at the thought. His own stupidity, his own viciousness—they were all he had to blame. He had driven her to it. As he thought back now, it seemed to him that he had actually been challenging her, taunting her, daring her to go that far. His own hurt pride—his stupid, damnable pride—had kept him from reasoning or even pleading with her. No, not for *him* to ask favors. The reconciliation would have to be on his terms. Reconciliation—no, that was wrong, that wasn't what he had sought at all. *He* had demanded utter capitulation. Nothing else would have suited his pride. He rolled his head back and forth in agony. Had he never even considered the alternative? Hardly, and even then not seriously. Her leaving him—it was unthinkable. That was why he had felt so confident in daring her to do it. But what he had failed to understand was that it was unthinkable only to *him*. For her—the thought knifed through him now with painful clarity—for her it must have seemed at first a temptation, a seduction, growing more and more alluring. And then at the very last it must have come to represent escape, a way out, freedom from the intolerable pain and disgust of seeing him. At the end it must have presented itself in such clear terms to her: He had nothing to offer her but himself, he *would* offer her nothing else, and if there were something more she wanted, then she would have to take it, not in addition to him, but in preference to him. And he, fool, had imagined that she could have no such other preference. In his blind self-confidence he had thought, up to the very moment when Christopher Gavin told him she had left him, that when the ultimate choice had to be made, she would choose him.

He had blundered here too. So often he had blundered. And always because of his damned pride. It had been the same story with Donald. Refusing to offer him what he wanted, fighting him even to prevent him from wanting anything, and then, when the boy had made it plain that nothing was not enough, shoving him away with a harsh word into the hands of—God? Gavin? Gavin and his God. It was his distinctive trait, he saw now, the inflated fatalism of invincible pride. He would not even try to pick up the pieces of his broken world, for to pick them up he would have had to stoop.

And now it was too late even to stoop. Too late. He hesitated. Why too late? He had to be very cautious now. His damned pride had betrayed him so often before—why not again? Was it now—he had to think this through clearly—was it anything but his pride again that made him say too late? No, there was real reason now to think that his opportunities had indeed escaped him—that was wrong: That he had declined to accept his opportunities. There, then. Reason to *think* it, but not to *know* it. How did he know what could or could not be salvaged even now, until he had once—he accepted the word with as much humility as he could muster—stooped to find out? He had lost a great deal, but perhaps—just possibly—not everything, and not permanently.

Mark opened his eyes and raised his head. The room was no different than it had been yesterday. And yet somehow, subtly, in ways beyond sense, it had changed. The silence in the apartment was oppressive.

It would be so hard to try. He was so very tired. He wanted only to lie down and sleep, accept a gracious oblivion. But his newly achieved perception had not left him. Even the act of despair was at bottom a gesture of pride. People had always told him he was a proud man, and he had accepted the comment complacently, almost as a tribute. But his pride sickened him now. It seemed something dead and atrophied in his spirit, which nevertheless steered his life with a withered hand. He rose, wearily but doggedly. It was Donald whom he had injured most, and so he would go first to Donald. The simplicity of the decision surprised and almost pleased him. He went back into the hall, picked up his coat from the floor and put it on.

It dawned on Mark on the way to the hospital that, if he announced himself, he would almost certainly not be permitted to see the boy. He imagined, in fact, with a shudder of chagrin, that his name was probably at the very top of the list of proscribed visitors. But hospital routine was often lax, and it seemed quite possible that he would be able simply to walk into the boy's room unchallenged. Thank God, someone at the school had done some fast talking and Donald had not been put in a mental institution. It seemed altogether likely that one could get into his room with no particular difficulty. The problem was, though, which was his room? And how to find out without giving himself away? He had actually reached the hospital and run through a renewed burst of driving rain to its door, before a solution occurred to him. Call Robbie. He found a phone booth in the bustling modern lobby and dialed the university. It was early afternoon. On a Monday Dr. Bond would be in the English department office at this time of day. After a moment, Robbie's uncertain voice said, "Hello."

"Hello, Robbie. This is Mark." A brief pause. He smiled grimly, for it was almost as if he could read the mind at the other end of the phone and see passing through it a variety of feelings—surprise, uneasiness, doubt, fear—none of which Dr. Bond wished to betray.

Robbie's voice said, "Why, Mark. How are you?" He was no actor. The exaggerated solicitousness of his tone was emphasized, rather than disguised, by the telephone.

"Fine," he said.

"Good, good, I'm glad to hear it. I was a little worried—but of course, I'm glad you took the day off. Did you a world of good, I hope."

"I'm sorry I didn't call you this morning."

"No need to, no need at all," Robbie hastened to say. "I quite understand. This whole business—what I mean to say is, it must have been quite a strain. I mean, it would have been for anyone. Naturally."

"Yes, it's been a strain."

"Well, I have one good piece of news for you."

"Oh?"

"Yes. About Gavin. He quit this morning."

"Yes, I know."

Another moment's hesitation. "You know?"

"He told me."

"Oh—really?" It was obvious that Dr. Bond was at a loss for what to say next. Mark, feeling sorry for him, decided to cut the conversation short.

"Robbie, I called to ask you a favor," he said.

"Oh, yes," Robbie said. "Quite." Mark noted with no particular bitterness that he was not committing himself to a thing.

"I'm over at the hospital now," he said. "I want to see Donald Reinhart, but I don't know his room number. Do you?"

The pause was pronounced this time. "Well," Robbie said at last, "I may have it somewhere."

"Could you get it for me?"

"Mark——" Robbie stopped, then started again. "Mark, it's none of my business of course, but do you really think—I mean, under the circumstances—well, *ought* you to?"

"I don't think I'll be certain of that until I've seen him. Right now, I think I should. I think I have an obligation to."

"Oh, I see."

"Robbie, I haven't gone off my rocker. I'm not going to say anything to upset him. At the moment, in fact, I'm not sure *what* I'm going to say to him. But I think I can guarantee that it won't be anything—anything indiscreet."

"Of course not, Mark."

"Besides which, I promise you no one will ever know you gave me his room number."

"Really, Mark! That hadn't entered my mind."

Oh, hadn't it? Mark shrugged. He did not care to argue the point. "Fine, Robbie, good for you. Then do I get the number?"

"You're quite sure——"

"No one will know."

"Just a minute." He heard the sound of a desk drawer being pulled open. After a moment Robbie said, "It's five-seventeen."

"Thank you, Robbie. I—I appreciate it."

"Mark——"

"Yes?"

"Please be careful what you say."

The telephone seemed almost magically gifted at giving people away. In this instance it laid bare in an instant a sincere concern in Robbie—for himself and the boy—which surprised Mark. And at the same time his own surprise made him rather ashamed. "I will be, Robbie," he said. "Thanks."

"Good-by, Mark. See you tomorrow."

"See you tomorrow, Robbie." He hung up slowly. It was a funny thing, he thought, but for as long as he had known Robbie Bond, he had never imagined that he was concerned about anything besides his own comfort. And now, almost by accident, he had discovered that Robbie liked and worried about—him, Mark Brodie. It was a day of revelations.

Mark rode the elevator to the fifth floor, trying his best to look inconspicuous and at ease. He had at the back of his mind the nagging fear that someone would suddenly challenge him, ask him who he was and where he was going. He got off at Donald's floor and looked as quickly as he could at the directional sign on the wall. He did not wish simply to be standing there as starched nurses and attendants bustled past him, for he had the fear that one of them might stop and, in a moment of misguided kindness, ask him which room he was looking for. Five-seventeen: down the waxed linoleum hall to the left. He walked briskly in that direction, glancing at the room numbers on the doors only out of the corner of his eye, so that he might give the impression of someone who had been there many times before. Then suddenly the number loomed up at him—517. Now, he had to stop for a moment, he could not help it. For he had first to be sure that there was no one else in the room. He waited, listening. The door was ajar slightly. There was no sound from inside. His heart was racing—like a schoolgirl's, he could not help taunting himself—then he pushed open the door noiselessly and stepped in.

It was quite dark in the room, surprisingly so. Just inside and to the left was another door—closet or bathroom. From where he stood, he could see only the foot of the bed. No light was on and, though the window shade was half raised, it was a dark gloomy day outside and the room was swathed in shadows. He took a step forward and paused. He saw the boy's figure now, propped up with adjustable mattress and pillow. He was half-turned toward the window—staring out at the steady rain, or perhaps sleeping. Mark saw with pain the wide gauze bandage, scarflike around his long neck, up even to his chin. It reminded him of what he had never seen, and yet could never forget.

"Donald," he said softly.

The boy did not move. He was about to speak again, when

slowly, in a rather hoarse voice the boy said without looking at him, "What is it?"

He realized that Donald had not recognized his whispered voice. "It's Mark Brodie," he said.

He watched intently to catch Donald's reaction. But there hardly seemed to be one. Carefully, as if it pained him, he turned his head and stared at him with lusterless eyes. "I don't think I'm supposed to have visitors, Mr. Brodie," he said. There was no animosity in his voice. It was only a statement of fact.

"Do you mind?" Mark asked.

"No."

"I just wanted——" He gestured vaguely. "I don't know what I wanted. Just to see how you were, I suppose."

"All right, thank you. They take good care of me here."

"Glad to hear it." Mark suddenly felt awkward standing there. He pulled off his coat, tossed it onto one of two straight chairs against the wall, and dragged the other up to the bedside. He sat down uncomfortably. There was no place to put his hands, so he lit a cigarette. Donald watched him with no perceptible emotion. They sat in silence for several moments.

After a while, Donald said, "Mr. Brodie." His tone was flat, dead. It was as if sometime in the last few days he had been wrung dry of emotions. His present lassitude contrasted frighteningly with his usual frenetic state. The change surprised Mark and unnerved him.

"What is it, Don?" he said.

"I wanted to tell you—I did something stupid before—before it happened. I'm sorry."

"I don't understand."

"I wrote a note. I don't know why. I don't know what I was thinking of. Anyway, I mentioned your name. I hope they didn't find it."

Mark hesitated. "No," he said, "they didn't."

Donald smiled faintly. "Good. I'm glad of that."

Mark paused again. Then he said gently, "Donald, could I ask you why you mentioned me in your note?"

The boy thought for a moment. "Because of what you'd done to Mr. Gavin."

"I see."

"Please understand me though, Mr. Brodie—I'm really sorry I did it. It was stupid. I even mentioned Eileen. I guess I was—" he made a small gesture with his right hand, which lay limply on the bed, "—a little bit crazy then. That's what they think here, I know. Actually, I'm not sure. It was just that—well, so many things seemed to happen at once. I'm just glad I didn't get any of you into trouble."

"Eileen and me?"

"And Mr. Gavin."

Mark stiffened in his chair. "Gavin," he repeated. "Was he—did you mention him in the note too?"

Donald nodded. "He said he wouldn't have anything more to do with me."

Mark ran his tongue along his lips. So he had been right after all, and Gavin had lied to him. "Did he tell you too that—that Eileen gave me that book list?"

Donald again nodded. "I see now," he said, "that you and she both thought you were doing what was right. But when I heard it then——" A look of pain passed suddenly over his face and he fell silent.

Mark reflected on the monstrousness of it. That Gavin would have said *that* to this boy—even now, knowing all that he did of the other man, the thought was only barely credible. What could he have been *thinking* of, what did he hope to accomplish by something that could so patently have no consequence except misery for Donald Reinhart? His own guilt toward the boy was real enough, he knew, but at least he had injured him through carelessness, not intent. But Gavin—what other reason could he have had but sheer pointless malice? What could he have hoped to accomplish but harm for harm's sake? Yet even as these thoughts passed through his mind, a more concrete question of fact presented itself to him. Donald said his note had mentioned himself, Eileen—and Gavin. But Gavin's name was missing from the note that had been found. The problem, then: where was the rest of it? But Donald's voice interrupted his thoughts.

"I must really have been crazy then, you know," he said. "I remember after—after *it* happened, I guess I was out cold, but I thought once that I saw something."

"You saw something?"

"I thought I looked up—from the floor, you know—and saw Mr. Gavin in my room. Can you imagine that?"

Mark's hand shook a little as he put out his cigarette in an ash tray beside the bed. It was all too fantastic—no, the right word was horrible. It was simply beyond belief. And yet, the conclusion seemed inescapable. Donald had mentioned Christopher Gavin in his note, but Gavin's name was not in the note that was found. Part of what the boy had written was missing, then. And now Donald remembered seeing—dreaming he had seen it, as he imagined— Gavin in his room as he lay half-conscious.

"One question, Don," Mark said slowly. "Your note—was it on one sheet of paper or two?"

The boy looked oddly at him. "I'm not sure," he said. "I don't remember. Why do you ask?"

Mark stared for a long moment at the boy, lying there in bed with a frown of concern on his face, a hint of fear beginning to dance in his eyes. What am I doing? he thought. He had told himself he wanted to help the boy, and yet now instead— "Never mind, Don," he said. "It's nothing important."

"As a matter of fact," Donald said reflectively, "I think it was two pieces of paper. Just from a desk calendar, you know. I guess my hand was shaking, so I must have scrawled it pretty large."

Mark realized that his hypothesis had moved from the realm of possiblity to that of probability. He supposed he ought to have felt elated at that, but instead he felt only a little sick.

"Why do you ask?" the boy repeated when he did not speak. There was a note of urgency detectable in his voice.

In all sincerity, he thought, shall I tell him? Will it help him or will it hurt him? "Donald," he said, "do you still believe in Mr. Gavin?"

The boy blinked in surprise. He did not answer at once, and it was obvious that the question was not a new one, that it was something he had asked himself many times before, and received no answer to. "I don't know," he said at last. "It depends on what you mean. You know how—how I depended on him."

"Yes."

"Well, I don't think—now—that I can ever feel that way again. I can't depend on him because—I don't know, I guess because he won't let me any more. He's not interested in me. Somehow—you know, I don't really know how—but somehow I think he felt at the very end that I'd failed him. Can you imagine? *My* failing *him*.

I guess in a way he depended on me. And when he felt I'd failed him, he decided he couldn't depend on me, so he wouldn't let me depend on him. Does that make any sense?"

For the first time Mark smiled. There was something of the old Donald in that. "Pretty good sense," he said.

"But that doesn't really answer your question, Mr. Brodie. You asked if I believe in him." Donald shut his eyes for a moment, concentrating. "It's hard to talk about that," he said, opening them.

"Don't then, Don, if you don't want to."

"Oh, it's not that I don't want to. I do. I mean, I'd like to be able to answer that—for myself. If I knew what I believed in now—well, it would be a start, wouldn't it?"

"It would be a lot more than that for any of us."

"It's so hard to tell. Maybe—please don't think I'm trying to be smart—but maybe it's not the right question. To ask if I believe in *him*, I mean. Well, of course you're right. It was him—really—that I believed in. I guess that's the sort of person I am—I have to have *somebody* to believe in. Not just something, *somebody*. And you know for a while it was you, Mr. Brodie. And then it was Mr. Gavin. And now—well, I'd like to think it was somebody else, only I'm not sure."

"You mean God?"

Donald sighed and frowned. "Yes," he said. "I know it will sound funny, but just before *it* happened, I thought to myself something like, 'Well, I'm finally going to find out if he's there or not.' And you know, that made me really *want* to do it, because I wanted awfully to know if there's somebody there to believe in. I still do. I'd like to—well, to go and find out."

Mark said nothing, but he could not keep his face from expressing something of what he felt. The boy looked at him and smiled a little. "You don't have to worry, Mr. Brodie," he said. "I'm not going to do it again. Before, I was just trying to run away from things. Now—well, now I guess I feel I can wait it out."

"I'm glad to hear that, Don."

"I suppose this all sounds pretty silly to you, Mr. Brodie."

Mark thought for a moment. Then he said slowly, "I guess it would have a couple of days ago, Don. I'm not so sure now."

For the first time the boy's face lit up with its old eagerness. "You mean you—you think differently than you used to?"

"Not the way you mean," Mark said hastily. "Don't expect that. I still believe what I've always believed. It's just that—I don't know." He lit another cigarette. "I guess that I'm a little more reconciled than I used to be to having you believe whatever it is that you want to believe. I can see some room for disagreement where I didn't before."

"Then we owe that to Mr. Gavin at least," Donald said.

A gust of wind sent the rain rattling up against the window. "I suppose we do," Mark said. How Gavin still possessed the boy's mind! He felt suddenly that he had to end his hold over Donald, once and for all. "We owe so much to Gavin," he said.

"So much?"

"Did you know that he's been trying to—to convert my wife too?"

Donald raised his eyebrows in surprise. "Mrs. Brodie?"

"You haven't been the only object of his attentions. As a matter of fact, he's been quite successful with Julie, too. He's gotten her to leave me."

"Oh." The look of pain returned to Donald's face. For whom? Mark wondered. Perhaps it was a mistake to continue. But would it not be more of a mistake to leave the boy with his illusions? The argument sounded familiar. Mark knew he could not depend on his own disinterestedness.

"Do you want me to go on, Don?" he said.

The boy did not answer at once. Finally he said, "You mean—can I take it?"

"Yes."

He considered for a while. "I think so," he said at last. "I have to sometime, don't I?"

"Not necessarily."

"You *have* changed, Mr. Brodie. You wouldn't have said that before."

"No. But maybe I have a little more sense than I used to."

"Maybe I do too," Donald said, forcing a smile. "Go on. What else has Mr. Gavin done?"

The thought—prayer, almost—passed through his mind: 'Grant that my intentions may be pure.' Then he said, "I'm not absolutely sure of this, Don—I can't be, because I wasn't there—but I don't believe you just imagined you saw Gavin in your room that night. You see, I told you that your note wasn't found. But it was."

"Mr. Brodie—I'm sorry!" he exclaimed.

"I know you are, Don. And after all, I can't say I blame you for writing it. Besides, I think you may have done me a favor. But what I'm getting at now is that there were only two people mentioned in the note that was found—myself and Eileen. There wasn't anything about Gavin. So you see, if he was in your room that night and if he did find the note, then——" Mark felt no desire to finish.

Donald nodded slowly, almost meditatively. "I see," he said. "It's hard for me to remember clearly, but I know there were two pieces of paper. And I think—no, I'm sure—your name and Eileen's were on one, and his on the other. So it would have been very easy——" He fell silent.

"Very easy," Mark repeated.

"Of course, he hated both of you so—it must have seemed like the right thing for him to do."

Mark could not help himself. "Anything Gavin chooses to do is by definition the 'right thing' as far as he's concerned."

"He believes in himself so."

"I asked you this before, Don—now I ask you again: Do you?"

The boy's right hand played with the edge of his blanket. "No," he said at last. "I believe in God."

He raised his eyes to Mark's and the two looked at each other for a long time. Finally Mark glanced away and stared at the streaming windowpane. "I'm glad for you," he said. "You're very lucky."

CHRISTOPHER SAW HER AT ONCE AS HE CAME THROUGH THE REvolving doors into the hotel lobby. It was odd, an experience he had never before had with anyone else, but she seemed to stand out for him in any surroundings. It was as if she had a peculiar radiance that drew his eyes to her unfailingly wherever she might be. He thought he could have picked out in any crowd her slim figure and her heart-shaped face with its hauntingly large eyes. The phenomenon never ceased to surprise him, and even to leave him a little awed. He was not yet ready to accept with complete equanimity the idea that she meant so much to him, though at the same time he realized that his desire for her was the strongest feeling, save only his desire for God, that had ever possessed him. She saw him now as he crossed the lobby—cheaply and vulgarly modern with its garish uncomfortable chairs and chrome shining out of every corner—and smiled at him, a smile that seemed to him to link them in an intimacy that excluded the rest of the universe. But as he came closer he saw he had been deceived and her smile was strained, masking insecurity and anxiety. The sight disturbed him and he was suddenly conscious of the two bus tickets in his shirt pocket. For it was to be now, he had decided, in the next few minutes that his fate would be determined—that he would ask her to give herself to him—and he could not help but feel that her nervousness somehow boded ill for his success.

"Hello, Chris," she said, rising from her chair.

He smiled back at her, trying to keep his own alarm from showing in his eyes. "Hello, Julie." They stood awkwardly for a moment, each waiting for the other to speak. "Have you had breakfast yet?" he said at last in desperation.

She nodded, then: "Haven't you, Chris?"

"Oh yes, of course." He lied. He had wanted to eat with her. It had seemed to him as if there would be something domestic and intimate about the small ritual. "But I think it's time for a second cup of coffee. How about you?"

She hesitated, and he knew that she wanted to ask him what had happened during his interview with Mark. They had made the appointment to meet here the day before, after he had phoned Mark, and he had not tried to get in touch with her since then. He had needed that time to himself, to make his plans. It was evident now that she was bursting to question him.

"I know what you want, Julie," he said in a low voice. "But let's sit down first. Come on—what about that coffee?"

She forced herself to smile again. "All right, Chris. Thank you."

They crossed the lobby and went into the hotel restaurant, which was nearly deserted at this hour—almost ten o'clock. The hostess showed them to a table by a picture window looking out on the downtown street. A waitress came and Christopher ordered two coffees. Outside a brisk wind was clearing away the few clouds remaining from the day before and drying the sidewalks. The sun shone with chilly brilliance in an intensely blue sky. He looked across the table at her and met her avid news-hungry gaze.

"I don't want to be rude, Chris, but could you tell me now?"

He ran his tongue over dry lips and looked away. "There isn't a great deal to tell," he said vaguely.

She twisted the end of her napkin in her fingers. "I know you would have called me yesterday if—if the news had been good. You didn't call, so—what I mean is, I'm not expecting good news, so you needn't worry about hurting me."

Her words frightened him. "I'm not sure what you would consider good news, Julie. From one point of view——"

"You aren't sure——?" She seemed genuinely baffled.

"No, I'm not," he hurried on. "It seems to me that what would be good news from one point of view would be—well, it might be bad news from another. But I'm sorry. I don't mean to delay telling you." He glanced out of the corner of his eye and saw the waitress returning. "Our coffee," he said.

The waitress set the cups down on the table, sloshing coffee into the saucers. When she left he slowly and methodically went through the routine of pouring cream and adding sugar, stirring with meticulous care. Julie left hers untouched. At last he put down the spoon and took a deep breath.

"Mark reacted as you might have expected," he said. "I tried to talk sense to him, to explain to him what you are doing and why you are doing it. I tried to make him understand that this is something in which he hasn't any right to interfere. But unfortunately he seems to think he does."

She looked down and bit her lip. "I know. I can't make him see that by becoming a Catholic I'm not betraying him."

For the first time his smile was genuine. "That's very well put. Betrayal. That's exactly Mark's idea of it. What you're doing, as far as he's concerned, is some sort of plot against him. He sees himself at the center of everything."

"Doesn't everyone?"

"It's what we all must fight against. We have to dislodge ourselves from the center of the universe and put God there instead. Otherwise we're living in a fantasy world we've created for ourselves."

She smiled faintly and shook her head slowly. "It sounds so easy, Chris—for you. But what about the rest of us?" She shrugged. "Never mind. The question is, what do I do now?"

"I think that's pretty obvious, Julie." He leaned forward.

"Yes." She sighed. "I'd hoped I could go back to him on some other terms—that it might all be a little easier for me. But there isn't any reason why it should be made easy, is there? We'll have to fight it all out from where we left off. God help me, I hope I'm strong enough."

"Julie!" He had listened with a sense of mounting horror, and now the words tumbled in disarray over one another as he sought to express himself. "What are you talking about? How can you even think of such a thing? Don't you realize what a risk you'd be taking? You just admitted you haven't the strength. It would be foolhardy——"

"But, Chris——" She looked at him in dismay. "What else can I do?"

He paused to get control of himself, then said slowly, "Leave him. You can leave him, Julie."

Her eyes widened. "Leave him," she repeated. "Chris——" She brushed her hand across her eyes as if she were uncertain whether she had in fact seen some monstrous vision which had abruptly loomed up before her. "You can't mean that. You can't possibly."

With a sense of sickening fright he saw that he had tried to move too fast. It was urgent that he backtrack now—but without withdrawing the suggestion altogether. "Don't misunderstand, Julie," he said quickly. "I know how it must sound to you. But I'm not suggesting you leave Mark for good—necessarily. Think of it this way. You need time to yourself to make up your mind about the Church—without interference—and then to do what you think necessary. But if you go back to Mark—just now, I mean—what chance would you have? Believe me, he's totally irrational on this subject. He wouldn't give you a minute's peace. He'd badger you and threaten you—and how do you know you could stand up under that?"

"I think it would be better for me to try," she said faintly.

"But would it? God doesn't want you to risk your soul for the sake of—well, for the sake of what? Not for Mark's sake, because you can't do him any good—any *real* good—by going back to him. By letting him torment you and deny you the faith you're only beginning to understand, you'd be helping him to damn his own soul as well as yours. Julie, leave him—for a little while at least. Until you know once and for all what the right thing is for you to do."

"Chris, if I thought I could know that——"

"You can. I'm telling you that you can. But if you put yourself into Mark's hands, you never will."

"So instead you want me to put myself into——" She did not finish.

He nodded. "Please, Julie," he said.

She was silent for a moment, then she said, "I don't understand, Chris—why do you do it?"

"Do what?"

"Take all this trouble. For me—for Donald—for anyone else. Why do you want so awfully much to make converts of us?"

The question put him more at his ease. He was on familiar ground once more. "Because there's nothing more important that I could do. You must know that by now, Julie. To be an instrument in bringing the truth to others, in helping them save their souls—what could be more important?"

"But is that really your job?"

"Of course it is. I'm a member of the Church. And that alone makes it my job—my duty—to help others to find the truth."

She did not reply. Instead, she seemed to think a minute, then asked again, "Haven't you ever thought you might be wrong?"

Christopher met her inquiring glance directly. "No," he said.

"Sometimes I've wondered," she said, "whether a faith that one has never doubted is a real faith at all."

Christopher straightened abruptly. "I'm afraid I don't see any sense in that." His tone was deliberately cold. "You ought to be careful, Julie, not just to play with words and ideas." He was pleased to see her eyes widen with regret in the knowledge that she had hurt him.

"I'm sorry, Chris," she said. "I didn't mean it the way it sounded. I'm not questioning your sincerity——"

"Thank you."

"What I was just trying to say—if I could only find the words for it—is that a faith has to be tested before it's really faith. Otherwise it's only—what can I call it?—only belief."

Christopher swallowed a mouthful of coffee. They were almost the only people in the restaurant now. Two waitresses were leaning wearily against the wall in a corner, chatting without enthusiasm. "What about you, Julie?" he said. "To use your own terminology—do you have faith or belief?"

She thought for a moment. "Only belief."

"And that means——?"

"I don't know what it means."

"What do you need to give you faith?"

She shook her head in confusion. "I don't know."

"Julie——" He took her hand. She did not protest. "I could give you faith."

"By a test——?"

"*No*. That's all nonsense—about testing your faith. It's wrong. It's sinful. No—I could help you to strengthen your belief, until it turns into—faith!"

"*Chris*." She jerked her hand out of his, and he realized suddenly that he had been squeezing it tighter and tighter.

"Julie—excuse me. On these questions—" he felt his face redden, "—I—I feel so strongly." He plunged his hand in embarrassment into his coat pocket. His fingers played about for a moment and then, unexpectedly, came upon a wad of paper. He knew suddenly that it was Donald's note. He had hardly given a thought to it since the night he had first found it by the boy's body. And now here it was again. What did that mean? he wondered.

Meanwhile Julie rubbed her hand. "Yes, I see you do." Then with a rueful smile she added: "Only, that just complicates the matter as far as I'm concerned."

"I don't understand."

"No, you don't—and that's what confuses me. On these things we've been talking about, Chris, you have such intelligence, such insight—but on the most elementary human questions you're hopeless, you don't understand a thing."

Once more he was hurt by her words. But at the same time his attention was distracted by the note in his pocket. He turned the wadded paper over and over between his fingers while an insane idea began to form in his mind. "Perhaps you could give me an example."

"This business of Mark," she said promptly. "You know everything there is to know about him—and about me, too—except the most important thing of all. How we feel about each other."

His jaw hardened instinctively, but at the same time he felt fright returning to the pit of his stomach. His hand was being forced. He could delay no longer. "Perhaps I'm prejudiced on that point," he said. "I only know what I want to know."

She looked at him in bewildered curiosity. "I don't think I understand."

"Could you——" He hated the triteness of it. "Could you ever love anyone else?"

A frown of confusion knotted her forehead. Then she seemed to divine his meaning. "You mean God?"

"No!" The sudden anger of his tone startled them both. One of the waitresses looked curiously at them. He paused to control himself. "No, not God."

"Chris, I don't understand you. What are you talking about?"

His fingers tightened around the ball of paper in his pocket. He saw now that she had to know everything. Only then would he be vindicated. He would not have her on any terms but his own. He wanted her to know for her sake too, so that she would have all she needed to make her decision. With something very like wonder he realized that he really did love her. Abruptly he pulled the note out and thrust it at her. "Here. Read this."

She took it hesitantly, keeping her eyes fixed on his. "What is it?"

"Something I want you to see." He turned his head away. He could not bear to watch, and instead looked out the window up at the sky. A few fragments of cloud were fleeting by. The sun shone brightly. God, have I done a stupid thing? he asked himself. No, it had to be this way. She had to know everything. And if he did not win—but that was stupid. He would win. He had always won. But he had to put it in her power to choose. He—even now, he could scarcely think the word—he loved her too much not to let her know. With an effort he brought his eyes back to her. She sat looking at him, the paper with its scrawled pencil message held unfolded before her.

"Well?" he said. His tone was harsh, but he would let himself speak in no other way. Her answer would mean so much to him that he could not bring himself to reveal his anxiety.

"What does it mean?" she asked in a low voice. He saw that she knew, but was afraid to admit it, even to herself.

"It's the other half of Donald's suicide note."

"The *other* half? I didn't know there was——"

"There was. I noticed it in his room that night. You see, I was the first one to find him."

"You?"

"Yes. I didn't want to—to get involved. So I left and called on the phone for him afterward—so they'd find him, you see."

"And you took this with you?"

"That's right."

"But it means——" She looked again at the scrap of paper. "You were to blame too for what he did."

Christopher shrugged. "In his mind."

"But what about Mark and that girl? Didn't you see what he wrote about them?"

"Yes. Of course."

"And yet you took the evidence that would implicate you and left the part of it that would——"

"Exactly."

"I see." She looked down again at the paper in front of her. He thought he saw her shudder.

"Julie——" He hunted for the words. "Julie, I know what your first reaction is. It seems to you as if I did a terrible thing, doesn't it?"

"Good God, Chris, what else can I think? Don't you understand what you've done?" There was disgust in her look, as if she had suddenly come upon some revolting animal.

"I know perfectly well," he replied as calmly as he could.

For a moment she continued to stare at him. Then abruptly she started up. "I can't stay here!" she exclaimed.

"Wait——" He grasped her wrist. For an instant he held her back, then she ceased to strain and he relaxed his grip. "Won't you even let me explain? Don't you think I should have that chance at least?"

"What could you possibly say?"

"Sit down and listen."

She hesitated, but he knew that her desire to find extenuating circumstances for other people would win out in the end. Finally she sat down, averting her eyes from his.

"Do you know why you feel the way you do about what I did?" She did not answer, and he went on rapidly. "It's because you're still infatuated with a neopagan ethic of sportsmanship. Play the game—that's your idea, isn't it? Well, I'll tell you something. When I saw that note there on the floor beside Donald, I didn't have any illusions about being involved in a game. It's no game, Julie, it isn't."

"No, it isn't."

"It's a matter of eternity. The eternal salvation or the eternal loss of a soul."

"Whose soul?"

"Yours."

She started. "Chris——!"

"Your soul, Julie," he repeated. "I had to do it for your sake. No, wait—before you say anything, think of this. Suppose I had been discredited along with Mark. Just imagine it. What would your reaction have been? Would you have been ready to leave him then? And if you hadn't left him, what chance would you have to save your soul? How could you come into the Church? I know what would have happened. You wouldn't have been able to see any difference between me and Mark."

"But now I can." Her voice was so low that he could barely hear her.

"Yes, now you can," he repeated enthusiastically.

"At least he was sincerely sorry for what he had done to that poor boy. But you——" She shook her head in disbelief but did not finish.

Her words filled his soul with terror, and he snatched her hand with a cry. "Julie!" She did not resist, but her hand was rigid and inflexible in his. "What had I done to him? I worked day and night to do for him what I'm trying to do for you. And what was the thanks I got? This note." With his free hand he took it suddenly, crumpled it, and thrust it again into his pocket. "Mark and that girl—they schemed and plotted to turn him against me. And they succeeded. But not as well as they thought. He knew what they were doing, and it drove him to try to kill himself. But they managed to confuse him about me, to poison his mind against me, so that in the end he imagined that I had betrayed him too. He didn't understand—" his voice almost sobbed, "—all that I wanted to do for him. And now you—Julie, do you know what I want to do for you? Have you any conception of what I'm offering you? Your soul, Julie, your immortal soul."

She stared at him for a moment with a look of horror. "What *you* are offering me?" She spoke very distinctly, with only a slight tremor in her voice.

He gestured almost despairingly. He wanted so desperately to find the right words, but they would not come, nothing seemed right, and with every further step he seemed only to be sinking deeper into a morass. There was so much he wanted to tell her. He tried to concentrate his attention. The look of terror and disgust in her eyes frightened him. "Julie, do you believe in God?"

"Yes."

"Do you believe in the Church, do you believe all that I've taught you?"

She nodded.

Then he could tell her without being afraid for her. "Julie, I love you."

"Oh no." She closed her eyes and shook her head slowly back and forth. "Oh no, Chris. Please."

"I love you," he said again. "I want to marry you."

She looked at him now, and he was shocked to see tears in her eyes. "Chris——" She hesitated. "Chris, I'm sorry for you."

He stiffened at the words. "I don't want your pity," he said.

"Don't you, Chris?" she said slowly. "Don't you think someone should feel sorry for all of us?"

"I don't know what you're talking about."

"Then try to understand, Chris." Her voice was gentle. She spoke as a mother might have. "Try to understand why you need someone to feel sorry for you——"

He clenched his fists. "If you mean because—because of what you——" He tried to force himself to go on, but the words would not come.

"No, I don't mean that," she said quietly. "I only mean—literally—God help you, Chris. I hope He will help you. I hope He'll show you all the harm and evil you've done—to yourself and to the rest of us. I hope He can make a human being out of you before you make something irrevocably inhuman out of yourself."

"Don't speak to me of God," he said with sudden passion. "What do you know of Him? What do any of you know? God hasn't anything to forgive me for, because it's God I've been serving all this time."

"Do you know what you're saying, Chris? Do you know what that would mean about God if you were right? That He is served by lies and selfishness and hatred—*your* hatred."

"What makes you think *you* understand?" He ground out the words. "It's always the same way—you drag in your stupid sentimentality, and then you condemn me because I spit on it, because I won't be bound by it. Well, I won't be. That isn't the love of God. He isn't served by weakness masquerading under the name of love."

"Is He served by all the suffering you've caused?"

"Why not? Why can't He make suffering His instrument? For some of those who suffer, suffering is good. It purges them of their lies and their lusts. And in other cases it's the instrument of His punishment, His means of doing justice."

"I see." She paused, then said calmly, "Tell me, Chris, into which category do you fall—the purged or the punished? Because I know you're suffering now."

"Damn!" Trembling he spat out the word. "How dare you? I'll tell you then—neither category. If I'm suffering, it doesn't come from Him but from you—all of you. This is your revenge, your way of getting back at me. But it won't work. My suffering will end. It will be over soon. Because you see I don't need you—any of you—I wouldn't have you—I——" Suddenly he choked and covered his face as the tears came. His shoulders shook with sobs.

She looked at him with immense pity. "Poor Chris."

"Julie—please——" he said brokenly. "Please—I need you so much." The tears ran down between his long fingers and dropped onto the tablecloth. He was like a belligerent little boy who suddenly had lost all his fight and was begging now for what he wanted.

She reached out hesitantly toward him, then stopped and with an effort drew back her hand. There was something almost grim in her air of resolution—as if she were forcing herself to do something painful but necessary. "I'm glad to hear you say that, Chris—that you need me. It's a sign, I think, that perhaps there's some hope for you. It shows what you would never have admitted otherwise—that you have feelings like the rest of us, that you *are* a human being. And believe me, Chris, you've been in danger of suppressing that fact so completely that eventually you might have become what you've seemed to be—a person without any of the human desires and sorrows and joys and pains and pleasures that everyone else feels."

"Julie, for God's sake——" His hands still over his face, he dug his fingers into the skin of his skull as if he wanted to shred it.

"What is it, Chris—that I'm making you suffer? Yes, I know that." Her eyes lowered and she hesitated a moment, but then she continued. "I'm saying these things because I want you to hear them and to suffer."

With a jerk he pulled his hands away. His eyes shone with hatred in a face from which the blood had drained. "How good of you, how kind," he growled between his teeth.

"You don't understand. But that isn't surprising. With your way of looking at things, Chris, you wouldn't. I know what you're thinking—you can only imagine that when I say I want you to suffer, I mean that I'm having some sort of revenge. But what sense does that make? Why should I want revenge?"

"Your precious Mark, to begin with——"

"Yes, you've hurt Mark—but so have I, I know that now. And I know too that whatever you might suffer wouldn't lessen the suffering any for him—or for that poor misguided boy who tried to kill himself, or for any of the other people whose lives you've dirtied and corrupted. So you see, it isn't for anyone else's sake that I want you to suffer, Chris, but only for your own."

He had control of himself once more. "Don't flatter yourself." His tone was ice cold. "I had certain ideas, certain infatuations, but now that I know the truth about you——" He swallowed, but could not go on.

"What you said before was truer, Chris—that you need me. I don't understand it, somehow it doesn't make sense, but you must need me terribly to have done so much——" She shook her head. "But I'm not flattering myself when I say that, despite what you think. I'm sure you don't need me for myself—because of who and what I am. It's just that I represent something to you, something that probably has very little to do with what I really am, and whatever that something is, it's *that* which you need. But whatever it is I represent, it's being denied to you now and that denial is making you suffer."

He wrung his hands in a paroxysm of stifled rage and pain. "And you like it. You enjoy it. It's your pleasure to see me suffer."

"Not a pleasure, Chris—not in the sense you mean. Although in another sense I suppose you're right. It is a pleasure in a way because, little as you'll believe it, I want to do something of lasting good for you. And it's only by this suffering that I can do anything. I told you before what I want for you—that you become a human being, with feelings like all the rest of us. And I think this suffering is the only way that will ever happen. Because, you know, when you suffer you're sharing all the pain felt by Mark, by that boy, by all the people you've hurt and trampled on. And, Chris, remember—by suffering you're sharing the pain that Christ felt——"

"Don't say that," he burst out. "Don't tell *me* about Him. As if I didn't know—I, His servant—"

"Chris, how can you?" Her tone was reproachful but mild, so mild that he looked at her in surprise, as if her gentleness were somehow a revelation to him. "After everything that's happened, do you really believe that? No, don't answer—" She interrupted as he was about to reply. "I know what you'll say—what you *have* to say— and I don't want you to have to bother lying to yourself any more. Instead of answering, just think about this—not how well you've served Him, but how well you've loved Him?"

"You're just playing with words."

"Am I? Perhaps so. If that's the case I hope you—and He—will forgive me. But try to think about it anyway, won't you? It might turn out that it's not *just* playing with words. After all, Chris, to do you justice, I think you're right, you *have* been a good servant in your own way. Don't think I'm calling you a hypocrite, because I don't mean that. It's so plain that you've done everything with a sense of dedication, a sense of service, and in some insane way you've really believed that what you did *was* service, that by lying and hurting other people you've been honoring God. But even granting that's so, what does it prove? There's not one bit of evidence in it all that you love Him. Just the opposite. Love has been so absent from all you've done that I think it's nonsense for you to claim now that it ever played any part in it. How can you pretend to have loved God, when there isn't any love in all of your life? Don't you think that if you had that love it would simply brim over in you and fill your whole life, so that it would be impossible for you to do the slightest action without love shining out from it irrepressibly on every side? You see, don't you, that I'm agreeing with you? You could have done everything you did, caused all that pain and suffering, and still have done it out of love for God. It would be an odd sort of love, a mad sort of love, one that saw life through distorting lenses—but it could be real love all the same. Only, if that had been the way things were with you, everyone would know. Even though we called you a madman and a fanatic, we would have to admit that you loved God. It would stand out all over you, and all over everything you did, no matter how hare-brained or superficially cruel it was. But that's not the way it's been. There's no hint of love about the things you've done, Chris. They have a different trade-mark on them. Your actions are touched with something cold, something inhuman, something—dead. You're God's servant all right, Chris, but you don't love God. There isn't any love in your service, because there isn't any love in you."

He sat impassively for a moment, not moving a muscle, not even blinking. Then slowly he raised his hand and rubbed it reflectively across his mouth. He reached mechanically into his coat pocket, took out a dollar bill, and dropped it on the table. Then, not looking at her, quite as if he were unaware of her presence, he rose and, without glancing to either side, walked slowly out of the restaurant. As Julie watched him her lips moved soundlessly in a prayer.

JULIE TURNED THE KEY IN THE LOCK AND LET HERSELF INTO THE apartment. She set down her suitcase on the floor, went to the closet, and hung up her coat. Then she turned and saw Mark standing in the doorway that led to the living room. She hesitated only a moment.

"Mark—I'm sorry——"

In one stride he reached her and caught her in his arms. "Julie—Julie." He repeated her name over and over, while she caressed the back of his head, held herself tightly to him. After a long while they pulled apart slightly, their arms still around each other, and exchanged a wordless, almost solemn look. Each knew that the other was thinking how close they had come to losing everything.

"Can you ever forgive me?" she said at last.

"Julie—as if *I* had to forgive *you!*"

"Let's go in there." She nodded toward the living room. He kept his arm around her waist and they sat close together on the sofa. She had been away less than a day, but somehow the room had a strange, unfamiliar look to her. It was as if she were seeing everything here for the first time. She shook her head a little confusedly. "I don't know how I could have done it," she said.

His face hardened slightly. "I know how," he said.

"Chris?"

"Yes."

"Don't blame him, Mark. He——" What could she say? She felt as if she had been given a glimpse into Christopher Gavin's soul that had never been granted anyone before. To reveal what she had seen would be some sort of betrayal. And she had no wish to betray him. "He's awfully confused," she said simply. "Try not to hate him."

Mark did not answer.

"I wanted to tell him I would pray for him," she continued. "I wanted to tell him I hoped—someday—both of us would."

"Then you still—you believe all he told you?"

She smiled. "Not all. But I want to become a Catholic. I believe that part of it. Can you bear that, Mark—that I should be a Catholic?"

He was silent for a moment. Finally he said quietly, "I haven't any right to tell you that you shouldn't."

"Thank you."

"As for Chris——" He swallowed, almost painfully it seemed. "I don't think I hate him. I think I only feel sorry for him."

She touched his hand gently. "Thank you," she said again. "He's only a tool—an instrument, you know."

A faint smile broke out on Mark's face. "Then I hope his owner takes good care of him."

She looked at him in surprise. "That's a prayer," she said.

Mark started to shrug, then stopped. "I suppose it is."

It had not been his intention to go into a church. Probably, had he thought about it in advance, he would have planned deliberately to avoid doing so. But now that he was there he found the dim light and the silence, in which sounds from the downtown street outside were muffled, restful and refreshing, like a cup of cool water. There were very few other people there—an old man kneeling as if asleep before the larger-than-life crucifix by the altar rail, a couple of other old men and women scattered about the pews of the church saying their rosaries to themselves. From time to time one of the doors at the back of the church flapped open and there was a clack of heels or the thud of a knee striking the floor in genuflection as someone stopped briefly at the holy water font to bless himself and mutter a prayer, and then the door would flap again, letting in a honking of horns or squealing of brakes from outside, and the brief passer-by was gone. But the old people and Christopher stayed where they were, as if time were of no very great importance to them—in the one case because there was so little of it left that it would have been foolish to worry about it, in the other because there was suddenly so much of it that it was impossible just now to begin to think of filling it. He was in no hurry to go. The bus tickets in his breast pocket were a reminder of an engagement, but he had no need to worry about that. He could just sit there against the wall, halfway up the aisle on the gospel side, lulled and bemused by the votive lights which flickered in hundreds from many corners of the church like friendly little red eyes saluting him with winks. He sat very quietly, as someone might who had suffered a grave internal wound and knew that the moment he moved the searing pain would come and with it the warm gush of blood flushing his life away. To a casual observer he would have seemed wrapped in devout attention to his own pious meditations. But in fact there was no particular thought in his mind, unless it were concentration on the exclusion of thought. He was simply sitting as quietly as he could in this obscure dark corner to wait for his anguish to subside to the point at which he could begin rationalizing it, moulding it into something other than it was and redirecting it at some object other than himself. That anguish was his wound, the jagged, bloody mouth he kept closed only by sitting so very quietly and trying not to let himself think of anything, but only allowing the votive lights to dazzle and blur before his eyes.

It was not, he knew, that his thoughts were so terribly bitter. They would be eventually, of course, but for now he was too stunned, too dazed by all that had happened, to have any very coherent thoughts at all. Rather, what he was trying to suppress and overcome was an emotion—call it chagrin, self-disgust, whatever it is one feels when he knows he has unwittingly and irrevocably given himself away to someone else, laid bare the entrails of his soul, permitted a curious and alien gaze to survey him in a slow stare of obscene intimacy.

He was sickened and repelled by what he had done, by his immense, incredible stupidity in breaking down before her, pleading with her—— His fists clenched once more as he recalled the scene, felt his hands over his face, the hot tears in his eyes, the constriction in his throat. To have let her see him like that was more than he could bear. He felt betrayed by—by whom? By himself. True enough, by himself, but more than that—by something in himself he had not known was there. Even more than disgust at his weakness he felt fear, fear at the sudden revelation of this weakness whose existence he had not suspected. That he had desired her he had known for a long time, but that the roots of his desire went so far and were capable of dragging him to such depths were facts he had never dreamed of. For the first time he could remember he felt fear, and the fear sprang from the fact that he could no longer trust himself. He had always been able to count before on his own strength, the imperviousness and resiliency which, he knew, again and again had left his enemies with the frustrated realization that, try as they might, they could not really reach him and that he was therefore invulnerable to the strongest assault they could bring against him. But that was no longer the case. Now he could depend on nothing. His weakness had been made manifest to him, and already he felt obscurely that he would live out the rest of his life in secret dread of the power which that soft core within him had to bring him low in the dust.

There was a clatter of small change being dropped into one of the metal poor boxes at the back of the church and Christopher realized with a start that despite himself he had been drawn into thought, reliving that scene, feeling himself succumb once more to that sudden sickening-sweetish surge of weakness. But to his surprise and relief he found that the pain did not accompany the recollection. Perhaps it was too soon for the pain to return; that might after all be a delayed reaction. But in the meantime it was possible for him to probe and explore, and the knowledge filled him with a certain perverse eagerness. For he was anxious to go back over what she had said, to refute it, to prove her wrong, to fling her words from their pedestal of self-righteous assurance and trample them underfoot.

So. But now that he had lifted up his weapon, he had the unpleasant sensation of not knowing where to begin. What had looked so easy a moment ago seemed now more difficult than he had supposed, and he hesitated uneasily. Best to get clearly in mind what it was she had said, the lies she had spewed out in her frenzied attempt to hurt him, acting as the instrument of revenge for her poor precious Mark. All right, what *had* she said? The usual nonsense: Because he made others feel pain, he could not really be serving God. As if that made any difference, as if pain were not His own favorite tool for cleansing.

But that reminded him of something else—what was it?—something unpleasant. Then what about his own pain? she had asked. Perfectly simple to answer that, perfectly simple. Only, what was the answer? Obvious: his pain was inflicted on him by his enemies, it did not come from God but from those who hated Him and His servant. He hesitated. It was a good answer, it *was* a good answer, it *was*— His eyes drifted beyond a cluster of flickering lights, tongues of flame floating on tiny waxen seas and no longer bringing courage and conviction in an upper room, farther and farther to the altar and to the tabernacle itself. It was a moment of epiphany, an instant of justification when all that he had done and all that he was should receive some word of approval, a pledge, a sign. But nothing happened. One of the old women blew her nose loudly. He lowered his eyes nervously.

He knew he was right. It was impossible that he should not be. But to his consternation he felt a thin edge of anxiety begin to wedge its way into his vitals. Suppose—the thought shook him to his foundations—suppose there were an element of truth in what she had said? Then for all these years he would have been living a fiction, deluding and deceiving himself, perverting the truth, tampering with reality to serve obscurely depraved ends of his own. He shook his head unbelievingly. Where did these thoughts come from? His eyes searched the tabernacle again, a little desperately, but it was shrouded in a churchly dusk, silent and inaccessible. He wanted to think no further, to stop now before he had gone too far with this suddenly frightening train of thought. But he knew he could not stop, he had to push on, to reason his way through this tangle of lies and regain the assurance which had so abruptly been snatched from him.

He had, he realized now, to face the ultimate challenge which she had thrown up to him, the one challenge he had not even dared to repeat over to himself. That, he saw, was where his thoughts had been tending all this time—to that final confrontation whose outcome held the key to this obscure and nameless conflict which had begun to rage within him. The challenge had been (he forced himself to look at it carefully and calmly) that there was no love in him, that he did not love other people and that, most important of all, he did not love God. He smiled thinly as the ready answer came to him: sentimentality again. She could not recognize his kind of love for what it was, any more than any of the others had. Their love was something effete and perfumed, a sugared emotion whose deadly sweetness dulled all strength and self-possession in voluptuous surrender to self-indulgence. Their love was a caricature of the real thing, a bawdy, sniggering parody like something scrawled on the wall of a urinal. But his love, he told himself, was a clean flame, burning away the tangled underbrush of trivia between self and the loved object, and at the same time burning oneself clean of all distractions, all minor lusts, all the myriad petty encumbrances which threatened to make that ultimate union less than perfect. If that flame caused pain—that simply was the nature of fire. It burned, after all, in imitation of the great roaring blaze of heat and light from which it had been tossed off and toward which it was returning relentlessly and unerringly—that is, in imitation of God Himself. Yes, there was the answer, he reminded himself triumphantly, his love was an offshoot and portrait in miniature of God's love. She and all the others like her could not understand it, because they had no conception of that greater love.

He waited confidently for this formula to take its effect. Always before, this, his ultimate justification, had not failed to reassure him, while at the same time it increased his determination to continue along the hard path he had chosen for himself. This thought had often been his consolation, a guarantee that he could trust his inclination as if it were a bit of metal being drawn toward some great lodestone from which it had been chipped off and to which it was returning. He waited then for the feeling of self-confidence which had before invariably followed hard upon this rewarding exercise. But now nothing happened. There was no surge of invigoration, no feeling of certitude and communion. Instead, to his horror, he heard her voice, clearly and close at hand, repeating her last words to him: "There's no hint of love about the things you've done, Chris. They have a different trade-mark. Your actions are touched with something cold, dead. You're God's servant, but you don't love God. There isn't any love in your service because there isn't any love in you."

"It isn't true!" he exclaimed half-aloud, bringing his fist down on the seat beside him. The thump of fist against wood reverberated through the church, and he looked about in sudden chagrin. No one had noticed. The old men and women still mumbled their rosaries. The only change was at the altar rail. The old man who had knelt there had gone away. The great crucifix hung in desolation, plaster eyes staring with unreturned compassion at the almost empty church. An uncertain smile flickered across Christopher's face. "It isn't true," he murmured experimentally. No one denied the statement, but no one affirmed it either; the crucifix looked unmoved. In that frozen moment of pain and abandonment and absolute giving of self, the whole issue seemed somehow superfluous. The only relevant response was to give something in return, give oneself.

Give oneself. Christopher rubbed his hand across his eyes. He was surprised to find his hand shaking a little. He wanted desperately to get up, to leave the church, to forget these insane thoughts. But if he were to leave now, he knew he would find himself frozen in this moment of agony, as Christ was in His, and quite without the promise of resurrection. He had gone too far now; it was impossible to draw back but intolerable to remain where he was. The only thing to do was to continue.

No hint of love about what he had done. Those were her words. But it wasn't true. Everything he had done—done for love—of course. Donald's purplish face, the necktie tight around the throat, passed before his mind's eye; Mark's face, white with rage and pain. Love. Without knowing what he was doing he doubled forward, his hands over his face again. No, he mustn't. With a huge effort he sat up, his arms at his sides, the muscles of his jaw knotted fiercely. The crucifix caught his eye, the plaster gaze radiated compassion at him. He looked away hastily. Julie—he had loved her at least. All he had done was the result of that love. If it had been immoderate, so be it—immoderation in love was a sign of one's essential warmth, the basic rightness of one's soul, into however wrong channels it might be turned. (He did not bother to reflect that these were arguments he would have scorned days—hours—

ago.) So that at least there was his love for her standing as a powerful refutation of her argument. He loved her—he wanted her. Wanted, desired. "You don't need me for myself. I represent something to you, and whatever it is, it's *that* which you need." Needed, taken, conquered, possessed, enjoyed. He groaned, a low grunt of pain and self-loathing.

So it was as simple as that. His own gratification had been his motive all along, in this episode and in all the others. The satisfaction of his sensuality or his egotism, of his desire to dominate or to revenge his injured pride, had driven him into these excesses which she called inhuman. He looked now in desperation at the figure on the cross, and his eyes locked with the plaster ones in a long gaze. Why did You do it? he asked. Why did You let me? He waited hopefully, but still there was no answer. Or rather, the answer came once more from himself, in a new, hard, insistent voice he had not heard before. You did it to yourself, the voice said. All these years and years he had been choosing over and over the path he would take, shaping himself too so that he could travel no other. Unmistakable in the finished product was the artist's hand—his own. God, he said now looking at the tabernacle, God— God, what? What was it he wanted to ask? He did not know. There was a response called for which he had not mastered. Sorrow perhaps, the begging for forgiveness, repentance. But he felt no sorrow. Having schooled himself for so long not to, there was no way in which he could. The channels of repentance were dry, clogged with debris, and at their head stood a wall of stone, unmistakably of his making. He would have liked to have felt something, felt sorry. "Forgive me," he whispered softly, trying the sound of the words. It was false. The words meant nothing. He did not want forgiveness. He wanted nothing. He had everything he wanted, all that he needed; already within him he could feel it begin to form—the hard kernel, the grain of sand gathering increment, the little knotted tumor of gall and bitterness and hatred. So that was how it would be. You understand me, don't You? he asked the tabernacle. He looked once more at the crucifix, and suddenly he felt something dissolve in him, something without a name, something he had not known was there whose dissolution now was like the removal of a great weight, a pressure he had borne for years and which had been dragging him down, wearing the life out of him. I feel so sorry for you, the plaster eyes said to him. Please let Me feel sorry for you. It is the only thing that will help, the only thing that will make any difference. Christopher nodded. Go ahead, he thought. Please, go ahead. He sat a while longer, but nothing else happened. He felt even more empty than when he had come into the church. He seemed to be an emaciated corpse, paper light, its veins drained, the flesh wasted away, the skin dried to a flaky film. There was no feeling in him and no thought. The thing that had dissolved in him was gone, and there was nothing to take its place.

Then, tentatively, half fearfully, he tried the words again: "Forgive me." And almost to his surprise he found he could go on. Forgive me for hating them all, for not seeing them with Your eyes. Forgive me for doing so much evil in Your name. Forgive me for distorting and dirtying every clean and decent thing I could get my hands on. Forgive me for presuming to think I knew so much more than the others, when all along I knew nothing and was stumbling in the deepest dark of us all. *Us all.* He turned the words over on his tongue. He could hardly remember when he had thought of "we" and "us." It's always been "me" before, he thought. For the first time he could recall he saw himself joined to others, part of a struggling crowd bungling its way through a self-imposed fog of ignorance, falling down, being hurt, rising again, and moving on. And now suddenly he felt himself to be so very close to all of them—to Robbie and Donald for whom he had felt contempt, to the priest whom he had envied, to Julie whom he had loved. And to Mark. To Mark whom he had hated and tried to hurt with every weapon at his command. They were all joined together and he with them, linked inextricably by a design whose whole pattern he could not yet see. He had imagined that it was he who was guiding the movement of events, but the outcome had opened his eyes. He too had done no more than play his part—badly and with ill will— but play his part nevertheless in a long, incredibly complex pageant of love which had been planned unrelentingly to bring some immense goodness out of turmoil despite the blindness and petty hatreds of its actors. He knew that love would not be denied, and that viciousness and apathy and lust and greed and selfishness and all the other varieties of human nastiness were only so many twists and turns which love incorporated into its own grand and ruthless design. Your design, he said to the figure on the crucifix. He felt an immense gratitude welling up in him—not for anything that had been done for him or to him, but simply for the wisdom of that love which, no matter what his own rash and selfish inclination, kept him from stepping irrevocably outside the pattern and doing some lasting harm to mar it. Dear God, he thought, I have done everything I could to resist You and to thwart You, to keep others from knowing and loving You. But You would not let me succeed, and for that I thank You a thousand times over. Christ, help me to begin to know You. I thought for a long time that I did, but instead I knew and served only myself and called myself You. That's funny, isn't it? It's hard to believe anyone could make that mistake, but it was easy for me. And so You hung here all this time waiting for me to stop looking at myself and come to take a look at You instead. Well, here I am now. I see myself and I see You and I finally see the difference—all the difference in the world, in the universe, if only I had bothered to look before. But blindness is an awful disease. The one single thing you ever know well is yourself. Only once you do begin to see, it becomes so simple. And so complicated. So hard to understand Your love when the only thing you've known and understood has been self-love. Dear Christ, You've brought me this far against my will. But now I surrender my will to You, and I only ask You to take me the rest of the way just as You wish. He looked intently at the crucifix, at the tabernacle. There was no illumination, no moment of epiphany, but only that endless calm compassion that flowed over him and through him like a healing lotion, radiating love.

He stopped praying then and sat a little while longer. He felt terribly tired, but satisfied too, as if he had fought and won an exhausting and decisive battle. Finally he stirred and rose, genuflected in the aisle and walked quietly out of the church.

Christopher pushed through the swinging door and heard it go slip-slop behind him. The sun shone between clouds outside and he hesitated for a moment squinting in the brightness before he went down the steps. The street was alive with traffic and people, and he walked slowly in the direction of the bus station, all the while looking in surprise at the people around him as if he had never really seen anyone else before.